A SUSPICION
OF SILVER

P.F. CHISHOLM is an author and journalist. She is a graduate of the University of Oxford with a degree in History. Her first novel, *A Shadow of Gulls*, published when she was eighteen, won the David Higham Award for Best First Novel.

By P.F. Chisholm

The Sir Robert Carey Mysteries

A
SUSPICION
OF
SILVER

P.F. CHISHOLM

HEAD
ZEUS

First published in the UK in 2019 by Head of Zeus Ltd

9 7 5 3 1 2 4 6 8

A CIP catalogue record for this book is available
from the British Library.

ISBN (HB): 9781788549783
ISBN (E): 9781786696205

Printed and bound in Great Britain by
CPI Group Ltd (UK), Croydon CR0 4YY

Head of Zeus Ltd
5–8 Hardwick Street
London EC1R 4RG
WWW.HEADOFZEUS.COM

Contents

CAST OF CHARACTERS

in no particular order

* historical person
in parenthesis: mentioned, not met

Marty, Whitehall stableboy
The Hochstetter family:
Daniel*, Radagunda his wife née Stamler*
Sons: Emanuel*, (Daniel*), Joachim, David*
Daughters: Annamaria*, (Veronica*,
    Susanna*), Radagunda*, Elizabeth*
Sir Robert Carey *
Sorrel, Blackie, his usual hobbies
Lord Scrope, Warden of the English West March*
Lady Elizabeth Widdrington, Carey's love*
(Sir Henry Widdrington, her husband, Deputy
    Warden of the English East March)*
Henry Dodd, Land-Sergeant of Gilsland,
    Carey's henchman
Whitesock, his favourite horse
Sir Robert Cecil, Privy Councillor*
Jonathan Hepburn/Joachim Hochstetter, an engineer
Simon Anricks, a merchant and toothdrawer
(John Napier)*, mathematician
Mr Menzies, a Scottish lawyer
Wattie Graham of Netherby, Border reiver*

Young Hutchin Graham, nearly a Border reiver*
Bangtail Graham, man-at-arms, Carlisle castle guard*
Red Sandy Dodd, man-at-arms, Carlisle castle guard
(Andie Nixon, man-at-arms, Carlisle castle guard)
  (Kate, his wife)
Leamus MacRom, Irish kern
Janet Dodd
Widow Ridley
Ritchie Graham of Brackenhill, gangster*
Bessie Storey *
(Nancy, her wife)*
Mark Steinberger, Schmelzmeister*
John Tovey, Carey's secretary
James Stuart, King of Scotland, 6th of that name*
(Mrs Hogg, midwife)
Shilling, a horse
Joshua Davidson*, possibly a hallucination
Wee Colin Elliot, headman of the Elliot surname
(Roger Widdrington, son of Sir Henry)*
(Lord Burghley) *
Frau Magda, barmaid
Long Tom Graham, unfortunate messenger
Maria, maid
Matthew Ormathwaite, carpenter
(Sir Thomas Carleton)*
Cuthbert "Skinabake" Armstrong*
(Earl of Essex)*
(Niall of the Nine Captives)*
Mr Lugg, barber-surgeon
Alyson Elliot, chatelaine of Stobbs tower
Aloysius Allerdyce, Mayor of Keswick
(Mr Nedham, shareholder in the Company of Mines Royal)*
John Carleton, smith
Rosa Carleton, his wife, and Josef, his son

(Trevannion, Carey's Cornish cousin)*
(Journeymen smiths: David Butfell,
   Tom Atkinson, Melchior Moser*)
(Apprentice smiths: Short Jemmie, Matty, Jurgen, Rob)
Betty, a milkmaid
Ian Ullock, merchant apprentice
Poppy Burn or Radagunda Hochstetter
Mary Liddle, a wetnurse
James Postumus Burn, a baby
Pastor Waltz*
Ulrich Schlegel, mine captain*
Hans Moser, mine captain*
Jane, a dairymaid
Herr Kauffmann Hochstetter
(Dr Hector Nuñez, Simon's uncle)*

A Suspicion
of Silver

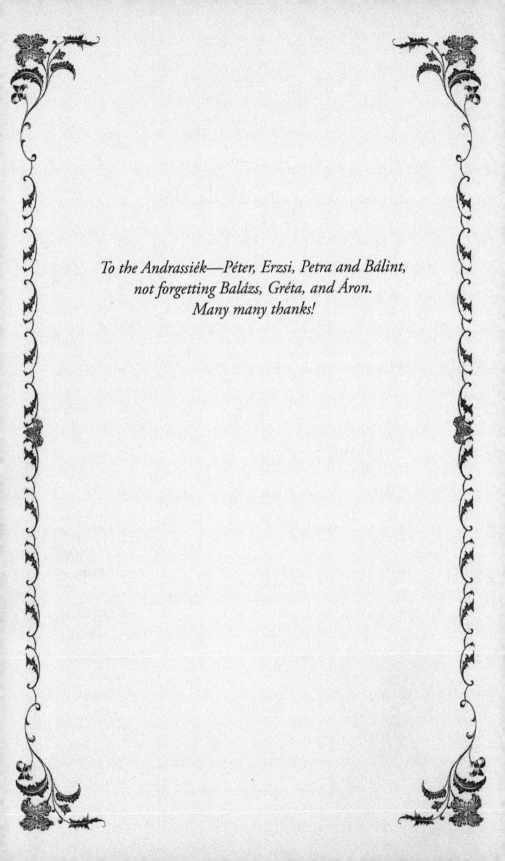

To the Andrassiék—Péter, Erzsi, Petra and Bálint,
not forgetting Balázs, Gréta, and Áron.
Many many thanks!

NOVEMBER 1571, LONDON

The stable boys stood around their fallen hero, silent and staggered at the impossibility of what had happened. Marty couldn't be dead, he couldn't! Now he would never sail the seas to find gold or fight the foreigners as he had boasted he would. He had ruled them with justice and his fists for a year and led them in wonderful adventures that yielded apples and sweetmeats and stories. He hadn't explained why he wanted a rich boy's clothes, but that was all right, he never explained anything and it always turned out well. Now this.

The youngest of them knelt, tears running down his cheeks, to shut Marty's eyes, and the eldest suddenly turned and ran to find the Head Groom.

EARLIER

At last, after the usual chaos of getting warm gowns on and cloaks and then spending half an hour looking for Joachim's hat which turned out to be on the top banister, the Hochstetter family of Augsberg were ready to see the famous sights of London.

Daniel Hochstetter and his four eldest children would walk to the Tower Gatehouse to see the lions and perhaps the armouries, but not the Mint which they had seen by special royal permission the week before. They would walk back, perhaps taking a detour to look at the goldsmith's shops on Cheapside and perhaps even going on London Bridge as well to see the draper's shops there. The baby would stay at their lodgings in Dowgate by the German Steelyard with her nurse. Daniel's wife, Frau Radagunda Hochstetter, her eleven-year-old son, Joachim, and her daughter, Little Radagunda, would actually go to see the wonders of Whitehall palace.

Daniel found his wife a boat from Dowgate watersteps, a double-ended skiff rowed by two muscular men in the famous red boatman's livery with their pewter badges on their shoulders. He lifted Little Rady into the boat while his wife nervously stepped onto the boards holding the boatman's hand in a vicelike grip and the boat wallowed. Joachim hopped in and grinned, sat down on the cushions at the back like a lord. Radagunda sat rigidly in the middle, gripping the sides.

It was a long trip upriver. Little Rady wriggled and knelt on the seat to dabble her fingers in the water. She was told to stop it at once by her mother, who was deathly afraid that she would fall in and die and go to limbo because, of course, she was only a child and as yet unbaptised. In their religion, only adults could be baptised.

It was too far to walk, but Radagunda wished and wished she had not asked to see the Queen's palace, for the terror of tipping the boat over filled her heart. It hadn't occurred to her they would have to take such a dangerous route as the Thames. She muttered prayers the whole way, feeling sick, seeing nothing of the proud palaces and churches and gardens going past, nor the newly built Bearbaiting Ring on the south side.

Little Rady wriggled the whole way and Joachim pelted the boatmen with questions in English. Radagunda couldn't understand him at all, although she had taken lessons in English too. Her lord and husband had insisted because they were moving from Augsberg to England, where there was copper ore but the people had no idea how to mine it. He had arrived back home from England in the summer, looked around the countryside, talked to some people, and by October they were in London. She supposed it was a wise decision, seeing how the poorer sort of people in Augsberg were starting to die of sickness and the harvest had failed again when they left. But she was nervous of going to the strange town of Kes-wick—where she knew nobody, and which was full of the peculiar English—though her lord was readying an island in a lake for her to live on and planting an orchard and building a mill and brewery there. That was a comfort.

"Haug and Company can afford it," he reassured her over their first dinner in England, picking up a feebly spiced bread-stuffed English sausage on his knife. "And we will be mining copper and silver and gold for Her Majesty of England and the new Company of Mines Royal."

She almost smiled with pride at this thought because her husband was an important man, never mind the constant difficulties with shareholders over money, and lazy English carpenters, and getting assays of the ores correct. He had told them stories of where he had been in England for so long, stories of the northern English who were hard to understand and lived in Cumberland. They didn't know anything about mining, poor souls, but had incredibly rich veins of copper ore in the hills right next to them.

Some of the stories were a little frightening: the evil servants of the evil and Catholic (of course) Earl of Northumberland had actually killed Leonard Stoltz, their preacher, for being an Anabaptist. But then God had punished him through his own actions because he rebelled against the Queen and ran away to Scotland, where he was now imprisoned and it was only a matter of time before he was executed.

There was a shout and a clatter and one of the watermen waved an oar at another boat that had come too close. The sound of the shouting was ugly and frightening and Radagunda clasped Little Rady to her, though the child was trying to escape to see what was happening. Joachim was kneeling up on the seat, laughing at the people on the other boat who had got splashed.

The older waterman said something gruff to Radagunda, who had no idea what it meant, and bent to his oar again.

Her heart was beating so hard she felt as if it was actually outside her chest. The horrible wallowing of the boat seemed to slow a little and as the speed picked up, she felt a breeze. Her hand cramped on the side of the boat and she had to let go of Little Rady for a second to ease it. Rady instantly got up on her knees again so she could see and wobbled so that Radagunda had to hold her tight again, despite her muffled protests.

Joachim was laughing at her. "*Mutti, Mutti, Mutti,*" he said, shaking his head, "it's only a boat."

"Sit down and hold your hat on," she snapped at him. He slowly put his hand to his hat and clamped it onto his head, deliberately insolent. She sighed. No, not insolent, he was a boy and a boy didn't see these things the same way: despite how ill he had been with the measles last year, despite how his little brother had died of it and gone to limbo, despite the way he had been dazzled by even dim lights and she had had to keep the shutters closed, despite the nights she had sat up with him as he fought his way through delirium and far more frightening deathly stillness, it seemed he wasn't frightened of death. He should be. Until he had been safely baptised, he could go to limbo at any time and she would never see him again, ever. Until she had children she had never doubted that the Anabaptist way, which followed Jesus Christ Himself in baptising adults, was right. Now? It was terrifying. If she let herself think of little Leonard whom she would never ever see again until the end of time and beyond, she couldn't stop the tears from rising.

At Westminster steps, the boatmen were still tying up when Joachim jumped from the boat to the steps which nearly stopped Radagunda's heart again. She told him off and he just stood there smiling. Well, he was eleven. Boys were supposed to be bold. One of the boatmen picked Little Rady up and deposited her ashore, so she didn't have to get her lovely green brocade kirtle wet. Radagunda climbed out of the rocking boat trembling, holding the other boatman's calloused hand as tight as she could. She gave Joachim the 6d to pay the boatman, because the man should pay.

They walked up the steps and through into New Palace Yard with a still fountain in it, across to a towered gateway, and then turned right into King's Street, away from Westminster Abbey. At the end was an impressive towered gate where they had to pay sixpence each to the Queen's servant in his black-and-white livery in order to go through. Then they came to another courtyard where they had to queue up to go through the next elaborate gate. Other people were already queuing up, French people and some Low Dutch-speakers from the Netherlands, probably, and a couple of Scots and some English as well. They joined the queue and waited to pass through the famous Court Gate. There was an oddly pointless fence that they had to queue round.

Men in good woollen doublets were waiting nearby and one of them instantly attached himself to the Hochstetters, explaining in a loud slow voice that the gate they had just come through, yes, that building with the round towers and flags, was the King Street Gate. He pointed out interesting places over the walls: the Queen's Privy Garden and the Privy Gallery on one side; on the other the Great Close Tennis Court, the Great Open Tennis Court, the Whitehall Bowling Alley, and in the distance the Little Close Tennis Court and the round roof beyond it of the Whitehall Cockpit. Yes, young sir, the courtiers enjoy playing tennis. No, young sir, bless you, you can't go and try it.

Finally they were allowed to pass through the Court Gate into the Court itself, cobbled and swept clean; they went into the Chapel Royal which had not been badly damaged by Reformers and still had its roodscreen, to Radagunda's disapproval. They did not go into the palace kitchens behind it whence curled pleasant smells of venison, chicken, and potherbs. They came out into the Preaching Place and the guide told them how many famous preachers and ministers had preached there, but they hadn't heard of any of them. They looked into the Council Chamber which was panelled in pale yellow oak and had a long table with Persian rugs on it and comfortable chairs, but no councillors.

They went through the mazelike passages of the Court to the Great Hall and stared at the hammerbeam roof and the minstrels' gallery and the portraits of the Queen and her father, Henricus VIII. A single small table and chair were on the dais, with a Cloth of Estate over it. All the people they had been queueing with were there, and they watched as four dazzlingly dressed and exquisite courtiers entered in procession. One in tawny damask and green velvet announced that the Queen's Majesty would be at the dinner although Her Royal Person was absent. Then the courtiers attended the empty chair which four red-and-black-striped Gentlemen of the Guard were guarding. Each courtier collected a large silver or gold dish from a kitchen servant, brought it to the chair, knelt on both knees to the chair, lifted the cover off the dish and waved it over the chair, put back the cover, stood up, took three paces backwards as if the chair actually had the Queen sitting there instead of empty space. Then the courtier turned and carried the dish down from the dais to the door to the kitchen and gave the dish to the same servant who took it away and reappeared a moment later with another dish. Joachim had to swallow a laugh because it was totally ridiculous.

The food was real, though, and smelled surprisingly good. There was pork and chicken and venison and potherbs and cheese and sweetmeats and a jam tart, and each dish was announced in a brazen voice by one of the Gentlemen of the Guard.

Joachim let out a snort when a courtier laid an unused napkin beside the clean plate to indicate that the mad show was over. His mother shushed him.

"Quiet, Joachim, show some respect. Did you think the Queen would be there herself every day for visitors? She has other things to do. I wonder what the recipe for that pork with apple and cider might be…"

From there, as a special treat, according to the man, they were allowed into the actual Privy Gallery where the Queen lived when she was in residence. They were shown into the Queen's Audience Chamber where there was a gilded throne with the Cloth of Estate over it like a little roof, bearing the arms of England. The French visitors raised their eyebrows at the *fleur de lis* quartered on it, in token of the Queen's claims to French soil which King Henry V had so nearly conquered. This room was Radagunda's favourite because it wasn't big and impressive but small and intimate and she could see embroidered velvet cushions on the white rush mats for the Queen's ladies-in-waiting and maids-of-honour to sit on, and the beautiful walls covered with white embroidered silk. The Queen met ambassadors and other important people in the room, explained the guide.

Something shouted "God save the Queen!" in a strange croaky voice. She knew the phrase but was appalled when she saw that the speaker was a bird, grey and red, with a big beak, sitting on a perch in the corner.

"That's Jacob," said their guide. "He's a parrot. Would you like to feed him some apple, young sir?"

Joachim translated this for her, though in fact she had understood, and asked her if he could. When she reluctantly said yes, he took the piece of apple, approached the bird and teased him with it, then threw it up and the bird caught it neatly in his beak.

Little Rady started jumping up and down wanting to do the same. Radagunda didn't like it; the parrot was worryingly clever for a bird. Was it infested with a demon?

The guide took Rady to another bird, this one smaller, and green and red. He got it to perch on his finger and brought it close to the little girl's face. Radagunda was terrified the bird would peck her or bite her but the guide looked up and said, "This is Sandy. He's sad because his wife died last month. Do you want to stroke him, young mistress?" Joachim translated it for her.

Little Rady's small face was concerned. "Poor parrot," she said in English, and actually dared to stroke the bird on his neck and he bowed a little and made a chirrup.

"There," said the guide, "you've made him feel a little better." He put Sandy back on his perch and Little Rady smiled her beautiful sunny smile, though Joachim was sniggering again.

Then they went into the Princes Lodgings, next to the old Stone Gallery and from the first room they could look at the Privy Garden with its formal short box hedges and winter rose trees and at the river on the other side.

"Birds don't get married," Joachim sneered to the guide and the guide said quietly, "Parrots do, they marry for life and are faithful too."

Joachim shrugged and marched into the next room. That was where the gowns were, three of them, behind a wicker screen you had to peer through and they were on wicker stands so they looked as if the Queen had turned to twisted wood.

Radagunda was fascinated by the gowns and peered through the screen which was presumably there to stop people stealing the pearls and jewels. She stared hard at the nearest gown and established to her satisfaction that all the gems were in fact paste, which made her snort. Little Rady was standing on tiptoe to look but couldn't see past the screen and so their guide kindly picked her up.

Of course Radagunda liked the green one best and admired the velvet and the forepart to the petticoat and then wondered why Joachim was being so quiet. She looked round and couldn't see him.

Where was he? She couldn't see him! When had he gone? Where had he gone? Sweet Jesu and his Mother, what could she do?

Joachim had found a little unlocked door in a corner that looked like the panelling on the walls. Looking back at his mother who was hypnotised by the boring gowns, he slipped through and shut the door behind him, found himself in a roughly boarded servants' passageway. There was a smell of mildew and mice. He trotted along it and came out in an orchard with bare trees, crossed it and went in through the first unlocked door he came to and found a small yard there surrounded by higgledy piggledy houses. Some boys a bit larger than him were standing around drinking beer and playing dice. He could smell it was the terrible English beer and lifted his lip in a sneer.

One boy was squatting by a watertrough. Respectably dressed in a woollen doublet and hose of blue that looked as if it was only secondhand, he didn't look like a stable lad, but maybe he was. He stood up and bowed quite low to Joachim who touched his velvet cap in response. The boy said something in English which was too quick and strongly accented for Joachim to understand. He smiled a little at the boy who said something like "parlyvu fronsays."

"*Entschuldigung*," said Joachim and turned to go, but the boy grabbed his arm.

"Want see Queen?" said the boy loudly and slowly. "SEE THE QUEEN?"

Joachim wondered why he was saying that when the Queen wasn't there—but maybe she was? The boy gestured for him to follow and ducked down a small alleyway between the houses. Behind him, Joachim heard a snigger and that warned him, made the world go slow for him.

He already had his dagger out when the boy suddenly turned and struck out at him with a stick he had picked up. Instinctively Joachim ducked and stabbed with the knife, missed and the boy put his hands out, said something about only joking. But the world was still slow, so Joachim stepped towards him, caught his shoulder and stabbed as hard as he could. It felt just like stabbing a dog or a cat, which was interesting.

Red flowered suddenly on the boy's doublet and when the boy lurched towards him, Joachim backed, tripped, and sat down hard in the mud of the alley. That pulled his dagger out of the boy with a slurp, so he got up and ran back the way he had come. His last sight was of the boy staring in disbelief at the blood pouring out of his stomach.

He sprinted up the alley, through the yard where the boys laughed at him and shouted catcalls, across the orchard, up the servants' passage. Just in time he stopped and looked at his knife which was still in his hand and bloody. So he pulled out his handkerchief and wiped it off carefully before sheathing it, then cleaned his hands too and tucked the dirty hanky into a mousehole. He paused to exult in what had happened. He had killed dogs before, they were so stupid, they just let him do it once he had convinced them he was their friend with a bone or two. He had killed a cat by wrapping it in a sack and bashing it with a rock. But this was the first time he had killed a person. And he had got away with it. And it had been utterly correct because the boy was trying to rob him. Joachim conscientiously thanked God for the chance to kill and hugged the deed to himself, replaying his quickness and ferocity and the blood in his mind's eye.

Then when his breathing had quieted, he went through the door into the room with the incredibly boring gowns.

THURSDAY, 4TH JANUARY 1593

Henry Dodd was burning, burning. The flames in the church rose higher and higher, licking everything wooden, the old worm-rotten roodscreen, the benches for the old folk by the walls. People were screaming and shouting, running around, most of them women and children. Flames everywhere. Hoofbeats outside, thumping in his heart.

He was lying on the floor on his face, pinned by a fallen rafter that was burning its way into his back, feet running past every now and again. The roar of the flames beat in his ears, as he tried to move but couldn't. He wasn't chained, he was just too weak, like a newborn kitten.

He panted for breath, everything was too hot, everything inside him was burning too. He tried to put his elbows under his shoulders and lift himself up. Pain ran in molten leaden streams up his back and down again. He heard an annoying noise, whimpering like a beaten dog. Was that his voice? He clamped his teeth, tried to stop the noise but couldn't, the sounds trickled out between his lips, dripped on the straw under him.

He got one elbow under. Panted. More burning. And the other. He had to wait and pant a minute. He tried to move away from the fire, but he could not. He was stuck.

He hunched his shoulders, strained every muscle. He knew which church this was. This was the old church filled with hiding Elliot women and children, and he had set light to it himself all those years ago. Now he was trapped in the fire in the church, that he had set. There were hoofbeats in the distance…he had to get away.

Someone moved near him, dumped something on him, soft but burning cold. The cold ran through cracks in his body, between the lumps of fire. He screamed, he didn't want to, and the sound came out as a groan.

He looked up and over his shoulder at a terrifying gargoyle's face, lit by a candle, a face which might have been a woman's once but was now melted and destroyed. He cried out at it, and the fire enveloped him.

He understood. The church was Hell. He was in Hell, where he deserved to go.

TUESDAY, 2ND JANUARY 1593, LEITH

In the afternoon of the 2nd January, Carey rode the two miles to Leith, carrying a warrant for the arrest of Jonathan Hepburn and his servants, signed by my Lord Maitland of Thirlstane, the Lord Chancellor of Scotland, because King James had decided to go hunting. He took with him ten men of King James' bodyguard, Leamus, the Irish kern, who happened to be hanging around the stables and a procurator fiscal, on general principles, a lawyer friend of Maitland's. At Leith Carey found that three ships had left the port early on New Year's Day: a Danish ship, a French ship, and a Dutch Protestant Sea Beggar, which had sailed for Holland when the Court was still at sixes and sevens, and had probably already reached Amsterdam. The other ships were still in harbour because the weather was awful, with the sleet and a bone-chilling wind bringing more snow from the north-east. Again, on general principles, he nevertheless searched the few ships in the main harbour from nose to tail, including rummaging in the holds, and found in a French ship some contraband barrels marked as brandy, which he confiscated.

The objections from the captains were silenced by a blizzard of legalese from the lawyer and the arquebuses of the King's Gentlemen. Mr Anricks joined him, having received a note of invitation at John Napier's house where he was staying to entertain himself with the *Ars Mathematika*, however you did that.

Together they went with the procurator fiscal and the King's Gentlemen and knocked on the gate of the little steelyard. When eventually it was opened by a young man, Carey said coldly, "I wish to see Herr Kaufmann Hochstetter, immediately."

"The Herr Kaufmann is at home and…"

Carey produced his warrant from Maitland which had some firm words about the King requiring assistance from any and all aliens or foreigners to catch evildoers, on pain of instant ejection from the realm. The young man took it, read it, and swallowed.

"*Jawohl, Herr Ritter*," he said. "Would you care to come in and wait somewhere warm?"

"Thank you," said Carey, "however last time I found your hospitality a trifle hot for me so I prefer to wait here."

The young man coughed, and shut the gate. A few minutes later a messenger boy came out, took off his cap to them, and set off at a firm jogtrot in the direction of some houses set back from the road. Carey stood with his back to the gate, his cloak billowing, and the Gentlemen lined up on either side and prepared for a long wait. Anricks already had a notebook in his hand and some blacklead making his fingers filthy and seemed to be calculating, while Leamus was looking with interest at some hoofprints in the snow.

"Sir Robert," said the procurator fiscal, with his hands behind his back and his comfortable stomach straining his beltbuckle. "may I ask whit ye think tae our legal system here?"

"Mr Menzies," said Carey, "I cannot tell you how happy I am that I have not yet enjoyed the experience of litigating or appearing in your courts." Mr Menzies gave a dry little laugh. "All I know is that the whole is based on Roman law rather than the Common law, which might have given me a clue about it, had I not been so idle as a boy and learned a little Latin rather than playing football."

Mr Menzies smiled and shook his head. "My tutor broke several birches on me wi' the effort of trying to instill the Latin."

"Mine couldn't run as fast as I could. How did you become a lawyer then?"

"I found Virgil's *Aeneid* and decided to read it for my own pleasure, which I fear embittered him further because at the end I knew more classical Latin than he did. I read Justinian's work on Justice as well and was inspired by it, and also by the fact that I am a younger son."

"Ah," said Carey, "me too. But I took the soldier's path to wealth, which is why I'm the Deputy Warden in Carlisle."

"I know," said the lawyer. "I wanted to ask you about the Border law and how it differs, but…"

"A complex subject, Mr Menzies. I suggest you ask the Lord Warden's clerk, Mr Bell at Carlisle, since he knows far more about it than I do." Carey spotted the heavyset merchant Hochstetter coming towards him, trailed by a secretary and, yes, his own lawyer. Carey repressed a sigh and then took thought of his warrant which he produced again. Menzies and Hochstetter's lawyer immediately began arguing over whether so general a document as a general warrant could be held to apply in this case to the very particular circumstances of a Hansa Steelyard with its very specific privileges and if, which was not admitted, it could, then exactly how far could the warrant be said to extend…

After he had had about as much as he could stand of sentences so long they seemed to disappear up their own arses, he said, "Jonathan Hepburn." Both lawyers were in full flow but Hochstetter looked uneasy.

"You know the name," Carey said. "All I want to know is whether the man is here."

"He iss not," said the Kaufmann.

"Was he here early yesterday, on New Year's Day?"

A hesitation. "He voss."

"We shall have to search the Steelyard to be sure he isn't hiding here, although I am sure he isn't, Herr Kaufmann, since that would be remarkably foolish of both you and him, and I am betting neither of you is a stupid man."

Herr Kaufmann Hochstetter said nothing.

"How did he leave? Which ship did he take?"

The Kaufmann made a circular gesture. "Off all the ships in Leith harbour, only the Sea Beggar has gone to Amsterdam."

Carey was staring at the man with interest. "Are you telling me that Hepburn left on the Sea Beggar along with his assistants?"

Herr Kaufmann Hochstetter shrugged and was silent again.

"Mr Menzies," said Carey, "can we execute the warrant to

search the whole Steelyard now just for the fugitive Jonathan Hepburn, suspected of being in the pay of the King of Spain, of plotting with the Maxwell, the earls Huntly and Angus, to bring Spanish troops to Scotland and also suspected of so hideous and outrageous an attempt at Court that I am not at liberty to describe it? Just one word, please."

"Ay," said Menzies.

"I assume, Herr Kaufmann, that you have no objection to such a limited search by warrant of the King, despite the privileges of the Hansa?"

Herr Kaufmann Hochstetter bowed shallowly and then nodded at the young man to open the gate fully. The Gentlemen marched in and split up to search the buildings and storehouses and even the two cranes which were still at the moment.

Anricks looked up from his calculations. "Obviously, he has long run from here," he said abstractly in French to Carey.

"Obviously," said Carey, mindful that Menzies and the other lawyer probably spoke French and quite possibly the Herr Kaufmann too. He sauntered into the compound, not sure what he was looking for but knowing he would recognise it when he saw it, followed by Leamus, who was tracking something in the snow.

Leamus squatted and examined some fresh hoofprints, heading for the stables, frowning over them as if they were a chess problem. Carey went and stood behind Leamus, careful not to disturb the shod prints.

"What have you found?" he asked.

Leamus said something in Irish and then paused as though he was calculating like Anricks. "There's something awry with these tracks," he said. "See, the front part of the hoof should be deeper, but it's the back part that's deeper."

"Hm," said Carey, wishing Dodd was with him instead of gallivanting around the Border, up to no good. "Yes. Where do they come from?"

The prints came over unmarked snow from the gate and beyond the gate they came along the Leith Road, often in the fresh snow to the side of the trampled road.

"From Edinburgh," Carey offered, "perhaps Hepburn..."

"Sorr, why would he take such trouble to ride on fresh snow?"

"Good question." Both of them looked at the prints and then Carey and Leamus both said it together. "The horse was shod backwards."

Leamus laughed and loped along the trail a little. "See sorr, the beast stumbled here and put his back hooves down first, not likely, I'm thinking."

Carey was grinning. "It could be someone else..."

"Who, sorr?"

"Quiet now. We'll play the game a little longer."

The whole of the Steelyard was searched and nothing at all was found out of place, not even the normal crewmembers' contraband. Herr Kaufmann was looking pleased with himself underneath the grave public displeasure on his face.

"My company vill request the League to write to the King about this infringement of our privileges," he said.

As the King's Gentlemen gathered themselves together and prepared to march out, Mr Anricks snapped his notebook shut, put it away and looked coldly at Hochstetter.

"I note that you have bales of tobacco in your warehouse, Herr Kaufmann," he said to the merchant. "May I ask who supplies them?"

"That is a mystery off my trade," said the Herr Kaufmann promptly, "I could not possibly..."

"I recognise the seals as being those of my uncle Dr Hector Nunez who imports tobacco from New Spain to England. However, I was not aware that he was also supplying Edinburgh. Given that the King is implacably opposed to the herb, I surmise that the tobacco is an unauthorized side deal? Hm?"

The Herr Kaufmann said nothing again. Anricks waited quite

a long time and then said, "I will be writing to him. What would you like me to tell him?" More silence. "I will also be informing Mr Secretary Cecil that you were given a prime piece of intelligence regarding the King of Scots, which you suppressed instead of bringing it to the attention of the authorities."

"I did not sink it was important…"

"You were wrong. And you tried to lay violent hands upon me and Herr Ritter Carey, also something I object to."

"Er…A mistake…?"

"Yes," said Anricks, turning his back on the merchant and going to a block to mount his pony.

They rode back past the links where a couple of golf-mad noblemen were arguing over balls lost in the snow, and Carey and Leamus tracked the reversed hoofprints all the way to Edinburgh and a little way further. At Hobson's stables they found a nag that had been completely reshod the day before but it wasn't conclusive even though at Hobson's nobody usually shod a horse that hadn't thrown a shoe, because it cut into the profits. The groom claimed it was for the snow and the nag was indeed now roughshod.

WEDNESDAY, 3RD JANUARY 1593

The next day, Carey took Leamus out on the Great North Road to try to find more traces of Hepburn, but there had been heavy snow in the night and all footprints were erased. That trail was literally cold. And as Carey said, there was no proof of where Hepburn had gone, Amsterdam or south, because either the Sea Beggar or the reversed shoes on the horse could have been a feint. From Amsterdam he could have gone anywhere at all. From Edinburgh he could have gone south to London, southwest to Carlisle or Keswick, he could even be somewhere in the Highlands, biding his time before he circled round and took ship from Leith. His name was read out at the Market

Cross in Edinburgh and at Leith, with the horn being blown thrice, putting him at the horn, making him an outlaw and any man's prey, but of course that only held in Scotland. The King's letters to Mr Secretary Cecil in London would take a while to reach him, even if Cecil reacted immediately. Besides, after the blizzard on the night of the 2nd to 3rd of January, all the roads were covered in deep snow and nearly impassable.

They were waiting for Dodd now. Whitesock and Dodd's hobby had been gone from the stables since New Year's Eve, his jack and helmet and sword were also gone, and when Carey asked Janet Dodd if she knew where he was, she said she thought she did and would like to stay in Edinburgh until he came back, if possible.

Carey was enjoying himself, playing cards with all the hangers-on at James' Court and taking their money, so he decided to give Dodd another week to finish whatever his business was.

THURSDAY, 4TH JANUARY 1593, DERWENTWATER

Radegunda Hochstetter liked to breakfast very early in her own kitchen, in her beautiful house on her island. The maid, Maria, had already gone out in the dark and snow to where Frau Radegunda's bakery was giving good smells to the air. She brought back a selection of breads, one made with almond flour which Radagunda particularly liked. She had butter to go with it, heavily salted and past its best but still edible, and cheese and some slices of proper sausage and mild ale from her own brewery. She couldn't shake the habit of being first up and first out and first at work because she was the mistress.

The snow had stopped for the moment and the sun was coming up at last, sliding its rays under the grey lid of clouds promising more snow. She felt restless so she stood and went out into the courtyard where she could see the sun between the outbuildings, ignoring the new white blanket covering the countryside, and the cold wind. She had her fur-lined gown, didn't she?

She stood and watched as her two youngest children came to breakfast. There was David, a hard-working quiet twenty-year-old, though regrettably spotty, and her youngest daughter, Elizabeth, aged eighteen, unaware of her beauty and quite shy. Both had been born in England, although David was not her youngest son. That was Elijah, who had been born six years after they came to this strange wet land, and her second child to die. He had always been fragile and fretful and a lungfever had eventually carried him off to limbo, no matter what she did, because he was, of course, unbaptised. She would never see him again, not even in Heaven, because his soul had not been brought into Christianity. Like his older brother Leonard, he was lost forever. The thought always shook her, brought back the doubts that could take her to Hell. Yet, Jesus Christ had baptised only adults: how could they do differently? She sighed and forced herself to think of something else, although she wondered sometimes if Elijah and Leonard were warm and dry in limbo? And at least they were safe from Hell.

David and Elizabeth prayed briefly and broke bread in the old style. Her heart warmed a little at that; it was good to see some of the old ways continuing. The two of them spoke Deutsch as she insisted in her house, on her island. The little island, sometimes known as Vicar's Island, in Derwentwater, would never hear the mongrel tongue of English while she lived.

Mark Steinberger, the Schmelzmeister, was already at the smelthouses where they were starting a new campaign. His wife, her oldest daughter, Annamaria, was in her house near Crossthwaite which was nearer than the island to the smelthouses in Brigham, and also near to the road to Gottesgaab mine, their gift from God. It was carefully placed to avoid the acrid continuous smoke from both places, as much as possible. Veronica and Susannah were married and with their husbands in Newcastle and Hawkshead.

Emanuel, her oldest son was currently at Workington to supervise the cargo that was due to go out in the next few days, and of course the essential cargo of good (she hoped) Irish charcoal coming in. She was impatient to see samples of it, the last lot had been terrible and so she had sought another supplier further south in Ireland, where there were more trees.

Joachim was…still absent, along with his disgraceful sister. He had been absent for years. She had trained her heart to think of her wicked daughter, Little Radegunda, who called herself by the ridiculous unscriptural name of Poppy, as dead and in Hell. Sometimes she caught herself thinking of her middle son the same way, as dead. But as far as she knew, Joachim wasn't dead, only absent, only gone from her side despite being such a clever boy, such a credit to her, such a skillful engineer. She allowed herself to think of him only once a day, feeling the longing in her heart for him only once a day, even allowing tears to rise to her eyes, although she never allowed them to fall.

He was her little Joachim, her little curly-haired child, running around with his mop of hair and his cap always lost, birds-nesting, climbing, stealing pointless things for fun, always in trouble. She didn't think of him when he had the measles. She closed her eyes and imagined him with all her strength, a warm shape in her arms, before they came to England, nuzzling his face into her neck and saying "*Mutti, Mutti, Mutti…*"

She walked out of the courtyard and went to the boatlanding at the north side of the island. She didn't do this every morning, exactly, only occasionally. She looked towards the dirty scatter of houses, the main street and English church just visible on the other side of Crow Meadow. You couldn't actually see the smelthouses or the road to Gottesgaab mine from here, they were on the other side of town. You could see the smoke, of course; there was always smoke from the smelthouses and the acrid yellow smoke from the ore-roasting at the mine. It gave the town a prosperous air, she thought.

There was a man at the Keswick-side boatlanding, talking to another man there, paying him. For a moment she felt a stab of hope in her heart, that this would be Joachim, but she was sure it could not be, although she didn't know who it was, she couldn't seem to recognise him, her eyes were no longer good enough. The man got in the boat by himself, shipped the oars expertly, started rowing himself across in the small skiff and she watched his back with its covering of white cloak, her heart beating hard for some reason. That was a very fine cloak—was it velvet?

She didn't move to help him tie the boat up but as he looped the rope and tied it, hopped out of the boat onto the landing stage and came towards her smiling, she felt her heart beat even faster and her heart knew him before her mind admitted it or her old eyes could really see him. She took a step towards him, holding her arms out and he came to her and bowed and she reached up to embrace him, hold him, feel the heft and strength of him, her son, her little Joachim, the child inside, always inside, the body of the man around it but her little son, there in front of her, in her arms. She couldn't believe it, had to believe it, didn't dare trust that it really was him, had to trust because it was him, it truly was him...

"Oh, *Mutti*," he said fondly and gave her his handkerchief to mop her face and she was annoyed at herself for crying. In God's Mother's name, what was she doing? She hadn't wept all the years he had been gone and now here she was, like a foolish old woman...

"Joachim," she said, stroking his face. "*Geht es dir gut? Wo bist du denn gewesen? Was hast...*"

He put his finger on her lips and said, "Shh." And then he asked something strange. "Is there anyone here from the Scots King's court? I'm expecting a message."

"No," she said, "nobody since before Christmas."

"No news?"

"Just that the harvest was bad." And that statement always sent a chill down her back.

He looked down, his face stiff with concern. "Surely…" he began.

"Surely what?"

He paused and then smiled at her, what she always thought of as his trouble-smile, the smile he smiled when he was expecting trouble but wasn't going to tell her what or why. She had seen it so often when he was a youth and she had needed to protect him over and over again, now she thought of it. It stole some of her happiness at having him back. She did not have him back, that was impossible. He was a man now, fully baptised, with his own fate to carve. She shouldn't think of him as her little boy anymore. But she couldn't help it.

"Is there any breakfast?" he asked, touching her shoulder lightly and she smiled at him despite everything.

"Of course, and the baker has made some loaves with almond meal in them."

She slipped her arm in the crook of his to go back to her house, leaning a little as she had done with Daniel Hochstetter, her dear lord and husband, dead nearly ten years.

FRIDAY, 5TH JANUARY 1593, EDINBURGH

Carey was eating a very good breakfast of porridge and a cold goose leg, which counted as fish for the fish day, because geese hatched from barnacles. He washed down the salty porridge with ale. He was eating in Holyrood Hall, once the monks' refectory, along with Red Sandy Dodd, Bangtail Graham, and Leamus. All around him racketed the usual din of a Court at breakfast, people helping themselves to porridge, salt cod, and soused herring, because breakfast was always less formal than dinner, here in Scotland.

Red Sandy and Bangtail were talking and laughing quietly together, Leamus was staring into space, and next to them some men-at-arms were quietly playing dice on the bench, one of them cheating with highman and lowman dice.

Carey was just wondering if it would be worth the effort and expense to take part in the Queen's next masque, but decided it wasn't. He could find as many opportunities to flatter the King more cheaply in the hunting field and that would actually be fun.

Carey liked hunting. He was not as crazy for the sport as the King but few people were. He had just decided to take part in a hunt planned for the morrow when there was the sound of running clogs and Young Hutchin Graham burst into the hall through the double doors to the kitchen and sprinted up to Carey.

"Sir, sir, Sergeant Dodd's horse just come in. He's wood, he willna let naebody touch him, and he's got a bloody saddle."

Carey was already on his feet, his heart thumping.

"Jesu," he said and followed Young Hutchin out of the hall at a run, Red Sandy and Bangtail close behind him.

In the stableyard there was an enraged squeal from the horse standing there trembling and wild-eyed. They could see the smears of brown all over the saddle, in his mane and tail. Carey tried for the bridle, which was half broken, and nearly got bitten.

"Red Sandy, would you try?"

Red Sandy nodded once, his tough young face shadowed. He stepped forward at an angle to the horse, his shoulders turned. Whitesock snorted and squealed. "Bangtail, will ye try and get the saddle off him whiles I distract him?"

"Ay," said Bangtail, moving the other way. "Happen it's the smell o' blood mithering him."

Red Sandy moved cautiously forward while Bangtail circled the other way. Leamus arrived and backed Red Sandy moving counterclockwise. Whitesock showed his teeth.

"Now then, now then," said Red Sandy quietly, "now then."

Bangtail slipped in behind, got two of the buckles on the girth undone before the horse felt him and kicked out viciously. Bangtail dodged the hooves; Red Sandy advanced.

"Now then, Whitesock, ye knacker's nightmare," whispered Red Sandy. The horse looked sideways at him, his ears right back and squealed again. Bangtail got the last buckle undone, pushed the saddle and blanket right off onto the cobbles on the other side while Whitesock skittered away from him and sideways, kicking. Red Sandy dived in and caught hold of the bridle, was nearly lifted off his feet as the horse tried to rear and Bangtail caught one of the other straps. And then Whitesock seemed to recognise Red Sandy, and suddenly stopped still, his broad chest heaving and every part of him shaking.

"Ay," said Red Sandy, "whit are ye at, ye great lummock, whit are ye at? Eh?"

Hutchin darted forward with a waterbucket, which Red Sandy caught up with his left hand, set it down, dribbled water on the horse's nose and after some more tense moments, Whitesock dropped his head and started to drink in long thirsty gulps.

"Young Hutchin, will ye go fetch...?"

"Ay, a mash for him, I will." Hutchin ran off, his clogs thundering.

Red Sandy picked up a whisp of hay and started to rub down the horse's muddy withers and the hay reddened with the blood there.

Very gently, Bangtail brought up a rope halter, got it over Whitesock's nose, and took the remains of the bridle and the bit off.

Carey stepped round behind him, well away from the hooves, and inspected Dodd's saddle.

"That's a very bloody saddle," he remarked neutrally.

"Ay, Ah dinna think it's the piles," said Hutchin as he trotted back with a full bucket. Nobody laughed.

Carey looked at the sky. "Red Sandy, could you track Whitesock's hoofprints in the snow?"

"Ah can try," said Red Sandy, his jaw-muscles clenched, "but Ah'm no' as good as my brother. At least the nag's shod, that'll help."

"Right. We'll saddle up now and see if we can find him."

Carey went to see the seneschal and explained where he was going so he could buy some supplies. Dodd had been gone nearly five days and so they might need supplies for at least five more. He went to his room, still found no Hughie Tyndale, who had also disappeared, and called his clerk John Tovey to act as his valet, at which Tovey was hopelessly unskilful and getting no better.

An hour later they trotted out of Holyrood gate and found a nice clear line of shod hoofprints in the snow going straight across country past Arthur's Seat and then circling round to the north.

THURSDAY, 4TH JANUARY 1593, DERWENTWATER

Joachim sat down to breakfast and ate like a man who was hungry but had a lot on his mind. Now the light was stronger, his mother could see he looked tired and worn out. She hadn't seen him like that before, she couldn't remember a time. He looked sad as well. What was wrong? Had his wicked heretic sister done something?

She began to probe, asking after Little Rady or Poppy as she liked to call herself now, asking after his work at the King of Scots' Court where he had been helping a courtier build his castle more strongly, according to his last letter. She knew each one by heart, kept the rare missives in a small carved wooden box. Of course she didn't keep his sister's letters, she burned them unopened and the undutiful little cow hadn't sent any for two years anyway, since she had married that heretic minister of hers, choosing her mate for herself as if she were a peasant.

Alas, tactful though she was, Joachim became more and more monosyllabic. Yes, Sir David Graham was the Gentleman of the Bedchamber to King James that he had been working for. Yes, he was an astonishingly ignorant fool, yes, he was married, yes, he was unfortunately a Catholic. No, Joachim had not married, he would not do that without her consent. Yes, he had helped again with the fireworks, his friends had gone to Amsterdam and eventually he would go there too…if no news came from Scotland. Oh just news. Important only to him. About the King of Scots. To do with the Court. Yes, in a way it was about an office, but it was secret. No, he couldn't tell her. No, he could not tell her under any circumstances, didn't she understand the meaning of the word "secret"? He stood, balled up his napkin in a way that had always annoyed her, and stalked outside. She shook out the napkin, folded it neatly and put it with the others. Then she went outside to join him. She found him taking out a small clay item, tamping some dried leaves into the bell-shaped end and then to her horror, setting light to it, drawing the smoke into his lungs and blowing it out of his nose!

"What on earth are you doing?" she asked, honestly nonplussed.

"Drinking tobacco smoke," he told her, "This is a pipe. It's becoming fashionable in Edinburgh as well as London and Amsterdam and Brussels."

She had never seen anything like it and made an expression of disgust. "How can you bear it?" she asked, "Don't you want to cough? We have chimneys now, so we don't have to breathe smoke anymore. Why do you…?"

"*Mutti*, it's only a medicine," Joachim told her in a patient voice. "Dr Nuñez's pamphlet says it's extremely healthy for the throat and lungs because it stops an oversupply of phlegm." He puffed at the stem. "His Highness doesn't like it though, perhaps he'll ban it—or tax it." He laughed then, a short laugh, that made her feel uneasy so she left him and tidied her spotless kitchen and swept away the crumbs, although Maria should do that.

And then she went to her husband's office and sat down beside the desk on a stool, never the chair with arms which was now for her eldest son, Emanuel, and pulled the sheets of paper and the receipts and invoices towards her and began putting them in order. She had two sets of books to see to, after all.

She heard Joachim wandering around restlessly, heard him tapping something. She heard him go into the furnace room on the servants' side of the ceramic stove that she and her husband had imported from Augsburg at hideous expense when they got tired of inefficient English open fires. He fossicked around and then opened the little door in it for adding fuel. What was he doing? He wasn't a servant. It sounded like he was using the poker, pushing the coals around, then he put in more wood and slammed the little door, opening the grate below for the draught to light the new wood. She heard him sigh as if there was something heavy in his chest, and then heard his boots going upstairs to his bedroom in the loft.

She had to do it. She got up, went round to the servants' side among the untidy piles of seasoned wood, opened the fire door in the ceramic stove and poked around. There were the remains of paper there and something yellow that smelled bad. She poked it all until it turned to ash, her heart beating. She didn't know what it was and she would not ask, but it made her feel the old fear. She put in some more wood, turned and saw Maria staring at her, so she smiled haughtily and said, "There you are, the fire was going out," and walked out of the furnace room again.

She could hear the creaking as Joachim paced in his room and she smiled because he would find it exactly as he had left it, except clean and tidy, and know from that how much she loved him.

SUNDAY, 7TH JANUARY 1593

The next couple of days hunting for Dodd were frustrating and cold, though at least it didn't snow again. They lost the trail and asked at every tower and farmhouse, checked every ominous lump in ditches, found what Red Sandy thought was the trail again, lost it again.

Leamus disappeared for an afternoon and came back looking

exactly the same, shaking his head. They stayed the second night at a tiny village inn and Carey asked at the pele tower where they said that no one had seen a man, wounded or otherwise, riding a gelding with one white sock.

Carey trotted back, wondering how much longer he dared give it, maybe one more day and they could go hungry on the way back. Red Sandy had been casting around and had found another trail, coming up from the south and west, of two horses, one unshod hobby, the other one Red Sandy swore was Whitesock hisself but laden. That went near a sheepfold built of stone and before that there were only the heavy-laden shod hooves, stumbling often. Leamus followed it on foot, but it was easy to see and wambled around the moors, stopping sometimes where there were tussocks of buried grass.

On the offchance they kept on following it, climbing into the moors where there were little hills all over the place and finally Leamus saw an ominous lump in the snow on one of them, and under it, red, where the birds had disturbed it. They dismounted. Carey paused and gestured for Red Sandy to go first. He gritted his teeth and went forward, bent and brushed the snow off the man's face.

His breath came blowing out of him and he brushed the snow again. Yes, it was a man wearing a morion, but no, it was not Dodd.

"Hughie Tyndale?" said Red Sandy, his voice full of puzzlement. "Whit the hell…?"

Carey came up behind him, and with his gloved hands brushed more of the snow off until they could see the corpse of Hughie Tyndale, staring eyeless at the blue icy sky, his belly pecked and his throat gone, but still quite recognisable. The crows had given up trying to peck through his leather buffcoat.

"Damn it!" Carey burst out. "Another valet gone!"

Bangtail swallowed a snigger.

Carey kept brushing the snow and found blood all around,

mixed in with the newfallen snow and frozen, brutally red like a stained glass window.

Carey looked at Hughie's hands and found his sword still gripped in his right hand, found a discharged crossbow on the ground next to him. There was something bright poking out from under one of Hughie's legs.

Carey moved the leg and found Dodd's dagger still stabbed deep in the calf, at an odd angle.

"Red Sandy," he said and found Dodd's younger brother at his elbow.

"Ay," said Red Sandy, thickly, "it's Henry's dagger. He's had it since he were eight."

Carey stepped back, looked at the scene. "Interesting," he said. "The sword has no blood on it but the crossbow has been used. And I don't see Dodd stabbing someone..." He looked again at Hughie's leg, where the knife hilt was downwards of the blade, "Yes, the angle says it was stabbed upwards. So Dodd was on the ground, possibly on his face. Hughie was standing. Dodd had the bolt in him somewhere, probably, since the blood doesn't seem to have come from Hughie, no holes in him. Except his calf which didn't bleed much. What killed Hughie?"

"And where's Sergeant Dodd's body?" asked Leamus softly.

They looked around as the sun westered and dropped, found nothing, not a trail, not a crossbow bolt, not a corpse. They circled outwards from Hughie's body until they came to the deeper snow that was virgin to the ground, nobody had troubled it.

It was getting dark. Carey came back. "I think Sergeant Dodd may have survived long enough to walk somewhere," he said, "but there's nowhere to go. There's nothing but moor hereabouts. He's probably curled up in a ditch somewhere, covered in snow."

"And deid?" asked Red Sandy.

"I think so. I'm sorry, but the blood didn't come from Hughie..."

"Maybe Hughie were at summat different and..."

"How do you explain Dodd's dagger?"

Red Sandy was silent.

"And it took us two days to get here, so probably the same for them, add a day for Whitesock wandering, us coming out, this is the third day at least…"

"Ay," said Red Sandy, his chin to his chest. "Ay, well, will we bury your man?"

"The ground's frozen," Carey said thoughtfully, "he's got Dodd's dagger in him. I'll take that, on the offchance, but… We could put some rocks on top of him, to stop him walking?"

"Let him walk," said Red Sandy savagely. "What did he wantae kill ma brother for? He can walk all he likes across the moors."

Carey said nothing.

"Sure and I'll have his buffcoat," said Leamus, "I need one."

Carey made a gesture with his open hand up.

They waited while Leamus and Bangtail struggled the buffcoat off Hughie's stiff body, having to break the frozen shoulders, and Bangtail decided to have Hughie's good woollen doublet and get it altered to fit him. He undid the laces and started pulling it off and then stopped.

"There's summat funny about his chest," he said. "It feels a' soft."

Carey helped remove the doublet, found two letters in the front pocket, but it was already too dark to read the cramped Secretary script. Bangtail pulled up Hughie's shirt.

There on his chest was the print of hooves, several prints, easily visible even in the twilight.

Red Sandy stared at the brown marks, touched the jellied ribcage.

"Did Hughie kill my brother and the horse killed him?" he asked.

Carey looked again at the trampled red snow, the blurred marks. "Perhaps."

Red Sandy was silent a moment. "Well, good," he said, "that's a good horse."

Leamus also quietly acquired Hughie's sword and tutted because it was a little pitted with rust. There was nothing he could do about that immediately, so he slid it into the scabbard with difficulty and wrapped the belt round his waist twice, the baldric went once. Hughie's buffcoat was much too wide for him but not too long. Bangtail folded up the doublet and put it in his saddlebag. When they had finished they looked at each other and nobody had anything to say.

Carey felt his heart heavy in his chest, as heavy and sore as if it was full of lead shot. Dodd had been something of a trial in the last few months since Dick of Dryhope's tower. His stubborn loyalty had been bought by Jonathan Hepburn to kill Carey himself, although he hadn't been able to bring himself to do it. And yet Carey already missed the man, felt nothing but sadness for his death.

They mounted up and Carey took them in a wide circle, looking for footprints, a strange hump in the snow, in a ditch, anything.

There was nothing.

At last with the dregs of the day fading from the sky and the cold sharpening its teeth on their ears and noses and fingers, Carey turned their faces north-east towards Edinburgh. It was full night before they found the drover's road, but all of them had good nightsight and the stars bit down on them from a black sky so when he tried to give somewhere else for his sadness to live by going up to a canter on the straight bits that had once been Roman, they came with him, to a canter, up to a gallop, dangerous on a frosty night with snow lying, but he didn't care and nor did they. In his imagination, Carey could see Dodd galloping grimly alongside them.

There were a few lights shining from Edinburgh castle and Holyrood house and Carey dropped his speed when he saw them, astonished to be back so soon, though he thought it was close to dawn. The hobbies were all breathing hard but seemed happy to run and make themselves warm on such a cold night, shaking their heads and blowing out as they came up the paved bit of road to the King's palace.

The gate to the palace was shut, of course, but there was a watchman who sent for the seneschal who eventually allowed as how they might be who they said they were and could come in, this once, so long as they didn't expect such disorderliness to be ignored again.

Red Sandy was hanging back. "Ah canna..." he said, taking a careful lungful of freezing air. "Ah canna tell Janet."

Carey nodded. "I know," he said sombrely. "I'll do it."

THURSDAY, 4TH JANUARY 1593, STOBBS

The church was still burning. The roof had collapsed again and Dodd was alone under the beams. His back was still burning fiercely and his breath came short and every single breath burned. He tried to stop breathing so he could die and be out of the pain, but it didn't seem to help and the fire in his back was getting worse.

"We have tae get the bolt out," said someone clearly, close to him. "Tonight."

Somebody answered, further away. Nobody was there. Clearly they were demons.

"I'll do it then," said the voice quite calmly, "Hold him down."

More rafters landed on his shoulders and hips, someone else held his arms. He tried to fight them but was too weak. Why was he so weak? What had happened? Was he wounded?

Maybe so, said an objective part of him. Or dead.

The church carried on burning silently around him, the roof starting to catch. Hadn't it fallen yet? Rush lights and candles were there too, heating him up.

"Very still now," said the woman's voice.

Another white hot pain attacked his back, running straight down into the red fire in the middle. Reflexively Dodd brought his knees up, curled and more strange sounds came out of his mouth.

"Can ye move the light a bit…Ah. I can see the point of it," said the woman's voice, "I'll cut it out. It's stuck in something that looks like suet."

Somebody else said something.

"Well he canna live with a crossbow bolt in his back," she said, "and if I take it out, I might as well take all of it. One of the plates of his jack turned it aside a bit, but it's deep."

More white hot pain cut through him, filling his body.

"It's good he's curled…ah now…"

The pain grew and grew until it filled all the world, above and below, till it walked into his heart and stuck a spear in it. He couldn't breathe.

Then it relented a little, just a little, went down to only agony. He breathed in sips. He heard somebody puffing a little. "Ay," said the voice, "Now then, where's the wad?"

More agony, more spears in his heart, more talk. "No, see ye, if ye dinna get all the bits of shirt and doublet and maybe jack outta him, he'll die o' the rot, certain sure, even if he disnae die of whit I'm doing now. There!"

What felt like fingers delved in the fire in his back and more white hot pain exploded. He tried to run away, escape, but all he managed was a movement of his shoulders which made him pant again. Ye've nae blood in ye, said the objective amused voice somewhere deep inside him, stay still, ye fool.

"Damn. Ah now, I've got it. Linen, cloth, ay, and leather. I think I'll pack it wi' moss and bandage him."

More pain of the red kind and they somehow lifted him to bandage his stomach. He tried to fight the demons, hit out blindly.

"Jesu, Henry, will ye stop fighting, just the once? Just once, eh?" The voice was amused. "Save yer strength."

He realised he knew the voice, but couldn't recall the name. But he knew the voice and for some reason it made him feel afraid and sad, all at once. His mind shied away from remembering whose it was.

There was the smell of dried herbs, clown's allheal, feverfew, he was laid back on his stomach again. The pain jangled and throbbed, the feeling of stickiness from the blood flowing. Somebody was snuffing out the candles thriftily.

Another mutter. "I dinna ken," said the familiar voice, almost merry. "He could bleed to death tonight. He could die o' the rot next week. Who knows? But Ah've done my best for him. Maybe he'll live. More likely he won't."

He heard the sound of water or broth in a pot, they lifted him again, broth came into his mouth on a spoon, he gulped.

"It's amazing he lasted long enough to get here, the way he wis bleeding. Did they catch his horse?"

He couldn't hear the other person, couldn't see the one who owned the voice he feared.

"Ay well, I didna think anyone would catch him, the beast's wood. Come down, we'll hae some supper and see how he is later."

Dodd was left alone again in the church as it burned and crackled around him like straw. Soon enough the roof fell on him again and buried him under massive timbers in the dark, all of them burning red and red and red.

THURSDAY, 4TH JANUARY 1593, DERWENTWATER

Joachim's eldest brother, Mr Emanuel, should be told about his return, but he was at their quay in Workington, waiting for the charcoal supplies to arrive. Mark Steinberger, the Schmelzmeister, came in to dinner late at two, along with David, who was learning the essential art of smelting and assaying from him. Steinberger stopped still when he saw Joachim, froze like a deer facing dogs, then put his gloved hand down and touched the table with his forefinger, as if he needed support.

"*Grüss Gott*," said Joachim, seeming amused and he smiled at Mr David, who smiled back, a little nervously.

"*Grüss Gott*," rumbled Steinberger carefully, "I see you have come back to us."

"Yes," said Joachim, "I've had enough of the Court and Amsterdam for the moment. How are you?"

"Much the same," said Steinberger. "Are you planning to stay?"

"I don't know," said Joachim, "It depends…"

"There's a chance he might be appointed to an office at the Scottish Court," put in his mother. "Isn't that wonderful, Mark, that little Joachim might have…?"

"Or something like that," said Joachim, his face freezing for a second. "I am waiting for news of it, as a matter of fact. Has a messenger arrived from Edinburgh?"

Steinberger shook his head. "No one new has come into town because of the snow—except you now, of course. That's since before Christmas. The packtrain is due, but it might be delayed. Where will you be staying, Joachim?"

"Here, I think," said Joachim, "with *Mutti's* permission." And he smiled at Steinberger because his brother-in-law could do nothing about it, although his mother was obtuse enough to think that the smile was a friendly expression.

She smiled at him. "Where else? Though when you marry, of course, the company will build you a house."

Joachim was irritated again. "I see no reason to hurry into marriage…"

"He is still the same," she said to Steinberger, shaking her head, "still a boy. I've got my eye on a few girls for you already, Joachim, but we must look at some of the older ones that will bring a better dowry too." Steinberger still stood as if he were made of stone. "When you get your Court appointment, Joachim, you can go to Court to serve the King while your wife will stay here, of course…"

She loved finding wives for her sons. Young Daniel had

married Jane Nicholson two years ago, although he was younger than Emanuel. Unfortunately, it was a love match, although luckily the girl was the daughter of a local gentleman, so quite suitable. Emanuel had finally got married in the summer to Thomasine, Jane's younger sister, a very pleasant young woman, Frau Radagunda thought. Now she was happily going through lists in her head of suitable girls of the right social status and the right dowry for Joachim.

For some reason, Joachim had turned monosyllabic again. He sat down, put his napkin on his shoulder and drank some of their own beer and listened while David told him a long and winding tale of the last cupellation campaign and how bad the charcoal had been and how they had had to do the whole process again with some very expensive Swedish charcoal which had caused Emanuel much lost sleep, and made him very bad-tempered.

After dinner, they said their prayers of thanks but Joachim sat silent, not bowing his head nor clasping his hands. Much as she loved him, it hurt and frightened Radagunda to see that, although she tactfully waited until Mark Steinberger and young David had gone before she talked to him about it.

"Joachim," she said, in her very gentlest voice, "it makes me sad to see you do not pray as we do."

"Well, *Mutti*, I can pray if you want, but my heart isn't in it. I've pretended to be a Catholic on occasion and frankly I prefer Latin prayers because you don't have to understand them."

She was so shocked, she felt the blood draining from her face. "You pretended…to be Catholic?"

"Yes, of course, when I was in the Spanish Netherlands. Why should I get myself burned for heresy?"

"You must trust in the Lord Jesus, Joachim, He will keep you safe from harm…"

"No, He won't. Did He save Pastor Stoltz? Did He save Himself?"

"The Crucifixion was part of the Great God's plan for…"

"Sure, fine. But the fact is, Jesus Christ didn't save Himself, did He? Pastor Stoltz was a martyr, and the fact is, the Lord Jesus didn't save him either. The fact is, the Lord Jesus never even said He would save anybody from harm. He said that those who suffer in His name will have eternal life—a very different thing, in my opinion."

She was staring at him, tears welling in her eyes. "But, Joachim, we are the Chosen People…"

"Ach," said Joachim, jumping to his feet and throwing down his napkin again. "I am not martyr material and so in the Spanish Netherlands, I pretended to be a Catholic, in Scotland I pretended to be both a Catholic and a Calvinist, depending, though never at the same time like the King, and if I went to Turkey, I would probably pretend to be a Mussulman. And stop gaping at me like that, *Mutti*, most people will do the same thing." He stalked out, annoyed with himself for telling her so much truth and with her for…for being exactly as irritating and stupid as she had always been since he was a youth. The island was already starting to suffocate him.

He was in a bad temper anyway. Where the devil was that messenger from Sir David Graham to tell him that the King was dead?

MONDAY, 8TH JANUARY 1593, EDINBURGH

Carey dismounted and led his hobby and remount across the Holyrood courtyard, followed in a line by the other men, Red Sandy at the back. He thought he might appoint Andy Nixon to the Sergeantcy but would see what the bribes came out at first. He was clear he wanted his own man in that position and not some unknown quantity, probably working for Sir Richard Lowther, the other Deputy Warden of the West March, but still, money was money and the office would probably amount to a pretty penny. He must ask Mrs Dodd how much the Sergeant had paid for it. Though perhaps not today.

He sighed as he led his horses into the small stableyard, separate from the much bigger one for noblemen's horses and nowhere near the size of the magificent stableyard for the King's horses.

Jesu, what would Mrs Dodd say? His mind skittered instinctively away from that. They would soon need to go home from Edinburgh, as soon as the roads were better for her cart, either frozen solid or melted and dried out. He would escort her, of course, she didn't need to risk Skinabake again.

And why in God's name had Hughie Tyndale taken it into his head to kill Dodd? Why? Carey had begun to think the Sergeant was unkillable, especially after what happened near Oxford, but of course no man was. So why? And it was bloody inconsiderate of Hughie to get himself killed too, really it was, he didn't want to have to find or train yet another valet. And Hughie had been better than most. Although at least he wouldn't have to pay Hughie's back wages or hang him, that was some comfort.

The sky was lightening, the grooms already at work. He stood near a closed lantern and drew out the letters that had been in Hughie's doublet pocket, squinted his way through the cramped Secretary script.

The letters were from a Mr Philpotts who was paying Hughie the surprisingly generous sum of a shilling each for some ciphered reports of Carey's doings. That didn't worry Carey, he was used to being spied on by servants. However he knew that "Mr Philpotts" was one of Cecil's own *noms de guerre* and wondered why he had dealt with the matter himself rather than delegating it to someone less busy. But why did Hughie kill Henry Dodd? There was no clue in the letters.

He shook his head, folded and put the letters away. What would he say to Mrs Dodd? Jesu, he hated this part of being a captain and there wasn't even a body, although they would be out on the hills again with more eyes the minute the snow melted.

So maybe Dodd was not dead? He shook his head again. He was being stupid. Hughie didn't have any hole in him big enough to put so much blood on the snow and Whitesock's saddle as well. That much blood…No. Dodd was tough, but he was human.

Somebody had taken Sorrel and Blackie in for him and he went in to find Leamus picking Blackie's unshod hooves while Sorrel drank and pulled hungrily at the hay in the manger.

"Did ye find him?" asked Young Hutchin, running past Carey with a bunch of bridles and a saddle on his shoulder. Had he grown another inch while Carey had been looking for Dodd's body?

"No, Young Hutchin," said Carey, suddenly weary amidst all the activity of a stables at dawn. "We found Hughie Tyndale in a patch of blood, Dodd's dagger in his calf and his chest caved in by a horse's hooves. Shod hooves."

Young Hutchin stood stock still and stared. "Ye mean yer tailor attacked Sergeant Dodd?" he asked incredulously.

"Probably with a crossbow," said Carey, stripping off his gloves which he had just realised were dirty with blood, "almost certainly from behind."

"Jesu, how did he dare?"

"I have no idea."

"Ye think the Sergeant's deid?"

"Yes. Though we couldn't find his body."

"Nae wonder Whitesock's still upset. He's no' a warhorse."

"No, but he kicked Hughie to death. We found the prints of his hooves on Hughie's chest."

"Ay?" said Young Hutchin and there was a glitter in his eyes. "He did tha'?"

"I think so. He did right by his master."

"Ay, he did."

Young Hutchin sprinted away and Carey waited and heard the trumpet sound as Young Hutchin blew his nose on his sleeve.

THURSDAY, 4TH JANUARY 1593, STOBBS

And still the Elliot church burned around him. The roof collapsed and Dodd was alone under the beams, somehow always alone. His back was still burning fiercely and breath came short and every breath burned. Something bitter came into his mouth from another world,

He knew. He was in Hell, wasn't he?

There was no one to ask, he was alone. In any case he couldn't speak, his mouth and throat were too swollen.

Voices moved around him. "We'll bring his fever down," said the decisive voice, "If it goes any higher it will kill him."

Something very strange happened then, his teeth clenched and his body contracted and for a few seconds he was somewhere else, in a black place.

"Fetch some snow," said the voice. "Now."

There's no snow, Dodd wanted to snarl, it's summer, that's why the church roof burned so well.

Another black moment as the fire burned on and on, never consuming the beams holding him down, never ceasing, hellfires. Then there was something freezing cold covering his back and as it melted, it was wiped off with linen cloths. He gasped when it landed and for a second it felt good, it felt kindly to him. Then he felt the fire come back again. And another shock as more snow landed, melted, was wiped off.

It went in cycles, more and more heat, the shock of the cold, a little relief and then the heat rising again. The fire boring into his back kept up a steady agony, only increasing. Sometimes spoons would come into his mouth to tip broth or small ale into him. Sometimes his bum would be wiped and more clouts wrapped around his hips.

The fire got hotter and hotter until there he was back in the burning church with burning beams falling on him, in Hell.

There was a galloping of horse hooves thundering from Dodd's chest, and into the burning church came a tall man with a bullet head in a worn jack with his favourite Jeddart axe on his shoulder, breaking down the burning door with a boom.

The man walked in, looked around at the smoke rolling in great gouts down the aisle, walked over to Dodd.

"Dad!" gasped Dodd.

"Ay," said his father. "Whit the devil have ye got yourself intae, ye fool?"

The monstrous unfairness of this broke Dodd's heart.

"Did I say, take revenge on the Elliots till the end of time? Well did I?"

"Ye didn't," said Dodd's mother behind him, "And even if ye did, ye didna mean it."

Dodd's father, or the demon who was pretending to be him, bent down and lifted a broken rafter off Dodd's back. His mother poured snow on it.

"Get awa' from me," snarled Dodd. "I ken ye canna talk for the Elliot spear went straight through yer throat."

"It did tha'," said his Dad. "I wis never so surpised in me life to be deid."

"And ye did sae well at first," said his Mam in reproachful tones, "keeping everybody together, getting the Elliots back a little."

"But then it went sour," said his Dad.

He plucked the last rafter off and Dodd suddenly felt lighter than ever he had before. Slowly he stood up, which somehow seemed possible despite the terrible wound in the back of the man prone beside him on the floor.

There were more hoofbeats, the sound of a goodly company arriving. Was it the Castle guard, turned out to help him?

"Ay," said his Dad, "that's Davidson. Will ye meet him, son?"

"Nay," Dodd said through his teeth, "I'll ha' naething to do wi' him...Where was he when Ah burned the church, eh? Why did he let me do that?"

His mother giggled suddenly. She looked plump and young

in her best blue Sunday kirtle and hadn't she wasted away to nothing in the months after his Dad died and his older brothers were killed, wasted away and died, leaving him, abandoning him.

"Och," she said, "ye're still my thrawn angry Henry," and she moved to hug him but he shook the demon off and brushed past the one pretending to be his Dad as well, heading for the burst door and the bright sunlight.

Through it came another man, tall and dark and strong-built, with a strong dark beard and hair to his shoulders and a jack like any fighting man. He hadn't drawn his sword, which was odd. At his back was his henchman, who did have his sword drawn. There was something wrong about that sword, a shining blue glint to it that didn't belong. He looked a right fighter though, the hard jaw and the jack and morion said that, and never mind the blurred impression of wings from his shoulders.

His father dipped his head, his mother curtseyed as they might have to their headman if Dodd's Dad hadn't been the Dodds' headman himself.

Dodd stood and stared the man in the eyes.

"What?" he said rudely, feeling for his sword and ready to take on the both of them if need be. His sword had disappeared which was typical.

"Mind yer manners, son," warned his Dad, "this is…"

"I ken who it is, or who it's pretending to be," he grated. "So?"

The dark man smiled and held out his hand. "Joshua Davidson," he said, "and you're Henry Dodd, at last."

"Sergeant Henry Dodd, of Gilsland."

"Yes, that's a pity," said Davidson, taking his hand back unshaken. "The freehold reverts to the Crown on your death, I'm afraid, since there are presently no heirs of your body nor likely to be, and you've not made a will. Still easy come, easy go, eh?"

Dodd said nothing.

"Will ye sit and have a quart of ale with me then, Sergeant?" said Davidson, seemingly not put off by Dodd's rudeness.

Dodd's lips were cracked with thirst. "Ay," he said unwillingly.

Davidson sat on a bench which had suddenly unburnt. Dodd's Mam brought a jug and poured ale into four silver cups, all very lordly.

They all took the cups and toasted each other, drank, while Davidson's henchman stood behind him, turned to the door, wide stance, arms folded, looking businesslike. Dodd would have given him a position in the Castle guard and not charged him a penny.

Dodd had never tasted ale so fine. It was as if he was drinking what all ale aspired to be, but wasn't. Next his Mam put a platter of stottie cakes on the bench beside them and Dodd took one, tore off a bit and tasted it. That too tasted finer than it had any right to.

He scowled and chewed. He knew his Dad and Mam were dead, he knew he was in Hell and the demons were tempting and taunting him and he would not be fooled.

Nobody spoke and Dodd realised that the flames were utterly still, frozen around him. They licked the air as if they had been painted there in the round. The smoke was still too. He stood up and waggled a hand through it and it didn't move.

So he came back, sat down and poured himself more ale, drank it down. It was just as good as it had been the first time.

"Prove ye're not a demon," he said to Davidson.

"Prove *you're* not a demon," laughed Davidson. "How many men have ye killed?"

"How many…How should I know? It's ma trade."

Davidson laughed again. His laugh was deep and infectious and it took effort for Dodd not to laugh with him. "So it is!"

"Are ye telling me I shouldnae have killt them?" said Dodd. "Ye should tell them too cos maist o' them were tryin' the best they could tae kill me."

"Fair enough, but not all of them." Dodd shrugged. "In the church for instance," said Davidson, "since here we are." His tone had suddenly hardened. "No fighting men in here, only women and children."

Dodd shrugged again uncomfortably. He always did his best not to think of it, had succeeded for years, but it was hard now. He had fired the old church, himself, personally, he had set fire to it with a burning torch, laughing to think of the Elliot women and children and old men inside, while Red Sandy had stood and stared, his mouth hanging open in horror, but some of the rest of the Dodds cheering him on.

"I wis young…" he said, "jist seventeen and…"

"And?" said Davidson, steepling his fingers. There were odd bone-shaped marks all over the backs of his hands, a gnarled scar at the wrist under his shirt cuff.

"And it seemed like a good idea," said Dodd heavily, knowing that this was justice and justice was justly coming to him and he would stay for eternity in the agonising Hell of the burning church because he deserved it.

Davidson nodded. "Why?"

"Why?" How could he catch in words the rage and sorrow and vengeance that had been in him as a youth? "Because the bastard Elliots had taken my Dad and my Mam and my brothers and my little sister who died of hunger, they had taken so much from me and it was time to take it back."

"Did you in fact get your Dad and Mam and brothers and sister back?"

Dodd glowered at him.

"Did it make you happy to do it? Afterwards?"

Dodd stared at the flagstones. "No."

"Did you ever think of forgiving them?"

Dodd spat. "Dinna insult me! Whit's that but a weak man's blackmail, a mewling spewling 'och, I forgive ye, so now ye'll allus feel guilty.' Nay, I'll tek me chances wi' vengeance, me."

Davidson smiled a little. His henchman fixed Dodd with a stern look.

"Ach," said Dodd in a paroxysm of disgust, "and now ye're gaunae forgive me too. I'll die first, ye soft bastard!"

And he stood and went back to the still fire, flicking Davidson two fingers as he went and sat down in the flames so he could get hot again.

MONDAY, 8TH JANUARY 1593, EDINBURGH

Carey pulled out Dodd's dagger, a plain steel blade eight inches long, with a leather hilt and a small bronze crosspiece, oiled and sharp and nicely balanced. Would he give it to Dodd's wife? He knew he should, but…No, he would keep it just in case, or put it in Dodd's shroud when they found and buried him.

He sighed and thought perhaps he could go and make an appointment for a final interview with the King…No, he had to get it done, stop procrastinating. Mrs Dodd deserved better of him.

Sorrel and Blackie had been seen to by Leamus, unasked, the dawn was come and a fine cold day, she would be up by now and Widow Ridley and he could find them easily. He didn't want to.

He walked slowly out of the stables and went in the direction of the old refectory that he had left in a hurry five days before and as he came through the main door, there were Janet Dodd and Widow Ridley, sitting to their porridge and mugs of ale, chatting in Scots with some of the chamberers and dairymaids at one of the lower tables.

She saw him, rose and dropped a curtsey to him. Mrs Ridley started climbing to her feet as well, so he inclined his head to Janet and waved to Mrs Ridley to save her poor knees.

"Mrs Dodd," he said formally as he came near, "may I speak with ye privately, please?"

She looked up at his face once and she knew. So did Widow Ridley for she caught Janet's hand and gripped it fiercely so she wouldn't fall.

Silently she gathered her kirtle and stepped over the bench, helped Widow Ridley get to her feet as well, and Carey led them both out into the lesser courtyard where they stood in a patch of pale morning sunlight.

"Mrs Dodd…" Carey began and then stopped, not knowing how to go further.

"Was it the duel?" asked Janet, "Did he fight Wee Colin Elliot and lose?"

"No," said Carey, puzzled. "Was there a challenge?"

"Ay," said Widow Ridley, "Mrs Dodd was ta'en by Wee Colin so she could bring it to the Sergeant."

"Wee Colin Elliot challenged Sergeant Dodd to a duel?" said Carey slowly.

"Ay," whispered Janet, "to end the feud, one way or another. Did he lose? It was tae the death."

Carey paused to get his thoughts together. You had to keep duels very quiet even on the Border, for the other party, the survivor if there was one, would be at the horn at least. For a while until everything quieted down.

"That's where he were going," amplified Mrs Ridley, "when he left the Court on New Year's Eve, to find Wee Colin and fight him."

Carey nodded. "Ah," he said and explained what he had found, out on the lonely white moors.

Janet shut her eyes and clenched her fists. "He was shot wi' a crossbow bolt from behind by Hughie Tyndale?"

"If the evidence of the blood and Dodd's dagger stuck in Hughie's calf is anything to go by."

"How did Hughie die, then?"

"I think Dodd's horse, Whitesock, killed him."

"What? How d'ye make that out?"

"Hughie's corpse had shod hoofprints on his chest and all his ribs broken."

"Whitesock killed Hughie for killing my man?"

"I think so, yes."

"So where's Henry's body, then, Sir Robert?"

"I don't know. He was out on the moors, miles from anywhere. We looked as best we could and found nothing, no footprints, nothing. We'll go back when it thaws, I think we'll find him then. There was heavy snow that night."

Janet stood ramrod straight, her fists in balls.

"He's still oot there, in a ditch somewhere?"

Carey didn't like to think of it either. "Or maybe he found shelter in a sheepfold."

"It's been gey cold," said Janet. "Wounded, he'd not have gone very far."

"Well, this is Henry Dodd we're talking about."

Janet put her fists together and clasped her hands tightly.

"Thank you, Sir Robert," she said. "I'd be grateful if ye could bring his body in when ye find it, if ye find it, so I have something to bury."

Carey nodded. "I'll do my very best," he promised. Janet walked like a blind woman back to the room she was sharing with Mrs Ridley and three dairymaids, at the back of another courtyard full of cows and cowdung.

Widow Ridley paused before following her. "Courtier," she said to him, boldly using the name all the men called him by where he couldn't hear. "Sergeant Dodd's no' dead. If ye havenae body, he's still alive."

"Well..."

"You mark my words. He's still alive and he'll turn up again like a bad penny. A tailor kill Henry Dodd? Tha's funny, that is!"

FRIDAY, 5TH JANUARY 1593, STOBBS

Dodd sat in the still flames while Davidson and his parents watched him. He felt they were laughing at him and scowled all the harder—demons, they were demons.

After a bit he got bored, stood up, went over and shouted at all of them.

"Ah ken ye're a' demons," he snarled, "so dinna try to talk me round. Where's the pit? I'll gae down maself."

His Mam shook her head. "Oh, Henry," she sighed.

"Ye're no' in Hell, Henry," said his father patiently, "Ye're in between. Ye can go back or stay."

Dodd thought for a minute. "This isnae Hell?"

Davidson shook his head. "Unless you make it so. But then ye've made a Hell of Earth itself on a whim."

Dodd grunted. "Then I'll go hame to Janet," he said, "and ma tower of Gilsland, and ma brother, Red Sandy. I'll waste nae more time on ye."

And he broke through a skin and found himself lying on a bed on his stomach, with the fire still glowing in his back but his body covered in sweat dripping into his eyes. He was naked except for some clouts around his hips.

People were talking above him, daylight came through a narrow window, an arrow slit, in fact.

"Ah," he said on an outbreath. At least there were no blazing roof timbers on him.

"The fever's broken at last for the moment," said the firm voice he had heard before. He craned his neck and saw a woman with a linen veil over her face. It left only one eye to look out, a green eye and wasn't there something familiar about it too?

She moved and somebody else lifted him and she put a shirt over his head, pulled his arms through as if he were a wean. "There," she said, "he's decent now, ye can come in."

He saw the man standing by the door in his jack and forgot about everything else.

"Wee Colin!" he gasped.

They had met before, although mostly in skirmishes at the other end of a lance. Wee Colin took his helmet off.

"Whit happened to ye, Sergeant, do ye recall?"

"Ye ken verra well what happened."

Wee Colin looked honestly bewildered. "Whit?"

"Ah wis coming to fight ye and ye sent your wee brother Hughie to trick me, to lead me out on the moors and then put a bolt in ma back," said Dodd, only his rage at the betrayal letting him speak so long.

"Ah did not!"

"Ye did so!" shouted Dodd, panting and trying to get up and punch him, only his arms and legs were like straw and wouldn't obey him as he heaved himself up and then fell flat again.

"Go!" said the veiled woman to Wee Colin. "He's started bleeding again."

Wee Colin nodded once and then left the room, his brow full of thunder.

"Och, Henry," said the woman, "now it's all to dae again."

MONDAY, 8TH JANUARY 1593, EDINBURGH

Janet sat on the bed she shared with Widow Ridley with her hands still clenched round each other until the knuckles showed bone white. She could not cry. She didn't know why, but she couldn't. Henry Dodd had found the death he had certainly been seeking, not honourably in a duel that might end decades of deadly feud between the Elliots and the Dodds, but stupidly, sneakily of a crossbow bolt. She didn't think even Henry could have survived the winter cold and heavy snow on top of a serious wound. She forbade herself to hope because that was soft. Everything was a disaster. She would lose Gilsland, that her father had won off Thomas Carleton at cards and made her dowry, though Carleton himself had only held it on a lease from the Earl of Cumberland. It had been given to Henry freehold by the Queen, but as Henry had no heirs of his body to inherit and no will, it would likely revert to the Crown or the Earl who would put in their own man. Maybe the new freeholder of Gilsland would let her stay, but more likely she would have to go back to her father's tower, because she was childless. No son could inherit, no children for her to take care of and take her mind off Henry. Her heart had frozen into a dirty lump of snowy ice and she couldn't cry.

Widow Ridley had got back in bed after breakfast since her joints were complaining at the cold, and she was sitting up against the bolster knitting socks. She had a long list of orders from the many young men at Court, so far from their mothers and not good at darning and was now charging ten shillings a pair. Scotch shillings so only worth a fifth of a real shilling, yet still not to be sniffed at.

"Och, hinney," said Widow Ridley, as she clicked her way down the new sock she had cast on the night before. Janet had been staring into space for an hour.

"Shh," said Janet softly, "I'm thinking how I could mebbe keep Gilsland."

"Ye canna."

"No," she said, and looked as if she was going to add something interesting but changed her mind. "I want his body."

"Ay, o' course ye do."

"But I canna see how he could ha' lived."

"In that cold? Nay, he's no' one o' the faery folk. But still, I think he might have."

"No," said Janet bleakly and with finality, "I'll no' think that way."

Widow Ridley started turning the heel, knitting the backflap. Janet had asked her once how she always made the socks the right size for the young man, and she had looked at her in puzzlement and said, "I look at his feet and then I know."

"Ay," said Janet, quietly, to herself. "Ay, it's worth a try."

"What?"

"Nothing."

Widow Ridley shrugged and went on knitting, checking on her from the corner of her eye occasionally. Janet continued to stare into space, her face hardening under its winter pale scattering of freckles.

FRIDAY, 5TH JANUARY 1593, DERWENTWATER

Joachim went to bed early and slept till the next dawn, by which time everybody else in the house was up and working. He lay there and listened to them moving around downstairs, enjoying the sounds of industry that he was not a part of.

But soon enough the worry came back, the worry about the messenger. Where was Sir David's man? It was impossible that his two carefully laid plans could both have failed, but...He needed confirmation before he could put the next part of his overarching plan into action: recruit soldiers here and in the rest of Cumberland—miners made excellent soldiers—and then go north to meet the first Spanish ships putting into Dumfries in the spring, to take advantage of the assassination and the civil war that would follow it. The Spanish King had approved his plan and promised him gold and land in New Spain if he succeeded in killing the Scottish King and leaving both England and Scotland without an heir. He thought he could do better than that: in the empty hole left by the death of James Stuart, he would be the most powerful man in the kingdom, if he could grasp the opportunity.

He also wanted to build at least one of the battle-carts he had in mind so that the Spanish King's general could see how brilliant they were. It was an idea he had got from an account of the Hussites in Bohemia a hundred years before, but much more possible now gunnery had advanced so much. Guns were lighter, balls were heavier thanks to better gunpowder. The battle-cart concept was no longer just a cart with a cannon on it, well though even those primitive carts had worked for Jan Zizka during the Hussite rebellion against the Holy Roman Empire.

He could see it now, a closed-in armoured cart with a gun sticking out of the front and arquebuses along the sides. The difficulty was with the wheels and the weight. If only there was a way of dealing with the inevitable mud of battle…? Unfortunately, with the cannon at the front pointing forwards, where it would do the most good, you had to be careful you didn't kill the draft horses. The recoil was a problem too but he thought he could modify the sailors' flail, the ropes and pulleys that controlled guns on board English ships and had given them their advantage against the Spanish ships during the Armada. The whole point was that the gun should fire while it was going into battle, not only when it stayed still.

There were creaking footsteps up the spiral stairs and some-body knocked and came in. It was Maria—all his mother's maidservants were always called Maria, no matter what their given name might have been. This one was shy, carrying a tray of bread, cheese, butter, and beer for his breakfast, and she was standing there, trembling slightly. He looked at her and found a wide pink face, with whispy blonde hair and a terrible number of spots on her cheeks, so there was no point in trying to get her into bed, which would be a much better way to wake up than just breakfast.

"Put it on the chest," he told her and then realised he had spoken in Scots, which was why she was looking at him bewil-dered. "*Entschuldige, Maria. Stell es einfach auf die Truhe.*"

"Yes, sir, thank you, sir."

She stumbled at the threshold from which Joachim surmised she was short-sighted. How absolutely typical of his mother that she would pick such a shortsighted, clumsy, spotty numbskull for her maid. Mind you, she was almost certainly still a virgin which made her more interesting. Still, the spots were offputting.

Joachim got out of bed in just his shirt and looked through the dormer window which had ice flowers on the inside, opened it so he could see out. Thank God for his mother's insistence on a proper ceramic stove that warmed the whole core of the house. Its warm chimney passing through the floor to the roofridge stopped the attic from being damp and miserable though it was still quite chilly.

He looked to the north and saw nothing, no horsemen, no people waiting near the Derwentwater landing stage. Had Sir David played him false? What was going on in Edinburgh? It was enraging and terrifying to be here in provincial Keswick and know nothing. He should have stayed nearer Edinburgh. Was the King dead yet? Were they keeping it secret while they chose one of the nobility to be king? That was possible, although the first of his plans had been public enough to make it difficult. Did that mean it had failed?

It couldn't have. The two plans together were too ingenious, too well thought out.

It was time to go and find his messenger, Sir David Graham's man, a respectable Graham, Long Tom was his nickname. Joachim got up and looked through his old clothes chest, found breeches, socks, hemp shirt, a jerkin that a miner might wear under his miner's coat, and a blue statute cap to finish it. As a precaution he took his flask with him, because you never knew. His mother didn't keep a stable on the island, although they had an entire string of packponies kept very busy between Bolton, Keswick, Workington and…Scotland. So he would have to walk and he felt nervous of being seen…just in case something had gone terribly wrong in Edinburgh. He felt more comfortable as just one of many young men in the town, not exactly disguised but less conspicuous. It had done very well years ago, before he left home, for Keswick was just big enough that not everybody knew everybody by sight and it was easier to chase and catch girls if they didn't know immediately that he was one of the Hochstetter boys and it was also much easier if his mother didn't find out either.

Mark Steinberger had found out about one of the girls because she was his niece, at which point his miners' clothes hadn't really helped. However he had been too clever for the Schmelzmeister. Throttling her and then setting her body up to look as if she had hanged herself had been a brilliant idea.

He smiled reminiscently and dodged carefully out of the kitchen door when there was nobody there. He went to the boat-landing and took one of the family boats, was hailed by the miller who was new and found himself being paid 2d to carry some sacks of flour to the Keswick boat landing which amused him, though he took the money.

Once over the water, he started walking quickly towards the smelthouses, keeping his head down and his back bent, looking out for anybody new who might also be Sir David's messenger. It had occurred to him a little late that any messenger would know him as Mr Jonathan Hepburn which would mean nothing to anybody in Keswick, and that might well account for the lack of sign of him. He really hoped the man hadn't decided to head home, but also hoped that the five shillings Long Tom was expecting for the message would encourage him to try hard to deliver it.

Friday, 5th January 1593, Keswick

Joachim walked swiftly to the northeast part of the town, where the Penrith road led away from the town alongside the usefully fast Greta River, and the smoke clung tight to the lower slopes of the hills. Once he was out of the main part, on the scrubby common land between the houses and the northern part of the river, he relaxed a little. His ludicrous mother had been upset as he expected at his refusal to pray, but he was so tired of pretending to be pious. Lip service was never enough for her, she insisted that you had to believe exactly as she did, that you had to be an Anabaptist as she was, that you had to be baptised as an adult in a cold river that was stupidly renamed the Jordan for the occasion, that you had to pray to the Lord Jesus all the time, whining and nagging Him for help, that you had to pray to His Mother as well, the Theotokos, which wasn't very Protestant at all and much more like the Catholics his mother hated so well, that you had to pray all the bloody time and listen to endless sermons from people less clever than you, who had clearly not even read the obscure texts they quoted and generally preached complete nonsense.

He remembered the endless irritation throughout his teens, like a physical pain it was, under his breastbone. Why did everybody he knew insist on praying and listening to long stories about God and Jesus? What was the point of it? In his experience, God never answered back and if you asked Him for something, sometimes you got it and sometimes you didn't, so why bother?

And then there was his cave. He had found it by accident, the year after the family came to Keswick. He was exploring the west bank of Derwentwater, parallel to Goldscope mine at Newlands, but on the other side of Cat Bells fell. He had found an opening in the rock and gone in, for the same reason he had gone through the unlocked door, long ago at Whitehall. He had climbed up through a narrow crack in the rock to something extraordinary, a huge cave. He had shouted and thousands of alarmed bats went past him into the daylight, and the echoes told him the size of it.

He had come back that night with lanterns and a stolen pickaxe and as soon as he had lit the lanterns and looked up, he had stood, stunned and astonished at what he had found. There was a crowd of painted animals above him, all shapes and sizes, all running towards a flat piece of rock where something else was painted.

It was the Devil. He knew it was because it was a man's face but it had horns. The face didn't look like the woodcuts of the Devil in prayerbooks, but somehow noble. He had stood and stared, his mind unable to take it in, unable to understand.

Was the cave an entrance to Hell? He didn't think it was

because it wasn't hot; in fact it was quite cold. With his lantern and pickaxe he had climbed up to where the Devil was and found there was a rubble of rocks hiding the Devil's body. Tentatively he pulled out a few rocks and found part of a painted shoulder.

He climbed back down and stared in the flickering light of the lanterns until one of the candles guttered and went out. And then he had carefully picked his way out over the stones, and found steps carved, going a different way down to join a small stream that came out under an overhanging rock a little below where the opening to the bat cave was. It was a gift to him and much easier than crawling up through the chimney.

It was as if the Devil had shown him a way to come back.

And so he did come back, and the Devil's Cave became his sanctuary, his refuge from the nonsense of his mother, the strangeness of other people, even before he found the Devil's Gift. He had gone to the local school for a while to learn to read English as well as Deutsch; he already knew how to calculate with Arab figures. Then he had been apprenticed to his father to learn the making and care of machinery, to be an engineer. He had liked that, found it fascinating the way the force generated by water power or animal power could be directed and aimed to move waterwheels and stampers and bellows. It was so much easier and more predictable than people, there were rules of thumb you could use, ways of calculating how many cogs you needed. It was so satisfying. More and more he felt alone among his large noisy family, alone among the miners. People were a mystery to him: why did they sometimes weep for no reason, why did they sometimes get angry for no reason, why did people sometimes embrace him? When his father died in 1581, taken after a short illness that made his breath rasp and his face swell, the family had gone into mourning. His mother had been impossible, weeping and wailing and calling "Daniel, Daniel!" as if his father could answer back. He couldn't. He had been alive and now he was dead. It was a pity because there was so much more Joachim could have learned from him, but what could you do about it? Why did weeping help?

Long before that, he had found that the enormous cave led back through interconnecting tunnels and caves to a place right next to one of the main mine tunnels of Goldscope mine. Nearby he had found what he thought of as the Devil's Gift. Using it, he had recruited a miner who drank a lot, to help him break through and then when the job was done, he had got the man drunk in the little alehouse. On the way back to the bunkhouse in the dark, Joachim had tripped him and hit his head hard with a pickaxe so he had snored for two days in his bed with his anxious wife and sons and daughters around him, and finally died.

That was when Joachim had realised that if there was a God, He really was not interested. Nothing happened. Joachim had waited with bated breath, his heart beating hard, for the lightning to strike, the voice to come from Heaven. He had made a false wall to hide the opening to his cave and he had waited for that to be discovered as well. And it wasn't discovered. It was not like the boy at Whitehall which had been self-defence, this was a murder pure and simple and he had done it to keep the Devil's Cave and more importantly, the Devil's Gift, a secret, nothing more. Day after day passed; the miner, whatever his name was, had been buried. Nothing had happened.

He had gone back to the cave and pulled some more rocks away from the Devil's body and stared at the painting. It was as if the Devil was smiling at him, though that was the lantern light, the painting hadn't moved, of course. If, as he had always suspected, God really wasn't interested in what he did, he could do what he liked. So long as people or his family didn't realise what he was doing, why he was doing it, he could do whatever he liked. It didn't matter that he didn't believe adult baptism was better than infant baptism, that in fact, he couldn't care less about Anabaptism, that he found the Bible boring and the character of Jesus both mad and weak. He could do whatever was more convenient, was best for him. It was a moment of pure liberation.

He had laughed with relief and gone back to the island and agreed to be baptised with his face contorted into an expression so holy, he felt sure it would be spotted as fake. Instead his mother had embraced him with tears in her eyes. Stupid bitch. And his father, still alive then, had shaken his hand. Why?

And he had treated God fairly. If anything had happened during his baptism, then he would have reconsidered. It was an experimentum. He went seriously through the whole business, firmly resisting the urge to laugh, wearing a white shirt, getting ducked by Pastor Waltz in the Greta which was bloody freezing, saying all the prayers and the whole time thinking, here I am, God. Do your worst.

Nothing happened. Nothing ever happened afterwards either. Here he was, he had lost count of the people he had killed or had had killed by the useful Hughie Tyndale, and he was better than ever. He had learned how to manipulate people as well, so they did what he wanted. Once he had found out what had happened at Court, he would make the next play in the long game that would make him, not just an engineer, but a power in the land, perhaps even the King. At worst the Spanish King would make him richer even than the Devil's Gift had done.

He skirted round the smelthouses carefully, not wanting to be seen by any of the workmen. Most of the older men knew him by sight, which was awkward, though some of them liked it that he wore their kind of clothes when he was in Keswick, and not the usual furs and brocades of his family. They seemed to think he was sympathizing with them, somehow on their side. He had encouraged that, although he had not realised why at the time. Now he knew it was to make it easier to recruit them as soldiers. Anyway he hoped that the years he had spent in the Spanish Netherlands and in Spain and Scotland had changed him enough.

He was heading to a little hamlet just beyond the smelthouses, where some of the workers lived. It had an alehouse and he hoped Long Tom would be waiting there for him. The other likely place was the Oak Inn, right in the centre of Keswick, but that was expensive and far too public.

He walked into the alehouse which had a small ceramic stove that turned a tiny cottage into a haven of warmth from the cold. There was an old man dozing in the corner and the woman who owned it, Frau Magda, was standing tapping herself some beer. She knew him and there was no point pretending he didn't know her. He knew her very well indeed, in the Biblical sense, and she had been his second woman.

"*Grüss Gott, Frau Magda,*" he said to her in Deutsch. "I'm looking for a man with a message for me? Have you seen him?"

She clasped her heart and smiled at him. "Jesu, Mr Joachim, you gave me a turn, I didn't know you were here."

He smiled back, although he had tired of her plump tits and obedience when he was still in his teens. "Well, I am, just staying for a short while. Have you seen my messenger?"

She frowned. "A man came in yesterday, said he was a merchant's servant, wanting to buy copper."

Joachim nodded brightly. That's what Long Tom had been told to say, at least partly to have some fun at Steinberger's expense who was always worrying about the vast quantities of useless copper they produced as a byproduct.

"Oh, he's still upstairs," she said. "He'll be down soon…"

Joachim went to the familiar staircase beside the stove, leading to the two upper rooms under the thatch, went upstairs and knocked on the door, put his head round and saw Long Tom sitting on the edge of the bed with his head in his hands.

"Good morning, Long Tom," said Joachim and for the first time felt a little tickle of discomfort, a tiny thrill of fear that the Devil had played him false. Because there was no reason why Long Tom should be in despair, no reason at all.

"Och, sir," wailed Long Tom. "Och, it's terrible, that's wha' it is, it's..."

"What's wrong, Long Tom, was it hard to get away...?"

"Ay, oh ay, it was, it was, the King's men wis everywhere, and poor Sir David's under arrest and like tae be hanged and..."

Well you'd expect some disruption to a court with the King dead or gravely ill, but...why was Sir David...? Joachim sat down on the bed next to the man and shook him, not very gently.

"What happened?"

"Ay, well there wis summat went wrong wi' the Queen's Masque but nae damage done tae the King then, jist his throne and a robe burnt, but New Year's morning wis a disaster, so it was..."

Joachim suddenly felt cold. It was ice radiating from his core, and it made him colder than the Baltic, colder than a winter's night in the Netherlands. "Tell me what happened?" he asked very calmly, wanting to shout and rage but the ice always in his heart helped him.

It was a long and complex tale, made worse by the fact that Long Tom was terrified of the fact that the nobleman he had helpfully bought belladonna for had turned out to be the King and that his master and distant cousin Sir David was clearly guilty of high treason and would, at the very least, hang. He had no interest at all in whatever might have gone wrong with Joachim's elaborate plan for the masque.

At last Joachim leaned back and looked at the thatch where the daylight came in under the eaves. There was enough light that they didn't need a candle, snow was reflecting and magnifying it. Long Tom had got away from the Court, despite the feeble attempts at security, by eavesdropping on the doings in the King's Great Bedchamber and immediately it started to go wrong, walking out carrying a hawk on his fist. That had been his excuse to be there at all. He had taken the hawk to the mews and left it there on a perch, gone to the noblemen's stables next door and taken two horses, which he told the head groom were for his grace the Earl of Huntly who had promised him a job if all went well. He had ridden out of Holyrood house by ten o'clock and waited for news at a coaching inn in Edinburgh, by which time there had been a hue and cry for any men of the name of Graham as well as a day of fasting and abstinence to celebrate the King's deliverance from the toils of the unGodly. That had caused enough confusion, considering how many collateral branches of the Graham clan there were, for him to be unremarked as the Liddle he claimed to be until the next day. And on that day he had headed for Newcastle and then Carlisle and finally Keswick, hoping to lie low in England until the whole thing had blown over.

All in all, Long Tom had handled himself well and got away when he could easily have been scooped up as one of Sir David's relatives. There was after all much less confusion at Court than there would have been if all had gone well.

If all had gone well. Why hadn't it worked? Why now?

He sat there staring into space for so long that Long Tom started to recover from his fear and was putting his doublet and hose on, hopping around in his stockinged feet and tying his garters and wondering aloud whether the Netherlands would be far enough away.

"Well, Tom," said Joachim slowly, "I think you're right. We need to think of leaving England as well as Scotland." He had no intention of leaving Keswick yet, but Long Tom certainly needed to leave the country one way or another because he knew far too much about Joachim. In fact the Netherlands were not far enough.

"I'll help you," he added, "of course. There's a small port near here called Workington and there are regular ships from Ireland and Scotland and Bristol, mainly coastal traders. I'd say you should take the first ship that will let you on board…"

"I'll need money, sir," said Long Tom. "Ah spent all ye gave me getting awa' from the King's men and to stay here a couple of days."

"Of course, of course," said Joachim with one of his easy smiles that let people trust him and occasionally got women into bed. "I'm just thinking aloud. With the snow at the moment and more on the way, I think it would be dangerous to try and get to Workington today. The hills are treacherous, local people call them man-eaters."

Long Tom shuddered.

Joachim got up and nodded his head. "Thank you for bringing me this news," he said, "I won't forget that you took the trouble to do that when you might have gone to Leith…"

"Nay, sir, the day after, that bastard Englishman was searching the port, that's why I went back into Edinburgh."

"Ah. Which particular bastard Englishman..?"

"Ye ken, the one the King likes, the one that wis at the Disputation with his friend the philosopher and then he was the man Sir David Graham invited to give the King his first wine cup of the day…" Which Sir David had done at Joachim's suggestion, in fact, so that the nosy Englishman could be blamed for the death of the King.

"Sir Robert Carey?"

"Ay sir, that's his name a'right. I think he knew the taste of the poison despite all the sugar and spices."

Joachim sighed heavily. Inside he was feeling utterly bewildered. Outside he kept his face smooth and pleasant. What was going on? Was it that he should have killed the Englishman when he had the chance, while Carey had no suspicion of what would happpen?

Maybe. Maybe so. Well, he wouldn't be so tentative next time. Or ever again. He had ended the life of the man who had been his best friend in Keswick, almost like a father to him after Daniel died. It was right to do it, despite the strange feeling of heaviness he had carried just under his breastbone afterwards. He didn't know what you called the feeling, which was odd because usually he felt nothing at all when he killed. He had used a new and complicated method to see if it would work, a way of killing someone without showing that he had been killed, and more reliable than poison. It was logical to kill him because he knew so much about Joachim's equipment. And he should have killed Carey as well.

"Let's hope he doesna come here..."

Joachim said nothing to that either because he was rerunning the casual conversation with Carey that he had had on Christmas Day, the conversation in which he had let out where he came from and what his real name was, the conversation in which he had denied that he knew Hans Schmidt, the man who had claimed to be an expert gunfounder, in which he had also denied all knowledge of his sister. He had been helping with the fireworks, not that the Han artificers really needed any help, and he had decided not to kill Carey after all, once he had convinced him that the Earl of Huntly was the man to watch. Killing him then would have been so easy to do, because Carey had been behind the scenes at the firework display, checking fuses and tubes to be sure none of them were pointing at the King. One charge, one hidden fuse and Carey would no longer have been a problem.

But he hadn't done it because he thought he had the man fooled. He had thought that with two elaborate plots to kill the King, nothing could go wrong. He had given Carey for free all the information Carey could have wanted to find him, and he had done it because...

Because he had thought he was safe. Dear stupid Jesus, how could he have been so...so mistaken? How could he have let so much out? Years of caution blown away in an afternoon, talking. Had he been mad? Insane? He started to sweat, thinking about the ramifications. Carey knew his right name was Hochstetter and where he came from. It was only a matter of time before he arrived in Keswick.

Long Tom was still talking, hammering out the question

of whether to go to Dublin or Bristol. He didn't know it was irrelevant; Joachim knew he couldn't afford to make another mistake like Carey. Unlike most men, he could learn from his mistakes, just as he had from the one he had made with Steinberger's niece.

He left the alehouse just before noon and as he was walking back to town, he saw a crowd around the Keswick marketplace, a boy with a drum and the broad new Mayor standing with his thumbs in his belt, making a speech. He instantly knew what that was about and turned casually down a lane that skirted the town to the south, cut through Castlehead wood and Cockshot wood until he came to the Derwentwater landing stage and took the boat back to the island, tied up and went into his mother's house and changed his clothes. He hoped the hue and cry wouldn't find Long Tom, that would be inconvenient. At least he was safe. He knew the Keswickers would stop at the landing stage on the Keswick side so the yokels wouldn't find him. Joachim smiled and went down to dinner.

MONDAY, 8TH JANUARY 1593, EDINBURGH

When Janet came to bed that night she was late. Widow Ridley was already tucked up and the three dairymaids snoring in the other bed. She unpinned her cap slowly, loosened her laces and took her kirtle off over her shoulders. Her shift was linen of her own spinning and weaving and was a credit to her, even without the embroidery of the cuffs in black silk, very expensive and elegant. Then she unplaited her plait of wild red hair and found a wooden comb in her petticoat pocket as she untied the back and took that off. She started combing her hair until it lay shining, melted copper, on her shoulders.

"Ye could marry again," said Widow Ridley judiciously, from her pillow. "Ye're not young but ye're a good looking woman, so you are."

Janet gave her a piercing look. "It's a little soon tae be thinking o' that," she said very staidly.

She lay down next to Widow Ridley who outed her candle. She lay on her back, and stared into the darkness listening to the soft snores and deep breathing that was so reassuring, that helped her to sleep. But she didn't sleep.

In the depth of the night she got up and put her shawl over her shoulders, lit the candle again from the watchlight and left the room with its snoring cargo of dairymaids and Mrs Ridley.

She knew where his room was and as far as she knew only his clerk would be sleeping there, the toothdrawer having left the Court and Carey's valet dead. Of course, he might have locked the door.

He had. She tapped softly on it, her breath coming short and her heart quailing in her breast at what she was about to do. But she knew fighting men. He'd wake to her soft sounds, if he was asleep at all and hadn't been drinking and playing cards with the other courtiers.

Carey didn't disappoint her. The door unlocked, opened and there he was in his shirt with his naked poignard in his hand.

"Mrs Dodd," he said, utterly surprised.

"Ay, Sir Robert, can Ah talk to ye? Now?"

"Now?"

"Ay."

He frowned, but after a moment's thought, he closed the door, and re-emerged wearing a fur dressing gown, slippers on his feet. Under his arm was some kind of rug from the bed.

"It's freezing," he said conversationally. "Wrap this round you. Come in. John's taken to sleeping down in the stables with the other men. Apparently I snore loud enough to wake the dead."

She crept in, and sure enough Carey was alone in the small dusty room, sleeping all by himself in the half-testered bed, not even a dog with him, poor man. It must be hard to sleep alone like that.

She sat on the truckle and he sat on the bed.

"Well?" he said at last, wrapping his fur dressing gown round his knobbly knees.

She looked at him, his chestnut hair messed, his blue eyes intent. Inside her a great tidal wave of tears threatened to rise up and overwhelm her, but it didn't. She pushed it away.

"Courtier," she said, "ye ken how I'm placed. I've nae childer fra Henry and now I'll get none which means Gilsland will be taken fra me, the freehold will revert. But…but now I'm a widow…if Ah can find a man…And I could…I mean i…if ye were willing…tae…er…"

Understanding dawned in his eyes. Some men might have laughed or made some smutty comment. Carey silently poured her a cup of whatever it was in his flask and she gulped it down, lighting a grateful fire in her belly.

"Ye ken I wouldna…"

"If the freehold of Gilsland wasn't at stake."

"Ay." She gulped more of the strange drink and blinked down at it, since she had never tasted the stuff before.

"Whishke bee," he said, before she asked. "Mrs Dodd, are you certain?"

"Ay. Ah would ha' asked his brother Red Sandy but I didna think he'd be able for it. Then I thought o' you. Henry said chances were that the babe that musician woman in London was carrying was yourn."

"It might be my father's," said Carey with a smile.

"I'll ask naething else of ye," said Janet seriously, "I'll ask nothing if there's a babe, nothing for myself. He'll be a Dodd."

Carey also looked serious. "But, Mrs Dodd, are ye sure?"

She took a deep breath, stood and dropped the rug and the shawl round her shoulders though the room was cold enough that she could just hear the water in the washbowl creaking as it froze.

Carey took her hand and brought her to sit beside him on the bed, and now his blue eyes were nearly black and he was smiling.

"Sir Robert, if he does come back fra the dead, ye willna tell him…"

"I'm not an idiot, Mrs Dodd, and I don't want to die." He poured some more whishke bee for her and she drank. The fire inside did seem to help.

Carey was stroking her hair and she shuddered a little at the familiarity. "I've wondered so many times why women always hide so much of their beauty. Caps on their heads, stays to hide their breasts, endless skirts and petticoats to hide their beautiful legs…"

He leaned down and tried to kiss her but she pulled back instinctively. That was too personal. Only Henry had rights to her mouth. He paused and she wondered if he would be offended, but somehow he wasn't and she ran her hands down his shoulders and back, smiled a little at him, feeling as if she was a maiden again. And, indeed, this was only the second man she had bedded in her life. He was breathing hard now and his hands were on her breasts, gently circling her nipples in the fine linen she had woven.

She had liked the look of him on her hay cart in the summer and now, as he stood up, dropped his dressing gown and despite the freezing air stripped off his shirt, she liked the look of him even more and had her curiosity satisfied for his lower beard was chestnut too and his shoulders had pleasing dimples in them. There was the mark of a bullet graze on his shoulder blade and the scar of a dagger marred his stomach, but she couldn't have loved a man without battle scars. She was an Armstrong, after all.

He undid the ties of her shift, found a breast and put a hot mouth on her nipple and started to suck while his hands went fluttering down to her own fur below.

Janet arched her back and pulled her legs up. It was over quite quickly but then Carey grinned at her and stayed where he was and sucked her other tit until she felt him in her again and that time was altogether better.

Carey dozed while Janet stared at the tester and wondered at it all. Gently she moved him off her and kissed his cheek. His eyes opened and he smiled at her, a smile full of satisfaction and complicity. She smiled back. Then she got up, pulled her shift back down and put her shawl round her shoulders.

"Thank ye, Sir Robert," she said formally.

"Thank you, Mrs Dodd," Carey said, equally formally, "for honouring me with your request."

She ducked her head, thrust down the tidal wave again, and went to the door. Carey came with her to the door and locked it after her. But first he took her hand, bowed over it and kissed it as if she were the Queen.

She walked back quietly with her burned-down watch candle through the maze of the sleeping Court, wrapped bodies everywhere there were bundled rushes. She outed her light before she came to the little room where the dairy maids were still sleeping, and climbed into bed where Mrs Ridley was sleeping quietly, a warm body that Janet was careful not to touch until she had warmed up a bit.

She lay and thought of Mrs Hogg and what she had said after Ellen lost her babe, back in the autumn. How if a man caught the mumps when he was grown, it did something to the stuff in his balls so that he couldn't make a baby, according to Mrs Hogg's long ago 'prentice-mistress, Mrs Maxwell. And Henry had caught the mumps when he first came to soldier in the Carlisle guard, to get him out of Tynedale, back in 1582. And although they had rejoiced in each other as a married couple should, it had been nearly ten years and there were no children. So she had followed Mrs Hogg's advice as she had said she would not, and she had done what she could and now she felt strange to herself, as if her body was somebody else's. Henry was dead but perhaps…

To her astonishment, Janet dozed off quickly, the damp

happiness between her legs making her feel like a traitor, and the print of Carey's mouth on the back of her hand like a Queen. But at least she might get a babe. Maybe.

TUESDAY, 9TH JANUARY 1593, EDINBURGH

In the morning, when he knelt to say his prayers, Carey wondered if the whole encounter in the night had just been a more than usually erotic and vivid dream. Lord knew, he had dreamt of Janet before…No, he saw the rug dropped on the rushes. By the time he was eating his morning bread and beer and cheese, he knew that it had been real. Extraordinary. Had it been another of his many sins of fornication? Well, yes, technically, but oddly he didn't feel like he had sinned: he felt he had done a favour for a friend, had helped Janet with something that was easy for him but hard for her. Of course she had chosen carefully and well. He didn't quite understand why Red Sandy was not suitable—perhaps he would have been too shocked at the idea—but failing Dodd's own brother, in accordance with the Bible, he felt he was by far the best man to father Janet's child. He could keep his mouth shut, he understood discretion and…well, clearly he was the right man. Henry VIII's Blood Royal ran in his veins and he didn't even have the French pox. And yet he wasn't quite sure why, but there was a tincture of sadness to his normal happiness after a night spent doing what he had, but there it was.

He was still staring into space and remembering, when a pageboy came up to him and said that the King of Scotland wanted to see him and would he come to breakfast?

If such an invitation had come from the Queen he would have run back to his chamber to shift his shirt and put on a clean ruff at the very least.

James VI of Scotland was not nearly so particular, to put it mildly, and in fact rarely shifted his own shirt and had never been known to bathe. So Carey simply followed the boy to the

King's privy parlour where he found the King eating partridge and venison and manchet bread and a dish of fried exotic roots from the New World, washing the whole down with red wine which he preferred to ale.

Carey took three steps in and went immediately, gracefully to his knees, partly out of habit, partly because there was nothing wrong with keeping up a little flattery. Many of James' own subjects barely bent their necks to him and also tended to harangue him about sin and vestments if they were ministers, and sometimes, even if they weren't.

"There ye are, Deputy Warden, how are ye, have ye braken yer fast? Guid, guid, here, have some wine."

The King waved expansively at a table with a flagon and silver goblets on it. Carey stood, bowed, went over and served himself some wine, took the napkin on his shoulder, came back to pour wine into the King's own goblet. He then lifted and tasted his goblet, found nothing there but surprisingly reasonable Italian wine, so he bowed again and drank more.

"Now, now," said the King genially, "sit ye doon, Sir Robert, and have a read o' this."

Carey sat on the stool, took the letter handed to him which had several grease stains on it and a wine blot. The King's black velvet doublet had grease spots from the venison too.

Carey sipped the wine and focussed on the letter. It was from Sir Robert Cecil in London, probably dictated to Mr Phelippes, thanking King James for his confidential explanation of the doings over Christmas and the New Year at his Court, and their connection with the northern Armada of the ailing Spanish king. Cecil didn't feel the danger was fully averted, seeing that the guilty Catholic earls were still at large, etc., and so on.

"Ah wrote tae my brother-in-law of Denmark to warn him in case Jonathan Hepburn turns up there. I'll wager he's gone tae the Netherlands to get back into Spanish sovereignty."

"Quite possibly."

"And it seems Hepburn was really an Allemayne fra the miners at Keswick. Did ye ken that, Sir Robert?"

"Hepburn told me himself on Christmas Day," said Carey.

"He did? Hm. No plans to go back there, perhaps. Now whit was it I...ah yes, here's a letter to ye fra Cecil himself."

Carey took the letter which was also in clear. "You are hereby warranted and ordered to go to Keswick and investigate the Dutch strangers there and find out how serious is their treason and sedition, whether Her Blessed Majesty should expel all of them. She is most unwilling because of the gold she receives as her share from the copper mining there, although it has gone down in quantity in the last ten years."

There was a second warrant, giving him authority as Deputy Warden to inspect the mine workings in Keswick and anywhere else in Cumberland that he thought fit. Carey nodded thoughtfully.

"It's impossible to know where Hepburn went on New Year's Eve."

"Not sae very hard," said James with a twinkle. "Ainly three ships left the whole of Leith that night, one was a Sea Beggar, one was a Danish ship, one was French."

"He probably went in the Sea Beggar. They would ask the fewest questions."

"He's a Catholic."

"How would they know that? He probably wouldn't tell them."

"My brother-in-law tells me he wasnae aboard the Danish ship."

"He might have taken the French ship as well."

"Ay," James sighed, "d'ye think he might have gone back tae Keswick?"

"No," said Carey positively. "Why go there? It may be in England and so out of your authority, but I think Cecil does not want someone who tried to assassinate Your Majesty twice anywhere on English soil. Jonathan Hepburn, or whatever his name is, can work that out too. And furthermore he actually told me he was from there. No, he's gone to the Netherlands."

"Ay, but Keswick is home ground to him. According tae his cousin at the Steelyard who has just spent a couple o' days in the Tollbooth for the guid of his soul, tae warn him, ye follow, he's a full Hochstetter, son of the man who first came over with the miners in the 1560s. D'ye not think he'd run to earth?"

"I don't. I don't find it at all likely: he's an engineer, he can make a good living anywhere in the world. Why not go to the New World and work at Potosi, for instance? Or the Netherlands, or the Spanish Netherlands or France…"

James sighed again. "Ah really want him dead. I dinna like the thought of him running about the world."

"Nor do I, Your Majesty. I would infinitely rather see him dead."

"Ay, and I could ha' done without the days of fasting and abstinence the ministers ordered in thanks for my escape by God's grace," said James gloomily. "It disnae exactly encourage my people to rejoice at my deliverance, especially as nobody has explained what from."

"A policy with which I wholeheartedly agree, Your Majesty."

James waved a hand. "Ay, o' course, we canna let the Catholic earls know how close they came, but still."

"A wise decision, Your Majesty."

"My Lady Widdrington is still at Court, ye ken?" said the King with his sleepy canny eyes hooded. Carey said nothing to this. "She's a fine woman, and my Queen is verra happy wi' her." Carey inclined his head. The King was appallingly nosy and loved gossip, everyone knew that. "Her husband isnae happy though. He's leaving for Widdrington on the morrow but I've asked if she can stay here as one of my Queen's ladies-in-waiting."

"I'm sure Sir Henry is sensible of the honour you and Queen Ann do him."

"Ay well, he says, he'll leave her here only if ye've left the Court before he goes himself."

Carey bowed a little. "Your Majesty, I came to ask your leave to depart in any case. I must escort my late Sergeant's widow home with her woman and her cart—I was only waiting until the roads were a little easier."

"I shouldnae think they'll get easier than they are now, with the hard frost. And I can help with that, nae problem, I'll lend ye a couple of my draft horses and ten men to see to it that naebody raids her—though I'd gae the long way round by the Faery Road, even so, with the Borders as tickle as they are."

"That's wonderful, Your Majesty, thank you very much."

It was not wonderful. It meant he would have to say goodbye to Elizabeth again, which took more and more effort to do each time. At least she would be safe at James' Court. He could concentrate on that.

He had already written to Cecil with an account of the New Year's attempts on the King's life, carefully filleted. Now he decided to write again and explain what had happened to Dodd and Hughie Tyndale, in case Cecil felt inclined to shed any light on the matter of Hughie and Mr Philpotts, and also to make it clear that he would go to Keswick as soon as he could, although he thought it more likely that Hepburn would make for the Netherlands. The King called a clerk for him and he dictated his letter while admiring the book on the *Venerie of Twytie* which he had apparently given to the King for his New Year's present, thanks to Mr Anricks.

SATURDAY, 6TH JANUARY 1593, KESWICK

Very early the next morning, before anybody was up and about except the bakers and the other Hochstetter brothers, but not his mother, Joachim rolled out of bed, dressed himself in the good dark grey wool suit from his chest that was five years out of fashion but still eminently respectable. He had refused to help his brothers with the midnight pack train, but had still woken about an hour before, unable to sleep any longer, and had spent the time thinking about what he needed to do today. He was looking forward to it.

According to David, the hue and cry had found nothing and the Mayor had adjourned the inquest. Everyone was speculating on what had happened with wild tales about a secret gang of reivers from Carlisle scaring everybody. The sooner he could get Long Tom out of Keswick, the better.

He took a boat in the dark from the boat house and rowed himself to the Keswick landing, tied up and hopped out. He had forgotten what a bloody nuisance it was to live on an island, but at least he could still row quietly and tie up by feel. He walked up the cobbled path to Packhorse Court and took a couple of his family's ponies. They had just come in from the usual long walk from Scotland and the Debateable Land, carrying heavy packs, carefully tied up in cloths so they wouldn't chink. The packs had been unloaded in the middle of the night by his brothers Emanuel, Daniel, and David, and by Mark Steinberger, because they were contraband. The Grahams who came with the ponies were put up at the Thistle alehouse because the Oak wouldn't have them, and were paid extremely well in new-minted silver.

The ponies were deeply displeased at being taken out again when they were trying to sleep after their long trip. Joachim tacked them up with saddles and bridles, rather than packs. Then he went to the Oak where Long Tom was supposed to meet him in the common room where the packpony drovers congregated. Joachim had given Tom enough money to spend the night with Frau Magda, if he chose, and the man was tucking into pork collops and fried sippets with a vigour that boded well.

"It's kind o' ye to show me the way tae Workington," said Long Tom. "Or are ye coming wi' me overseas?"

"No," said Joachim, "better not. I'll be leaving later, probably to Dublin."

"Are ye no' scared o' King James?"

"Not at all," said Joachim. "The man's a notorious coward. Has he even executed any of the earls who were involved in the Spanish King's plot? Probably not. He didn't execute them the last time they committed treason. His writ doesn't run in England anyway." Even if he hadn't had business with the Devil's Gift to finish, he wouldn't have been in any hurry to leave Keswick. So what if he was at the horn in Scotland? He wasn't outlawed in England or Amsterdam or New Spain, for that matter.

The road to Workington had been built by the Hochstetter family company. It had taken many cartloads of stone from the Giant's Wall to build and Joachim had gone to watch the men mending it as a lad, listening to his father explaining how detail mattered in every enterprise and an unmended bad road to a port might end by costing you twice or three times as much as a good road. He had admired the way the miners worked—they found moving stones in the sunshine much easier than in the dark of a mine. The road wasn't straight as Roman roads were, but wound up and around the brutal hills to ease the packponies' work and make sure they could find water in the summer.

It wasn't as good as it had been, he found; the road had been robbed of stones by farmers who wanted to build newfangled sheep pens, and the weather had broken up other parts. But it was still a lot better than most of the roads in the country, which dated back to the monasteries of two hundred years before, where they didn't date back to the Romans themselves.

Their ponies could pick their way perfectly well and in fact knew the way better than Joachim did himself, insisting on a detour to avoid a place where it turned out that a mudslide had almost taken the whole road out where it was so steep by Whinlatter pass. He and Tom laughed about it and the weather was cold and grey but at least it didn't snow again.

They stopped a little further on from there to have their bread and cheese, and Joachim offered Long Tom some spiced wine from his flask, then suggested they could climb up to the hill's brow through the woods and look at the fells to the south and see how far they were from Workington. They toiled upwards, Joachim's heart beating hard, until they stood on the edge and Long Tom swayed because of the belladonna in the flask, and Joachim stepped up behind him and pushed him off the cliff.

He shouted, slid to the edge, grabbed at Joachim's boots and Joachim stamped down on his fingers so he fell two hundred feet, then slid head first, crashing into rocks and trees until he reached the road and lay still. Joachim scrambled down to him, found him still breathing and stove in his head with a rock so Long Tom stopped breathing. And then he rolled Long Tom on down the hill until he ended with his head in the Whinlatter Gill, hard to see from the bushes and trees round about.

Joachim looked at his handywork. He was panting and his hands were filthy with blood and brain from Tom's crushed skull so he washed them in the Gill and then breathed deep, stood up and shook himself. There was no sign of anything except Tom Graham being unlucky in a fall from his horse, and that made him smile.

He untied Tom's pony and drove him off into the woods, then climbed back to the road, mounted his own pony, and headed slowly back to Braithwaite and Keswick. So it was not true there was a simple way to kill somebody, just push them off a cliff. He had been advised that that was the best method by a lawyer, so he shouldn't be surprised that it didn't work. None of the methods he had tried were ever foolproof, no matter how simple or complicated he made them. People were both fragile and tough, they fought back. Look at Rosa—she had spotted what had happened to her husband when he really would have thought that that method was foolproof. Maybe he would try a pistol next time, despite their inaccuracy and noise. Or perhaps Hughie Tyndale had the best idea, a garotte. He thought he might offer him his old job back when he had finished being Carey's *valet de chambre*.

Now that was a good idea, why not tell Hughie to get on and earn his thirty shillings by killing Carey? That was a very good idea. Joachim would give him the good news as soon as he turned up with Carey, as he surely would.

Joachim was whistling as he pottered down the road back into Keswick, past the made road leading to Newlands valley and the Goldscope mine, the jewel in the Hochstetters' crown, or rather the crown itself. He paused there, wondering about going to visit his cave and do a bit of peaceful chiselling, and then decided against it because there was always a risk and the miners were all working, and the massive wooden machines too, the ore-stampers thundering and the ore-roasting putting plumes of bad-smelling smoke in his way. Some of the men would be glad to see him, some not. Best to keep his head down and pretend to be the dutiful son for his mother to find a nice wife for, best not to make too many waves until he had decided what to do next.

Also there was Carey to deal with, Carey who had made a fool of him and thwarted all his carefully laid plans. He needed to plan Carey's death very carefully.

TUESDAY, 9TH JANUARY 1593, EDINBURGH

After leaving the King, Carey went to the Queen's suite of chambers and found that all the ladies were walking in the snowy garden and enjoying the sugared twigs and frosty hedges. Carey watched them through the window of the passage. Elizabeth was talking to the other women in what sounded like a mixture of Scots and dreadful Danish, colour in her cheeks and a sparkle in her eye. Her cap was pinned as firmly as usual with a new tall-crowned beaver hat on top and she walked quickly with the younger and more vigorous women.

James came up behind Carey and laughed. "Ye look like a mooncalf," he said. "God's sake, Sir Robert, go out and tek yer leave of her."

Carey bowed and went out through a garden door and found himself picking his way straight across the formal box hedges and dead flowerbeds to get to her sooner, rather then wending his way along the gravel paths. He came to the knot of ladies and bowed low to Queen Anne, slightly less low to the other ladies, including Lady Widdrington in that group. She coloured when she saw him and smiled back at him.

"It rejoices my heart to see you so well, my lady," he said, bowing again over her hand and suppressing the unwelcome memory of last night and Mrs Dodd. James had gone to greet his Queen and was giving her a smacking kiss on the cheek.

"I like the Court, and Her Highness is very kind to me," said Lady Widdrington. "Are you going to Keswick now?"

"Not immediately," he said with a rueful smile since it seemed James' Court was even more porous as to information than the Queen's. "First I have to take Janet Dodd back to Gilsland." He felt his ears redden and really hoped that Elizabeth couldn't read his mind. She didn't look as if she had noticed.

"Of course," she said with concern. "How is she?"

What could he say? "She's as well as you might expect. There was a duel arranged between the Sergeant and Wee Colin Elliot which was why he left the Court, but why Hughie Tyndale should have taken it into his head to kill Dodd is still a mystery. I'm hoping Mr Secretary Cecil can cast light on it, since he was paying him for news of me."

"Hm," she frowned a little at that. "Tell Mrs Dodd that I'm sure Sergeant Dodd is still alive," she said. "I simply can't believe he is dead, and you haven't found his body yet, have you? The King said he might send some men out to see if they can find him when the thaw comes, since you'll be inspecting the mines in Keswick."

"Well...."

"Frankly, I wouldn't be sure Dodd was dead if I were looking straight at his headless corpse."

He laughed. "Death comes to us all, my lady."

"True. Tell her I'm sorry, for I am. And not just because without Dodd to guard your back, you're in even more danger from the Grahams."

Carey answered this with a shallow bow because he was quite unreasonably certain that the Grahams would not manage to kill him, even though Ritchie Graham of Brackenhill was now apparently offering fifteen pounds English for his head.

Obviously they could not kiss in full sunlight in the open garden, although King James was kissing his Queen, but it was a near thing. Elizabeth, rested and not tense, was not nearly so forbidding as usual. She smiled at him as he bent over her hand again and then whispered, "I wish I could give you my ring, my mother's handfasting ring, and take yours, but I can't for Sir Henry would spot it, even if I split it and just gave you the man's hand..."

"Oh, my lady," he whispered back, "I will marry you, come what may and all the demons of Hell against us."

She laughed. "I'd watch out for the Widdringtons."

"Them too."

It was so hard not to kiss her, especially with King James a few paces from him, kissing his Queen in a way that boded optimistically for the succession. He moved away with a sigh and then stopped because Elizabeth had put her hand on his arm and thrilled his skin even through the velvet of his doublet sleeve.

"Wait!" she said, and she was smiling. She ran over to Lady Schevengen, talked quickly to her and the lady gave a disapproving frown but handed her a small embroidered pouch full of sewing things. Elizabeth took a pair of snips out of it, ducked behind a round bush with a hat of snow balanced on it, and after a minute came back to him looking mischievous but no different.

"Here," she said. "You can make a ring of this or just spend your last penny on a locket to contain it—or keep it in a bit of paper."

She held out something that shone red, was springy with curls, quite wiry…Good God, it was a lock of hair. Her hair? He stared at it and then at her. "Your hair is red?"

"Embarrassingly so, carrots," she said. "If it weren't for the Queen I couldn't bear it!"

"But your eyebrows…"

"I know, brown. I colour them a little."

"Oh." Carey shut his mouth and stared down at Elizabeth's hair, which he had never seen because she always kept it tidily under her married woman's cap. He took the lock of hair carefully, between his fingers, and twisted it to knot it. "Thank you, my lady," he said, taking his notebook from his doublet pocket and putting it between the first pages, where he had copied out a prayer. It shone there, a vigorous bookmark. "Thank you," he said again, quite unable to think of anything courtly to say, and put it away in his breast pocket.

"How I used to pray for brown locks when I was young," she said, her eyes laughing, her face straight, "despite the Queen's fiery hair. But Sir Henry won't notice that a bit is missing, he's always complaining about my ugly hair and how much of it there is."

There was another reason to kill Sir Henry Widdrington, piled on the top of a teetering heap, that he was rude about Elizabeth's hair.

As the Queen had come out of her clinch with the King, he bowed low to her again, to Elizabeth and the other ladies, and walked away as fast as he could, feeling the lock of hair glowing and burning in his notebook like an ember. He wished and wished he could do as Dodd had often suggested, to wit, raid the Widdringtons, kill Sir Henry, put her in front of him on his horse (though he'd need something bigger than a hobby since Elizabeth was tall and well-built) and carry her away with him. He didn't, not because he was frightened of the Widdringtons or Sir Henry, which he wasn't, but because he was genuinely terrified of the Queen's wrath.

Maybe the Queen would understand…No. She wouldn't. Queen Anne might, but Queen Elizabeth would be fatally offended and angry: he would lose his office, he would have no chance of another, he would never be received at Court again and his only means of living would be by his sword in the Netherlands or Ireland, neither of which were places he could take Elizabeth.

It was so hard.

TUESDAY, 9TH JANUARY 1593, EDINBURGH

To take his mind off his disastrous love life, he went into Edinburgh to John Napier's house where he found Simon Anricks stuffing his smart brocades into his toothdrawer's pack, with the lurid picture of a worm emerging from a tooth painted on the wooden top that always put Carey off his dinner.

"Mr Anricks," said Carey, midway between laughing and horror, "I fear I must return your compliment of rating me for sleeping in an unlocked room and rate you for treating your duds so ill."

"Oh?" said Anricks, looking at him in surprise. "Why?"

"They are silk brocades, sir, and cost you a pretty penny. You should at least shake them out and fold them and wrap them in something to keep the damp away which might make the colour run and besides make them smell of mildew, and so be able to wear them again if you should so desire, or perhaps sell them at not too much loss if you should be tired of them."

"Ah," said Anricks, and pulled them out again. "I have had a *valet de chambre* in the past but still know not how to proceed, sir, for I never paid attention to what he did."

"Fortunately, I have been a penniless courtier and can demonstrate at least something of the proper care of doublets and hose…I suppose you have not hung them up and burned incense inside to clean them a little?"

Anricks' blank look was very funny but Carey managed not to laugh.

"My wife usually takes care of that sort of thing, if there's no valet," he explained with a helpless gesture. "Or one of her women."

"Well, let's see if we can do something to the purpose," Carey said, and emptied the pack out. He found a snarl of shirts, under-breeks and stiff socks and hose, wrapped around something luridly green which turned out to be a forgotten half loaf of bread, and a leather wallet holding Anricks' toothdrawing tools.

"Hm," said Anricks, "They need cleaning. I wonder why it is that tools stored with blood on them rust much sooner than tools cleaned and oiled?"

"I have no idea," Carey answered, "but I would be very unhappy if any of my men put his sword in its scabbard with blood on it because the next time he tried to draw it, the rust would stick. Maybe it's something to do with rust having the colour of blood and so the blood changing its nature to rust in its turn?"

"Hm, on the doctrine of like-signatures? Perhaps."

Anricks went out with the wallet and came back a half hour later with his tools gleaming and covered in beef tallow of which Napier's household had a good store for tapers. Meanwhile Carey had shaken out the shirts, thrown the green bread into the street where an urchin had delightedly picked it up at once, and carefully folded the doublet inside one shirt, the hose and stockings inside another and put them into the bottom of the pack. The sleeves he rolled up and put down the sides and the small falling band he wrapped in a kerchief donated by Napier's housekeeper and slid into the front.

Anricks was wearing his lamentable old wool suit with the motheaten gown and the frankly disgusting twenty-year-old greasy tawny velvet cap on his balding head. His tools went into the pack next and on top were his collection of clotted rags for stopping the blood when he'd drawn the tooth, wrapped round two bottles of the magic sweet oil of vitriol that made men fall asleep so he could pull their teeth more easily. They might provide some defence against the rain.

Anricks tried the pack on his back then and nodded approval. "It's much less lumpy," he said. "Thank you, sir."

They went out into the watery sunlight and sat on the bench outside the front door where Anricks took out a clay pipe and filled it with tobacco, started drawing the smoke into his lungs and coughing occasionally as the medicine drew out the phlegm, of which, he explained, he had an excess.

Carey shared the pipe and took a draw of it carefully, enjoying the lightheadedness it gave. Edinburgh clattered by on wooden pattens against the mud, pert maidservants with white aprons and caps, severe-looking ministers in sombre greys and blacks, a few yards of woad-blue sky showing between the clouds.

"Well, Mr Anricks," he said, "I'm returning to Carlisle by way of Gilsland with Mrs...with the Widow Dodd."

"I had heard that the Sergeant had been killed, but not how."

Carey told the tale as he had deduced it and Anricks nodded, blew smoke through his nose, made no comment on the likelihood of Dodd actually being killed by a tailor.

"I'm for Widdrington," Anricks said. "As I promised Mrs Burn I would do when once she was lightened of her babe and had been churched, I will accompany her and her woman to her hometown of Keswick in Cumberland. I should think we will get there sometime around the middle of February, depending on how well she is after her childbed."

"I will go there as well because the King thinks Hepburn will head for his hometown."

"From your tone, you do not."

Carey shrugged. "I'll go to Keswick, investigate as best I can, and try to find him. Now the trail's cold he could go anywhere, change his name again. Why should he go to Keswick to make my work easier? But still, he might, and so I'll do my best. At least Cecil is also doing his best to help, he's sent me written orders to go and investigate the possibility of sedition among the Deutschers and a warrant that gives me the right to inspect all the mine workings, smelthouses, and machinery."

"And if you find him, you'll arrest him?"

"No, probably not, especially since his family are likely to back him up. I'll kill him, if I can."

Anricks did not object to this way of proceeding, only nodded and tapped his underlip with the mouthpiece of his pipe.

"Then I will probably see you in Keswick," he said. "And then from Keswick I will go home to Bristol and see the new son my wife has presented me with."

"My hearty congratulations, Mr Anricks."

Anricks smiled. "I truly hope that Mr Secretary will not find a new conspiracy against the Crown that I must lollop over hill and dale to find out about, although I may well come north to Scotland again to visit Mr Napier and his magical Bones. But I may use a coach next time."

Carey grinned. "How are you with seasickness, Mr Anricks? The Queen says she is always stricken with it any time she goes in her coach."

For an instant there was an iron look on Anricks' face but then he relaxed. "I do not suffer from it," he said simply and Carey remembered the scars on the palms of his hands. "In fact, now I think about it, I think the best way to come north would be in a ship, a coastal trader. With the right winds that would also be very much the quickest route."

"Ye-es," said Carey who was long experienced in flinging himself up and down the country at the Queen's command. "The only trouble with it is if you have a deadline, because then you can be certain that all the winds will be contrary. Riding post you can do London to Berwick reliably in three days and in 1589 I did London to Berwick in twelve days on foot."

"Why on foot?"

"It was a bet," said Carey, "with pretty much the whole of the Court, to rescue me from my creditors. The book was immense with the sidebets running to hundreds of pounds and I'm happy to say, I won three thousand pounds. Although I still have creditors, I'm really not sure why."

Anricks took breath to speak and then thought better of it and sucked smoke instead. Carey was grateful for that because he was tired of being lectured by well-meaning people about compound interest. Instead he broached a problem he had with Young Hutchin, and Anricks listened carefully.

"You're worried that Young Hutchin will abscond while you are on your way to Gilsland and inform his uncles, particularly Wattie Graham of Netherby, about Mrs Dodd's cart full of grain and horsefeed, and that the Grahams will then raid you in force."

"Yes."

Anricks nodded. "I assume Young Hutchin is as easily bought as any of them."

"Yes. I thought of sending him with a message for the King, but of course that then puts him in the path of Lord Spynie again. He isn't anything like as pretty as he was last summer but still…"

"Hm. And I think it would be better if his mission were dressed up as something else, so he doesn't suspect anything and decide to head for Brackenhill anyway."

"A good point."

"I have the very thing," said Anricks.

They gathered themselves together to get packed up and the cart ready—it could have done with new axles after its ordeal over the drover's roads, but Carey had the Court's wheelwright look at it and after considerable tooth-sucking, the man opined that the axles were well enough and the wheels too and he thought it would do if they stayed on the Giant's Road. Just on the off-chance, Carey invested in a spare axle which was balanced on one of the packponies' backs and strapped down carefully.

James' ten men were the usual gutter-sweepings of Edinburgh and Leith, his two draft horses at least strong-looking and not obviously sickening for anything serious like the glanders. The cart itself was full of grain and fodder and there were five hired packponies as well. Janet had turned almost all her worthless Scotch shillings into far more valuable food. Whitesock was tethered to the cart since he would not have a man on his back and had bitten the groom who tried to put a pack on him. Nobody had dared to try and put the spare axle on his back since even an experienced packpony didn't like it and needed blinkers.

Carey found Young Hutchin sucking a dairymaid's tit behind a stable wall, raised his eyebrows and said nothing as he went out again and waited in the yard. Young Hutchin came running out, adjusting himself and full of excuses which Carey waved away. Carey gave him a letter to carry to Mr Anricks at John Napier's house in Edinburgh and a verbal message, promised him thruppence and sent him off at a fast jogtrot into Edinburgh. Carey watched him go with a distinct feeling of relief. Whether he would in fact have told his uncles about the valuable fodder and grain on the cart was a moot point, but at least, with luck, Carey wouldn't have to face a raiding band of Grahams. Gilsland was sixteen miles east of Carlisle and nowhere near the Grahams' lands stolen from the Storeys, but he thought Ritchie Graham of Brackenhill's reward of fifteen pounds English for his head might inspire them and there were plenty of Elliots in the area too. Luckily, the pele tower at Gilsland was extremely strong and well-built and had withstood several attempts to burn it down.

Young Hutchin came back an hour later to say that Mr Anricks had offered him a temporary job and could he take it, which impressed Carey because he had bothered to ask. Carey then spent half an hour complaining about his shortage of grooms and messenger boys and only grudgingly said yes, when he heard how much the wages were to be. Young Hutchin trotted off, looking happy.

WEDNESDAY, 10TH JANUARY 1593

They set off before dawn the next day, with Janet riding Shilling and her green eyes narrowed and anxious.

"Word will ha' got out about Sergeant Dodd," she said. "Whit'll we do if Skinabake hits us for the grain?"

"Fight him," said Carey who was in his jack and morion, "or anyone else that wants to take us on."

He had had a quiet word with Leamus, and had sent the man out early in the morning to find out where the reivers were. Leamus went in Hughie's buffcoat, but with bare lower legs and feet which looked very odd indeed. Carey was particularly interested in Skinabake who needed a set-down for the way he had sold Janet to Colin Elliot. The fact that Wee Colin hadn't harmed her or even held her very long was not Skinabake's fault.

And so they clattered and creaked their way along the Great North Road, heading south through the usual scattering of peasants and craftsmen and the occasional messenger galloping past, shouting at them to get out of his way. They started collecting travellers going to Berwick and Newcastle almost at once. The road had big potholes but was relatively safe, thanks to the Earls Hume who were Wardens of the Scottish East March and had beaten and terrorised it into relative calmness. Which was to say, not really safe at all by the standards of the rest of the country, and so lone travellers tagged along with them.

They took a right turn by a drover's road and got into a coaching inn some time after sunset. The place was a post stop on the way to Edinburgh with regular trade from the King's messengers riding north with the sealed packets of letters from the Queen's Court in London and others via Newcastle, so it was bigger than a village inn. Still they overwhelmed it, with their cart and Carey's followers, John Tovey and Red Sandy and Bangtail and Leamus and Mrs Ridley and Janet Dodd and King James' men and the taggers-along who dossed down in the courtyard, since the common room and the stables were all taken. The innkeeper, a wide man wearing a jack and helmet with a Jeddart axe at his belt, was deeply disapproving of the women, put them in the smallest of his three rooms, with barely space for a bed in it. Carey and Tovey shared a bed in the biggest room along with a stranger who took the truckle, a stern bald silent man in grey wool and a falling band who spent a remarkably long time on his prayers.

Carey went out in the depths of the night and found the door to the women's room locked from inside, and so he sighed and visited the jakes and went back to bed feeling chilly. He supposed it would have been a little snug in the bed with Widow Ridley there too and the crowd of men-at-arms from Edinburgh dossing down in the common room underneath, at least one of whom was likely to be King James' informer. Tovey was full of some news about the man sharing the room who hadn't bothered to introduce himself and had closed the curtains.

"He's got which book in his saddlebag?"

"*Malleus maleficarum!*" hissed Tovey. "Hammer of evildoers. It's about witches, sir. I wonder if there are any round here."

"He's probably heading for Edinburgh," said Carey. "King James is very interested in witches, especially since the Earl of Bothwell nearly put a spell on him a few years ago."

THURSDAY, 11TH JANUARY 1593

Before dawn they were off again on the dangerous leg of the journey. Around sunrise they came onto the Giant's Road, south of the Wall, the one that had been built by the Fay, the Giants, or the Romans, take your pick. Most of it was patched, often badly.

Leamus turned up as they passed the remains of a mile castle, sitting on one of the snowy walls like a troll. He came trotting softly up to Carey, smiled and said, "There's a big clan of men, north of you and shadowing you."

"Friends?" asked Carey cynically.

Leamus smiled wider. "If your friends are likely to cut your throat."

"How many?"

"I saw twenty."

"Sounds like Skinabake again," said Carey. "Are they armed?"

"Carrying lilies and roses, sure."

"Guns?"

"None that I saw."

"Where will they hit us?"

"When I was listening at their campfire a while before dawn, they had made up their minds to take us between milecastles, but they were still arguing it out over which."

"Where are they now?"

"Last I saw of them, they were camping in one of the mile-castles."

"Can you take us straight there?"

"Sure, sorr," said Leamus and his teeth gleamed.

Carey took King James' men and Bangtail, leaving Red Sandy and John Tovey in charge of the cart and the women. He bunched the men round him and loaded and wound his pistols while he told them that he couldn't pay them extra for fighting, but they could have any plunder they found, to which they agreed. He was taking a big risk because another band of Border robbers such as the Scotts or the Kerrs could happen on the cart, or even the Grahams without Young Hutchin's help, but on the whole he felt it would be safer to take out the main problem in one go. Word would spread and as none of the local reivers were any braver than they had to be, that would help keep other vultures off their backs. The snow was lying and looking worn but it hadn't snowed again yet, which would have helped. The bracken was frozen and too wet to fire. So speed would have to do.

Leamus loped next to Carey's horse as Carey took everybody off up a path to the north, his bare feet and lower legs as sure-footed as an unshod hobby.

"Aren't your feet cold?" Carey asked the Irishman, thinking about Dodd's suffering with his feet in the autumn.

"Not while I'm running, sorr," said Leamus. "And I take them for a little run a few mornings a week, now."

They came to the first milecastle, nobody there, cantered up to the next and as they came up heard shouts of "A l'arme!" Carey kicked his horse to a gallop, felt Leamus let go of his stirrup and saw him sprinting like a goat over the fallen stones of the wall, unplaiting his hair as he went. Carey opened his pistol case and took out his pistols, felt Bangtail close behind and King James' men not nearly as fast, as he galloped into the middle of Skinabake's little band which was mostly engaged in making a late breakfast of porridge. One man stood staring and stock still with a spirtle halfway to his mouth for a taste.

He stood in the stirrups to aim, shot the one with the spirtle in the face, shot at another who was diving and may have hit him, dropped the smoking pistols back in the case, and swept out his sword. The bunch of King James' men charged, not very enthusiastically, at a knot of Skinabake's louts, who swapped blows and then tried to run. They might prey happily on lone travellers and women, but they didn't fancy an actual fight with even odds. Which was good because Carey suspected King James' men felt the same way.

He stood up in the stirrups again, looked around with his sword bloody, he had no idea how, saw Skinabake in the distance, fighting one of James' men and driving him back. He sent his pony scrambling over the stones and snow and knocked Skinabake over with the flat of his blade and saw Leamus jump down on the man with a bloody knife in his hand.

"Don't kill him," he shouted, as he dealt with a couple of Skinabake's men and then jumped from his pony.

Skinabake was rolling his eyes as Leamus knelt on his back, his long knife digging in Skinabake's neck, whispering in his ear.

"Get him off me!" he shouted, "Chrissakes, get him off!"

"Why?" asked Carey, as Bangtail came up and tied Skinabake's hands behind him and took his sword and helmet, tried the morion on.

"Bastard kern said he'd eat mah heart!"

"Don't be daft," said Carey, "you haven't got one, otherwise you wouldn't have sold your own cousin to Wee Colin Elliot. Do as you like, Leamus."

Leamus grinned broadly, turned his head and bit Skinabake's ear, then got up and let him go, yelping.

"Ow! Och!" shouted Skinabake, staring wide-eyed at Leamus who licked his lips and said "Yum." Skinabake scowled and shuddered.

Most of Skinabake's twenty hard-faced tough lads had run. A couple were dead and a couple more were wounded and bleeding. They flinched when Leamus passed them to stab his knife into the turf and rub it dry with a cloth. He hadn't drawn the sword he had taken from Hughie's corpse.

Carey got them organized with King James' men guarding Skinabake and the other lad who had a broken arm and was crying quietly. The ones with holes in them ran away. Two corpses lay on the ground, not even worth the robbing. Then he headed back to where Janet, Red Sandy, Mrs Ridley, and the cart and packponies and Whitesock of course, were rattling along. Mrs Ridley was still on the cart, knitting away, Janet was astride Shilling looking like a mother fox defending her cubs because half her hair had escaped from her cap.

Carey took his helmet off to her. "Mrs Dodd," he said formally, "here is Cuthbert Armstrong, known as Skinabake. Shall we find a tree and hang him?" Carey looked about. There weren't any trees. "Or maybe we could hang him off a milecastle's wall."

Janet skewered the cowering Skinabake with a look and lifted her chin.

"I dinna ken," she said. "I'll think aboot it."

THURSDAY, 11TH JANUARY 1593, STOBBS

Dodd was fighting a monster on the moors, it was invisible and it kept coming up behind him and before he could get a good blow on it, digging its claw deep into his back. He was hot again and exhausted because he had been fighting it all his life, forever, he couldn't remember a time when he hadn't been fighting it, and once he caught a glimpse and thought he knew the man but couldn't think of his name. It wasn't a man, really. It was a grim-faced giant, twice, thrice his size, and seemed to be playing with him.

Over and over he wondered what would happen if he just stopped fighting and let the giant kill him, but he couldn't. It simply wasn't in him to give up.

So he blinked sweat out of his eyes and tried to stand and something pulled him down and stabbed him in the back. He heard women's voices and the sound of someone sniffing hard, close to him.

"God, he's got an abscess," said the firm one wearily. "Well that'll kill him right enough. Maybe we should call Mr Lugg?"

A man's voice again, he knew the man, but he was too battle-weary even to feel rage at the Elliot headman.

"Mr Lugg, the barber surgeon. Ay, I've heard he's good. Well, if you think it might help…"

"I do—so far as anything can help."

"I'll send a boy to fetch the surgeon," said Wee Colin Elliot. "It's the least we can do."

Thursday, 11th January 1593, Derwentwater

Joachim had spent several days happily checking all the mining machinery with the carpenter, Matthew Ormathwaite, who was far more expert than he was at making the wooden cogs and wheels and straps, but had never had an original idea in his life. They decided to straighten the course of Newlands Beck and bank it, to make it run faster and give more power to the ore-stampers and persuaded Hans Moser, one of the mine captains, to lend them three men to do the digging. It was a good opportunity since the snow had locked up a lot of the water that usually ran through it down to Bassenthwaite Lake, parallel with the River Derwent, but of course the earth was frozen which was why they needed three men.

Joachim was standing watching as the men dug, listening to the rough music from the ore-stampers a little way from the mine, when he felt himself being watched and looked up. He sighed. It was inevitable but it had been pleasant to pretend it wouldn't happen: his eldest brother, Emanuel, was watching from the back of a pony with Hans Rössle beside him on a fat donkey.

Joachim bowed to his brother and his brother came and immediately started to ask anxious questions about the works in Deutsch, why was he interfering with Newlands Beck, didn't he know how important it was, he should stop immediately until he had authorisation from Emanuel himself.

Just for a moment Joachim boiled with anger and then he let it go. He had learnt to do that when stupid patrons and employers couldn't understand why something needed to be done. Emanuel was no different. So he told the men to stop digging and go back to the mine, they would get a full day's pay from Emanuel for what they had already done.

Then Joachim put his hat back on and stood there with his arms folded, breathing deeply to try and quell his anger.

"We should go to the alehouse," said Emanuel. Joachim thanked Ormathwaite elaborately in English for his tour of the mining machinery. Emanuel looked even more worried about that, as if Joachim would deliberately interfere with the machines, which showed how little Emanuel knew his younger brother because Joachim was far more willing to kill a man than to damage a machine.

Emanuel sent Rössle on to Keswick and they walked to the small hut where the miners got their beer and sausages and sauerkraut. With two pewter mugs of the best ale at their elbows, Joachim and Emanuel sat opposite each other. Emanuel was going bald, Joachim noted, who wasn't. His thick yellow hair wasn't as thick as it had been and there was a little island in the middle of the straw and two encroaching areas of bare skull on either side. Heroically, Joachim didn't twit him on it.

"Did you get my letter?" asked Emanuel after a long silence.

"Yes, I did," said Joachim. That was the letter from Emanuel in a simple cipher asking him if he was planning to kill the Scottish king, since their cousin at the Leith Steelyard had been worried enough about it to write to Emanuel. "I thought it a remarkably stupid thing to do, all things considered. Did you get my reply?"

"Yes," said Emanuel, "but I heard a worrying rumour at Workington that there was an attempt made on the King at New Year, although it didn't work. Was that you?"

"No," said Joachim, smiling at him, "that was the Deputy Warden Sir Robert Carey's attempt."

Emanuel said nothing but drank ale unhappily. "Then why are you still here?"

"If I had tried to assassinate the King and failed, I would be safely in the Netherlands by now," Joachim said. "But I might be falsely accused and I wanted to come home to my family, who, of course, would back me up."

"I would rather you went to the Netherlands as well," said his brother. "You've been here for a week, why not go to Workington tomorrow and take the ship that brought the charcoal, the *Swan of Dublin*, which is leaving in a few days?"

"Why should I?" asked Joachim, very quietly. "Yes, I probably will go back to Amsterdam but I'll go when I choose, not you."

"I don't want you here."

Joachim tipped his tankard to Emanuel and tutted. "*Mutti* was very happy to see me," he said which made Emanuel frown. As far as their mother was concerned, Manny could never do anything right, although he had spent his whole life struggling to make their mother love him, poor fool. "I will go when I'm ready and not before and I'll come back if I want to, when I want to."

"That can change."

"You mean when my beloved mother dies?" Joachim hooted at him. "She'll outlive you by decades."

Emanuel looked into his beer as if it could tell him something, his lined forehead creased. It wasn't just that he had had all the responsibility and worry about the complex business of the mines since their father had died, it was that he couldn't admit that their mother was the most annoying woman on the Devil's Earth, and utterly determined to have her way, which was very unsuitable to a woman. It seemed he loved her and was still trying to get her to love him, whatever that meant.

"Look at you," Joachim went on because he couldn't help it, "you're going bald, you look fifty though by my reckoning you're thirty-eight, and you never have any fun, ever. What's the point of a life like that? Harassed by *Mutti*, harassed by your wife—if I ever felt sorry for anybody, I'd feel sorry for you."

"Why are you so scoffing, Joachim?"

"Why are you so dull, Emanuel?"

Emanuel's jaw clenched. "I may be dull, but at least I am not a murderer."

"Phooey," said Joachim confidently. "Have you been talking to Mark Steinberger? The silly bitch committed suicide, that's all, even the inquest found that."

"Don't you care about anybody except yourself?"

"Why, who else should I care for?"

"Us. Your family."

"You care for me, do you? Well that's wonderful news, Emanuel and I'll look forward to receiving some of my dividends soon. In the meantime, I suppose I had better tell you that the man who actually made an attempt on the life of the Scottish King, Sir Robert Carey, will possibly be arriving here with a cock and bull story about how I did it, not him."

"Lord Jesus, Joachim, did you really try and assassinate the King...?"

"No," said Joachim loudly and patiently, "I told you, Sir Robert Carey did and is trying to make me into the villain. If he arrives I want you to keep him in the dark and hide me from him until I can...get rid of him in some way."

Emanuel was silent, and looked like he wanted to cry, the pathetic old stick. "Or?"

"The usual terms, my dear brother, the usual terms concerning silver."

Emanuel shook his head slowly from side to side, like an old man. "Dear Christ," he said, "don't you have any fear of Hell?"

Just for a moment, Joachim played with the temptation to tell his idiot brother what he really thought of Hell, now he had worked it all out—Emanuel would surely have a nervous breakdown, which would be fun to see. He almost heard himself saying, you fool, Emanuel, I don't worship anyone. I certainly don't worship God nor the insipid madman, Jesus, and certainly not the Theotokos, the little tart who bore Jesus. He could just see the shock, the grief, the fear on Emanuel's face, the shaking voice, the horror of it...Yes, it was very tempting. But he resisted because he did need them to shelter him from Carey until he could kill the man and then leave Keswick again. Or perhaps stay and take over the mines from Emanuel...Yes, but could he stand to live here for two, three years, with his mother fussing over him and Emanuel worrying? No, he didn't think he could. Once the fuss had died down, and he had done more chiselling for gold, he would be off again.

Well, in any case he couldn't tell Emanuel the truth about his beliefs or the Devil's Cave, and that was that. He wasn't going to be stupid the way he had been when he had chatted to Carey at Christmas. He just shrugged.

Emanuel said nothing for so long that Joachim got up to go. He was bored of the whole conversation anyway but then Emanuel said in a voice thick with frustration, "Why are you here? What is there here for you?"

Joachim shrugged again. "I'll tell you when it's all over," he said, finished his ale and walked out of the shed.

He stood outside for a while, undecided, while Emanuel went to talk to the mine captain about the problem of getting new tools since the sad and mysterious death of John Carleton, the Keswick blacksmith. The funeral would be on Sunday, at Crossthwaite church, and Joachim knew he would be expected to attend. He did not like the prospect of a long dull service with more ridiculous emotion and weeping and wailing from the women, but if he was going to be respectable for the moment it was necessary.

Eventually he strode off in the direction of Keswick, letting the action of walking a couple of miles along the packpony paths move his mind towards seeing Carey killed in some way that would in no wise implicate himself. He spent some time thinking about ladders in the mine, but abandoned that as too likely to kill one of the miners instead, or even himself, then considered an elaborate trap designed for the stupid English courtier specifically, so he would be unable to resist it. Joachim had no plans whatsoever to confront the man directly—he wanted something that wouldn't put himself in danger.

At least he had an idea about the bait for the trap—if there was anything that was reliable about courtiers, it was their attitude to gold.

Crossbow? Gunpowder? A tragic fall from a high place, like Tom Graham? A gun? All I have to do, Joachim thought, is stay hidden while he's here, if he dares to come here, and then act boldly and unseen. The thought of that pleased him, a sense of being godlike again, looking down on the world at the ant-men and snuffing them out as he chose.

THURSDAY, 11TH JANUARY 1593, THIRLWALL CASTLE

Carey and his party creaked tediously along the Giant's road. Nothing else happened all day except several other travellers attached themselves to them and the front axle on Janet's cart predictably gave up the ghost and died just as they were climbing a hill, splitting with a loud crack as the wheel rolled over a stone. Carey was delighted with himself for investing in the spare axle, instead of believing the Court wheelwright. They had to fetch a wheelwright from Hexham, but after that, replacing it only took a few hours—unloading the wagon, turning it upside down, taking the broken axle out, putting the new axle in and reloading the wagon again.

At nightfall they stopped at Thirlwall castle, which belonged to Sir Thomas Carleton and, short of an attack by massed cannon, was pretty much impregnable. King James' men camped in the bailey which was stinking full of cattle and Carey dumped Skinabake and the other lad into the convenient old cellar. Red Sandy, Bangtail, and Leamus organised themselves in the stables, Janet and Widow Ridley went into one of the rooms on the top floor, and Carey and Tovey got the best room with a four-poster bed and old-fashioned bastard swords and big shields on the wall, since Captain Carleton wasn't there. The steward was used to men-at-arms turning up and needing shelter and even recognised Carey, to judge by his grunt. Carey paid him with a harbinger's warrant signed by Thomas Lord Scrope, Lord Warden of the

English West March, which made his expression even sourer.

After seeing to his horses and swallowing a meal of pottage and gritty bread, he went to take a look at Skinabake.

The reiver had eaten some bread and pottage and was sitting sulking on a stone in the little cellar. He hadn't even bothered to help his follower put a splint on his arm. Carey found this annoying and so took the lad out and gave him to Janet and Mrs Ridley to deal with, came back to find Skinabake still sulking. He was rubbing his ear which had snaggled toothmarks in it.

He tried a few questions on general principles and got nothing except grunts and scowls, so left Skinabake and went to find his men who were drinking horrible ale in the hall and boasting about how they had taken on and bested Skinabake Armstrong's famous outlaw gang.

Leamus was sitting near the fire, staring into it. He had his boots and hosen on again. Apart from his lanky way of moving and the plait of dark hair down his back, he looked quite normal and almost Christian. He wasn't drinking much, just a sip of ale now and again.

Carey was curious about him and sat down near him, on the bench. Leamus made way for him and filled up his beaker without a word.

"Thank you for your excellent scouting today, Leamus," Carey said.

"Sorr," said Leamus, tilting his head.

The fire crackled in its enormous fireplace.

"I've never met an Irish kern before," said Carey. "Or a gallowglass. Well, I have if you call it meeting, in France, and killed some too. I've never talked to one."

Leamus didn't say anything but he smiled.

"How did you come to be fighting with my lord Earl of Essex's men?"

Leamus didn't say anything for a while and Carey was about to give up the attempt, when he said softly, "I was wounded and they captured me. When he found I spoke English, the Lord Essex promised me money if I would scout for him and I said yes because I needed a surgeon. And he offered more than the Guises. I got the surgeon but otherwise it was a mistake, sure."

Carey said nothing. His lord, the Earl of Essex, was notorious for promising the world to his soldiers and never paying up.

"When some of them decided to head for England to try and get their backpay from the man who had left them to die in France, I thought that was a fine idea and so I went with them."

"Why?"

Leamus shrugged. "It's closer to Ireland," he said after a while.

"Would you really have eaten Skinabake's heart?" asked Carey, only half-joking. There were some nasty rumours about the Irish.

Leamus looked sideways at him and smiled slowly.

"My ancestors might drink his blood, but only if he was a brave man, to get his…his strength, his virtue for themselves. They drank the blood of kin dead in battle to keep their virtue. So even if I was one of the pagan Irish, I would not drink Skinabake Armstrong's blood since he has no strength nor courage nor virtue. But my ancestors would take his head as a…what is it? A prize?"

Carey lifted his eyebrows. "A trophy? Like a stag?"

Leamus nodded once. Then came a flood of incomprehensible Irish.

"What does that mean?"

"I am Leamus of the clan Maic Rom. Most of my brothers and sisters' sons are harpers and singers and once we sang for Niall of the Nine Captives and we are descended from Lugh Longhand, the Sungod of old. But my singing and playing is not good enough and so I fight."

"I can sing," said Carey. "I still fight. I like it."

"Myself too." Leamus said something else in Irish but didn't translate. He went back to studying the fire as if it were telling him stories.

Later that night, Carey was alone on the top of the keep,

looking out over the businesslike battlements to the north and east where Elizabeth was. Then he felt someone's eyes on him and turned. He recognised her at once, despite the darkness of a night that promised more snow, stepped towards her and stopped, uncertain. Would she..?

She smiled slowly at him, took his hand and led him into the little turret where they kept the tallow and the rocks to drop and one small and ancient cannon, pointing due north. Carey lifted Janet up and propped her on the cannon, fumbled at his laces while she held her petticoats up and out of the way in a bunch. Neither of them said anything, word or grunt, though he thought he had made her happy again. When it was finished, Carey lifted her down from the cannon, helped her to rearrange her kirtle, kissed her hand again and they walked separately out of the turret. He nearly tripped on a rammer lying on the floor.

FRIDAY, 12TH JANUARY 1593, GILSLAND

The next morning they continued along the road that paced close to the remains of the Giant's Wall and Carey sent Leamus out ahead to scout again. For convenience they tied Skinabake's hands to the cart and he walked along at its side, alternating between sulking and complaining to Widow Ridley that he should ride beside her while his nephew should walk, despite his broken arm. The nephew dozed the whole way and Widow Ridley kept on knitting and occasionally saying, "Fancy!" Janet ignored him.

Finally, some sixteen miles from Carlisle they topped a rise and found the Giant's Wall below them like a giant snake and some of Janet's cousins taking stones from it and piling them into another cart. Leamus was sitting on the wall, his legs clad again, playing a small whistle with a sprightly little tune. Janet's tower and its bailey was full of wintering animals; they could smell it from a mile away.

Janet rode straight up to the open gate where her Armstrong

brother was arguing with Big Clem about the best place to put the new goatshed.

"It's going there, in the corner near the postern gate where the little girls can milk the goats in the morning," she said to them as she slid from Shilling's back.

"Janet!" shouted her brother and hugged her.

Janet pushed him away.

"Did ye hear what happened to Sergeant Dodd?"

"The Border's full of rumours about him, that he's dead, that the Elliots have him, that he was taken by the Fae on New Year's Eve."

"He's dead."

Jock shut his mouth with an effort and stammered, "B…but are ye sure?"

"He wis ambushed fra behind by Hughie Tyndale wi' a crossbow, out on the moors a day or two after New Year's and there was a heavy fall of snow that night. We've not found the body yet, but…"

"Then mebbe he's still alive?"

Janet shook her head and said sadly, "Jesu, Jock, I hope so but it's no' likely, is it?"

Jock set his jaw. "Where's this Hughie Tyndale then?"

"Lying out on the moors for the crows," said Janet. "The courtier found him wi' his crossbow discharged and Henry's knife in his calf."

"What killed him?"

Janet pointed at Whitesock who was pulling at his tether and showing the whites of his eyes. "He did, Whitesock. Ye mind, Henry reived him in London? He kicked in Tyndale's chest, there wis hoofprints on it."

Jock's eyes were wide. "Ay?"

"Be careful on him, Jock, he's no' the sensible beast he was, he's wood."

"Small wonder," said Jock, shaking his head. "I'll see to him last and maybe get some oat mash intae him."

"He's not short of fodder, is Whitesock," said Janet cynically. "Red Sandy's been feeding him like a king."

Red Sandy smiled wanly and nodded.

They opened the main gate wide so they could get the cart in and Janet's cousins and brother started unloading it and the packponies. Despite the loss of the Sergeant, some of them couldn't help smiling as they carried the heavy grain sacks into the half-empty storage huts.

Carey took King James' men into the keep where the remains of the huge Yule log were coals in the great fireplace. Two girls came in and started piling on kindling and small logs to get it going again. At least they could thaw out before they went to Carlisle the following day, though Carey thought he would send King James' men home to Edinburgh over the drover's roads since he did not need an escort to get to Carlisle. The five packponies could stay until they had loads to take to Berwick or Newcastle; he saw them being led out to the infield where they set to finding something to eat among the pawed snow and sour grass.

The girls came trotting back with piles of bread trenchers and jugs of ale, which was promising. Widow Ridley brought Skinabake in behind her, his hands still tied in front of him, and now they were chatting like old friends. She came right up to Carey.

"Tell the courtier what ye said about the man the day after New Year's Day," ordered Widow Ridley. "It might save yer neck."

"Why?"

"Do it and dinna argue."

Carey sat down in Dodd's own chair with the carved arms. Dodd had carved them himself with his knife, or said he had.

"Ay, the carlin says, but whit does the courtier say?" grumbled Skinabake.

"Information might save your neck," said Carey. "Luckily it doesn't have to be very valuable information, to match the neck. Let's hear it first."

"Och, I dinna ken why she thinks it's important."

"Or we could just hang you, which frankly I'd prefer."

"It was naught but summat my lads saw a day or two after New Year's, which was a man by hisself on a good horse, riding fast."

Carey shrugged. "What was special about him?"

"Ye mind what the weather was like hereabouts, snowing again. Not even the Queen's messengers were riding. He had a remount too."

"And where was this?"

"We wis staying with some…er…friends for New Year," said Skinabake, "and the lads had only gone out to fodder the horses and they didna like it, and they didna stay out long and all three of them saw him."

"Where?"

"About ten miles south o' Carell city."

"Ten miles *south* of Carlisle?"

"Ay," said Skinabake. "And he wis heading south and west."

Grahams, Carey thought instantly, a lesser branch, possibly Bangtail's family or cousins. So this man hadn't been heading for Carlisle, which was at least interesting especially as the weather was so bad.

"And both horses had been ridden a long way."

"Anything else?"

"One said he thought it was a ghost for his cloak wis white."

"Thank you, Skinabake," said Carey. "That's interesting." It was, though there was no guarantee it was Hepburn.

"Will it save ma neck?"

"That's for Mrs Dodd to decide since it was her you sold to the Elliots and not me."

"Och," said Skinabake. "He said he wouldna harm her and he didna."

Carey tilted his head. "It's a neck-verse," he said. "I'll talk to her."

Skinabake looked miserable. "I'm allus unlucky, me," he whined. "Tisnae fair!"

Carey left him and went back out to the bailey where Janet was deep in conference with her sister-in-law over the stinking retting tubs. He waited a little way off and then drew her aside as she hurried past.

"Mrs Dodd, will I hang Skinabake or ransom him?"

She scowled and then said, "Och, naebody will pay a penny for him, they'd likely pay you to keep him. I'll keep him here a couple of days and then I'll let him go, he's ma second cousin and I ken my kin even if he disnae."

Although Carey privately thought it would considerably assist the tenuous peace of the Marches if Skinabake wound up kicking on the end of a halter, he only nodded.

They ate well that night, beef stew from the autumn and bean pottage and the last remaining wrinkled apples which must have come from afar since there were no surviving fruit trees so close to the Border. The beef was good with carrots and parsnips, and a herb suet bag pudding to soak up the juices. They all did their best not to notice Sergeant Dodd's empty chair, where not even Janet would sit. Nobody said a word, though some people tipped their alemugs to it.

SUNDAY, 14TH JANUARY 1593, STOBBS

Dodd was more exhausted than ever with fighting the monster behind him, he was hot and he just wanted to stop, but he couldn't.

Voices called him back from the borderlands where he was stumbling about tripping on tussocks, nearly falling in a stream. There were the firm woman's voice and a man's voice he recognised but couldn't put a name to. At least it wasn't that bastard Wee Colin Elliot.

"Well?"

"Ay, I'm amazed he's still alive. I can lance the abscess and drain it and then cauterise the site, but I dinna ken whether he's got another abscess further in. Just cauterising it could kill him."

"But, Mr Lugg, if it disnae kill him, he may get better."

"Ay."

"That's as good as we can hope for. A'right, let's dae it. I'll have the blacksmith put an iron in the fire, give it an hour until it's hot enough."

While Dodd writhed sweatily and feebly in the bed under the digging of the monster's claw in his back he heard the two women and Mr Lugg talking between themselves, how the courtier was now back in Carlisle and James' troops had gone home directly to Edinburgh with a safeconduct from Carey.

"Has anyone sent to Sir Robert to tell him where his man is?" asked Mr Lugg. "I heard tell he was planning to go out again with the entire Castle guard to find Dodd when the snow melts."

Carey? thought Dodd foggily, I know that name. The woman gave him a beaker of a thick syrup mixed with brandy which made everything distant and the claw in his back almost stop hurting. Then the giant grabbed him and laid him down on the bed bent over on his side, and the wound in his back oozing pus. The claw went in again, deeper than before and he screamed and tried to fight but his hands were tied together. There was a feeling of relief as foul-smelling stuff poured out of the wound and the woman giant mopped it up with a cloth that smelled of aquavitae. Mr Lugg held the wound open and said he thought he'd got all of it.

Then there was a thunder of feet on the stairs and a feeling of heat passed over him.

"Hold him," said Mr Lugg and somebody put his weight on his shoulders and somebody else held his arms. Then the heat came into his poor sore back and he screamed again and again at the red bar of agony driving right through him.

The woman's veil slipped but she couldn't put it back because she was holding his arms down.

"Jesus Christ, Henry!" she gasped. "Stop fighting!"

And the linen cloth slipped some more and fell off and

showed her monster face where it had been destroyed long ago by the burning rafters of a church, taking one eye and some of her nose, the skin still red and tender fifteen years later. But he knew her, knew her too well. She had been buried deep in his mind because he had known Alyson was dead and he killed her, and here she was still alive.

All the breath gasped out of his body and he lay still and stayed still, staring at her, despite the smell of roast pork and she looked straight at him with her one good green eye and knew he knew her.

And then darkness took him from below and he fell into it. He fell down and down and down, a lifetime of falling.

MONDAY, 15TH JANUARY 1593, STOBBS

And then he landed on the same bed with fresh sheets on it and with more bandages tight around his middle and the claw in his back turned to just a spike.

He gasped, breathed deep. He was on his side, covered by blankets and was no longer hot, in fact he felt cold. The light coming through the arrowslit was luminous and white so perhaps more snow had fallen. A fire was chuckling to itself in a brazier and the veiled woman was sitting beside the bed which had a respectable half-tester over it, though it was old.

"Good morning, Henry," said Alyson, "How are ye?"

"Uh…" his lips were bone-dry. He felt as light as an autumn leaf. "Ah've been better."

She tilted her neck, lifted his head and gave him some warm chicken broth. It tasted good. He slurped greedily from the horn spoon, trying to lift his own head rather than letting her do it, but he couldn't.

"What happened?"

"I think somebody shot you with a crossbow…"

"Ay, I remember that and I remember getting on Whitesock's

back as it got dark, though I dinna ken how. Then it's a' black night and snow."

"Ah well, the day after the snow, a tenant of mine, a Turnbull, was out to find his sheep and bring them into the infield, and couldna find them and went further and came upon you on your horse with the white sock, and you were lying on his withers with a crossbow bolt sticking out of yer back, not quite dead. The horse wouldn't let the man near enough to take the reins but followed him when he headed for my tower, which pleased him because he marked yer jack and that the horse was shod so he wondered if there might be a ransom for ye. Which nae doubt is why he didna dump ye in a ditch and tek the horse. When I saw who ye were, I gave him an English shilling for bringing ye."

Dodd submitted to more spooning of broth and gathered his strength for more talking.

"Is ma horse here?"

She shook her head. "Once we had got you down from him, he bolted and nobody could catch him."

"Och." Dodd was annoyed to find tears pricking his eyes. God, he was weak. He dimly remembered lying on his face with snow and mud in his mouth and the long shape of the horse on his belly in the mud beside him, nickering anxiously. He had spent what felt like at least an hour mountaineering up the side of the horse to get his leg across, while Whitesock waited patiently, only flicking snowflakes off his ears.

What had happened to Hughie, the man who had dared to try and kill him from behind? He couldn't say. One minute he was there riding behind Dodd, the next minute he was towering over him, talking about how he was an Elliot while Dodd fought the breathless agony in his back, managed to pull his knife out of its scabbard and stick it in Hughie's calf. Then he caught the iron smell of a sword, heard the outraged scream of the horse and thought he could hear sounds of fighting which made no sense, until it went to silence. Then he had the horse-mountain to climb until finally Whitesock scrambled to his feet and he clung with his hands and teeth in Whitesock's mane and the saddle pommel digging into his stomach and the claw in his back. No more, there was only endless clinging to the horse's warm back in a black night full of snow, the life in him leaking away slowly but surely, until it was all black. And then the heat of the burning church woke him.

"Why?" he whispered to Alyson. "Why are ye looking after me? Why didn't ye kill me?"

Her face behind the veil was unreadable, even if it hadn't been burned into immobility.

She didn't answer, just spooned broth into him until he slept.

MONDAY, 15TH JANUARY 1593, CARLISLE

Carey was sitting in Bessie's while the place racketed with a grand shove-groat competition that Bangtail was near to winning. The prize was worth having, since it was free beer for the winner for the evening. Carey was not as talented as Bangtail at shove-groat and couldn't get anybody in Carlisle to play cards with him anymore, so he was watching the proceedings, thinking about who he would take to Keswick with him and fantasizing about Elizabeth and Janet co-operatively in the same bed with him, which was about as likely as…hills flying, crows turning white, oceans running dry, as they said in ballads. Well, it may not have been realistic, but it was a very nice idea, so long as it never left the safety of his own skull.

A solid black-haired man came and stood in front of him and took his cap off, so Carey returned the courtesy with a tilt of his head. "It's Mr Lugg, isn't it?" he said with an effort, thinking back to haying and his man that had had his hand blown to pieces by a badly made caliver, before the disastrous trip to Dumfries.

"Ay, sir," said the surgeon, smiling a little. Carey gestured at the bench and Lugg sat down, set his pewter mug in front of him. "I've some news for ye, Sir Robert."

Carey raised his eyebrows. "Oh?"

"Ay. Yestereven Ah lanced an abscess in the back of your man, Sergeant Dodd…"

"You did?" Carey was almost on his feet, laughed aloud. "He's still alive?"

"He was when I left Stobbs this morning, cannae say if he still is for he's been bad wi' a crossbow bolt in his back nigh his kidney, but ay. Happen he's still alive."

"Good God!" Carey paused just long enough for the fleeting unworthy thought to pass across his mind that now Mrs Dodd was untouchable again and that was a sad thing. Then he laughed again because of course Dodd was still alive, that man was unkillable by anything short of a halter or an axe. Even a petard at Oxford hadn't done it. And fighting men of Dodd's quality were not common even here on the Borders, where right fighting men were two a penny. "God's Blood, Mr Lugg, that's the best news I've heard since New Years' Eve. He's at Stobbs tower, you say?"

"Ay, Mistress Elliot took him in and Wee Colin Elliot sent for me."

"Elliots took him in?"

"Ay, and looked after him—Mistress Elliot is a fine horse-leech and kens when summat's beyond her, too."

"I'm…I'm astonished."

"Ay," said Lugg with a pull at his ale, "I wis surprised meself, but there ye go. He's at Stobbs and likely to bide there a while."

Carey felt in his purse and found a stray sixpence, gave it to Lugg who touched his cap. "Thank you," he said, standing up and looking round for Red Sandy who was sinking another quart and shouting for Bangtail in the competition. "Thank you for treating the Sergeant and thank you for taking the trouble to tell me."

"Nae bother, sir," said Lugg, finishing his beer and getting up to go to Bessie again for a refill.

Carey got up as well, and struggled through the excited crowd as Bangtail slapped the board again and got his groat further than the other finalist in the last round of the game. Half the watchers cheered, half groaned and then the business of settling the bets started while Bangtail stood up, raised his jack, and downed his quart of beer in one before holding it out to Bessie.

Carey put his hand on Red Sandy's shoulder, who was grinning drunk and cheering the victor. He had to shout and say it twice but eventually Red Sandy got the message.

"Are ye telling me ma brother's no' dead?"

"I am," said Carey and explained what Lugg had told him. Red Sandy stood stock still for a moment when he heard where Dodd was, with a very peculiar expression on his face, and then a slow smile lit it up.

"Ay," he said, "ay."

TUESDAY, 16TH JANUARY 1593, STOBBS

Dodd woke again and found Alyson standing by the bed with a long-necked glass pot in her hand.

"Now, Henry," she said, "could ye see yer way clear to filling this?"

Piss in it, she meant. He was in fact desperate to piss but it was hard and embarrassing, because the clouts round his hips had to come off and then he had to go to all fours because he couldn't even sit up and she had to hold the pot and then he had to let go which at least felt good. At last the pot was full of piss that was a funny colour. She put a shirt on him afterwards, his own, it was washed clean of the blood and the bolt hole carefully darned.

Alyson lifted the pot to the arrowslit and squinted her one good eye at it like a physician. "I think that's old blood," she said, "not fresh. We'll keep it to show Mr Lugg when he comes tomorrow."

She put the pot down and helped him to lie on his side and then started spooning more broth into him. He was very thirsty and gulped and then suddenly he was full.

"Now, d'ye feel strong enough for visitors?" she asked and her voice sounded as if she was smiling, though how could she smile? "Mr Lugg said he'd tell yer Deputy Warden where you are last night and sure enough, here he is. But ye have to bide quiet and not fight anyone, Henry, d'ye understand? No fighting yet."

He felt weaker than a baby, panting for breath, a newborn kitten could have mauled him. "Ay," he croaked.

She opened the heavy door and there stood the courtier in his jack, his morion in his hand, his Court goatee nicely trimmed again and his chestnut head brushing the ceiling.

"Och," said Dodd to himself.

"Sergeant Henry Dodd!" said Carey, coming forward wreathed in smiles. "I'm delighted to see that you're clearly born to be hanged, since it seems that not even a crossbow bolt in the back an inch from your kidney can kill you."

For a moment Dodd tried to hold onto the grudge he had been enjoying against the courtier since Dick of Dryhope's tower, but it now seemed a distant and a dead coal, no longer smouldering in his heart. He was surprised at that. Somehow, when he wasn't looking, so to speak, he seemed to have forgiven the courtier for giving the Elliots a second chance. Then he relaxed and pulled a weak smile back.

"Ay."

Carey put his morion carefully on the table next to the piss bottle and sat down on the stool next to the bed. Alyson stood watchfully by the arrowslit.

"D'ye ken what happened to yer servant, Hughie Elliot?" Dodd asked.

"Elliot? You mean Tyndale?"

"Nay, Elliot. He told me he was Wee Colin's younger brother after the bastard shot me."

Carey's face cleared and he smiled with enlightenment. "Aha," he said with great satisfaction, "now I understand. Well, we found his corpse on the hills and I found this in his calf muscle."

With some ceremony, Carey put Dodd's knife on the table and Dodd tried to reach for it but couldn't manage, and had to settle for looking at it lovingly. It was his, had been his since he was a wean and his father had given it to him. It was like seeing an old friend.

"In his calf, eh? So I got him fra the ground while he wis jawing at me?"

"You did. And your horse…Whitesock killed him. He was lying on his back with Whitesock's hoofprints on his chest."

"Och," said Dodd, emotion swelling in him and making his chest feel thick. "Ye're telling me ma horse killed ma enemy?"

"Yes. It's all over the Border and I'll bet someone is making up a ballad about it right now."

Dodd couldn't speak for a moment. "Did ye ever hear the like?"

"I didn't. I have heard of trained warhorses killing men in battle but never anything like that."

"Did ye find him, ma horse, Whitesock?"

"Yes, that's how we knew something had happened. He came back to us in Edinburgh with a bloody saddle."

Dodd was silent again. Was there ever such a horse? He had killed Dodd's enemy, taken Dodd to safety, and then gone for help. Plenty of men wouldn't have done so well.

There was wet on his face and he lifted his hand to wipe the stuff off and saw a stranger's wet hand, frail and bony.

"He's in Carlisle stables now," said Carey, "though he's too wild to ride. But how are ye yerself, Henry?"

"Ah cannae hardly move but my back doesnae hurt so much now," Dodd admitted. Carey took his hand, felt it, smiled again. "I can't feel any fever," he said. "Can you move your legs?"

It took concentration and a lot of effort but he managed to bend his legs and straighten them, wiggle his toes.

"Or possibly you're fated to be beheaded like me, because I honestly can't think of another reason you survived a foul snowy night like that one with a crossbow bolt in you."

For some reason Dodd found the idea funny, that he might lose his head to the axe when hanging was so much more likely. He began a laugh, then winced because it hurt him.

"Ay," he said.

"Now I'm riding straight to Gilsland to tell Mrs Dodd you've turned up. Mistress Elliot says you can't move back there for a week at least because the wound might open up, but after that we'll take you to Gilsland on a litter…"

"Ye will not," snorted Dodd. "Ah'll ride my horse, Whitesock, so I will."

Carey tactfully said nothing to this preposterous plan but clasped Dodd's almost transparent hand and left the room with a courteous bow to Alyson.

He clattered down the spiral stairs and came down to the first floor hall, where a short man in a jack and falling band stood warming his hands at the fireplace.

Carey stealthily loosened his sword and then went forward and smiled.

"Mr Colin Elliot, isn't it?"

Wee Colin turned and did the fighting man's instant measuring up of Carey as a possible opponent.

"Ay," he said and showed his teeth in a smile. "Sir Robert Carey, if I'm not mistaken, now officially Deputy Warden."

"The same. I'm pleased to meet you at last and not behind a gun."

"Ay."

"Mr Elliot, are you responsible for seeing to it that my man, Sergeant Dodd, was cared for and his life saved?"

Wee Colin considered this for a moment. "Ay," he said, "ma

sister is chatelaine o' this tower and took him in first. But I was happy she did it."

"Even though you still have a blood feud with the Dodds?"

"Ay."

"May I ask why?"

"Ay," said Wee Colin, his face hardening. "I challenged Sergeant Dodd to a duel, man to man, body to body, to settle the old feud in a new way and pit an end tae it."

"To the death?"

"Ay, o' course. It wisnae the Sergeant's fault that he didna come to meet me and it isna his fault that he canna fight me now. So as it wis my ain half-brother, bad cess tae him, that snuck up behind him wi' a crossbow, I'll see the Sergeant healed and well and in his strength again, and then we'll fight."

Carey tilted his head. "That's very...chivalrous of you."

"Nay, I canna be bothered wi' sneaking up on the man, that's a tailor's game."

"I'm afraid your half-brother is dead. We found his corpse on the hills where he shot Sergeant Dodd."

Wee Colin lifted his shoulders and dropped them. "Guid riddance. When I kill Sergeant Dodd, it'll be despite all he can do tae stop me."

"Thank you, Mr Elliot. I have business to despatch for the Scotch King and Sir Robert Cecil. Would you please wait your duel with the Sergeant until I can get back and be his second?"

"Ay, Sir Robert, nae trouble," said Wee Colin. "He'll not be strong enough to have a chance agin me for months yet, mebbe not for a year. But when he's ready, I'll be there."

Carey tipped his morion to the headman of the Elliots, who bent his neck slightly. Then he went out the door and down the creaking steps to the bailey, where he waited patiently by the water trough while Red Sandy went and visited his brother, his blue eyes fixed thoughtfully on the middle distance.

A couple of hours later they were cantering a bit less than thirty miles as the crow flies across country to Gilsland. Red Sandy jumped from his horse and fairly ran into the yard and found Janet spinning with her gossips and shouted the news to her.

"Janet, Mrs Dodd! Yer man's found and he's not dead, he's wounded but he's mending." The Widow Ridley spinning wool in the same group just tossed her head.

Carey felt Janet's eyes go to him once for a fraction of a second and then her face lit up and she rose and clasped Red Sandy and kissed him.

"The Elliots looked after him?" she said to Carey, once she had sorted out Red Sandy's somewhat incoherent tale. "There's a surprise."

"No. It's so Wee Colin can fight him when he's better," Carey explained. That caused a shadow to cross her face.

"Can ye take me to him?"

Carey gave a shallow bow. "That's why I'm here, Mrs Dodd. We'll take you tomorrow since it's a good way into Scotland."

Janet went and called together everyone there and told them the good news, ordered the last barrel of double double beer to be breached so they could drink the Sergeant's health properly.

In the hall, Carey sipped his beer and watched her. She seemed genuinely delighted at the news, laughing, her face vivid with colour. Carey felt melancholy. He had enjoyed their trysts, he liked Janet's uncomplicated lust and joy in their coupling which had been such a businesslike arrangement, could understand why the Sergeant loved her, although it was less clear to him why she loved the Sergeant.

Was he doomed always to be a bachelor, always the bull, never the mate? With the persistence of a tongue seeking a hole in a tooth, he thought of Elizabeth Widdrington at Court, her face softened and pretty because Sir Henry wasn't bullying her, how she had given him a lock of her infinitely precious red hair. He took his notebook out, hiding it, hoping no one would notice, looked at the small shout of colour lying on the prayer. He touched it delicately with his forefinger, tried to imagine Elizabeth in her smock, with her cap off and her hair down around her shoulders on their marriage night, how he would lift the shift off over her head like a priest unveiling something sacred, how he would kiss her mouth and then her cheek, and her chin and her throat and her collarbones and her chest and her breast...How much longer would the bloody man live, for God's sake?

Carey spent some time on a further satisfying fantasy wherein he flogged Sir Henry until his back was bloody and killed him with a bullet to the head and then took Elizabeth up against a wall. He sighed and looked down at Janet's face, come to pour him more beer.

"How is he, Courtier?"

Carey told her again about the crossbow bolt and Hughie Elliot also known as Tyndale and the horse as well and she smiled and said, "Ay, that's my Henry, wounded and flat on his face in the mud and he still stuck his knife in the man."

"It certainly is," said Carey, praying he would never have to fight a duel with the Sergeant himself. "He's weak and thin now but he's still insisting he will not go home to Gilsland in a litter but on his own horse."

"Huh!" grunted Janet, deep in her throat. "We'll see about that."

Carey smiled. It made him happier than he would ever have thought that Dodd was not a corpse, despite the dangerous complication with Janet. Dangerous for him certainly and quite possibly dangerous for her too, depending on how Dodd took the whole thing if he ever did find out. But of course Dodd would never hear the story from him. He was long experienced at adultery which was so much safer than seducing maids-of-honour like that arrogant idiot, Sir Walter Raleigh. He had got away with it before and surely he would again.

Sometimes now he thought of the young French aristocrats aged around ten who might possibly be his and wondered wistfully how they were shaping with their swordplay and whether any of them had telltale chestnut hair and blue eyes. And maybe there were others he had no idea about, that he would never meet, never know, all the children who called another man "father." When he had been a heedless youth and a lusty young man full of vim and vigour, it had never occurred to him to wonder whether his widely sown wild oats would sprout. Now, for the first time, it did.

He ate supper with Janet Dodd and her household, good thick pottage enlivened with bacon in honour of the occasion. His eyes kept returning to Janet's face, who ignored him studiously. She looked beautiful, her cheeks pink, her eyes sparkling and her summer freckles gone into hiding for the winter. She looked relaxed and happy, bountiful as a Queen.

Inside his chest, he felt it. Certainty that she was with child, his child, filled him up and spread through everything. Another child, another little stranger, as they all were, and not one to call him father. The melancholy overtook the happiness about Dodd suddenly and covered it with a black pall. What if Janet got an attack of conscience and told Dodd what she had done? Christ, he'd be in trouble then, the Netherlands wouldn't be far enough, maybe even the New World wouldn't be safe.

He drank more beer, wrestled with the melancholy and finally succeeded in clapping it in irons. What was the point in moping or melancholy? So he had sinned grievously with Janet, just as he had with so many other married women. He would simply have to rely on the mercy and forgiveness of the Lord Jesus Christ.

He would have liked to try...Perhaps he still could...? No, don't be ridiculous. He finished his beer and Janet refilled it for him with a smile that said nothing.

WEDNESDAY, 17TH JANUARY 1593, GILSLAND

He slept the night in a spare room filled with spare weapons and a startling number of longbows and arrows, but then Dodd was old-fashioned about guns. He didn't sleep well and Janet didn't visit him, of course, for now it would be adultery. Well before dawn he gave up the struggle and left to climb the spiral steps to the top of the tower, where he hoped the rising sun might give him a boost, or the icy wind shake him out of his mood.

He found Red Sandy and Bangtail there, talking quietly and intently and wondered what they were about, if they knew about him and Janet...No, he didn't think so. Neither was a good actor and he knew there would be grins and sly comments if they even suspected. They knuckled their foreheads and clattered down the stairs noisily in their hobnailed boots and pattens covered with sheepskin against the ice and snow.

He looked over the parapet and saw Janet and her gossips heading into the bailey to milk the cows. There wouldn't be much milk but it was worth getting what they could to turn into cheese, with dearth on the way unless the next harvest was wonderful.

He watched Janet and then turned away deliberately because he must never think of her again if he wanted to make old bones. He wondered if he would be able to command Dodd as he should, once Dodd came back to the castle guard, given that he was now so full of complicated feelings of jealousy, of envy, of sadness. What he needed was his own wife, Elizabeth Widdrington nee Trevannion, that would settle him. Why could he not just take her from her husband, why couldn't he just...?

Janet and some of her women came back to the dairy, carrying the heavy buckets on yokes. It was far too early to tell, of course, but still Carey was more than ever sure that there would be a bastard boy or a girl in nine months who would grow up to call Henry Dodd father. And would he be a batchelor still or married or dead? Would he ever be able to marry Elizabeth or would she die herself? Killed by her God-damned husband's cruelty or some chance fever? He didn't think he could bear that, just the thought made his stomach clench as if at a blow. He would go to the Netherlands for sure if that happened and either drink himself to death or fall pointlessly in some pointless sordid skirmish.

On impulse he knelt on one knee, facing the watery sun as it rose, praying incoherently for Janet, for Elizabeth, for himself, even for Dodd, stubborn bastard that he was.

As happened sometimes, he felt something, the warm pressure of hands close around his; a workman's hands, callused in the places that a carpenter's hands were and quite different from fighting calluses like the ones he had. Somehow that made him feel better, as if he had been heard by the Lord Jesus, as if the Lord Jesus had received his fealty as a lord receives it from his man or a king from his vassal.

He stood up, his heart unaccountably lighter, and saw Janet's head coming up the wooden ladder and the rest of her following like the rising of a human sun. She was pinning her married woman's cap on again because it tended to be pushed off by the wiriness of her springy hair.

He took out his notebook, opened it at the beginning, touched the lock of hair with his forefinger. The colour was a little darker than Janet's hair. Then he closed the book with a snap and put it back in his doublet pocket.

Then because there was no one there to see, he bowed to Janet as he would have to Lady Widdrington or a lady of the Court and was rewarded by her pleased flush as she dropped her curtsey.

"I'm ready to go now. Where is he exactly?"

"In Stobbs tower."

Janet laughed. "That's where Wee Colin took me at Christmas-tide. There's a veiled woman there—I think it was Wee Colin's sister—though it was his wife, Mrs Elliot, who received me."

He went down the stairs first with habitual chivalry, though there was very unlikely to be danger there in Janet's own tower. Shilling and two packponies were waiting in the inner courtyard. One was loaded up with grain, the other with mysterious packages and Red Sandy and Bangtail were standing nearby drinking their morning beer.

"You're planning to stay, Mrs Dodd?"

"Ay. I know Henry. I'm the only one that can keep him in his bed till he's well enough to travel."

"I think you are. I certainly couldn't keep him from riding after he took a bad beating in London from Sir Thomas Heneage and his men."

Her nostrils flared. Clearly she had heard the story from Dodd, and Carey suspected she was only mollified by the very satisfactory revenge Dodd had taken for the insult, of which Whitesock had been a part.

An idea came to him. "Mrs Dodd, I'll keep Whitesock at Carlisle for the moment and when you tell us that Dodd is ready to ride, I'll have Whitesock sent up to Stobbs. You can tell him that the horse needs to recover, not him."

Her smile struck him in the chest, because all of its fondness was for Dodd.

"Ay," she said, "that'll dae it. He'll spare the horse when he willna spare hisself."

They rode out and went northwards and without a cart, made much better time and reached Stobbs by evening. The veiled woman came out to welcome Mrs Dodd and put them up for the night, though Carey and his men had to doss down in the hall on the rushes since the guest chamber was occupied by Dodd and his wife.

THURSDAY, 18TH JANUARY 1593

The next day he, Red Sandy, and Bangtail took their horses and remounts and went south and west thirty miles to Carlisle. Carey upped the pace and upped the pace as if he was escaping from something, until they were galloping across the snowy moors and risking death. He wanted to take a shortcut through the Debateable Land, but for some reason Red Sandy and Bangtail refused to contemplate any such madness with only the two of them there and so they got to Carlisle late at night.

MONDAY, 22ND JANUARY 1593, KESWICK

Carey waited a few days to see if the snow would melt, but the cold was still bonechilling and it got dirtier and more worn, but stayed obstinately where it was. In that time he received another letter from Sir Robert Cecil, this time coded by Mr Phelippes, explaining who Mr Philpotts was with an elaborate apology in bad verse which at least made him laugh. With it was another fuller warrant, which authorised him to inspect the mining works and all machinery and warehouses appertaining thereto in Keswick or any other mine worked by the Deutschers, their agents or assigns, and also a very welcome banker's draft to provide him with money. It seemed Cecil too wanted the death of the man who had so nearly succeeded in killing the Scottish King.

He appointed Andy Nixon his Acting Sergeant and rode out of Carlisle immediately after church service on Sunday with Red Sandy, Bangtail, Leamus, and Tovey his clerk. He didn't need more men than that for peaceful Keswick and it was the raiding season and the Maxwells and Johnstones at each other's throats over the Border, and Scrope was shorthanded as it was. He still had no valet. All the young men he had interviewed for the post were unable to tell a pair of hosen from a woman's cap and utterly cackhanded at tying up laces. Of course not one of them could sew. He was annoyed about it. Would he have to send to London to find a valet? Did Cecil really expect him to manage without one? Surely not. Well, maybe he would find somebody to keep his clothes and jack and boots in order in Keswick.

It was sixty miles to Keswick as the crow flies and further by road, rolling country and a road in very poor condition. So they took it slowly and stayed the night at a tiny inn at Penrith. The next day they got lost and then luckily found a shepherd who pointed out the pathway leading up into the hills that shouldered their way through the mist, their flanks covered by fur gowns of winter forest. They picked their way through the woodmen's paths through the trees that were at all stages of growth from being cut for charcoal, slender stalks protected by deerfences and thicker withies and then branches as thick as your wrists. But then they crested a rise and looked down towards Keswick and saw that there was some disease of the trees, for many of them were sick or dead, some still holding onto their leaves as though they had forgotten to drop them in the autumn, with bare branches and trunks naked of lichens. Some of the mountains were bald and ugly too.

At least it was easier to navigate through the sick forest and they could see the smoke of Keswick ahead where some of the fields had already been plowed and there were orchards that looked sick and sorry for themselves as well. Red Sandy and Bangtail were looking around in wonder and Leamus had his hand on something hanging round his neck inside his buffcoat, muttering in Irish.

Carey had seen something like it before and was racking his brains to think where and when. Finally he got it—the place was like the Forest of Dean, where most of the English cannon were cast. Interesting—was there some tree-sickness that came from metals, perhaps? Nobody hailed them on the road, though there were peasants trudging along. They came into Keswick along the road that followed beside a river busy with weirs and mills. There was a lot of sour-smelling smoke coming from a number of large buildings behind a fence. They left that behind and crossed the town meadows, finally coming to the town with a scatter of cottages first, and then the tightly packed townhouses, built into the gardens of older houses. Bangtail and Red Sandy were shocked again when they realised that Keswick had no walls, being protected by its hills and distance from the Borders. They reached the main inn, the Oak, and went into the small courtyard. The innkeeper came out, a skinny man with a settled cautious expression on his face.

"I am Sir Robert Carey, and I am here on the Queen's Warrant," he explained blandly to the innkeeper's questions. Their horses were stabled and Carey given a small guestroom to share with Tovey while Red Sandy, Bangtail, and Leamus went into the dormitory downstairs.

The supper was dispiriting, an oatmeal pottage with too much salt to disguise the fact that it was on the turn and a piece of salt beef floating in it which Carey suspected of having been condemned before the Armada.

As expected, the town Mayor turned up as they struggled through the stale bread and thin ale, complete with his crimson gown in the style of Henry VIII. He bowed to Carey and introduced himself as Aloysius Allerdyce.

Carey bowed back and eyed him. He was short and wide-built and smiling broadly so Carey too painted a smile on his face and sat himself down on the bench with the wall at his back.

"I am Sir Robert Carey, knight, Deputy Warden of the English West March at Carlisle."

"That's what I heard. Are ye here on a hot or cold trod, Sir Robert?" asked Allerdyce with a frown. "I don't think there are any cattle raiders here except for…well, there aren't any and he's respectable enough when he visits."

"Who?"

"Oh, just Mr Graham. They say he's a notable reiver but…"

Carey narrowed his eyes. "Which Graham?"

"Er…" Clearly Allerdyce was wishing his tongue hadn't run away with him. "Mr Walter Graham."

"Are you talking about Wattie Graham of Netherby, by any chance?"

"Happen I am."

Both eyebrows went up. "Really? *Respectable?*"

"He owns some woods hereabouts in Borrowdale, nearly the only good-sized timber left and he often comes to…er…inspect it."

Carey blinked and did his best to hide his instant fascination. What was Wattie Graham doing, owning woods like a lord? The Grahams famously didn't even legally own or rent the lands they lived on, but were squatting on Storey lands. They had driven that family off in the 1520s when the original five Graham brothers came south from wherever the devil they came from, probably Hell.

"Ah," he said. "Well, no, I'm not precisely on a trod. I am interested in the mines and miners hereabouts."

Very deliberately, Allerdyce spat into the fireplace. "The Dutch miners?"

"Yes. Can you take me to their headman or captain?"

"Why d'ye want to talk to they, they're not even Christians?"

"Oh?"

"Anabaptists and devil-worshippers, I heard."

"Really? Well, I have been directed by the Queen to inspect the mines, make sure that the Queen is getting her rights and so on."

An interesting expression crossed Allerdyce's broad face, equal parts disappointment and disgust. "Ay well, we thought ye wis something to do with the murder."

"The murder?"

"Ay, the murder of one of my aldermen, three days after New Year's Even."

"I am also, of course, warranted to investigate any and all breaches of the Queen's peace," Carey lied briskly, "so certainly I would want to find out who committed such a terrible crime. Do you have anyone locked up?"

"Nay, it's still a mystery."

"Ah. Perhaps I can assist you to find the guilty party."

"Hmf. And the miners?"

"Who is the headman of the miners? I believe it was originally a man called Daniel Hochstetter of the Augsburg company Haug and Co, but that he died more than ten years ago and Haug and Company have gone bankrupt."

"Ay, he did. There are the shareholders in the Company of Mines Royal, but they're in London now. I suppose the nearest to a headman would be Hans Loser but really ye should talk to Frau Hochstetter, Radagunda Hochstetter, Mr Daniel's widow, or mebbe her son, Mr Emanuel."

"Ahah. And when can I meet the widow?"

Allerdyce moved uncomfortably. "Oh, I don't think there's any need. She doesn't speak English, ye ken, even after all this time in England. Mester Daniel did, but not her."

"Are there any shareholders at all here in Keswick? Surely there should be at least one to keep the accounts and so on?"

"Ay," said Allerdyce, clearly thinking hard. "Though Mr Nedham's awa' from the town at the moment. I heard tell he's gone to Bristol, looking for good charcoal." There was a short silence.

"Well," said Carey, "if you haven't buried your murdered alderman yet or had the inquest, perhaps you could tell me what happened and then I could view the body?"

"Ay, o' course, ay."

"So what happened?"

"Eh?"

"With the alderman. What was his name to start with?"

"Oh, it was Carleton, not from the riding Carletons, ye know, the southerly branch and it surely is a mystery."

Carey steepled his fingers, hooded his eyes and waited.

"Ay, John Carleton. It's hard to think who could have done it, he wis found in the morning, stone dead and his smithy fire out for he hadn't curfewed it. That was shocking."

"He was found in his smithy?"

"Ay, he was a plumber too, very clever man, he could make

lead pipes and sheets for the church roof but mainly he was the smith and he could make all kinds of new things with iron and copper and lead and such. He made a little thing to help with whisking eggs for his mother, a very respectable woman, and she died last year of the stomach ache."

"You say he was found in his smithy? Why did you think it was a murder? Perhaps he just dropped dead from an imposthume?"

"That's what we thought at first and it was only when Mrs Carleton laid the body out with her gossips and washed it that she found…she discovered." Allerdyce was almost purple. "…er…a bruise on his skull under his hair and…"

To Carey's horror, Allerdyce had tears in his eyes.

"He was a good man, ye ken, allus willing to help, would allus put hisself out for his friends, he didn't deserve such a… such a death."

"What kind of death?"

Allerdyce took a deep breath, put his two fists together in front of his chest and whispered, "A heated swordblank or…or a spit…up…up his arse, Sir Robert, it were all burnt…and…" He stopped.

Carey was silent. "That is indeed terrible," he said quietly.

"Somebody said the like wis done tae a king once, but he wis a pervert and deserved it."

"I think it was but I don't remember which king. There's a poet down in London who was writing a play about him too. Good God."

"But John…he wasnae a pervert, he was a right fine man." Tears were coursing freely down Allerdyce's face now. "And that was how we knew he'd been murdered by somebody, but nobody else was there. And everybody in the town, every man, even the apprentice boys, was in bed that night for it was snowing."

"I suppose you've buried him by now?"

"Ay, poor fellow. We had a funeral as soon as the snow stopped and we could get the grave dug for he wis a big man too, we had paid mourners and all, it were quite an occasion. Even some of the Deutschers came for he spoke Dutch and he was married to one of their women too. Everybody was sad to lose him."

Carey was deep in thought. "Perhaps I can view his smithy?"

"Ay, his son will have it in the end, though he's ainly young, still an apprentice. We're on the lookout for a good smith that isnae a drunk to teach the boy until he can take over."

"The murder happened after New Year, when there was snow on the moors?"

"Ay, and here too, there's been snow since November. We looked for cloven hoofprints or some such but there were so many from everybody who came to see, all scuffling around before we realised he hadna just up and died…"

Carey nodded. "You weren't to know. Had anyone new come to town, since New Year's Eve?"

"There's allus a coming and a going here, especially if there's a good freeze in the winter, so the packponies can move more easily. But not in a blizzard. There was a maidservant who claimed she saw a ghost on horseback during that night but Betty has more phantasy than most and likely she was dreaming."

"Hm." Carey was tapping his teeth thoughtfully.

"Well, Sir Robert, if ye'd help us find the man that did such a horrible murther, we'll not be ungrateful. The last murder we had in Keswick was that Deutscher preacher, Leonard Stoltz, back in 1566 and nobody hanged for that either, though we all knew Toby Fisher that was the Earl of Northumberland's reeve was the man who killed him right enough, though it took twenty more of Northumberland's tenants together to pull Stoltz down."

"Hm. I would like to know more about that as well."

"It was a'cause Stoltz was an Anabaptist preacher and the Earl of Northumberland was a Catholic who didn't like any of that sort of stuff."

"I have heard something about the religious wars in Allemayne, but that was back in the 1520s, wasn't it?"

"Ay," said Allerdyce, dismissing the whole deadly war with his shoulder. "That's furriners for ye. I'll bid ye welcome tae Keswick, Sir Robert, and yer men with ye and I'll be with ye in the morning to bear ye company to poor Carleton's smithy."

For courtesy's sake, Carey went with him to the main door of the inn and then went across the yard to the snug with its roaring fire where Bangtail and Red Sandy were playing quoits with four hard-bitten weather-beaten men who turned out to be the packpony drovers. Everybody was doing their level best to get rid of their money as fast as possible. He sat down with a cup of red wine, a smart silver cup in honour of the Mayor probably, but the wine was so awful he slung it in the fireplace and got some of the beer which was much more drinkable and nothing like the thin ale they had had with supper which the innkeeper clearly kept for strangers. In fact the beer was so good, he complimented the innkeeper on it, who immediately looked guilty, as well he should.

"Ay, it's fra the Deutscher brewery on the island, ye ken. Ye can say what ye like about the furriners but they do know how to brew beer, that's for sure."

Carey toasted him and took another quart, sat down again by the fire and watched the proceedings. Bangtail was pretty good at quoits and Red Sandy was adequate, and the drovers were drunk but surprisingly accurate and so the game ended at evens.

The bed in the private room was lumpy but at least not damp though the room was cold with no fireplace. Tovey was deep in some book he was reading by the light of two candles, in his shirt and wrapped in his threadbare scholar's gown. He came hesitantly to help Carey take off his arming doublet, fumbling irritatingly at the laces and forgetting the right order. Carey bit his lip to stop himself shouting at the youngster because shouting at him only made him more clumsy and he was at least trying.

When the whole process was finished and Carey in his shirt

and fur dressing gown against the sharpness in the air, he looked at the large tome Tovey had put down carefully marked with a bit of paper.

"What are you reading?" he asked, "It looks...er...heavy."

Tovey's shy smile lit his pale bony face. "Yes sir, it is," he said eagerly, "but it's fascinating and I was very lucky to find a copy in Carlisle cathedral library and they let me borrow it too, though I had to leave my cloak as a surety."

"So what is it?"

"*De Re Metallica* of Agricola, sir," he said. "All about mining and smelting metals and so on."

"Really? I'd like to read that myself."

"Well...er...it is in Latin, sir..."

"Damn. As so often happens I find myself stymied by my youthful idleness." Carey often wondered if he could have learned Latin the way he learned French and caught himself in a promising fantasy about the legendary harlots of Rome who spoke very good Latin because all their best customers in the Vatican were bishops and priests...

"Yes, sir, but see, sir, there are pictures, lots of them. It's a very expensive book, it cost the cathedral a whole five pounds and that was back in the 1550s."

Carey was squinting at one of the woodcuts. "What on earth is that?"

"It's a waterwheel sir, powering the hammers that break the ore into smaller lumps."

"Ingenious. A good way of saving on workmen."

"Yes, sir."

Carey flipped to the end. "And is that a kind of furnace?"

"Yes, though it's a cupellating furnace to use when separating silver and gold from the copper."

"So there is gold here?"

"Only very small amounts and the Queen gets half of that."

He had helped his cousin Trevannion out over some Cornish

mines in the early eighties but had been busy at Court and couldn't recall the details. He thought it had been very expensive but Trevannion had got what he wanted.

"And silver?"

"It depends how rich the ore is."

Carey looked at the very clear, detailed, and neatly labelled pictures until Tovey coughed apologetically and said, "Sir, if I can read through all of it, I will be able to help you much better with the Deutschers in the morning."

"Certainly."

He dozed off with the bedcurtain drawn and the candles still burning, but no sound because Tovey read even Latin internally.

WEDNESDAY, 24TH JANUARY 1593, KESWICK

The morning was equally irritating as Tovey helped him put on his olive brocade doublet he had brought along, fumbling short-sightedly at the points again. So Carey clattered down to breakfast in slightly less good a mood than usual, for Carey was a man who rejoiced in mornings, the earlier the better.

The inn was already serving breakfast because the drovers needed to get their packponies back to Goldscope mine in Newlands valley with food and gear for the miners. Not all of them were laden which helped with the climb, according to a drunken drover who was explaining to the host, how the unladen ponies went ahead to help pull the laden ones along.

Carey and a heavy-eyed Tovey tucked into a new kind of meaty sausage with plenty of pepper, black pudding and bacon and fried bread sippets, no fancy New World roots from Newcastle here. Red Sandy and Bangtail appeared, followed by Leamus, and they also tucked in.

"Did ye ken there was a man killed here the week after New Year's?" said Red Sandy to Carey. "And they'd no' had a murder in Keswick for near thirty years. Did ye ever hear the like?"

Bangtail shook his head. "I dinna believe it, me. Whit aboot the raiding season, whit aboot blackrent?"

"I heard there had been a murder, yes," Carey said, wondering if it would be worth the effort to explain to Bangtail about peaceful countryside and so on.

"Thirty years wi' nae killing!" jeered Bangtail, "it's no' possible."

"It is," Carey corrected him, "if you're far enough away from the Border. And sixty miles is far enough. And the hills help."

Bangtail was struck silent by this and Carey wandered out into the stableyard to check the horses who had been fed and watered by the men, or more probably by Leamus who was technically the most junior and foreign to boot.

He came back and met Aloysius Allerdyce, resplendent in his Sunday best of dark grey wool with expensive velvet trim, who smiled and bowed, so Carey bowed back. "Ah'm pleased to see ye, Sir Robert. Will ye come and see the smithy now?"

Bangtail was standing behind him in the yard, looking puzzled so Carey asked, "Did you want something, Bangtail?"

"Ay, sir, it's what ye said. Ye said if ye're far enough from the Border, there isn't much murthering."

"Yes. There's also hardly any cattle raiding, sheep-rustling, kidnapping, and arson."

Bangtail gulped. "Ye're telling me that the normal killing and fighting and reiving is just on the Border."

"Yes."

"But why?"

"Er...perhaps it's because England and Scotland have been at war most of the time since about two hundred years ago. The Borderers...well they couldn't beat the soldiers and men-at-arms, so they joined them."

Bangtail nodded slowly. "So if I got maself a farm, say, sixty miles from Carlisle, south, say, I might hold it?"

"Yes, if you had bought it fairly."

Bangtail's eyes were big, a child looking at a confectioner's window. "And naebody would raid me nor burn it nor kill me."

"Probably not."

Bangtail shook his head. "Jesus!" he said and rubbed his face. "Jesus Christ. Ah'm moving." He went into the stables looking like a man who had been hit on the head.

Carey took Tovey with him to the smithy since the lad was clearly eager to make himself into an expert on metals as well as herbs—at least intellectually. Men with the practical knowledge from apprenticeship and journeying would obviously be better at making swords and tools and perhaps even guns, though that would be more a specialist trade like they had in Dumfries. However men like that often couldn't read and weren't good at talking.

They went to Mr Carleton's house on the small high street, where his wife and young son were waiting for him in the hall, their silver all on display and freshly polished and both in their Sunday best as well. Carey instantly became the courtier again, bowed to Mrs Carleton's curtsey and gravely returned the boy's clumsy bow.

"I am so sorry to intrude on your grief, ma'am," he said to the widow who was a pale blonde and very self-possessed. The black veil did not suit her at all. She curtseyed again. "May I see your late husband's workshop please, in case I can help find the evil murderer?"

"Of course you may, Sir Robert, and I am honoured by your interest in my poor husband." Her English was perfect.

"And may I talk to you about it after I look at the smithy?"

She dipped her head.

"D'ye think there was more than one, like a gang of men?" asked Allerdyce eagerly.

"Was there a gang of men in town—like the drovers, for instance?"

"Nay, not them, we know them, they're friends. I meant, maybe a gang come down from Carlisle or summat?"

"With all the snow? I doubt it, Mr Allerdyce. And why would they go to so much trouble? They'd be more likely to lance him and then fire the smithy. But they would be much more likely to spot your house as being better than the others and come and take your silver and insight and maybe your wife for ransom. Reivers want money. Killing is just the quickest way to get it, in their view." Allerdyce shuddered a little.

They went through the hall to the little courtyard at the back which was full of pots with winter twigs in them. There were some more pots keeping warm in the stables in which the plants looked less dead.

Then they went into the large smithy which had two separate furnaces and an open fireplace and strangely no fires. The place was empty though there were tools on hooks all along the wall, and some half-made sword blanks in a pile and a stream burbling through a stone channel to a large quenching trough that was half full.

"Now, Mr Allerdyce," said Carey, wondering why there was nobody there, "could you tell me who found the body?"

"It were his lad," said Allerdyce. "He ran in to ask his dad to show him something and found him on the floor and couldn't waken him, so ran back to tell his mam."

"Where was the body?"

"Lying on his stomach apparently, but quite...er...decent, ye ken. It were his wife and one of the apprentices that saw to it. They took him in and laid him out upstairs, cos they knew he was dead o' course. Cold as charity, he was."

"So was the smithy fire still lit?"

"A dinna ken. O' course, with the blacksmith dead, I expect it was the journeymen put out all the fires."

"Why?"

"Why what?"

"Why did the journeymen put out all the fires?"

Allerdyce looked shocked. "Ye canna have the smithy fires lit if the smith is dead, specially if he died in the smithy, t'wouldn't be right, t'wouldn't be safe."

"Why not?"

"It just wouldn't."

"Would they have been lit before, when Mr Carleton came in?"

"Ay, or curfewed. He liked to be in the smithy early, the first, he was the master, he liked to make sure it were all stimmel..."

"What?"

"Er...right, tidy, proper for the sun to see. He'd sharpen up one of the fires usually to do some tinkering. Sometimes if the mood was on him he'd be at the smithing all night, making something strange. He made all the different tools and mattocks for the Deutschers, and he made them good and so did his journeymen and 'prentices. He had another forge down at Newlands too to make the parts for the machines and some of the bigger tools."

"Did he use ore from the mine?"

"Nay." Allerdyce grinned and Carey got the message he had asked something ignorant. "The rocks is all copper here, green copper with a little si...gold in it, ay, but nae iron, we get that fra Bristol. Copper's worth more than iron anyways, even now, but it's not so useful a metal, it's a little soft though it makes good pots and pans. Ye can make bronze to cast from it wi' a bit of Cornish tin added in at the smelting."

"I see." Carey started poking around the neat shop with its swept floor. "Why isn't the smithy being worked now?"

"Well...er...they're afeared of Mr Carleton's ghost, sir. Once they knew he was killt in his ain smithy, they all left and Mrs Carleton won't order them back for they won't go. A blacksmith is...well, they say he can work magic, sir, or his ghost can, and they wouldn't take the risk. They'll come back after forty days has passed since he died, but until then, no."

Was there something eery about the quiet cold place that should have been bustling and hot? The weak sun lit it well, passing through hatches in the roof with sliding shutters to let the heat out in the summer. All of them were open despite the cold.

"How many men worked here?"

"Well now, there was David Butfell and Tom Atkinson and old man Melchior Moser too—he's a Deutscher and a copper-smith. Still a journeyman, though Herr Moser should have been a Master with his own copperbeating shop, but he didn't want the responsibility."

Carey had his notebook out, noting the names. "And the apprentices?"

"Ay, there was Short Jemmie, Matty, Jurgen, Rob, and…"

"And me, sir," piped up a boy's voice. "Josef Carleton at your service, sir. I'd only started in the workshop last year so I havena made nothing yet and I wis just sweeping up and I havenae got my growth but…but I'll be a fine smith, sir, just like *Vater*."

Carey smiled at him gravely. "I am certain you will," he said and sat down carefully on the trough's edge because his back points were a little tight. "Now Josef, it was you found your father, yes?"

"Ay sir," said the boy, with his jaw as hard as rock, and his velvet cap crushed in his hand, determined not to cry. Carey signalled with his hand that Tovey was to take notes. Tovey started and fumbled out his pen and ink bottle from his penner on his belt and a new notebook from the breast of his doublet.

"Could you tell me exactly what you saw when you found your father?"

The boy swallowed hard. "*Jawohl*," he said. "Yes."

"Do you speak Dutch?"

"Of course. English und Deutsch together."

"I speak French, but not Deutsch alas."

"It's a beautiful language, sir. You should study it."

"Perhaps I will. Now, what can you remember?"

"I came running in because I had an idea for a thing we were making together, a special machine like the ones in the mine, but small and of bronze or perhaps steel because bronze is brittle… and I knew my father would be in the smithy as it was dawn already. Then I stopped."

"Why?"

"Sir?"

"Why did you stop? Did you see your father?"

"No sir, but…I felt frightened."

"Why? Think back. What was it frightened you?"

The boy's eyes went vague and then sharpened. "Ay, sir, it were the fire, sir."

"What was wrong with it?"

"It was…it was in a pitiful condition, sir. The other two were out, the end ones, no curfews on them, just the coals unswept, but my *Vater*'s favourite, Violet…"

"He named his fires?"

"Of course, ye can't smith without fire, can ye? That's Violet and those are Daffodil and Rose."

"Ah…so what was wrong with…er…Violet?"

"She were sick, sir. Somebody hadna put a curfew on the coals to keep them hot, just left her to burn down so the coals were down to ash grey and dark red, nearly cramoisie. I knew my father would never have neglected her in such a way so I come in more slowly, saying "*Vater*," ye ken. Anyway I rounded the trough and peered past Henry…"

"Henry?"

"Me father's favourite anvil, sir. That one."

The boy pointed. "Ah, I see. Henry. Yes, a good name for an anvil. Go on…"

"And that's when I saw him on the floor, wi' his legs drawn up."

"Was there any blood?"

"Nay, sir, nowt. It looked like he'd fallen asleep on the floor which he'd never done before though I've found him asleep on that bench, there, still in his apron and work clothes when he'd been tinkering with something all night."

"Did you think he might be drunk?"

"Nay, sir, he only drinks…drank mild ale when he was working."

"So what did you do?"

"Well, I went to him and shook his shoulder only it felt funny…"

"Did it feel stiff as if it were all of a piece with his whole body?"

"Ay, sir."

"Go on."

"I tried really hard to wake him, I got more and more…. afeared and then I saw his eyes staring at me and…I…ran to fetch my mam…"

"Was there any smell?"

"Sort of a burnt smell, like when the charcoal burners burn dung? It was terrible."

"Thank you, Josef, you've spoken bravely to me. Is there anything else you can remember?"

"Nay, I…." He frowned. "Yes."

"What?"

"There were two of our silver cups standing on Henry, with mulled ale in one."

Carey carefully kept the excitement out of his voice. "Two cups? One for your father and…"

The boy paled even more. "One for the murderer?"

Perhaps. It was very important not to make assumptions, but maybe. "And what does that tell you, Josef?"

The boy scowled, scowled some more and then gasped.

"He knew the murderer, sir, my father knew him."

Carey nodded. Josef said some explosive words in Deutsch which Carey suspected was swearing. "Please don't tell anyone or…"

"Ay, or the murderer hisself might hear. Yes sir, I'll keep stumm."

"Not even your friends?"

"Ay, sir, I understand. It's like a smith's mysteries. Ye dinna spread it all about or everyone will know and then where will ye be?"

"Exactly. Now one more thing. Show me exactly where your father lay. Where was his head? And his feet?" Josef showed him. "And you said he was on his side?"

Josef nodded.

"So how did he get on his stomach."

"I pushed him over trying to wake him...and so I wouldn't have his eyes staring at me." Josef swallowed. "Was that wrong?"

Carey's heart bled a little for the boy. "No, Josef, I understand. But you know when the eyes set like that, it means his spirit has departed, gone straight to God for Judgement. They can't see anything anymore."

The boy ducked his head, said nothing.

Carey stood and went with him to the door, found Allerdyce sitting and waiting patiently on the courtyard bench which had a number of clay pipe fragments swept under it.

"Thank you, Mr Allerdyce," he said as the boy ran off into the house.

"Think nothing of it. Ah wis curious to hear the lad's story too. So ye're reckoning is that Mr Carleton knew his killer."

"Yes."

"God's truth. That's worse than the idea there were a gang o' them come fra the Border."

"Indeed, though a gang would be much easier to track."

"A friend, ye say? That's hard. Every man in the town knew Big John Carleton and most of them were his friends."

"Or perhaps a respected customer. I think for a friend you'd use whatever was usual and to hand, a leather jack or a horn cup or perhaps pewter. But for a customer, you'd get your silver cups out of your locked cupboard. Unless it was some kind of celebration."

Allerdyce nodded. "Any notion what was in the cups? Wine?"

"No."

"Pity, there's only one place ye can buy wine hereaboouts, at the Oak Inn, and then ye might know when Carleton bought the wine."

"Good thinking, Mr Allerdyce, but according to young Josef it was ale, perhaps mulled."

"Ay, that's a friendlier drink than wine."

"I'm also interested to know why there was no blood apparently."

"Ay?"

"There's a possible reason but I need to speak to Mrs Carleton about that." Carey stood and stretched his back. Having ill-tied points always made his back ache. "Come on, let's get on," he said.

They found Mrs Carleton in the parlour with three silver goblets of wine poured for them and a plate of wafers sprinkled with sugar. In the corner was a solid-looking older woman in Netherlandish clothes, knitting away. Most women were busy knitting or spinning like the Fates at the turn of the year. Mrs Carleton and her woman got up to curtsey and Carey waved her down, bowed slightly and sat in the guest chair with the back but no arms. He took the goblet proffered him by Mrs Carleton's woman but avoided the wafers because of the sugar. He preferred them salted in any case, even if he hadn't sickened of the sweet spice of sugar since his tooth needed drawing.

Mrs Carleton was pale to her eyebrows, which were pale blond, her German-style cap was not far enough back to show any hair. Would it be thin blond or thick blond, Carey wondered absently as he gestured at Tovey to take notes. Tovey found a place to rest his notebook on a high chest and somehow made himself invisible.

"Mrs Carleton, can you tell me what happened on the unfortunate night when your husband died?"

She pinched the bridge of her nose, with dark circles either side, then braced herself.

"That night I went to bed with my husband, he was my usual bedfellow when he was in Keswick and we…" Her pale face coloured a little and then paled again. "We knew each other."

Carey tilted his head respectfully.

"We slept in each other's arms. Mr Carleton must have woken long before dawn as was his wont, for though he liked to be in bed betimes, you couldn't keep him in bed at all after the sky started lightening or earlier if he was excited about something he was making. So I don't know when he left me but it was probably very early." She took a deep breath.

"He must have dressed in his work clothes as he usually did and went to say his prayers in the smithy while he got Violet sharpened to work and put his aprons on, for he was wearing them when we…When my son found him. I don't know what he was working on, there's nothing in the smithy with a peculiar shape or half-finished."

Carey nodded.

"Anyway, when I woke up I said my prayers and went to see if the 'prentices were up yet, which they weren't, the lazy *Junges*. So I went to fetch fresh bread myself and came back to start to make breakfast which was some sausage and fried onions and the bread, of course.

"And then young Josef came running in, saying…he was stammering about *Vater* being ill, so I ran into the smithy and found my husband lying, almost on his stomach and…and he was dead." She took another deep breath and held it, but tears still came to her eyes and she scrubbed them with a white hand-kerchief. Carey had expected this and waited patiently, looking as sympathetic as he could.

Her lips firmed. "So I sent Josef to get the 'prentices and Rob and Matty came first and we all carried my lord up and Jock helped for he was heavy, and we put him in the parlour on the table on his back."

"Was there any blood?"

"No, none. His face looked quite peaceful, just as normal, though he favoured his own *Vater* in death, but he favoured his *Mutter* in life."

"Can you tell me anything about his clothes? Were they fastened properly?"

"What?"

Carey gestured apologetically. "Were his points at the back tied?"

"Oh." She coloured, swallowed. "No, he was wearing his leather working breeches which are held by a thick belt to support his back, his shirt was tucked in the way he liked it, his leather jerkin fastened. He still had his working gloves on. His cap had fallen off though."

She took a long drink of wine, showing some fortitude since it was white and sour. "Then we said some prayers and I left pennies on his eyes to keep them shut. We went downstairs again, heartsick, heartsick. Do you understand? He was not in his prime but still he was a large healthy man with a big laugh and…and I missed him already. We didn't know then what had really happened, we thought he had been taken by a fit or imposthume."

Carey nodded sympathetically again and waited.

"My gossips came that afternoon to help lay him out. Heidi Stamler…" She gestured at the older woman who inclined her head, "Annamaria Steinberger and Alice Bunting. We…we got his clothes off him, jerkin and belt and his shirt and then, when we had his leather breeches off it was Alice who noticed that his…his *assze* looked strange. I looked and it was odd. There was something…some metal thing stuck there and we couldn't get it out. Alice ran to the smithy to get a pair of metal pliers and we managed to pull it out a bit."

"What was it?"

"A half-made sword blank, with a point, what we saw later. It was firmly stuck." Mrs Carleton paused to swallow and shut her eyes and open them again. "It was a long sword, a rapier blade. It must have reached to his chest, at least."

And his heart, Carey thought but only nodded again gravely. "What exactly was strange about his rear?"

"It loooked blackened, as if he had sat on something dirty."

Carey suddenly had to gulp some wine. Tovey was looking at him with shocked eyes, he prayed the boy wouldn't throw up, he looked on the verge of it…That was why there was no blood, the sword-blank had been red hot and cauterised as it killed.

"So then we covered him with a sheet and I went personally that evening to tell Mr Allerdyce what we had found and when he had seen it for himself, he said he must immediately call an inquest since he is the Coroner."

"Ay," said Allerdyce who had sat respectfully silent through all this, sitting foursquare on the bench. "O'course we convened the inquest jury for the next day and found that Mr Carleton had been unlawfully killed and murdered by person or persons unknown. But we had no one we could even ask about it except the 'prentices and they were in their beds upstairs and the young men, the journeymen, live out."

"Mr Allerdyce helped. He called a hue and cry through the whole town but because of the snowfall there were no visitors and no strangers."

"What about the maidservant who said she saw a ghost rider?"

"We questioned her at the inquest," said Allerdyce, "but she said she saw him from her bedroom window and his horse's hooves left no print in the snow and he had nae face, just a yellow shape with holes and it frightened her so she want back to bed and hid under the bedclothes and her sister didn't see it, so we thought it were likely a dream."

"Hm."

"We waited a week in case anything else turned up and told us the guilty man, but nothing did and there was more snow and so we had the funeral and buried him in Crossthwaite churchyard. Everyone in town was there, and the Deutschers too, they came, they were right sorry at Mr Carleton's passing because he was such a clever smith. He made all the tools for mining, see? That's why he'd done sae well because miners need a powerful lot of funny tools and smelters need more and they wear out quickly."

"Is there another smith in town?"

"There was, but he wouldna take orders from the furriners and so his business went down and down and he died o' drink."

"What will you do about it?"

"We might go to Carlisle to find a master smith to come and train the journeymen and judge their masterpieces and the best can take over the smithy until the boy is of age. That's what I'm thinking, any road."

"Was there anyone at all you can think of who might have disliked your husband, Mrs Carleton? No matter how foolishly?"

She lifted her shoulders and shook her head helplessly. "No, you would think he would have enemies seeing he was so successful and had such a big smithy and he had come up from just a journeyman himself in the sixties. But everyone loved him, Sir Robert, honestly they did. He was such...such a funny, such a big funny man. The town seems so empty now."

"But somebody hated him enough to kill him, Mrs Carleton. Can you think of anyone at all?"

Both Allerdyce and Mrs Carleton shook their heads.

"But, Mr Allerdyce, somebody did. Somebody wanted him dead and did in fact kill him in a way...well, that is frankly so cruelly abhorrent I find it hard to think about. That argues hatred."

Tovey suddenly opened his mouth as if he had thought of something surprising to say and then shut it again. Nobody else moved.

Carey sighed. "Well, Mr Allerdyce, this is a pretty mystery and I own myself as much at a stand as your inquest jury. However I am here primarily to conduct an inspection of the mines around this place and the smelting houses and stamping houses in the north of the town. Perhaps I will also take a look at some of the woods being cut for charcoal. It must be a problem finding enough charcoal with the woods being so…so sparse and sick."

"Ay well, Frau Hochstetter now gets most of her coals for the roasting from the Bolton earthcoal mines. You can't use earthcoals for smelting, they're too full of brimstone, but they're good for roasting the ore. The packponies take the coals and charcoal straight to Newlands to the roasting houses there. She uses charcoal from Ireland for special jobs, like cupellation and some from Mr Graham's woods if she must, since he's very sparing."

Carey's eyes stretched at the idea of Wattie Graham of Netherby being worthy of the title of "Mr" but said nothing.

"Some people don't like to do business with the Deutschers and the dowager Lady Radcliffe has always hated them, since the old days, though she sold them fruit trees and dung from her stables when Mr Daniel was setting up the island for his family. So Frau Hochstetter often has to rely on Mr Graham." Allerdyce was looking a little tense and Carey got the feeling that he knew more about Wattie and his woodlands in Keswick, for God's sake, than he admitted to.

"Yes. Mr Graham. For instance," he pursued, "if you're looking for a man who casually commits murder for trifles and beats up poor farmers who can't pay his blackrent, then Wattie Graham is that man."

"I don't think he was in the town for a week after New Year's Day," said Allerdyce hastily. "He told me he usually celebrates with his brothers at Mr Richard Graham of Brackenhill's tower."

"Well, well," said Carey but left it. Instead he fished out and handed over the rather pompous second document that Cecil had sent, complete with the Queen's Privy Seal. Mrs Carleton looked at it with wonder and Allerdyce treated the document with appropriate reverence and spelled his way through it since it was a general warrant and so had an English translation from the Norman French and Latin.

"Ay," said the Mayor, "that looks all in order. Well, Sir Robert, I think the best thing would be for ye to meet with the Hochstetters and discuss how you can make yer inspection." He carefully folded the document and handed it back to Carey. "Perhaps you would do me the honour of bearing me company to dinner at the Oak and then we might go and see the Deutschers."

Carey agreed with this idea affably enough and they walked along the high street again where numerous women were busy sweeping their yards and men walking about purposefully, all pretending not to stare at the strangers. At the inn they found Allerdyce's aldermen lined up in their Sunday best, all full of bonhomie and feverish curiosity.

After dinner and feeling very full of salt cod since it was a Wednesday, Carey walked with Allerdyce down the long path to the boatlanding on Derwent Water. The island was close to the shore and the buildings on it clearly visible—and very odd they looked, being German in style and elaborately carved. There were a couple more little lake islands, covered in reeds and unhealthy-looking trees. The Deutschers' island itself was not very large, maybe two or three acres and there were bigger buildings there as well, including one that seemed to be the source of the rather fine beer Carey had drunk at dinner, since it had a malting tower.

Carey sniffed the air. It had an odd smell in it, woodsmoke to be sure, but also an abrasive smell which he recognised. It took him back to Whitehall palace and a winter when the Thames had frozen and he and the Earl of Cumberland were sharing a small, leaky, and ridiculously expensive room. Carey had won a lot of money at primero and had bought some earthcoals to try them out. Their servants had taken ages to get the coals to light but then once they were lit, they were warm for much longer than wood and curfewed better too. The only disadvantage was the nasty sulphurous abrasive smell—which was why the Queen refused to have anything but good seasoned oak or elm in her privy chambers or indeed anywhere she went at all.

There was smoke hanging on the still cold air over the whole town and it seemed to be thicker to the northeast where the smelting houses were. It clung to the lower slopes of the great ugly hills, covered in snow but shockingly bald of forests except for a few sick remnants here and there. Carey looked at them and repressed the impulse to shiver. What had hurt the forests so badly? They were taller hills than he had seen in England, though he had lived as a child some of the time in the Marches of Wales. These naked hills seemed somehow sulky and malevolent.

"Ay," said Allerdyce, following his gaze. "They're nae sae dangerous now, but Scafell there has eaten his share of men. In spring or summer you can go up in broad sunlight and not a care in the world and next minute the fog has come down, ye've lost your way and pitched off a ledge ye couldna see. At least now in winter ye can see them for what they are."

"I've always preferred tamer country," Carey admitted, "with signs of human life. Do you know what's wrong with the trees and why so many are sick and dying?"

Allerdyce gave him an odd look. "They were well enough before the Deutschers came, ye ken, came and dug out the mines and started smelting. Mebbe the trees dinna like them."

"Allemayne is full of trees, I'm told."

"Well maybe it's the kobolds from the mines."

"What?"

"Little demons that break machinery and ruin the bloom—kobolds. Mebbe they kill the trees too. I've often thought so cos it's not natural, is it?"

"Possibly."

Down by the boatlanding where the lake was flat and still with a fringing of ice, there was a small party of people drawn up to meet them.

"Won't we be going to the island?" asked Carey, a little disappointed.

"Nae need, they prefer to meet us here anyway and there's not so many of them that lives there now either. Most of the Deutschers live in the town because they're married to our women and some of us Keswickers work for them. There's not many of the old Deutschers left, most went home in the seventies when the mines here were failing of ore. They're still mining copper ore, mind, but I remember nigh on a hundred of them when I was first a journeyman mercer."

"Did you mix with them at first?" Carey asked, remembering how the Mayor had spat at the first mention of them.

"No, for there was all that trouble with Leonard Stoltz and the Earl of Northumberland's men and after it was all over, that's why they moved to the island, see. But it got better later, 'cause they were mostly young men that came over—fine big men some of them, that worked in the smelting houses, and all very strong with that fine yellow hair—ye can imagine the trouble we had keeping our Keswick maids from marrying them."

Carey laughed. They had arrived at the boatlanding. One of the Deutschers was a short stout determined-looking woman in a Deutscher cap and hat with a veil, very old-fashioned, two men who looked in their thirties, and one who was quite a young man. Everybody was wearing sober brocades, mainly green, and fur-lined robes in the Deutscher style. The bald boatman was sitting behind them in his boat, smoking a clay pipe and watching a heron that was standing sentry in the reeds of one of the other islands.

The man who stepped forward first, Allerdyce introduced as Mr Emanuel Hochstetter, the managing director of the family firm and old Mr Daniel's eldest surviving son. He had a slightly moth-eaten thatch of bright blond hair under his fashionable beaver hat and blue eyes, and a settled anxious expression on his face. Next to him was a thin balding man in a narrow tall hat, introduced as Mark Steinberger, perhaps a few years older than Emanuel Hochstetter. The woman bowed to Carey and Carey bowed back. Allerdyce murmured that this was Frau Radagunda Hochstetter and the young man was her youngest surviving son, David.

Frau Hochstetter said some words in High Dutch which the lad David translated into English, words of formal welcome and a promise of co-operation. Carey handed over his warrant to Emanuel Hochstetter who read it carefully aloud in Latin and Mark Steinberger also read it and gave it to Frau Hochstetter who didn't read the Latin, gave it to the youngster and the youngster scowled over the official English section. They gave it back with a certain amount of muttering.

"Master David," Carey said to the youngster, "would you translate for me?"

"Yes, yes of course," said the young man with no trace of an accent. And so Carey smiled and bowed all round and asked if he could have a guide to show him round the mines and smelting houses and so on since, alas, Mr Secretary Cecil had wished this inspection on him when he had more than enough to do at Carlisle and in the Debateable Land and he knew nothing at all of mines or miners. Not today of course, it was far too late in the day for that, but perhaps tomorrow or the day after if that was convenient to Mr Emanuel Hochstetter and Mrs Hochstetter?

It was. She said some more words in High Dutch and then all four of them got back in the boat and were rowed back to their mysterious island, where tendrils of fog were already preparing to take the houses back. Carey watched them and wondered what was wrong with them. Why did he have the feeling he had missed something important?

Tovey came close. "Why were they so tense, sir?" he murmered. "Even the lady?"

"That's probably because they're hiding something," said Carey, "and they almost certainly are."

"What?"

"No idea. It would be nice if they're tense because Jonathan Hepburn is in fact here, but I doubt it. Peculation to wholesale theft, I suspect. If, as Mr Secretary says in his letter, the main mine, called...er...Goldscope, I think, is exhausted, why are they still here?"

Tovey nodded.

"I'm looking forward to seeing the smelting houses," he said with a sudden eager grin. "All those wonderful machines."

"I am too," Carey admitted, "and the mines as well. I've never seen a working mine or been down one except siege mines, of course, which were damned small and dark and smelly and uncomfortable and apt to collapse at any minute."

They walked back up to the town through the dusk, wondering at the dirtiness of the buildings which were covered in a kind of black dinge that also speckled the piles of snow on every side where the small few streets of Keswick had been shovelled clear.

At the inn, Carey presided over all of them at supper in the common room and told Red Sandy and Bangtail of the surprising respectability of Wattie Graham, hereabouts known as Mister, which made them laugh. They agreed to have a drink with the drovers again and see if they could find out where Wattie's woods were and anything about them. After some ferocious games of shove-groat and quoits, Carey retired to his chamber and beckoned Tovey to follow.

"Mr Tovey," he said, "I have a job for you."

Tovey looked anxious. "Yes, sir?"

"It is not, you will be relieved to hear, a lucrative position as my valet. I'll find someone else as soon as I can. I want you to talk to people and report back to me."

"Sir, are you really here to inspect the mines?"

"Well, Mr Secretary has been remarkably co-operative, not to say speedy, in the matter of my warrant. No delay, no messing about, comprehensive. Why?"

"Does he actually want the mines inspected?"

"Yes. His father is a shareholder in the Company of Mines Royal and I expect he's happily killing two birds with one stone. Get the mines inspected anyway and find this would-be assassin for His Majesty at the same time."

"Oh."

"So while I'm shinning up and down ladders and inspecting smelting houses, I'm also expected to find Jonathan Hepburn or Hochstetter, if he's here, or get some kind of clue as to his whereabouts if he isn't."

"Why would he be here, sir? Surely he'd be safer in the Spanish Netherlands."

"Of course, though I'm sure King James will send men to all the uusual places in the Low Countries. No, in fact I agree with Mr Secretary. It's worth me coming here with a licence to poke around. There's something here that might have brought him back, something he can find nowhere else, wheresoever he wanders."

"What's that, sir?"

"His home."

Tovey was silent for a moment. "I hadn't thought of that."

Carey had started unbuttoning his doublet. "I really want to get onto that island too. What are they hiding there apart from a brewery and a bakery? Perhaps Hepburn himself?"

Tovey shook his head. "Could you arrest him if he is there?"

"Probably not," admitted Carey frankly, "since I only have four men and myself. That's going to have to be me killing him, I'm afraid."

Tovey looked shocked and Carey laughed as he unbuttoned his waistcoat and carefully took it off without untying the points at the back and bringing the canions and hose with them. Then he hung it on a hook, where it dangled looking like some kind of fashionable ghost.

"Let me explain something to you, Mr Tovey. King James gave me the commission, himself personally—find Hepburn and kill him. No nonsense about a trial. His Majesty doesn't want to frighten his people or make the commoners demand the execution of the bloody earl of Huntly nor Lord Maxwell. It seems that Cecil has found out or has been told by His Majesty that he's commissioned me and not only does not disapprove but approves enough to help me out with that warrant—and the banker's draft I exchanged in Carlisle too."

"What about the Queen?"

"I am quite sure that Cecil has only told Her Majesty what she needs to know on the subject, although…Well, she's as good at playing that game as he is, if not better. And so it's dirty work but I'll do it, because I personally object to assassination attempts being made on my liege, present or future."

Tovey's eyes were round. "It wouldn't be against your honour, sir?" he asked hesitantly.

"Good question, because, after all, King James is not yet my king. However if the Queen said to me, 'Find him and kill him,' of a would-be assassin like Hepburn, I would regard it as an honourable deed in the service of my liege. Odds are that King James will eventually be my liege, if he lives long enough, so on the whole, I don't think my honour will be touched if I kill Hepburn. And of course, I will be pleasing King James and possibly Cecil, which is no bad thing. I regard assassins as vermin anyway."

Tovey nodded.

"Also you should remember one other thing."

"What, sir?"

"Hepburn or Hochstetter may kill me."

TUESDAY, 23RD JANUARY 1593, STOBBS

Dodd was on his side on his pillows, bored and extremely grumpy while his back drove him mad with itching and his joints felt sore. He wanted to get up and walk around but both Janet and Mistress Elliot were adamant that he couldn't. Janet had gone downstairs to rest since she was tired and feeling sick, and so the veiled Mistress Alyson Elliot sat down on the stool and gave Dodd the spoon. He had insisted the day before he wouldn't be fed like a wean anymore, but he also remembered something from when he had been feverish and was wondering if it was the truth or a fever dream.

He spooned the usual pottage clumsily a couple of times and then stopped. "Och," he said, gesturing at her veil. "Will ye take that off?"

"Why?"

"Ah wantae see what Ah did tae ye."

"It's no' pretty."

"I ken that."

"Why d'ye want tae see it? Your gazing on it willna make it better nor even less sore."

"Is it still sore?"

"Ay, it is. Even if ye were to greet and say, 'Och, I'm sorry,' and all that, it wouldna make it better nor bring back my lost eye."

Dodd said nothing.

"Ay well," she said, "why not?"

She moved the veil from around her face carefully and then the rest of the way with a sharp angry movement so he could see the ruination of her face. He looked steadily for several minutes and then turned away.

"Och, God, ye're not greeting after all?"

"No," lied Dodd and blew his nose into the rushes. "I still dinna ken why ye didna slit ma throat when ye first saw me. I would ha'."

"Ay well, there's a difference between ye and me, Henry. Ye allus was a wee bit too quick to kill."

She wrapped the cloth around her face again, folding the fine linen with practised fingers so it hid the blind eye and the half-gone nose. Her working green eye with its long lashes looked at him consideringly.

"It was a beam that fell on me, or rather the end caught me," she said, "while I was holding up the trapdoor so the childer could get into the crypt and out by the nether door, while ye and yer surname were whooping and yelling around outside like savages. It was old Mrs Hall that dragged me out of there and so we ainly lost about ten people, plus Mrs Elliot that hated her husband and ran to Edinburgh with her young son Hughie."

Dodd nodded, his mouth drawn down and sour.

She was still considering something, watching him the way a cat watches a mousehole.

"What?"

"I'm wondering if I should tell ye or no'."

"What?"

"That when the church burned, I wis with child."

Dodd felt as if he had been punched in the gut. He struggled round until he could look at her. "Ye mean you and me...?"

"Naebody else to tek the blame. I was a virgin before I met ye at the haying. And I haven't known a man since, of course."

It had been while he was haying as a seventeen-year-old day-labourer for some Kerrs, over the Border, and she had been raking. As plenty of youngsters had done before and since, they had bundled in the hay after the dancing and the beer when the hay was in, not asking surnames for fear of learning something they didn't like. That was often the way on the Borders, where every surname lived cheek-by-jowl with their blood enemies.

He was sweating. "Did he live?"

"Ay," she said thoughtfully. "I thought I wis sure to lose him but I didna. And after I wis churched, I gave him away to a cousin that had just lost her wean, for by then it was clear that nae man of worship would take me to wife and I wouldna marry a clown nor a hunchback."

"Can...can you tell me the name?"

"Nay, Henry, I think not. Save that, of course, his surname is Elliot. He'll be getting old enough to ride soon. Maybe he's a big lad like you and he's killed his first man by now."

"Ye won't..."

"Ah won't. It's like a tale in a ballad, Henry, any Elliot ye meet that's young and around fourteen could be him."

Dodd's mouth was open but he couldn't think how to persuade her.

"Ye see, Henry, ye allus was one for the killing and the fire, but I think this is a fine revenge in itself. Ye'll never know. Even if ye come back when you're healed and batter me, ye'll never ken if I lie or no'."

And she stood with grace and finality and swept from the room, her well-spun and woven grey woollen kirtle whispering in the rushes.

With infinite effort and care, Dodd put the half-finished bowl of pottage on the little table and laid the horn spoon down beside it and then collapsed on the pillows, breathing hard.

Maybe she was lying. Maybe she had made the whole thing up just to vex him and make him doubt and weaken him. You could understand why, sure, but...no. He did not think she had made it up.

Jesu, it wasn't fair. Ten years of marriage with Janet and nothing, and one night under the stars with...her and...God!

He turned to take the weight off his side and lay there, wound-up tight as a spindle and unable to sleep as the pale light blazed to pink and purple through the southwestern arrowslits.

Suddenly decisive, he swung his legs over the side of the bed where they lay like withies. He planted them apart in his socks, braced his knees, and stood. He felt desperately dizzy, everything seemed the wrong way up. He grabbed the wall over the table and the painted cloth hanging with amateurish flowers and stars on it, clung to the painted cloth and shuffled his feet on the bundles of rushes until he could look through an arrowslit at the white moors painted with the pink and purple of the sun who had put his head down.

"Henry!" came a sharp voice behind him and he saw Janet pale and angry. "It's too soon to be on your feet…"

"I just wanted to look for Gilsland." How could he tell her that he had only wanted to see the sky, after day after day cooped up in a little room?

"That's too far away. We're in Scotland, remember." She came over and put her shoulder under Dodd's arm so he could use her like a crutch to get him back to bed. It was a struggle and Dodd was gasping and sweating again by the time he was lying down and Janet insisted on checking his bandages for blood, muttering to herself.

"Well I dinna think ye've made it bleed again," she said grudgingly, "which would be nae more than ye deserve."

He thought of telling her what he did deserve and why, and then thought she probably knew the story of what he had done to the church anyway. She had never asked him about it yet.

And of course he could never tell her anything about Mistress Elliot. He hadn't told anyone about it, not even Red Sandy who had been with him, a lad then and on the cart. Dodd had been a virgin too and triumphant and happy, but the news she was an Elliot, which he saw on the farmer's hiring list the next day, soured everything.

So he grabbed Janet's hand and wouldn't let go until she stopped her bustling and sat on the stool.

"What?" she asked.

He couldn't tell her, there was so much he couldn't tell her, it lay inside his chest like one of those pig's bladders you washed and blew up for boys to play football with barefoot, until it popped…his Dad had made one for him once. So he lay clutching her hand like a wean, somehow inexpressably glad that she was there with him, until he dozed off and his grip released. And still she sat there wondering how the devil he was going to kill Wee Colin Elliot with a sword when he could barely walk.

THURSDAY, 25TH JANUARY 1593, KESWICK

In the morning after a sprinkling of snow in the night, Sir Robert Carey could be seen in his fashionable olive green doublet, black velvet sleeves and canions, and a tall Edinburgh hat, walking up the high street with his clerk to Allerdyce's house, which had a warehouse in its basement and a line of patient packponies being unloaded. Allerdyce was standing to one side with his thumbs in his belt, watching the proceedings.

Carey changed course and went up to him and they both timed their bows to the second.

"Mr Allerdyce," said Carey, sounding to Tovey just a little more soft and Southern than normal, "I wonder if I could trouble you for the name of the maidservant who claimed to see a ghost rider and where she works."

"Ah," Allerdyce frowned. "She's a dairymaid, lives in town, works in the town dairy and takes the cows out as her first job o' the day. Betty's her name. Why? You don't believe her nonsense, do you?"

"Certainly not, but I do think she may have seen something she didn't understand."

"Ay well," said Allerdyce, grinning, "good luck tae ye."

Carey found the dairy down a sidestreet near the bridge and reeking of cowdung, where, to his surprise, the cows were lined up being milked. He talked to the woman in charge who was large and embittered by the flibbertigibbets she employed. He asked her why she was still milking and found that although there was very little milk now, the cows had been seen to by the local bull, what there was made good hard cheese. Then he asked her about Betty and the woman rolled her eyes. It seemed that Betty was the worst of them.

Eventually, a plump fair-haired girl was drying her hands and staring at him saucer-eyed.

"This is Mr Carey," sniffed the woman.

"Sir Robert..." Carey murmured, but she ignored him.

"Happen he's interested in hearing tall tales, eh, Betty?"

Betty curtseyed and clutched the damp rag.

"Don't keep him too long with all your nonsense. I've got three more cows needing milking and now we're one short." The woman stalked off to shout at another girl.

"First, Betty," said Carey cautiously, "can you show me where you live?"

She walked him there to the little cottage tucked into the lane behind Carleton's smithy, where she lived with her three brothers and two sisters. She pointed to her window which actually overlooked the street that led to the smithy.

"Isn't it noisy when the smithy is working?" Carey asked.

"Oh ay, it is," said Betty, "but I think it's a pretty noise, sort of like a song, and I share the top room with my little sister, and she likes it too, she said so. That's Sarah and she's a pretty little thing and such a sweet way with her, why only last week she asked me if chickens can give milk too and I did laugh..."

"So why did you wake in the middle of the night?"

Her broad pink brow furrowed. "I'm not sure, truth to tell, maybe little Sarah turned over and kicked, she's a terrible kicker in her sleep and I mind me she was worse when she was littler and..."

"So perhaps she kicked you?"

"Perhaps. It was too early for the birds to be up...there are pigeons that nest right next to my window and it's funny to watch them in summer when the cocks prance and dance..."

"Why did you go to the window?"

"I heard a funny noise, like *schssssh, schssssh schssssssh*. So I opened the shutters a little, they don't lock properly anymore because of our young Ben swinging on them last summer, ooh he did get in trouble wi' our mum…"

Now understanding Allerdyce's grin, Carey asked doggedly, "What did you see?"

"When, sir?"

"When you looked out of the window."

"Oh, I saw a ghost, sir! He had no face. Just a round thing with holes."

"Was he wearing a cloak?"

"Yes, sir, it looked like the snow…"

"So it was white?"

"White sir, white as the milk and heavy-looking because he was a ghost and he was walking funny, sort of *scchhssss schssss* and the horse was walking funny too."

The rider seen by Skinabake's men had had a white cloak as well. "Was the horse white too?"

"No, sir, brown."

"Can you show me how the ghost was walking funny?"

Betty took a couple of sliding large steps. "And his feet were huge, sir, he was a monster, a ghost, something sent from the Devil, for sure, and I was frightened and I shut the shutters and blocked them with a broom handle and ran back to bed and hid under the bedclothes so the ghost wouldn't get me."

"Before you went back to bed, do you remember which way the ghost was going?"

"Yes, sir, he was going down to the lake, to Derwent Water, maybe he was a poor soul drownded in the lake…"

"What colour was his face?"

"I told you sir, he didna have no face, it were all round and smooth and yellow…"

"Yellow?"

"It looked yellow his face, though there weren't no face there."

Carey nodded. "Is there anything else about this ghost that you can tell me, Betty, anything no matter how foolish?"

"He had dark hands. Black they were, like night."

"Gloves?"

Betty was a little annoyed. "Maybe," she admitted.

"Well, Betty, thank you very much. If anything else should come to mind, would you tell me? Or my secretary?" Carey gestured at Tovey who flushed to his ears at this promotion.

Betsy curtseyed again. "Ah'm no' silly," she said all in a rush. "I looked for hoofprints when I went out to work in the morning, which was only a couple of hours later I think, and the snow was flat and scuffled but no hoofprints where I saw the ghost rider and his horse, no hoofprints at all and I thought, well, it must be a ghost, I mean, what else could it be…?"

Carey nodded and gave her a farthing as well as one of his charming smiles which made her blush. She curtsied once more and hurried back to her cow.

Carey and Tovey went back to the Oak for more of the Deutscher beer. "Can I see your notes?" said Carey and found Tovey's notebook full of a chaos of Greek and Roman letters. "What's this?"

"It's a method that makes writing quicker and also harder to read," said Tovey. "I invented it myself."

"Ah, I think Mr Phelippes has invented something similar. That man is a genius with codes and he has his own alphabet."

"I'd like to meet him, sir. Maybe I could learn to make codes."

"I'm sure you could, Mr Tovey. I'll see if I can arrange it. In the meantime could you read me your notes?"

Tovey did so and Carey tapped his teeth and gazed into the distance or at least at the parlour wall which had a painted cloth on it.

"To me it's obvious," he said to Tovey, "but how am I going to tell Allerdyce that his good friend and alderman John Carleton, knowingly or unknowingly, helped Hepburn set up an elaborate plot to kill the King of Scots? Hepburn came here to await the outcome of the plot and incidentally killed Carleton so he couldn't inform against him."

"You think Betty's ghost rider was Hepburn?"

"Yes, of course, wearing some kind of mask and a white cloak from the masquing wardrobe, wearing pads on his own and his horse's feet. That's obvious."

"That might not have been him."

"True, it might not. Can you think of a plausible tale to explain why a citizen of Keswick on his perfectly lawful occasions, might have chosen to come into Keswick at around three or four in the morning, in the snow, wearing a mask and a white cloak, with his horse's hooves muffled?"

"Maybe something to do with Wattie Graham, sir?"

Carey paused. "Very true," he said. "Thank you, Mr Tovey, I hadn't thought of that."

Tovey flushed again.

"Even more clearly, I can't, without evidence, make an accusation to Allerdyce against a man who allegedly isn't here and another man who was his friend and is dead. What do you think the Mayor will say?"

"He won't believe you."

"More importantly, supposing he knows Hepburn is here and is hiding him and tells him that I'm in town and can link him to Mr Carleton's murder?"

"He might try to kill you, sir. Or he'll run, maybe to Workington."

"Which is?"

"It's the local port, in the west. That's where the drovers go with their packponies and some of the metal."

"Ah." Carey had his chin on his chest. "Well, in the unlikely event that he is here, I think he'll try and stay here. I think he has plans in Keswick, although I'm not clear what. And I don't think he's the kind of man to run. This is his home ground. We met his mother and his brothers earlier."

"Then he'll try and kill you, sir," said Tovey. "If he s...succeeds, then the man who can link the whole plot together is dead and he'll be free and clear."

"He won't be, because I have relatives too, but he might well think so. And King James has a very good memory. But yes, largely you're right." Carey sighed. "It seems that once again I'm painting a large round white target on my own back."

"We could go back to Carlisle."

"You've forgotten that Mr Secretary Cecil has taken an interest in the matter."

"Oh."

Carey sighed again and then brightened up. "Never mind," he smiled. "Let's poke the bushes anyway and see what sticks its head out."

It was a carefully edited story that Carey told with Tovey trotting along behind. They walked down to the lake edge where the boatman and two beefy looking Deutschers were unloading full beer barrels from the boat and loading empty ones. Mr Allerdyce was shocked to the core at the news that there had been a dangerous attempt on the King which Carey was not at liberty to disclose, but which involved alchemical matters and engineering. The man they were looking for was named Jonathan Hepburn, but he himself had told Carey that his name was Hochstetter.

Allerdyce stopped on the path, his eyes narrowed until he was squinting.

"So that's why you're here," he said. "I was telling Frau Radagunda that I didn't think you were really here to inspect the mines. I thought you were after Mr Gr...well, anyway."

"I still plan to inspect them and make a report," said Carey blandly, "but I am more interested in Jonathan Hepburn, or Hochstetter. Of course he may have been lying to me about his real name."

"Is he a gentleman?"

"Almost. He's a very skilled engineer, which is a profession he can take anywhere, and an alchemist as well. For instance, part of his plot involved large quantities of vitriol, which only alchemists know how to make…"

"And miners," muttered Allerdyce.

"So is there a man called Jonathan Hochstetter here, an engineer, curly light brown hair and beard, well-looking, soft-spoken, has an eye for women?"

Allerdyce took breath to speak, paused and then said, "Joachim Hochstetter, that's him."

"Do you know the man?"

"Ay, ay, Ah do. Clever. Good engineer, he cut his teeth on the mining machines and made several of them better when he were nobbut a lad. Mr Emanuel and Mr David's brother, he's a son of Frau Radagunda."

"Ah." Very gently and casually, Carey turned away from the lakeside where the men were working on the barrels and headed back to town.

Mr Allerdyce was shaking his head. "He's allus been a terrible worry tae his mother. And not very respectful to her either."

"Where is he? I'd like to meet him."

"He left home a long time ago, went to the Low Countries and Spain, I think. Last I heard of him he was working for one of the courtiers at the King's Court as his builder."

"Yes, that sounds like Hepburn. Mr Allerdyce, can I ask you to keep this matter of Hochstetter quiet for the moment?"

Allerdyce paused, shook his head and said, "He's not here."

"No?"

"I've certainly not seen him for years, ay, and not missed him either."

"Are you sure?"

"Ay, Sir Robert, although us Keswickers don't mix much with the Deutschers."

"Hm."

"If he were here, would ye arrest him?"

"How can I," said Carey, "seeing King James' writ doesn't run in this country? Mr Secretary Cecil has warranted me to report on the state of the mines, not Hepburn or Hochstetter's soul."

"Have ye any proof Hepburn did the attack?"

"It's good enough to try him since he was the Artificer of the props and scenery for the Masque and he disappeared from Court without permission on the night it happened. And there's evidence that he did it at the behest of the King of Spain and some Catholic noblemen of Scotland as well."

Allerdyce was silent and all around his head Carey could almost see the ghostly shapes of the things he wasn't telling. He sucked his teeth and made clicking noises with his tongue, as if talking to a horse.

"That's a bad business. It's all a bad business."

"If Joachim Hochstetter were here, where might he be?"

Allerdyce sighed. "The island," he said. "There's ten or eleven good houses on it along of the brewery and the bakehouse and the mill. Only the Deutschers go there. If Joachim is here, that's where he is."

"I just want to talk to him," said Carey reassuringly. "Quite possibly Joachim Hochstetter isn't really the man we're looking for. Even if he is, I can't arrest him, since he's done no crime in England that I know of. Unless..."

"Unless he killed Big John..." breathed Allerdyce.

"Why should he?" asked Carey. "He's a killer, but he usually kills for a reason." There was a very good reason why, but Carey wasn't certain enough yet to break the matter with Allerdyce.

Allerdyce shrugged uncomfortably.

"Is Joachim Hochstetter also a killer?

Allerdyce looked very unhappy but he didn't answer. Finally he said, "I didna like Joachim, never got on with him, even if I saw him grow up along of his brothers and sisters, even if he wis allus his mother's favourite. I wis glad tae see the back of him and his sister."

Poppy Burn, Carey thought instantly, what happened there, I wonder? "And anyway," he put in, "he isn't here."

"No," said Allerdyce with a guilty look on his broad friendly face. "No, he isn't. Well well, what d'ye want to do now?" he added with forced good humour.

Carey felt a thrill of excitement, just as he would at the first sight of fresh deer fewmets when hunting.

"I'm planning to see the smelting end of the operation and then if the weather holds, travel out to take a look at Goldscope mine tomorrow," he said. "And of course I want an excuse to visit the island."

"Ay," said Allerdyce, "I'll see whit I can do."

"You don't find it completely unbelievable that Joachim Hochstetter could be an assassin?"

"No, I don't and it's no' just because he's a Deutscher. I've got no quarrel with the Deutschers, me. There may have been some trouble when they first came but that was all settled a long time ago and most of it was down to the Earl of Northumberland anyway, dog in the manger that he was. He didna ken how to mine his lands nor know anybody that could, but he didn't want anybody else doing it either. I was glad when he met the executioner. They're all good citizens and they pay their taxes on the copper and the Queen gets her share of the gold they refine. It's true that something has been the ruination of the woods hereabouts and the land's gone sour and there's some superstitious folk that blame them for the kobolds, but…nay, I've got nothing against the Deutschers."

"But?"

Allerdyce's face tightened. "Mebbe I'll tell ye later."

"I wish you would tell me now, Mr Allerdyce."

"Why?"

"Because you may be mysteriously dead later."

Allerdyce shrugged. "Well, Frau Radagunda is the one

that'll have to give ye her permission and I suggest ye dinnna share your thoughts about Joachim, for he's the apple of her eye, so he is."

Carey sighed. "Thanks for the advice, Mr Allerdyce, I appreciate it."

He stood up, bowed to the Mayor and went out into the street. It was very cold and his ears tingled with the frost, and where there were cobbles, there was a sheen of ice on them and they were very slippery. Luckily there was plenty of frozen mud where his hobnails could get a better purchase. Tovey came trotting after him, looking through his sheafs of paper.

That was when Red Sandy and Bangtail came running up to him, very excited at something but having difficulty explaining what it was because they were so drunk. Carey concluded that they had spent the entire night drinking with the drovers and then gone on drinking in the morning on the grounds of hair of the dog or some other famous principle.

"Ay," said Bangtail, beaming fatuously. "Ah niver heard the like…Would ye credit it, Red Sandy?"

"Ah would no'." Red Sandy pronounced with one eye shut.

"Why's he here, eh? Answer me that?"

"Ah can no'." Red Sandy said, trying the other eye.

"Ay, and whit's he doing here, for God's sake?"

"Ah dinna ken," said Red Sandy sadly, sitting on the edge of the market water trough, tipping forward and puking onto the ground. Two skinny town dogs immediately stood up and took an interest. Then Red Sandy turned, took off his helmet and dunked his head in the trough but banged his head on the ice. He came up rubbing his head and cursing, found a rock, broke the ice, and then dunked his head properly and came up blowing. "Ay," he said, putting his helmet back on, "tha's better."

"Are ye aright?" asked Bangtail, holding onto his shoulder.

"Ay, Ah think the ale wis poisoned…"

"Nay, it were the fried sippets…"

"Happen. It could be," said Red Sandy, and both he and Bangtail nodded wisely.

Carey was standing with his hands on his hips, looking severe and clearly having a lot of work not to laugh.

"Tell me, goodmen," he said delicately, "did the drovers give you anything…unusual to drink?"

"S'funny ye should say that, sir," said Bangtail, wagging a finger. "They gave us some stuff that tasted very strong, though they all swore it wisnae."

"Ah, and what was the stuff's name?"

"Wishy?" said Bangtail looking at the sky for inspiration.

"Wishy kee?" wondered Red Sandy.

"Whishke bee?" asked Carey.

"Ay," said Red Sandy, hawking and spitting. "Said it wisnae stronger nor good beer and made from respectable barley in Scotland."

Carey sighed and nodded. "And who was it you saw?"

"Ay, it were a surprise to the baith of us," hiccupped Bangtail. "I never thought to set eyes on the like."

"Never," agreed Red Sandy. "Sitting in the alehouse over there wi' all his cousins and nephews and…"

"Who did you see?" said Carey at not quite a bellow.

Bangtail held his forehead and blinked at Carey reproachfully. "Och, sir, not sae loud. Ye said yerself. Wattie Graham's here in Keswick."

"What? Here now?"

"Ay," said Red Sandy, wiping his mouth with the sleeve of his jack. "Wattie Graham of Netherby. Here."

"Do you know why?"

"The drovers said he's often here for the special packtrain. And to check naebody's logging his woods in Borrowdale."

"Ay." Bangtail swallowed and looked green suddenly. A moment later he was puking by the water trough. "Ye ken, Red Sandy," he gasped, still bent over, "Ah think they drovers wis lying when they said the wishy wisnae strong."

"Ay, that could be it."

"Or the sippets."

"Nay, now I think on it, Leamus had some."

Carey sighed again and started unlacing his black velvet sleeves at the shoulder points, pulling them off one by one and giving them to Tovey who stood there looking puzzled. He handed over his tall hat. Then he rolled his shirtsleeves up to his shoulders as well.

Then he grabbed Bangtail and Red Sandy by the greasy scruffs of their necks and ducked both their heads in the trough while Tovey stood well back and stared in wonder. The sound of the ice crunching against the stone was alarming and some of the burgers of Keswick were watching and grinning.

Carey waited until the struggles became violent, let them up and shoved them away so they tripped over each other. "I want you sober right now and I haven't the time to wait for it to happen naturally."

"Ye told us to go drinking with the drovers..." protested Red Sandy, saw the nasty glint in Carey's eye and added a hasty "sir."

"I said drink with them, I didn't say, get stinking and uselessly drunk with them. I want to catch Wattie before he leaves and I need men at my back, which has to be you two ugly louts since Carlisle's sixty miles away. And where the devil is Leamus...?"

"Here, sorr," said the Irishman who had been leaning against a doorway on the other side of the street.

"Are you drunk too?"

"No, sorr," said Leamus. "I have drink taken, ye might say, but we have the whishke bee in Ireland too, and I know the stuff of old."

"Well, why didn't you warn Bangtail and...?"

"I tried, sorr, but they didn't listen."

"Arrgh," growled Carey, drying his arms with a kerchief from his pocket, unrolling his shirtsleeves, and beckoning Tovey to put the doublet sleeves on again, which took some time. The town dogs approached Red Sandy and Bangtail's leavings cautiously and then ecstatically started gulping up the puke. Leamus strolled past them saying something hospitable-sounding in Irish.

Carey clamped his tall hat on his head and said, "Where's Wattie hiding, then?"

"He's still in that alehouse, sign of the Thistle," said Leamus, pointing to a cottage with red lattices some way up an alley. "He seemed a little upset."

"Ay," said Bangtail, as he finished spitting frozen horse trough water. "He wis fair mithered to find ye in the toon and no mistake..."

"Did you tell him..?"

"Nay, sir," protested Red Sandy, "we wouldna do that, but he knew me, o' course and he asked the alewife wis there a long Court pervert wi' pretty clothes in town and o' course the alewife said, ay, happen there is and he said, wi' dark red hair and a stupid Southern way o' talking and the alewife said, ay, and Wattie said, 'och God, what's that lang streak o' piss of a Deputy Warden doing here, for Christ's sake? That's all I need...'"

"And then we left because we hadna money left and naebody was buying any more," finished Bangtail.

"So he might still be here. All right." Carey lifted and dropped his sword and poignard in the sheaths. Leamus did the same. Bangtail finished banging water out of his ears and Red Sandy stood fairly straight and said, "This way, sir."

They walked in diamond formation with Carey ahead, Bangtail at the rear, and Red Sandy and Leamus at Carey's shoulders. Tovey trotted along, some way behind. At the alley they found five young ruffians with the long jaws and grey eyes of the Grahams, standing by the door doing their best to look hard—at which they were quite successful because they were hard. The Graham-pattern jacks and morions helped.

Carey ignored them and headed for the door.

"Where are ye going?"

"Into the alehouse," said Carey mildly, "to greet your master, Wattie Graham."

"And ye are?" said the other young thug with an insulting sneer.

"Ay, he's the Deputy Warden," said Red Sandy, "and dinna ye forget it."

The lad spat on the ground.

"We're no' in the Marches here," he said.

"Very true," said Carey cheerfully. "You're a long way from where you're squatting the Storey family lands too. Please tell Mr Walter Graham that Sir Robert Carey, seventh son of the Lord Chamberlain, Baron Hunsdon, nephew of the Queen, courtier, ex-MP and quondam captain of the Earl of Essex's troops in France, would esteem it a singular expression of friendship and good fellowship if he could speak with the said Mr Graham."

The lad banged through the door and they heard him say, "The Deputy Warden's here, Uncle Wattie."

There was a murmuring inside and the lad came back and held the door open, looking sulky. Carey went through smiling, followed by Red Sandy and Leamus. He gestured for Tovey to come in as well and nodded at Red Sandy to stand by the door.

Inside the small dark alehouse, Wattie Graham was sitting resplendent in bright tawny brocade, a remarkably fashionable hat on his balding head and a clay pipe in his mouth which was making him cough. The chair was the only one with arms and the alewife was standing behind him, looking nervous.

Carey pulled up a barrel table and perched on that, while Tovey did his best not to shake at the assessing stares from Wattie's Graham relatives, and Leamus leaned against the wall, watching with interest.

Wattie glared at Carey.

"Whit are ye doing here?" he demanded.

"Tut, Wattie, I might ask you the same question."

"Ah'm visiting mah woods in Borrowdale, the which I inherited fra me dad."

Carey's eyebrows went up. "Did you really?"

"Ay, Ah did."

"How did that come about?"

"He did a favour for Lady Radclyffe in the sixties. Ye?"

"I'm here on warrant from Mr Secretary Cecil to look at the mines and smelting houses and so on," drawled Carey, tipping his hat back. "Would you like to read the warrant, it has an English translation?" he added, knowing full well that Wattie couldn't read.

"Whit?"

"I really can't imagine why, since I know less of mining and smelting than a newborn babe. But there you are. I expect the Queen got a notion in her head, or some such."

Interestingly, Wattie Graham looked suddenly furtive when Carey said that, which was interesting because he had made up the detail about the Queen on the spur of the moment. Why was Wattie, of all people, worried about the Queen?

"So how's Netherby?" Carey asked solicitously, poking at one of Wattie's many sore spots connected with him. "Replaced the woodwork yet?"

"Ay," said Wattie, biting the stem of the pipe and breaking it and spilling hot tobacco all over his velvet trunkhose. He half stood and batted the coals away, leaving a couple of small holes.

"And your adventure this Christmas. With the cows. Were any of them found to be yours in the end?"

Wattie scowled even more mightily but didn't answer because, of course, none of the Graham kine were unstolen.

"It's nice you're so respectable now, Wattie...no, I'm sorry, Mr Graham," said Carey. "As a gentleman, perhaps I could call on your help with my report to Mr Secretary on the state of the mines."

"Ah'm busy."

"Of course you are, of course you are," sang Carey, standing up, sweeping off his hat and making a flamboyant but shallow bow to all the Grahams. "Good day to all!"

He walked out with Red Sandy ahead, Tovey beside him, and Leamus last, and found Bangtail engaged in a staring match with all the Grahams, who were in fact distant cousins of his. Carey gathered him up and swaggered across the cobblestones to the Oak where yet another string of packponies was lined up, nose to tail, munching at nosebags.

There he found the youngest Hochstetter brother, David, waiting for him.

"My mother and uncle sent me to guide you to Goldscope mine," he said, his slightly spotty adam's apple bouncing nervously. "You can meet the mine captain there. They think it will snow tomorrow or the next day so it is best to go now."

"Certainly," said Carey with enthusiasm. "I have never seen a working mine before and I hope you will tell me all about it, Mr Hochstetter." The lad flushed at being promoted from Mr David. "Give me a moment to change my doublet."

Twenty minutes later, back in his comfortable old arming doublet and jack with his morion on his head, Carey re-emerged from the inn looking as enthusiastically witless as you might expect a Court sprig to look.

As he explained to Hochstetter the younger, he didn't want to leave his vulnerable hungover men in the same town as Wattie Graham, so he took everyone, including Tovey. They made quite a party, though they didn't bother with remounts because the mine was only a couple of miles away. Hochstetter himself had a very nice black palfrey that was roughshod for the snow and ice. As they rode along, Carey wondered if a roughshod horse went better than an unshod horse in snow, and if they could have a race to see which was in fact the best system, and suddenly Hochstetter lost his shyness and started talking about making the race with two of each kind of shoeing to make sure it wasn't the peculiarity of the beasts that caused the winner and on second thoughts, they should unshoe the shod horses and shoe the unshod and run a second race for an even better measure…

"Yes," said Carey, "but it takes a while for a horse that's been shod to regrow his hooves."

"True. Perhaps then the second race should take place the following year…"

They passed close to Crossthwaite church and came to a made road that had cobblestones. They followed it and it led them out among the hills which were also bald and almost denuded of trees. They could see smoke from the mine furnaces lying in the valley they were heading for.

"So, Mr Hochstetter…" Carey said as they passed through a clutter of sheds and barns. Great gouts of white and yellow smoke also came up from the northeast of the town where the smelting houses were, the air smelled sour and abrasive, and they could hear a rhythmic banging and creaking from both places. "Can you tell me how the metals come to be so deeply buried in the rock and why do we find them next to hills and mountains? I have always wondered about that. Surely if they were intended for our benefit by Almighty God, they wouldn't be so hard to get at?"

"Ah…" began Hochstetter.

Tovey started to give them an explanation based on Agricola but found himself shhhed by Carey.

"Sorry, Mr Tovey," said Carey, "but I can hear your ideas whenever I like, whereas Mr David is of the famous mining family, Hochstetter of Augsburg, and I'd like to hear what he has to say." Tovey flushed and went silent because he and Mr David were close in age.

This unleashed a learned disquisition from young Mr David, the upshot of which as far as Carey could make it out among all the technical words in Deutsch, was that metals came from juices that flowed through the veins of the earth and hardened when they met the air at the surface.

"And are the metals separated or mixed together in these juices?" Carey asked respectfully.

"They are mixed," said Mr David, "always mixed in greater or lesser proportion."

"So is there iron in this mine?"

"Copper and gold and arsenic and lead, of course. And other metals in small quantities."

"Really? Fascinating! How do you know which metal is which if they're all mixed together?"

"It is a great art to assay them, but my uncle, Herr Schmelz-meister Mark Steinberger, can tell you more about it."

"So what is assaying?"

Off Hochstetter went about the colours and consistency of various ores and how you could tell them apart and how you needed to assay them frequently in a small furnace because the proportion of one metal to another in ore changed all the time. Carey listened carefully, asking more questions until they came down Newlands valley to the entrance of the mine. They heard it long before they arrived because there was a dull thunder as if a giant were hitting rocks with a hammer, constant creaking, and the sound of water.

Most of the wooden machinery was protected from the weather by wooden rooves, but water tumbled everywhere in channels. Some of the huge machines were still, some were working, and there were two patient blindfolded ponies walking round and round to drive some of it. Mr David waved at a long tall building where the worst noise came from, the giant crashing and crashing his boots on gravel.

"What in God's name is going on in there?" shouted Carey, riding a few frightened crow hops from his horse. Mr David's palfrey was stolid and unafraid, but Red Sandy and Leamus' hobbies started to buck and Leamus went off over his horse's shoulder and did a magnificent roll. He came to his feet, dusting off his buff coat and smiling with embarrassment. Red Sandy was still on his hobby's back and laughing at him. Bangtail's pony only twitched an ear.

"Sure and I'm no horseman," said Leamus, hopping back on his hobby.

"It's the stamping house," shouted Mr David. "We're using the meltwater from the hills. If it snows and freezes again we'll have to stop."

"Stamping house?"

"Yes, the....BANG...hammers...BANG...small pieces... BANG." Mr David's fairly thin voice was competely drowned.

"Can I see?"

"What?"

"SEE?"

Without waiting for an answer, Carey jumped down from his hobby and went towards a door. Mr David scrambled down from his palfrey and led him to another door. Tovey dismounted more cautiously and peered. Of course he knew in theory what would be there but was immensely curious. He hadn't expected the levels of noise for a start.

The stamping house was the tallest in the valley, twice as tall as the other sheds, built against the hill and vibrating with thunder. Inside, huge hammers made of treetrunks, some of them shod at the end with iron, banged up and down on the stones. The shed was built on an incline so there was a raked path for the rocks to roll along under the first stamper and then the second and so on. Boys were bringing baskets of rocks and throwing them under the top hammer and they broke and rolled down and were stamped by another massive hammer. The hammers were attached to a waterwheel by complicated cogwheels like the ones you would find in a flour mill and they rose and fell one after the other as if they were alive.

Two greybeards raked the rocks in and out as the hammers

came down and lifted. They had curious leather coats on, pointed at the back with pointed hoods which also covered the ears, which must have helped a bit with the noise. They were very skilled. Nobody lost a rake or a leg under the remorseless hammers.

The rocks and gravel were carried down a water channel which ended in a series of sieves. A tow-haired solid-looking boy collected the larger lumps out of the sieves and carried them back up the shed to the first stamper again. Nobody paid Carey any attention.

Mr David showed Carey out through a second door to another building, further up the valley, made of brick not wood, where large faggots of firewood were piled up against the walls as well as sackfulls of black earthcoals.

"This is the furnace house," he shouted, "where we give the ore its first roasting, which makes it easier to break up." This was where all the smoke came from. Yellow and acrid, it billowed out of the brick furnace chimneys and out of openings in the roof and was pummelled a little by the weak breeze. Most of it stayed where it was, making the air yellow and hard to breathe. Further on were long low sheds and another greybeard in his leather coat, his hood stiffly pointed above his grey head.

"This is Herr Steiger Schlegel," said Mr David. "He is one of the two mine captains."

"Herr Captain Schlegel, delighted to meet you," said Carey and shook the proffered hand. "I wonder if we can go in the mine?"

Schlegel said something in Deutsch to Mr David. "He says it wouldn't be safe for you, for you are not used to ladders and because of the frost, the ladders are very slippery."

Carey raised his eyebrows, to be met by bland looks from Schlegel and Mr David. So he smiled with pretended relief and asked, "Well, what's in this house?"

Mr David answered that eagerly. "It's the bellows house," he said. "We aren't working the mine at the moment because of the frost, so they aren't moving."

"Are they for the fires?"

"No, no, these are quite different. Here, come inside, you can see."

The lad seemed very relieved to get Carey into the bellows house. Inside there was a harness for the pony to go round and round and a rod that led down into the earth. Carey squinted down under the floor and found a row of bellows in a cellar.

"Good Lord," he said, standing up and dusting down his hose, "those bellows are huge. What are they for?"

"We must keep air blowing into the mine or otherwise the air becomes stuffy and bad and in the end men die of suffocation."

"Oh."

"The other house has bellows worked by paddles for men to use, and we're running those at the moment."

Nothing would do but they must go over to the other wooden shed and go inside where there was a continuous stamping and creaking as two men trod the boards that forced open a huge pair of bellows in front of them and then sighed shut, pushing better air into the mine.

"Very interesting," Carey declared, with some amusement as Tovey stared around him with an expression of delight on his face. "Looks like a lot of hard work, eh?"

"Yes," said Mr David seriously, "it is a lot of hard work. That was why we came from Augsburg: you need hard work and skill and machines to make a mine and the English have no skill at mining or knowledge of machines and…"

"Indeed," said Carey, coming out of the older bellows shed and finding a path that led up the side of the bare hill. He immediately started following it, trailed by Tovey and Mr David. Slightly short of breath when he got to the top of the hill, he looked around at the short grass and peered into the next valley which was equally bald. Some skinny sheep were wandering around, cropping the grass. "What happened to the woods?"

"They were all burnt for charcoal when we first came," said

Mr David, "before we found the earthcoal in Bolton about nine miles away and we're mining that. It's excellent and comparatively clean of brimstone too. But we still need charcoal and it's hard to find now the woods are gone. Mr Graham keeps promising to give us...well, sell us...some charcoal from his woods in Borrowdale, but he never does."

Carey came jumping down the rocks and smiled at Mr David. "Well, Mr Hochstetter, if I can't go into the Goldscope mine itself, I think I've seen what I can now, haven't I?"

Mr David was working hard not to look very relieved. "Do you want to go back?"

"Oh, I think we had better, it's getting dark now."

Carey and Tovey mounted up and they turned their horses around and started back behind the usual packtrain, heavy-laden with roasted and hammered ore. Behind them in the distance the mine bell sounded.

Carey kicked his horse suddenly and galloped ahead into the dusk when they came in sight of the faint and few lights of Keswick. The others caught up with him sitting at his ease by the fire in the Oak Inn's parlour, drinking mulled and spiced ale.

Mr David had gone on down to the lake by the curving path running through a large stand of sick trees full of arguing crows settling down for the night. The innkeeper came and announced that the ordinary was salt beef stew with neeps again and there was still some left. They all ordered some.

"Well, Mr Tovey," said Carey as they tucked into the thick salty stew, "I'm sorry I had to cut you off but I wanted to win young Mr David to me. What did you make of the mine workings?"

Tovey smiled shyly. "I am no expert..."

"You're the nearest I've got. Also I don't want the Deutschers realising that you know more than I do—I want them to think us both Court fools they can get rid of quickly and easily without us learning anything, especially whatever it is they are hiding."

"Oh. I see, sir. Sorry, sir, I should have realised. Well, the mines seemed very interesting and it accords with Agricola's account. You roast and stamp the ore near the mine if you can, because that makes it easier to pack on the ponies if it's in small pieces."

"Infernally noisy, though!"

"I suppose it is. I hadn't thought of that."

"And what do you think to the idea that the earth juices make the metals?"

"It is also Agricola's theory, very orthodox."

"They haven't mentioned Agricola's great tome either, not once. You would think they would when faced with such an ignoramus on mining as I am."

"Sir?"

"They could say to me, you should read about it in Agricola and then I might do that and leave them alone. So why are they silent about a book full of diagrams about mining? At least Herr Steinberger must have read it."

"I don't know sir," said Tovey unhappily. "I don't..."

Carey leaned over and patted his shoulder. "Thank you, Mr Tovey."

"Why?"

"I much prefer an honest statement of ignorance to the more usual piles of speculation and nonsense."

Tovey went red and buried his nose in his beer.

"They are hiding something. I know nothing of mining or smelting, but I know that. Possibly they are hiding more than one thing. What was that Allerdyce was saying, that Leonard Stoltz was an Anabaptist preacher? Sounds funny to me and they're from the right part of Germany, so they might well be Anabaptists."

"What are Anabaptists?"

"Terrible heretics that caused the religious wars in Allemayne in the time of Good King Henry."

"Oh."

"According to the Catholic church at least, which makes me

think more kindly of them. Though good English churchmen seem to be hot against them as well, for reasons I can't quite fathom."

"Why do you think they are hiding something, sir?"

"The Goldscope mine is described as being worked out and yet here they are still working it and spending good money on mining coals at Bolton to roast the ore. The returns are steady but miserable, according to their accounts. Yet here the Deutschers still are, able to afford brocades and furs, when they could go home. Depend upon it, Mr Tovey, they are hiding something."

Carey blinked at the fire, which had earthcoals in it, and rubbed his fingers. "I really want to get on that island," he murmured. "What have they got there?"

FRIDAY, 26TH JANUARY 1593, KESWICK

The next morning when they woke there was snow falling silently in soft permanent-looking lumps and the huge bald hills were hidden by the low clouds.

Carey saw no reason to stop what he was doing simply because it was snowing and persuaded the innkeeper's boy to show him the way to the smelthouses via a court where the ponies were lined up ready to go out to Newlands again, through a back lane and onto the Penrith Road. He left Red Sandy and Bangtail to exercise the horses and took just Tovey and Leamus.

The smelthouses were behind a stout fence with two gates in it large enough to let a pony through. The houses themselves were a clutter of ugly raw wood and raw brick buildings, separated by muddy yards that were nonetheless swept clean, and the thick metallic-smelling smoke was colouring the snow yellow and black as it fell.

The foreman there was another greybeard in a leather tunic with a pointy hood. His younger men were dressed in jerkins and hose and, from the way they talked in Deutsch and English mixed, they were the second generation.

Hans Altschmer, the foreman, was extremely offended at the sudden appearance of Carey, Tovey, and Leamus—Carey in a fur-trimmed cloak, Tovey shivering in his scholar's gown, and Leamus comfortable in his buffcoat with a scarf wrapped round his stringy neck to keep the cold snow out. He insisted that before anybody could venture into the smelting houses, he must first ask Herr Schmelzmeister Steinberger, and as Herr Schmelzmeister lived on the island, this would take all morning.

To Tovey's surprise, Carey smiled at the indignant Deutscher and said it was fascinating just to watch what was happening and stood around in the main yard where there were unlit furnaces, getting in the way and asking fatuous questions. He watched yet another packtrain arrive laden with earthcoals and thought it was unloaded with an efficiency and lack of fuss that argued a lot of practice. The snow fell gently the whole time and boys swept it up, red-nosed and red-fingered and shouting at each other in the incomprehensible coughs and splutters of Deutsch. From the laughter, he guessed they were saying rude things about him. He wandered among the ponies, slapping them and being nosed inquisitively and found that there were very few Graham brands, but plenty of Ridley, Storey, and Liddle brands, which meant the ponies had been reived once upon a time.

"Hm, interesting," he said to himself, scribbling with a piece of blacklead in his notebook. "Let's see. The packponies come from Bolton with earthcoals, they unload some here, they go up to Goldscope with coal and supplies, and come back down again with ore which they unload here. And then where do they go? Do they go to Bolton with supplies? Do they go unladen?"

"Why does it matter?" asked Tovey.

"Nobody ever sends a packpony train anywhere unladen if they can. They're ponies, they eat their heads off whether they're working or not. How do they get to Bolton?"

"Should we go and look? Or ask a drover?"

"Certainly we should go and look as soon as the snow stops."

Both of them looked up at the clouds and the way the dirty snow was disappearing under something whiter and the flakes kept coming in little flurries, as if someone in the sky was flinging them out of a sack.

Carey closed his notebook with an impatient snap. "I'm bored," he announced. "I suppose there's no hunting around here?"

Tovey shook his head. "I was asking the innkeeper if he knew of any useful herbs around here and he laughed at me and said there had been plenty when he was a lad and hunting too, but now there were no trees and no herbs, save grass and some weeds in the summer, and even the lake had hardly any fish in it, though the water was so clear and it used to be stuffed with fish."

"Did he say why?"

"He didn't know, only said it was the kobolds from the mines roaming around after dark and turning everything they touched to ruination."

"Ah. Kobolds again."

"They cause roof falls and poisonous airs too, and the water kobolds even poison the hill streams so there are no fish."

"Has anyone ever caught a kobold?"

Tovey shook his head.

At that point Herr Schmelzmeister Mark Steinberger arrived with young Mr David, his oblong angular face conveying grim acceptance.

"Ah, Herr Schmelzmeister," carolled Carey, "how kind of you to make time for me in your busy day. Will you be acting as translator, Mr Hochstetter?"

"I speak gut English," said Steinberger, with a tight smile.

"Splendid, splendid!" said Carey, "That's considerably more than I could manage with High Dutch, alas. Now then, perhaps you could explain the smelting process to me?"

Steinberger smiled a little. "It vood take at least a year to teach you efen the basic principles, Herr Carey."

"Herr *Ritter* Carey," smiled Carey. "I'm sure it would take at least that long if not longer. Could you just tell me the main outlines?" Once again Tovey had his mouth open to answer and Carey stared fixedly at him. Damn it, why did clever, bookish young men always have to show off?

Tovey caught the glare and shut his mouth, his spots going a nasty colour. Leamus was just staring into space, holding the horses, with no expression on his face, and Carey wondered if he knew how to play primero.

They spent about an hour going through the smelthouses, except for one section which was apparently closed for repairs although smoke was rising from a chimney in the centre. The whole place was full of smoke and hot despite the snow, and the rooves had melting water running off them into neat gutters and so into tanks.

It seemed that smelting was largely a matter of first roasting and pounding ore into gravel which they did near the mine. Then you put the gravel in a very hot fire until the metals melted out of it, to make a cake. Then you cooled the metal cake in water, chiselled the good metal from bad, and melted it again until you got something fairly pure.

Carey was full of happy interest and excitement. "So, most of the ore here produces copper once you have baked the sulphur out of it. What happens to the sulphur?"

"It becomes smoke which we collect and lead to a tank of water to make vitriol after air has passed through it."

"Wonderful! It sounds quite alchemical."

Steinberger tried not to sneer. "Nobody really understands why the things we do work, but one thing is certain and that is that alchemists do not know. Their theory of the Elements is childishly simple and does not work for metals. Those alchemists that are not outright frauds are fools and children, entranced by their texts."

Tovey was gasping at this. "But the theory of the Elements

is one of the most well-attested foundations of philosophy and medicine…"

"Maybe. It is nott at all well-attested and for sure it does not work for ores."

"Fascinating!" interrupted Carey, standing on Tovey's foot. "So you start with, for instance, that green kind of copper ore. You crush it, roast it, crush it again, roast it again. If you catch the smoke and pass it through water in an alembic, you eventually get vitriol which burns with invisible flames."

"Ach, you have seen it."

"Yes," said Carey, "it was impressive. Is there a use for it in mining?"

"Yes," said Steinberger. "It is said it can be used for improving gold ores."

"Ah, gold," said Carey, with greed glowing in his eyes. "How do you get the gold out of the rock? For Her Majesty, of course?"

"If the ore is rich enough you can find lumps of it. However usually the ore is not rich. Usually we find an uncium of gold to a truckle of ore. This much ore…" With his hands Steinberger sketched out in the air a box as wide as his arms that came to his chest. "…to this much gold." He held his thumb and forefinger an inch apart. "Or vorse."

Carey's face was comically disappointed. "Oh," he said.

"For gold you must put the treated stein to a different kind of furnace and heat it much hotter and then you pour off your first cakes."

"But you don't eat it," said Carey, laughing a lot at his wit.

"*Nein*," said Steinberger with another tight smile.

"And there's your copper?"

"No, of course not," said Steinberger patiently. "It's a mixture of copper, perhaps lead, perhaps even gold."

"Aha," said Carey, nodding his head. "The Queen's share?"
"Off course."

Tovey appeared to be about to say something else and Carey

stood on his other foot.

"Perhaps arsenic, perhaps litharge, you never know. You must test and try a sample and add fluxes such as glass or sand, melt again. Herr Gans, the Jew that came here ten years ago, greatly improved our operations by showing us the use of fluxes and thereby cut the amount of roasting and melting and so the cost of charcoal. A very skilled and learned man."

"I see," said Carey, obviously not seeing. "So how long before we have copper, or should I say bronze, for guns?"

"No, bronze is made of copper with a little tin," said Steinberger, not quite rolling his eyes at this. "As it happens we have great stores of copper cooking pots…"

Nothing would do but Carey must see the piles of cooking pots, some covered with verdigris, kept in a storeroom. Carey exclaimed over them and spent time thinking of a use for the copper.

"Surely these are valuable?" he burbled.

"It is hard to sell them," Steinberger admitted. "I thought noble kitchens and gentlemen would be glad to purchase them but they must be cleaned and polished after each use and the lazy kitchen boys would rather use an earthenware pan a couple of times and then throw it away than…Don't go in there!"

Carey had wandered through the piles of copper pans and opened a door which led through to another smelting house that had three odd-looking furnaces with round domed lids attached to chains. The heat was stunning and Tovey wondered if they ran the furnaces in summer too.

Steinberger slammed the door and smiled in a strained way. "Yes," he said, "that is simply a way of…er…making the copper a good red colour."

"Of course," said Carey, "I realised that."

They were guided through another brick building at a fierce heat where cakes of shiny metal were being poured from a furnace and then dunked hissing into tanks of water. Carey bent to touch one and had his outstretched hand knocked aside by young Mr David.

"Careful, sir, they are very hot, even after the water."

"Are they?" Carey laughed, rather a whinnying laugh which no one there could recognise as a deadly accurate imitation of the Earl of Southampton's laugh. "Bless me, thank you, Mr Hochstetter. And is this where you get the gold out?"

Steinberger and Mr David exchanged glances.

"Well…" began Mr David.

"In a manner off speaking," said Steinberger, "although there is only a tiny amount of gold in this ore, perhaps as I said, one or two uncia per truckle.

Mr David waved helpfully at a large truckle being mended in a corner of the yard.

Carey's face became comically downcast. "Is that all? Isn't there anything else of value in the ore? Lead, silver, arsenic?"

"Sometimes yes, ve haff lead and arsenic, sometimes efen silver."

"Ah yes, silver."

"But in this ore from Gottesgaab…I mean Goldscope, not fery much," said Steinberger and Tovey saw a bead of sweat on his forehead, probably because even with the door wide open, the heat and smoke in the smelting house was savage. "In Augsburg, yes, there are such ores. Efery ore is different."

"Oh. Well, gentlemen, I own I am set down by that. I thought there might be a lot more gold than that."

"It iss all in the accounts we gif the shareholders," said Steinberger in a stuffy voice. "The gold iss alvays a very small amount."

"Well, yes, but…" started Tovey and stopped with a squawk.

"I see," said Carey, looking thoughtful with a masterful expression of thwarted greed underneath. "And are there perhaps diamonds and rubies and pearls?"

"Not at this mine," said Mr David, "although they say there are rubies near Pot—" and suddenly Mr David squawked and went silent. Tovey rubbed his toe, Mr David rubbed his shin.

Leamus made a little noise like a grunt, turned aside politely and blew his nose with great vigor into the snow at the side of the yard.

"Vell," said Steinberger smiling, "perhaps ve can refresh ourselves after the heat of the smelting houses."

"Splendid idea," said Carey, "but it's a long walk back to town."

Steinberger looked smug. "Follow me, *meine Herren*."

"But…" Tovey was spluttering to Carey, "what about…?"

"Shut up," said Carey very quietly, "or I'll make you my official valet."

Tovey gobbled and swallowed, going quite purple.

"Ah, yes, your Deutsch beer," Carey said loudly and enthusiastically, "wonderful stuff, Herr Schmelzmeister, puts most of ours to shame, I'm afraid, how do you make it so fine?"

Steinberger smiled patronisingly. "I think, Herr Ritter, that the secret is in the copper vessels that ve use which can be made much more cleaner than wooden bucks."

"And that helps?"

"So I am told."

It was only a short way to a small alehouse tucked under the high cliffs on one side of the river which was lower than before and looking to freeze again. Two red-faced men were carefully keeping the sluice from the river free of ice. The alehouse had the statutory red lattices, but was empty and there was a plump woman there, with a pink face under her linen cap, and her kirtle a vivid blue. She brought all of them quart tankards of a dark brew which Carey sipped cautiously and then grinned and raised his tankard to Herr Steinberger.

Carey asked questions of Steinberger about the accounts and the apprentices, probing for something that would prise him open. As the day darkened, the mine bell rang in the distance and a closer bell answered and shortly afterwards came a rush of greybeards and young men from the smelthouses, who all had a fierce thirst and generally downed their first quart tankard in one and held it out for more beer. Some greybeards and young men went off to their families, and the rest demanded the ordinary which the woman, whose name was apparently Frau Magda, went bustling around to bring them. It was bread, spiced sausages, and some kind of salt-pickled cabbage which smelled very sour. Carey had found a large tub of it in the yard when he came back from the jakes, sneaked a bit from under the ice and found it remarkably edible. The woman warmed it up on the stove and he ordered the same ordinary for all of them.

Red Sandy and Bangtail were highly suspicious and refused to try the cabbage while Tovey tried some at least and Leamus plowed through his whole plateful and then finished Red Sandy's and Bangtail's. Tovey ate his way absent-mindedly through his cabbage as well, scowling as if he was trying to remember something.

Late in the evening, Carey was singing an old English round with a greybeard and two youngsters singing what was evidently the same song in Deutsch and making a truly lovely sound. Everyone else stopped and listened to them and then clapped like customers in a barber shop. Carey started singing another old song and the greybeard sang extempore and Tovey put his head on his arms and passed out.

He came-to breathing water and found his head in one of the water tanks, fought wheezing to the air. Carey was standing there looking stern with his arms folded and Leamus was dunking him.

A word was screaming at him through his headache and the fumes of the beer pulsing in his eyes. It was a Deutsch word and it came from Book III of the *De Re Metallica* of Agricola, or as his friends knew him, George Bauer. And he suddenly remembered the rest of the relevant paragraph.

He surged to his feet, shook Leamus off and started running through the dark streets of Keswick, slipping and sliding on the newfallen snow on top of the old. When his old habit of coughing caught up with him, he slowed to a walk and then trotted on when the coughing died down and so walking and running he came back to the Oak Inn, plunged through the side door and staggered upstairs to the little room he was sharing with Carey. He found the leatherbound volume of *De Re Metallica*, lit a candle with trembling fingers and flipped through the heavy pages full of woodcuts. Where was it, at the end of Book 3? He could see the words now…

He found it, breathed out fully at last and laughed for joy.

"Well, Mr Tovey," said Carey's voice behind him, not nearly as out of breath as he was, presumably because Carey had ridden back and Tovey hadn't even thought of his horse in the heat of the moment. "Perhaps an explanation would be in order?"

"Yes, sir," said Tovey, now feeling his chest tight and starting to cough as he often did when he ran, having a narrow chest and too much of the phlegmatic humour. "Look, sir, see…"

"See what? I told you, my Latin is desperate."

"The name of the mine here is Goldscope but in Deutsch it is Gottesgaab."

"Sounds similar."

"Yes. Gottesgaab means God's Gift in Deutsch, but anyway, here in Cumberland, Goldscope and Gottesgaab mean the same thing, the mine in Newlands valley."

"Ye..es."

"But there's another mine called Gottesgaab in a place called Abertham in Allemayne. Almost certainly our Gottesgaab is named after the one at Abertham, which came first. And they called that Deutscher mine God's Gift because…it says here…'for they have dug out of it a large quantity of pure silver.'"

Carey hefted up the volume and squinted in the bad light of the inn's muttonfat tapers. "Ah, *argentum*!"

His face was suddenly wreathed in a joyous smile and he chuckled long and low. "Well, well."

"And I'm sorry, I kept trying to tell you, but you didn't

understand. You know those funny-looking furnaces with the domed lids lifted by chains?"

"That they really didn't want us to see, though two of them were fired?"

"Yes, sir, well, they were cupellation furnaces, see here. Here's a picture."

There was and very clear.

"Cupe...what?"

"To get the silver out of copper, you first have to melt in lead which the silver prefers to stick to than the copper, you pour off a cake and cool it and then you chip off the lead and silver mixture. You put it in a cupellation furnace again, lined with charcoal—I'm still not sure how it works, sir, but the Athenians did it in the time of Socrates so it can't be new— that separates the silver and lead and then all you have to do is get the gold out of the silver by the same method of cupellation and then..."

"You have some gold to give the Queen her share which she is very particular about and then you have all the silver which is probably considerably more than the gold, being a baser metal, to do what you want with."

"Yes, sir."

"Which is why they did their best never to speak of silver and why Herr Steinberger didn't want young Mr David even mentioning Potosi, in case we thought of silver."

Tovey nodded.

"And which is also why they have all that big stockpile of copper pans they can't sell and keep sending pathetic letters to Mr Secretary Cecil about."

"Yes, sir."

Carey sat back on his bed and laughed again. "Wonderful, Mr Tovey," he said. "I saw something in you at Oxford and this confirms it."

Tovey blushed. "Th...thank you, sir."

Carey's blue eyes were bright with merriment. "They've been

cheating the Queen since they started or possibly since Daniel Hochstetter died. They are still here mining, so there is still silver in Goldscope mine and perhaps others of their mines in the area."

"Shouldn't we challenge them, sir?" Tovey asked, who was rather shocked. "Shouldn't we report back to Mr Secretary and…?"

"Oh no," said Carey. "I don't think that would be a good idea at all. No, no. You may have noticed that I was playing rather stupid today, eh?"

"You were?" said Tovey tactlessly. Carey sighed.

"Yes, I was. That's because fatuous ignorance is an awful lot better for prying secrets out of people than marching up to them and hitting them until they tell you. Not that there's anything wrong with the traditional way in its proper place, but here we are in Keswick, sixty miles from Carlisle, and whereas I have only four men, including you, Mr Tovey, the Hochstetters have at least twenty men accustomed to wielding picks and axes and probably a lot more."

"Ah." Tovey had gone white again.

"So we will remain tactful and quiet on the subject of the silver, until we find where they've got it hidden and until we get back to Carlisle as well. Eh, Mr Tovey?"

Tovey nodded.

"I bet I know where it is, too," said Carey thoughtfully. "It's on their precious island along with the brewery, the bakery, and the mill, and no doubt Hepburn or Hochstetter too, sitting on top of the pile like the dragon in a nurse's tale."

He leaned over and gave Tovey a slap on the back that started him coughing again. "Good work," he said, as Tovey's heart swelled. "I wonder what else you'll find for me, Mr Tovey? Come on, let's go to bed, if you can get my points undone."

SATURDAY, 27TH JANUARY 1593, STOBBS

Sergeant Dodd had spent most of the Friday stepping slowly down the spiral staircase at Stobbs, two storeys down, past the hall and down to the storeroom and stable on the ground floor, past the internal iron gate for stopping besiegers. He then slowly shuffled across the floor, watched with grave disapproval by a couple of lame ponies and a cow. Once on the other side of the floor he sat on a stone and pushed the thick barred door open a little so he could see was it still snowing in the barnekin, and get his breath back. Then he shut the door and doddered back through the comforting smell of horse and cow shit and straw, up the spiral stairs, past the entrance to the hall, up the stairs again, trying not to stop at the cubby hole for people to pass each other, though sometimes he had to, up the last few stairs to the third floor, through that gate, through one large chamber and then through the door to the one that had held him prisoner for weeks. There he fell on his stomach on the bed until his breath had stopped cawing in his throat and his head had stopped whirling. And then he got up and did it again. Janet had wanted to help him at first but he had snarled at her to leave him be and so after watching him intently through one entire journey, she disappeared to the kitchen which was in a separate building right next to the tower.

After a couple of full journeys, he had fallen asleep and woken to find a bowl of broth and a spoon on the little table, and so he had drunk the broth and started down the spiral stairs again.

After two more journeys, the snow had stopped and the sky cleared a little and he looked out at it longingly for a while before snarling at himself and setting off again. He passed by the ponies and the cow, which looked as if it was still in milk for a wonder, and climbed the spiral stair again. Everyone had been in the hall by the fire, but now they had all gone out and got on with the things they should have done earlier when it was snowing too much to see. This time he didn't fall on the bed, but sat on it and waited for his breathing to ease.

He got back down to the courtyard gate again, his legs feeling like lead and found Janet waiting with her arms folded. She insisted on turning him around and checking the bandages on his back for bleeding, but there wasn't any blood, he knew it. There was no longer a spike of pain there, but more a needle of itching which drove him crazy when he stayed still. At least while he was moving he didn't feel it so much.

She smiled at him and told him to wait and ran upstairs for something, came down again carrying a thick blanket and a pair of pattens to put on over his socks.

Then she opened the courtyard door and went out and swept the snow off the steps so he could venture into the open for the first time in he had forgotten how long. He walked the distance to the barnekin gate, which had its postern open for the men who were taking fodder to the ponies and cattle in the infield. The sky seemed enormous over his head, the giant white folded sheets of the moors and hills alien and threatening.

He felt suddenly weak and wanted to sit down, but put his arm on Janet's sturdy shoulders instead and tried not to lean too much. Janet looked up at him and smiled at him, such a beautiful smile, so full of hope and happiness that he stopped and said, "What?"

She hesitated. Then she said, "Ah'm no' sure yet..."

"Sure of what?"

"It must have been while we were at the King's Court after Christmas, and Ah'm no' certain but..."

"But what?" he frowned at her. "What are ye telling me?"

"Henry, I might be wi' child."

He didn't hear her words really, but understood the gesture as she put her hand on her lower stomach. "Ye're what?" he asked, his breath coming short.

"With child," she said again and he felt his chest lift and open as if the sun had risen inside him.

"Ye...ye think ye've got a babby?"

"I do, Henry, though it's too early to say yet, for I had my courses a week before Christmas and I might lose it yet but..."

She couldn't speak any more because he was kissing her mouth and then, very gently, her stomach and then her mouth again and he felt something stir in himself for the first time in weeks and then let go of her, lest he dislodge the wee manikin from her stomach.

"Och, God," he said, "Ah canna believe it, how did ye...?"

"I got a charm fra the midwife, ye mind her, Mrs Hogg?"

He wrapped his arms around her warm body and hugged her as tight as he could and found his eyes betraying him again and had to cough and snort to hide it.

"Ay," he said, "ay," and she turned him and pushed him back into the pele tower and up all the stairs, all the way while the rising sun inside him lifted and grew and its rays filled all his body, so he didn't notice how tired he was. Even when he had to lie down on his bed again, it was still there, warming him from his heart outwards. He fell asleep and later Janet got into his bed with him and held him all night. He knew she did because he kept waking and wondering why he was feeling so happy and then felt her arms around him and knew why.

And then on Saturday...Saturday was the prize. Today Janet had brought him his own clothes, a hemp shirt and breeches and hose and a woollen doublet and leather jerkin and a cloak to go over it all, smelling friendly of himself. He slowly dressed and put his boots on which were clean, strapped on his dagger that the Courtier had brought him, and found he needed to make another hole in the belt quite a way from the one he usually used. Janet went down and borrowed a leather punch from the tackroom and made the new hole for him. Then he stood up straight and felt like a man again and not a wean.

He went down to the hall and greeted the Elliots who were

there, Mistress Elliot with her linen veil and her friend sitting next to her and the cousins and lads and maids who helped her run the place. Dodd looked at the boys, wondering about them, but no, she wouldn't have her child with her, that would not be respectable at all. He thanked them all for helping him and they looked at each other and a few nodded, even if some of them scowled or stared into space.

There was a sound of some fuss in the barnekin, a horse squealing with anger and men trying to hush it and calm it. Dodd tilted his head to the sound.

"Ay," said Janet, "there's Whitesock."

"Whitesock?" Dodd said, standing up so fast he caught his back. "Why's he squealing? What's wrong wi' him?"

"He's wood," said Janet. "I tellt ye, after he came back to Edinburgh wi' your bloody saddle to show us what happened, he's been wood. He wilna let naebody back him nor groom him and now he willna hardly eat. I wouldna have brung him so soon but I'm afeared…"

By that time Dodd had walked out of the hall and down the stairs, past the ponies and the cow, out the door and into the barnekin where a horse in terrible condition was standing four-square, teeth bared, defying the two men holding leading reins. But he had a roman nose and a white sock and he was Whitesock.

Dodd tested the wind and moved round so it would blow from him to the horse.

"Leave go of him," he ordered the men.

"He's like to kill ye, Sergeant."

"Hmf," said Dodd and walked up to the horse from the side. "Ye'll no' kill me, ye clever bastard, will ye?" he said softly to the horse. The horse rolled his eyes at him, reached out with his teeth to bite. Then he stopped still as a statue and his nostrils flared. Then he nickered like a foal, and pushed his nose into Dodd's chest so Dodd was nearly knocked over. "Och," he said and patted the muddy neck and blew into Whitesock's muzzle.

Then Dodd reached up and started untangling the matted mane and Whitesock stood and closed his eyes and swayed a little, while Dodd unclipped the reins, rolled them up and chucked them in a corner.

"Did ye think Ah wis deid?" Dodd said to him, his fingers working on the crest of the mane, clearing knots. "Did ye think Ah wis gone? Ah wisna, and it's thanks tae ye, ye clever lummock, eh?"

Janet and Mistress Elliot watched from the door of the pele tower and then stepped away so that Dodd could lead Whitesock into the dim tower stable and one of the empty stalls beside the ponies.

SUNDAY, 28TH JANUARY 1593, KESWICK

In the morning, it was still snowing, though fine flakes now that stung the eyes because it had frozen hard in the night. Carey found that nobody was doing anything except going to church because it was Sunday, so he dutifully gathered his men and set off for the little church in the south of town where there was a scattering of the better folk, plenty of townsmen and no Deutschers at all.

Carey's eyebrows went up and after the service he went to talk to the pastor, a nervous young curate standing in for a courtier with a number of other benefices.

"So," he said, after congratulating the young man on his sermon which had not been about vestments nor the Four Last Things, but simply about the real difficulty with loving our neighbour, which is that our neighbour is normally not very lovable. "Where are the Deutschers? Are they Papists, recusants?"

"No sir, not at all Papist…in fact, no, not Papists at all. They have their own assembly on the island and my Lord Burghley gave them permission for it to be in their own language, so long as it wasn't Papistical, which it isn't. It's very simple, in fact, and on Sundays the men often meet in Crossthwaite church which is their official parish, so they don't have to row, which would be servile work on the Sabbath. They have readings from Scripture, prayers, sometimes a very simple Eucharist."

"Ah. Well, I'm pleased to hear it."

"They don't allow the bakehouse or the brewhouse to work on Sundays either, sir. They're very strict about it and there's no nonsense about vestments, just a simple surplice without lace and…"

Carey was already bored, but he was mollified. The Deutschers being Puritans was less worrying than their being Papists or indeed Anabaptists. "Do you know what the best way of gaining permission to visit the island might be?" he asked. "I'd particularly love to see the brewhouse—the beer in this town is wonderful."

The curate brightened up a little and said mournfully that it might be possible but that his honour would have to gain permission from Frau Radagunda Hochstetter. Carey sighed at this and went to join Red Sandy and Bangtail and pretended he hadn't seen them quickly hide their dice.

They headed for dinner at the inn and ate more stewed salt beef with neeps, which was universal winter fare, especially in a small town with only two butchers in it.

Halfway through, and deep in an argument about how the animals might have been stowed on Noah's ark and how in fact you stopped the lions from eating the goats, the sheep, the deer and so on, he realised that Tovey wasn't there and hadn't been for a while.

After Leamus said that Tovey had last been seen heading in the direction of the smithy, he went that way, paid his respects to the servants, and went in to find Tovey searching through a chest in the corner of the smithy, filled with odd bits of metal.

"What are you looking for?"

"Notebooks," said Tovey, sitting back on his heels and rubbing his hair the wrong way so it stood on end. His scholar's gown with its pathetic bits of rabbit was all dusty. "Some smiths use them, especially smiths that like making new things. I feel sure that Mr Carleton could read."

Carey helped him search but none of the various boxes or chests in the smithy had any such things.

They went to the house to ask the elderly woman servant if Mrs Carleton had any notebooks of her husband and found she was expected back from Divine service on the island, and shortly after saw her walking up the road that led from the lake with her young son, Josef. The apprentices seemed to have gone to the church at Crossthwaite.

Carey bowed, she curtseyed, and he asked, "Ma'am, did your husband keep any notebooks?"

Pain crossed her face and she said nothing for a while. Young Josef pulled at her skirt and said something urgent in Deutsch. "Yes, he did," she said slowly.

"I would greatly appreciate it if I could inspect the note-books—they might contain clues to his murderer."

"His notebooks? They are about smithying and making strange things of metal."

"Nonetheless."

More Deutsch from the boy and she shrugged. "Why not? I cannot understand them."

"I do," said Josef to Carey with a brilliant smile. "I have been looking at them, they make me feel closer to *Vater*, even though if he was alive he would never let me have them."

"Why not?"

"They are to do with the mysteries of smithing, the different colours of the fires, the different prayers you say. It is for the master smith to have them and he is dead, so I have them. I will be the master here one day."

The boy made a small bow. "If you will permit, I can show you the notebooks that are not about the mysteries but about things he made. He kept them in his study—it was really the parlour but he liked to eat in the kitchen with the apprentices, not separately as they do in so many smithies, and he needed a place to think, he used to say, and he did that in the parlour. I will show you his last notebook first."

It was a little leatherbound notebook, half full. Josef handled it gently and delicately, as if it could feel. "This notebook…" he began, "this notebook…" He tried again. "I have found that this notebook has had two pages torn out of it, the last two pages. My father would never have done that! Never! He always said that your mistakes taught you as much if not more than your successes, that an idea that didn't work one time in one machine might work wonderfully another time and in a different machine. My father never never tore a page out of his notebooks…" Josef's chest was heaving and he was fighting not to cry.

"Can I see?" said Carey, holding his hand out for the note-book. Reluctantly, Josef handed it over. Carey flipped to the end and found diagrams for some kind of fantastical machine which involved water and coalfire and a boiler to drive something that looked like a London waterpump. And two pages had indeed been torn out. Carey looked at it for a moment and then lifted the notebook up to the light and squinted sideways across the blank page. "Hm," he said, "do you happen to have any blacklead around the place, plumbago some people call it? Look, I have some for writing in my own notebook."

"Ah," said Josef, "waad. Yes, we use it for polishing, there's a waad mine near here at Seathwaite."

"There is? You must show it to me."

"My father used to get annoyed with how the waad dirtied his fingers and he was trying to come up with a way to protect the fingers and yet have the waad useable."

"I think all Christendom would be grateful for something like that. Could you fetch me some, the very softest? And a pestle and mortar."

A few minutes later Josef came trotting back with a small lump of blacklead and a pestle and mortar he had clearly got from the kitchen because it smelled faintly of pepper. Carey dropped a bit of the blacklead into the bowl and then crushed it into a fine powder. Then he took a pinch of the fine dust and blew it over the blank page following the two torn out. And there, ghostly in the sunlight, appeared lines and confused writing. Clear among them was a sketch of a half-sphere, and by the side some just readable Latin.

Silently Carey showed the words to Tovey who nodded and said, "*Plumbum. Contra vitriol.* Lead against vitriol."

Carey sketched what was there into his own notebook. Josef watched owlishly.

"What are the round things?"

"The two halves of a sphere made of lead. Real lead, the metal, not blacklead. It's important for reasons I can't tell you."

"Will it help to solve the death of *Vater?*"

"Yes. It means that the person who killed your father also probably had a hand in the…the outrage at the King's court."

"Do you know who he was? Or is?"

"I'm not sure. Do you know a man called Joachim Hochstetter?"

Josef made a face. "I remember him from a long time ago when I was littler; he used to help my *Vater* make tools and machine-parts for the mines. I didn't like him, he frightened me."

"Out of the mouths of babes and sucklings. Well, if you see him again, I want you to tell me immediately."

"Do you think he killed *Vater?*"

"I'm not sure. But possibly."

The boy seemed to want to add something else but stopped and just nodded. Carey gave him back his father's notebook. "Thank you, Mister Josef," he said formally. "Keep the notebooks safe."

The boy nodded again and then ran off into the house because there were tears in his eyes.

"We have to talk to Allerdyce now," said Carey and so they

walked to the Mayor's house where they found him at dinner eating salt pork, neeps, bread, and a chicken blankmanger with his wife and family in his parlour. Allerdyce waved his arm expansively and invited them to join him which after a bit of polite prevarication, they did.

The Mayor had a brown-haired wife and two polite children who budged up for Carey and Tovey without complaint. They discussed the sermon which Allerdyce had found funny since it was a well-known fact that the curate was embroiled in a dispute with a neighbour over some boundary markers which both sides were alleging had been moved by the other, although in Allerdyce's opinion, the River Greta had changed her course slightly and that probably caused the confusion. Carey wondered if the river could be called as a third party to the dispute and they laughed at the idea of a river appearing in court.

When asked his views on the matter, Tovey, who had been modestly silent until now, said that in his opinion the only person who could represent the river in court was the Queen, because in her Person, she represented all of the land of England, and that they should subpoena Her Gracious Majesty immediately. Everybody laughed at that, especially Carey who could imagine the likely royal reaction and gave a deadly rendition of the letter that would be received from the Queen in response to such a summons.

When the laughter had died down, Allerdyce's wife and children excused themselves and left, and then Carey could tell him what he had found sketched in the smith's notebooks.

"This half globe sketch by itself connects Carleton with whoever made the attempt upon His Majesty, although I think it's more than probable that Hepburn didn't explain what the lead half-spheres were really for and came up with some colourable tale. That man was clearly Jonathan Hepburn and we can make the connection between him and Joachim Hochstetter."

"How d'ye think it all happened?"

"I'm fairly satisfied that Carleton, no doubt unknowing, made the half-spheres of lead and the alchemical alembics to produce the vitriol. Hepburn took them to Edinburgh before Christmas. He came back in a hurry after New Year's Day, perhaps because he knew his attempt had failed, perhaps simply to wait here until the King's death had happened. At any rate somebody rides into town very early on a snowy morning two or three days after New Year, wearing a white cloak and the Apollo mask from the masquing chests, as seen by Betty. It was done deliberately so anyone who saw him would sound utterly mad—and it worked. Hepburn goes straight to visit his friend the smith, the man who had taught him to be an engineer, knocks him on the head and then…er…spits him on a red hot sword blank and leaves him so nobody can connect him with the attempt on the King. I don't think he expected the sword blank to be discovered, probably because he has never laid a body out."

Mr Allerdyce had his lips well-compressed.

"I'm sure I don't have to say that I'd rather this was kept confidential, Mr Allerdyce," Carey said, because he wanted to make sure that the Mayor passed it on to the Hochstetters.

"Ay. Ye don't."

Carey was already mentally drafting a complete report to Mr Secretary Cecil, although there was no point trying to send it because nobody was moving anywhere on the bald treeless hills, nor on the snowbound roads. The confirmation that Hepburn was indeed in Keswick, made the blood rise in his veins. Perhaps he would be able to kill the assassin after all, which would make the future King of England both happy and, perhaps, grateful. "My bet is that Jonathan Hepburn or Hochstetter is on the island, but…"

"Could ye find him if he was?"

"I hope so," said Carey. "We can't go into the island houses behind a boot and a hammer, the way we could if we were searching for a Papist priest. But I could at least look and learn where he isn't."

"Ye ken Frau Radagunda dotes on him. He's her favourite son."

"So you said."

"We could swear ye out a warrant because of the possibility…"

"The probability…"

"Possibility, Sir Robert, that poor Mr Carleton helped with the attempt on the King. At least it gives us a possible murderer when before we had to adjourn the inquest. I'm certain Carleton wouldn't have known it was against the Scots King…"

"So am I, Mr Allerdyce. I don't see Jonathan Hepburn sharing that tidbit with anybody."

Allerdyce sighed again. "I'm fair scunnered wi' all this," he said. "And I hope it wisna Joachim, but some stranger come down fra the Border country. But."

Carey did his best to look sympathetic.

Suddenly there was a peremptory knock on the door. One of Allerdyce's apprentices opened it and there stood Mrs Carleton looking enraged, holding tight to her son's hand. He looked frightened and kept trying to escape.

"*Was höre ich da..?*" demanded Mrs Carleton, "*Joachim ist der Mörder meines Mannes?*"

"Ah, Mrs Carleton, will ye no' come in and sit down…?" said Allerdyce smoothly. "And we can…"

With effort, Mrs Carleton switched to English and continued in a low furious voice, "How can you think Joachim killed my husband, it's a stupid idea, very stupid. My husband was like a father, like an uncle to Joachim, one of his family…Joachim was always in and out of the smithy, learning to make things, Mr Carleton loved Joachim like his own son…"

"Did Joachim love your husband back?" asked Carey mildly.

"Of *course* he did, they were so close…"

"Well, perhaps you can come up with a better explanation for what happened," said Carey, suppressing his first impulse which was to tell her that she was a woman and knew nothing and should be silent and let men do the thinking. Since he had met and got to know Elizabeth Lady Widdrington he had learnt that that approach never worked very well, even if the woman did in fact shut up at the time.

Mrs Carleton pulled up a stool and sat down.

"Mr Josef," said Carey, "do you still have the notebook?" Josef removed it from his doublet pocket and held it out to Carey, who took it. "Thanks to your son who let us see this, your late husband's latest notebook. Do you see how two pages have been torn out here?"

She nodded, suddenly looking uncertain.

"Did your husband often tear pages from his notebooks?"

"No, never. He kept everything, every sketch, even if it never worked. In his chest in our bedchamber he kept his notebooks going back to when he was an apprentice. He said you couldn't tell when it might come in useful."

"So would he have torn out the two pages?" repeated Carey. Mrs Carleton looked down and shook her head.

"*Nein,*" she whispered.

"Yet here they are torn. Now, Mrs Carleton, this is a method I learnt from the late Sir Francis Walsingham, to find out what might have been written that was later torn out. It only works for blacklead, where there is pressure of the point on the next page, not really with a goose quill and ink which is too smooth on good paper."

He proffered the notebook to her and she looked at the page with the faint lines on it. She paled and pressed her hand to her heart as if the sketching was elvish.

"Nothing magical here," Carey reassured her, "you just blow finely powdered blacklead or charcoal over the page and a little sticks in the grooves left by the pressure of your hand on the page before. Do you see?"

"Yes," she said slowly. "I remember the two half globes. He

made them of waste lead, out in the yard where the fumes could escape, eating butter to protect himself. Last summer. It took a long time to make the moulds and build the internal reinforcing since they were so heavy. Josef was staying with his grandparents."

"Indeed," said Carey. "This is a state secret, Mrs Carleton, at least in Scotland, so I beg you will not speak of it with your gossips, but those two lead hemispheres were used to hold vitriol which was to be poured all over His Highness of Scotland, thereby killing him or at best badly wounding him."

"But vitriol burns..."

"Yes, it does. It set fire to a throne and a velvet robe."

"*Heilige Mutter Gottes*," gasped Mrs Carleton, her hand over her mouth, her face as white as milk. "But Joachim would never do such a thing..."

"A man called Jonathan Hepburn did all that. It was his idea. He brought the leaden hemispheres and inside, the vitriol that came from the ore roasting process to Court in Edinburgh. He was the artificer who made the props and the scenery for a Masque. He brought it in, the lead globe covered with paper and painted as the stable Earth that the Sun and planets circle around, put it on a high stand above the King's throne. Then he left the Court with his assistants. I think they must have laid a trail to Leith and the assistants might well have gone on to the Spanish Netherlands, but I believe it's possible Jonathan Hepburn came back here, where he came from, because his true name is indeed Joachim Hochstetter.

"The first thing he did was to kill his old friend Mr Carleton to cover his trail and then he probably sat down to wait for the news of the King's death to get here—except that it didn't for the good and sufficient reason that the King, by God's grace and perhaps the poor efforts of myself and a friend, wasn't dead or even hurt."

He watched Mrs Carleton struggle to get control of herself. She looked as if there was an enormous battle raging inside her.

She had let go of her son who had his face screwed up with disgust and was moving away from her. Watching her, watching the son, Carey suddenly knew the reason for the battle. Jonathan Hepburn was after all the man who had also seduced Sir David Graham's fluffy-headed wife as part of his long plan. He had a taste for blondes too. Carey carefully kept his realization away from his face—and besides she would hardly admit to the five-year-old dalliance now, would she?

"I think Hepburn is here, somewhere, still here. He's gone back to being Joachim Hochstetter," he said very softly. "In fact, I'm sure of it. Do you…could you perhaps tell me where he might be?"

Mrs Carleton shook her head, her hanky pressed tight to her mouth. She curtseyed to Allerdyce and himself, and then left the house, almost running, followed more slowly by her son. Poor boy, no wonder he didn't like Joachim; poor woman, sinner though she was, Carey thought. It was supposed to be just a fling, an amusement when she felt neglected by her own husband, so wrapped up in his smithying. He carefully didn't think about Mrs Dodd, since that was a completely different circumstance.

"Ay, she's lonely for poor John," said Allerdyce who seemed to have completely missed the byplay. "And wi' the smithy shut she's naught to keep herself busy."

"When will they reopen it?" asked Carey.

"I told ye, not till February. They're waiting the full forty days before they start up the smithy fires again. That'll be a sight to see when they dae it, they'll fire all three up at midnight, wi' made-fire fra a drill, the auld way, ye ken, and all the other smiths fra round about will be here and they'll burn John's gloves, ay, and his hammer they'll melt down and set to and make summat in iron for to remember him by."

SUNDAY, 28TH JANUARY 1593, KESWICK

It was pure chance that led Carey to take one of the ponies out for exercise that afternoon, along with a young man called Ullock, who was one of Allerdyce's merchant apprentices to show him the way. There was no need of Red Sandy or Bangtail in peaceful Keswick and John Tovey was still reading his book in the Oak's parlour where there was plenty of light. Carey didn't have the heart to winkle him out.

They rode out on roughshod ponies, and Carey went and took a look at the village of Braithwaite, at the foot of some high and brutal-looking mountains, hidden in mist and their shoulders dappled with snow, rode back and around, taking a look at the mouth of Newlands valley where Goldscope mine was. He considered going north to inspect Bassenthwaite Lake, but was put off by Ian Ullock's laughing description of the likely mud on the bad road there and in the soft marshes between the two rivers, Derwent and Newlands Beck. So they rode sedately back over Derwent bridge, went southeast alongside Derwent Water where Carey got a view of the island with its freight of German houses from a different perspective and then continued round via Castlerigg where there was the remains of a castle, being mined for stone, and northeast again to a tiny hamlet called Goosewell where there was one of those mysterious stone circles built by the Druids with eldritch powers, according to Mr Ullock. Nobody would dare mine that for stone. They talked about metals and swords. Mr Ullock had Deutsch cousins that lived in Allemayne and was much taken with a story he had heard from them about a new way of fighting a duel, with guns not swords. Carey listened with deep interest and they were still discussing it as they rode downhill to the River Greta.

There were three mounted travellers riding sedately along the road from Penrith, two women and one man, one riding pillion behind the man, and the other riding sidesaddle by herself, and behind them a train of four packponies with a drover.

Carey blinked a couple of times and then galloped down to join them, flourishing his hat and bowing low in the saddle to the mounted lady.

"Mr Anricks, Mrs Burn!" he was saying as Ullock caught up. "I am delighted to see you safely come to Keswick…"

He bowed over Poppy Burn's hand and tipped his hat to Anricks who had bowed in the saddle. The woman behind Anricks was clearly Poppy's wetnurse, since she was holding a small white parcel that was already making angry noises, and chucking to it wearily.

"Now, now, little Jimmy, there there…"

"Waagh…" said the baby and Poppy made a wry face. "Uwaagh…"

While the baby warmed itself up with intermittent squawks and yowls, Carey looked along the line of patient packponies plodding along. "What's in there?" he asked Anricks.

Anricks smiled. "Mrs Burn's books."

"Just books?"

"Mostly. And clothes and baby things."

Carey looked in astonishment at the ponies who were carrying large heavy-looking boxes rather than packs. "Oh? Really?"

"Minister Burn, my husband's legacy to me," Poppy Burn said to him, "because he knew how I love them and had nothing else of value to give me than his library. I gave his jack and helmet and his weapons to his brothers who have more use for them. I sold some of his books to Cousin William Hume but I managed to keep all the books in Deutsch and some of the older English volumes. I was helping my husband by translating some of Luther's and Zwingli's works into good Scots and he quoted them in his sermons. We had to make a special trip to Wendron to get them all or we would have been here last week. Did you think I would leave such treasure to the next Curate? He can have the Scots Bible."

"Of course, Mrs Burn," said Carey. "It's just I never heard of a woman owning so many books."

"I understand that Her Majesty the Queen has an entire room at Whitehall just for her books. My Lady Widdrington loves books too," said Mrs Burn haughtily. "She has to hide them from her husband because otherwise he might burn them as being of no use to a woman. I hope you are not of that opinion, Sir Robert."

"No, no, of course not," he said quickly, instantly changing what opinion he had had, which was the simple assumption that books were for men. It was indeed true that the Queen had a library in Whitehall and could often be seen with a book in her hand. If Elizabeth Widdrington loved books, books she would have, as many of them as he could afford to buy her as soon as they were safely wedded. He was already thinking of some courtly phrases about books and flowers and books and jewels. Good Lord, it shouldn't be a surprise to him that Elizabeth was apparently something of a bluestocking, there was a serious side to her after all. He imagined her, sitting by the fire, turning the pages of a book and looking up when he came to her and kissed her...

He sighed. "Who paid for the packponies?" he whispered to Anricks.

"I did," said Anricks. "I love books too and if she can't keep them here, why, I'll have them. I want to learn Deutsch in any case."

"Ay, and I wish I could read Latin too," said Carey. "Young Tovey has found some very useful things in a great tome he brought from Carlisle, *De Re Metallica* by Agricola."

"There you are,"

He rode alongside Mrs Burn for a while, whose nose was in the air as she ignored him. She rode very well and he thought her courageous for the way she had dealt with her husband's murder and the violence she had suffered. There was no sign of that now, nor much sign of her pregnancy either apart from the baby-parcel. "Ma'am," he said finally, "whither shall I escort you in Keswick?"

She sniffed and said, "The Oak Inn, Sir Robert."

"But won't you be staying with your mother, Frau Hochstetter?"

She stared into the distance. "My mother hates me and has forbidden me from going on her island."

"Why?"

Mrs Burn shrugged. "I don't know," she said. "I went with my brother Joachim when he left five years ago, for the adventure and because I admired him then. My mother loves Joachim and now hates me—why is a mystery to me, but since she won't talk to me, I can't find out why."

"I'm sorry to hear it, ma'am."

"Yes." Poppy was looking at the smelthouses as they passed by the stout wicker fence. "I may not be able to stay in Keswick if she continues her persecution of me. She is a very stubborn person."

"Where will you go?"

"I have no idea, unless I marry again quickly."

Carey nodded. "Lady Widdrington likes you, I think," he said consideringly. "Perhaps you could become one of her gentlewomen, a companion to her?"

Mrs Burn looked at him sideways. "I think I would like that very much, Sir Robert," she said. "Thank you for the suggestion."

"And wasn't Roger Widdrington quite...er...sweet on you?"

She smiled sadly. "His father forbad the match since I have no dowry or jointure for that matter, apart from the books. Roger Widdrington would have to take me in my smock."

The first two things Carey thought of to say were lewd so he took refuge in silence. Or at least not speaking, since the baby had finished his warm-up and was now bellowing with rage. As they passed the gate to the smelthouses, Mark Steinberger came out to see what the noise was. He looked idly and curiously at Mrs Burn who was a pretty woman and looked well in her grey wool riding habit. He blinked, stared, and opened his mouth.

"*Grüß Gott und einen guten Nachmittag, Schwager!*" sang out Poppy, and Steinberger's mouth stayed open as he watched them go past. "Hmf. Well, Annamaria will soon know that the prodigal daughter has returned. God help me."

Ian Ullock returned to Allerdyce's yard as soon as he could, rubbing his ears, but Carey bore them all company down Back Lane and across Packhorse Court and so to the Oak Inn where there was a flurry as Anricks dismounted first. Carey was off his horse instantly to hand Mrs Burn down from the mounting block and then she went to the wetnurse and put her arms up for the very loud baby, while Carey helped the wetnurse down too. Poppy lifted the howling parcel, sniffed his lower half and made a face. "Lord," she said, "poor little James Postumus Burn."

The nurse nodded, curtseyed to Carey and said, "I'm Mary Liddle, the nurse. I'll need the parlour for to change the wee mite and to feed him in, what's more."

"Er...yes," said Carey, not sure how you broke this to the innkeeper. Anricks was ahead of him and already parting with silver to ensure the parlour was cleared for them. Mary Liddle retrieved the baby from his mother, and marched into the parlour with him under her arm, where she put him on the table. "I'll need a bowl of water, clouts of cloth, sphagnum moss..."

Anricks came past Carey with an enormous bag taken from the first packpony which Goodwife Liddle opened and started investigating, while the purple-faced baby roared from the table. Carey prepared to flee to the commonroom which was blessedly free from infants, but Mrs Burn stopped him. "Sir Robert," she bellowed, "would you be kind enough to order the ordinary for both of us and two quarts of small beer as well, please—oh and make sure it's from the Deutsch barrel in the kitchen, not the one behind the bar."

Carey retreated to the male sanctuary of the commonroom, bringing Anricks with him. He ordered quarts of double beer for both of them, because Anricks in particular looked as if he needed it. He did. Half of it went down in one while Carey made their orders and listened to the ever-loudening outrage from the parlour that went to a crescendo and then reduced a little before finally stopping completely.

"Jesu," he said, accepting two large bowls of bean pottage which Anricks laid into with a will. "How was the journey?"

"Urrgh," answered Anricks.

A little later he added, "Mrs Burn is extraordinary for a woman who has only just been churched, but the babe…"

"Objected?" grinned Carey. "Why has it gone silent now? Have they killed it?"

Anricks snorted. "No, the nurse is feeding it."

"Of course."

"That will hold him for about three hours and then it's all to do again."

"All night as well?"

"Urrgh," said Anricks again.

As he rubbed his bread around the bowl and cut some cheese from the wedge on the table, Anricks added, "Still, here we are at last, thank the Almighty, and it is no longer my problem. I will rest and recover for a few days and perhaps pull some teeth before I go south to my wife in Bristol."

Joachim came in through the kitchen door, lifting the latch quietly with his long eating knife and sliding round the door, shutting it equally quietly behind him. The fire was curfewed and the room very dark, but suddenly he stopped. He knew there was a person sitting waiting at the table. For him?

It was so dark, he couldn't think who it might be. His mother? She had done that to him sometimes, when he was a youth.

No, the shape was too tall. Emanuel? Mark?

"Joachim," came the deep dull voice of the Schmelzmeister. For God's sake, that was all he needed, he had already had an aggravating day and a worse night, and here was another pompous old fart telling him what he should and shouldn't do. "I want to speak with you."

"Oh, God, what now? Your niece Sylvia…"

"Committed suicide because you, Joachim, got her with child and then refused to do the right thing and marry her."

"It wasn't me. How many times do I have to…?"

"It was you, Joachim. I saw you."

"That was somebody else with curly hair. Not me." He was starting to feel indignant about the accusation even though it had been him. God, five and a half years had passed, couldn't the idiot forget it? She was just a girl.

"Well, never mind," said Mark Steinberger unexpectedly, "maybe it wasn't you. Maybe it wasn't just you, although she was a virgin. But it was you who killed John Carleton, our smith, a couple of days after New Year's Eve. Mr Allerdyce told me. Wasn't it? It was you who came to him wearing a white cloak and a mask, you drank with him before sun up while you waited for the swordblank to heat, it was you who knocked him on the head with a hammer and then…" Mark Steinberger shook his head and his voice was thick with disgust, "…then you stuck the spit up his arse as if he was a suckling pig."

Joachim stood still, he couldn't risk moving because he was wet through to the skin and couldn't afford for Steinberger to notice. He was starting to shiver as well and he clenched his teeth so they wouldn't clatter. It was very dark, maybe he would get away with it. Damn it, he should have gone to Pastor Waltz, not home; the Pastor was terrified of him thanks to his information from Frau Magda, and would do whatever he said.

"He was your friend and you killed him because he made the lead spheres for the attack on King James, so he couldn't betray you—as if he would have. As if he would ever have betrayed you because he loved you, Joachim, just as Frau Radagunda loves you. Why it is a man so utterly worthless as you can make so many people love and admire him, I do not understand."

He wanted to argue, wanted to argue against Steinberger's words, but couldn't squelch, couldn't move so much as a muscle, couldn't think what to say. There was a soft pitter patter of drops of lake water, falling on the floor. Damn it!

Mark Steinberger stood up. "Leave," he said. "Go away. Take your habit of killing somewhere else and leave us in peace. Emanuel wants nothing more to do with you, nor does Daniel nor David. Not even Annamaria wants to see you."

He creaked to the door that Joachim had just come through, opened it, paused. Had he noticed that the latch was wet?

"By the way, Little Radagunda, Poppy, is back in Keswick with her baby, I saw her ride in. I'll be very interested to hear what she has to say about you."

He walked out, shut the door gently. Joachim let his breath out. Maybe Steinberger hadn't noticed that the door was wet and the floor was splattered with water. Then he remembered what Steinberger's parting shot had been. Little Rady, Poppy was back in Keswick?

MONDAY, 29TH JANUARY 1593, KESWICK

Carey was sound asleep when there came a tapping on his door at around two a.m. He answered the knock with his sword in his hand, and found Bangtail and Red Sandy, looking excited.

"Hey, sir," said Red Sandy, not too much the worse for drink this time, "guess what?"

"What?" said Carey cautiously, rubbing his eyes.

"There's a packtrain going out of town fra the smelthouses, they've been loading them up since midnight, and I heard tell fra one o' the drovers that's a friend o' mine, that the packtrain goes out at night about every month and they end up in the Debateable Lands."

"Do they now?" said Carey, hauling on his arming doublet and leather hose and his jack at speed. "What's the load?"

"Metal and heavy."

"Gold?"

"Nay, sir, Leamus took a peek and it's white, no' yellow."

"Silver?" said Carey to himself as he slipped his flask of aquavitae into his doublet pocket and shook Tovey awake.

"You have to stay here and tell everyone I've got an ague, a quartan ague," he told Tovey four times. "I'm leaving you here too, Red Sandy, so someone will have some authority."

"Aw, sir…"

"You're in command until I come back. I want you to make sure everybody knows how sick I am. You can't get drunk. Where's Leamus?"

"He's hiding near the smelthouses, keeping an eye on the ponies. They havena gone yet."

"Good."

He hesitated over his helmet and then took Red Sandy's greasy statute cap since the tall beaver hat would hardly be better than a helmet and Red Sandy sighed and said he would have to buy a new one. Carey gave him sixpence from Cecil's funds to pay for it. He took his long poignard but not his sword since it would clatter and catch in brambles, though he felt naked without it. Red Sandy stayed behind at the Oak Inn.

The town was empty so early in the morning. Carey stopped at the side door of the inn and told Bangtail to run to the baker and get three large loaves of bread while he slipped into the common room and snaffled three horn cups. Bangtail arrived back with the three loaves still hot from the ovens in a hemp bag and then they walked quickly through the footprinted lanes to the northeast corner of the town where they could hear the stamping and occasional whinny of protest and the stealthy chink of metal. Then Carey and Bangtail crept as quickly as they could from building to building until they saw the line and the drovers hefting the small packs and strapping them on carefully. Wattie Graham and his relatives watched in the light of a couple of lanterns by the fence and Mark Steinberger and Mr Emanuel were next to a torch, making notes in a ledger.

Carey grinned wickedly and hunkered down. Leamus was there at Carey's shoulder. His legs and feet were bare, his boots hanging around his neck.

"I'm thinking no horses," Carey whispered.

"Best not, if ye don't want to be seen," breathed Leamus.

"Nice trail for us, though."

Leamus just smiled.

For all it was supposed to be secret, Wattie, it seemed, could not be quiet, though he tried to shout in a whisper. "Come on, come on," he was saying, "Ah wantae to get some land between me and Keswick, will ye get on?" Somebody said something about waiting until the bastard courtier was gone home and Wattie snorted. "Nay," he said, "they're running out o' silver and besides, yon courtier's tucked up and snoring in his bed."

Carey streaked his face with icy mud and did the same for Bangtail who didn't protest. Leamus already had mud on his face.

The ponies were lined up and the next moment they started forward with a jingling and snorting, heading along the Penrith road eastwards until they turned off left to go north and eastwards along a well-used drover's trail that soon led into sparse woodlands. Carey and Bangtail slipped through the woods to one side of the path and Leamus turned up every so often to warn them of turns and stops.

As the sky started lightening at last with the late winter dawn, Wattie turned aside a little to three small stone shepherd's huts. The ponies were circled and a watch set by the Grahams, so Carey pulled back a little way and prepared for an uncomfortable day.

Leamus had his knife out and was trimming two large saplings, pulling them down and pegging them and piling branches and bracken on top which made a kind of rough shelter. He rolled inside and Carey paused, then did the same, dozing off on his side until Bangtail shoved in and Leamus went out to keep watch on Wattie.

At sunset they took their cue from the Grahams and ate one of the loaves of bread between them, with water from a burn cleaned with a little aquavitae. Then the packtrain set off again, with much shouting from Wattie, climbing high into the hills, all the ponies tired and apt to kick, still heading north and east from the prickling stars. Carey kept further back since the woods were thinner so high up. When the train stopped again at sunrise, he wondered why Wattie didn't just keep going for a while. He supposed that Wattie had tried speed and decided secrecy was better and nighttime helped with that. They lay out on the moors under piles of bracken and hoped they wouldn't be spotted, but the Grahams were sleeping in a remote farmhouse with a small tower and only a couple of sheepdogs seemed interested. Carey gave them half a loaf of bread and the dogs decided that the three of them were friends and not after the sheep.

The third night, Carey knew they were near Carlisle itself, but the packtrain didn't use the Eden bridge. Instead it headed eastwards and forded the river at a place that was near unfordable since the river was so high. They slipped into the Debateable Land after dark, wet to the waists and freezing cold.

Carey was keeping as close as he could to the last pony and when the animal finally stopped he nearly collided with the beast's hindquarters, though the ponies knew they were there of course, and protested too. Just in time he threw himself full length into a stand of mixed bracken and gorse and watched the boots of the young Graham lad as he pulled up the straps on the pony's pack, swearing all the while. Luckily Wattie was not inclined to pay attention although the drovers were unhappy.

Wattie was shouting in a whisper again.

"Just a little way more," he was saying, "and then there's food and beds for ye at Brackenhill."

Carey nearly popped his head up at that but stopped himself in time.

"Brackenhill," he said to himself. "Why Brackenhill, not Netherby?"

And then he knew and it made such beautiful sense, fitted in so nicely with everything else, he had to bite his lip to keep from laughing like a loon.

He could have gone back then, but they stayed with the ponies until they had theoretically gone into Scotland, filed through the gate of the large handsome pele tower with all its outhouses that was Brackenhill, as the false dawn peered up through more snow clouds. There was Ritchie Graham, by the gate, the Graham headman and oldest of the four brothers, a large man, wide as Henry VIII and a lot less handsome, greeting his brother with a clap on the back. Leamus came loping through the undergrowth like a hunting dog, with a happy grin on his face.

When he came up to them, Carey and Bangtail started trotting alongside him. At least running would warm them up and maybe even dry off their frozen lower halves. They had ten miles of the Debateable Land to get through before they could win over the Eden Bridge and when Carey saw what it was Leamus was holding cuddled to his side under his buff coat, he sped up to a run.

"You stole one of Wattie's cakes of silver?" he said breathlessly, as they crested a rise.

"I did, sorr," said Leamus and added something in Irish. "I could not resist it," he explained, not very apologetically.

"Oh, Jesus," Carey laughed, "Wattie will be fit to be tied again when he finds out." And he kept laughing occasionally as they ran up and downhill in the dark along the well-used track that led to Carlisle, with Leamus ahead and Bangtail bringing up the rear.

They had the Eden Bridge in sight, like a caterpillar frosted with white, when they heard the ominous pounding of the Graham hoofbeats behind them in the distance and increased their speed. The cold dawn came up.

There was a mile to go and the Grahams were getting nearer fast. Carey craned his neck to look behind him, saw the ponies break from the woodland, five of them, thought about stopping to give battle, they were three against five, and the five mounted, maybe not...

Leamus was already ahead of him and he went to a sprint, impressed at the speed of the Irishman's bare legs. Perhaps running without heavy boots on was easier? Bangtail was at his shoulder.

"Rouse the watch," he said breathlessly to Bangtail as he went past.

They pounded across the bridge, Wattie and four Grahams galloping behind them, shouting and gaining fast. They couldn't make it to the gate so it was time to fight. Carey drew his poignard and stood in Wattie's path, the blood racing in his veins. Leamus scooped a couple of rocks from the ground and hopped up to the parapet. He threw both of them and hit one of the ponies which reared, causing confusion, while Carey threw a rock as well and missed completely but made Wattie duck. He could hear the banging on the gate and shouting as Bangtail roused the watch.

"Ye bastard!" shouted Wattie, drawing his sword and pulling his morion down, "Ye God-rotted thieving bastard, I'll hang ye for stealin' ma siller..."

Carey dodged a lance from one of the Grahams, dropped and rolled under one of the ponies' bellies, jumped up and just ducked in time as Wattie swung for his head and another rock from Leamus hit Wattie's pony on the hindquarters and started him bucking. Carey scrambled away and over the parapet at the Carlisle end of the bridge and Wattie stopped there.

"It's not...your silver," Carey bellowed back, hoping to make the Graham waste more time shouting. "It's the Queen's silver!"

Wattie's face went purple and he fairly gibbered.

City men were at last coming running out of the postern to Carey, several with arquebuses and others shooting long-bows.

Carey was crowing for breath, but took off Red Sandy's statute cap so Wattie could see him properly. The sheer disgust on Wattie Graham's face when he saw who it really was that had followed him for three nights was worth every snore of Bangtail's. Carey bowed, waved the cap and laughed breathlessly at the lot of them as they swore, milled their ponies round angrily and went back.

THURSDAY, 1ST FEBRUARY 1593, CARLISLE

They ate breakfast at Bessie's, which was the normal fare of oatmeal porridge since the Castle guard had not gone out on the trod that night and Carey decided to report to Scrope immediately before he went to bed. Scrope was looking very anxious.

"Yes, my lord," he explained, trying not to yawn in the warmth of the fire in Scrope's parlour. "The mine in Keswick produces a lot of silver as well as a little gold and plenty of copper—a fact they seem to have kept secret with some success, despite naming the mine Gottesgaab, God's Gift. It seems that the Deutschers have an arrangement with the Grahams, through Wattie Graham of Netherby. They send the cakes of silver north to Brackenhill, to Ritchie's counterfeiting operation there. Now I don't think he uses much of the silver for coining Scots shillings, because they're almost worthless. Clearly he's not going to waste a lot of good silver on Scots money. I would say he uses the silver to make English shillings and sixpences which he then sends all over the north and also uses for usury, certainly in Carlisle, Newcastle, Berwick, and probably Durham too. I'd guess that the English shillings are actually quite good value although I doubt he keeps them as pure as the Queen does. There will be a margin between silver as silver and silver as shillings, and he keeps that as if he was the King himself. The Hochstetters get the shillings back, less a large fee for the counterfeiting and the packponies and guards, and pay their miners and creditors with it. Which accounts for why the Grahams are so rich and powerful. I had wondered."

"Ehm…were you thinking of telling Her Majesty all this?" asked Scrope, looking even more nervous.

Carey hesitated a second and then smiled. "I don't know, my lord," he said carefully. "I think Mr Secretary Cecil may suspect something because, after all, he commissioned me to inspect the mines."

Scrope looked away and stared into space. "Only, you know, there is never enough Tower silver coin here in the North. That's why we use Scotch shillings too."

Carey's eyebrows went up. "Well, my lord," he said, "I shall have to be very careful when I report to him. It would never do if Sir Robert Cecil should take it into his head to come north, after all." Scrope shuddered and shut his eyes. "It would be very bad for his back."

Carey wrote a letter to his father that afternoon, using a private cypher, and after some thought decided not to send it off with the regular messenger, since Cecil was probably reading all those letters. Instead he gave it to Bessie for safekeeping until he could find somebody not owned by Cecil to take it. He ignored the noisy festival of Candlemas and fell into his bed in the Queen Mary tower shortly before sunset. As usual he woke before dawn feeling refreshed and only slightly the worse for spending three nights unnaturally on foot, though he had a couple of blisters and holes in his hose.

He found Bangtail and Leamus at early breakfast with the cake of silver between them, arguing over where to sell it and how much for, and advised a visit to the Carlisle silversmith and to check that the scales were fair when he weighed it. In the end, Carey went with them to make sure they weren't cheated.

The silversmith clearly recognised the cake of silver, complained that it wasn't pure and that it was sure to have lead in it…

"As well as a little gold," put in Carey, playing with his gold rings. The silversmith gave him a wary look and weighed the cake, finding there slightly more than a pound of mixed silver and lead…

"and gold…"

"…which would make about twenty shillings' worth of silver, not calculating the lead…"

"…or the gold…"

"…which would amount to 6s 6d for each man, more or less, after the lead…"

"What say you we agree on the twenty shillings English, and leave the silver and the spare 2d here?" put in Carey. There was silence. "Ay," said the silversmith. "Ay, I could dae that, it's fair enough."

Two minutes later they were in the street again with their shares, Leamus looking very happy and Bangtail quite thunderstruck. "Is it enough to buy land, sir?" he asked Carey. "Not round here where all the reivers are, but far south, doon in Keswick, or mebbe some ither town, away from the kobolds?"

"You could maybe buy a field for about forty shillings."

"Right. Ah see, sir. Right. Or save the Queen's life, like Sergeant Dodd?"

"You could, though you would have to go south to find her."

"Ay," Bangtail was stroking his scrubby beard and staring into the distance. "And then, once ye've bought it, it's yourn."

"More or less. So long as the man you buy it from actually owns it, of course."

"Ay. And nae reivers."

"Almost certainly not. Though you'd have the usual problems with the weather and murrains and…"

"Ay, everybody has those. So for a farm, I'd need about ten pound?"

"That would be a good start."

"It's no' impossible, is it? Ah mean, it's a lot of money, but if ye have the money and can find someone to buy from…It's like buying a stottie cake."

"Or you could try what the Grahams are doing, which is squatting on somebody else's lands and making as much money as they can out of it before they get turned off."

"Who's going to turn them off?" scoffed Bangtail.

"King James, when he becomes King of England."

"Oh."

"What my father would do, and probably already has, is buy up parcels of land on the Borders, here and there for very little money and just keep them rented out for the moment. Nobody wants land here because of the reivers, as you pointed out. But when the Scots King comes in, the reivers will be finished because there won't be a Border anymore, and then the value of all my father's little bits of land will go up."

Bangtail was staring at him in astonishment. "Jesus!" he breathed, "Jesus Almighty Christ! Do you think so?"

"Yes. Provided King James can stay alive long enough. If he can't, of course, there'll probably be civil war and so all the land values will go to hell."

"Och."

Carey left him behind to think and hurried down English street to the castle because he wanted to get back to Keswick.

They headed off to Keswick an hour later and in a hurry, with Carey, Bangtail, and Leamus all on sturdy surefooted Castle hobbies, with remounts, and Leamus with his boots and hose on for a change. So they made the sixty-mile journey in one long tiring day of mainly cantering, saving time by not getting lost, changing mounts every ten miles or so. They followed the dull red fires of Keswick and the smell of acrid yellow smoke to come past the smelting houses late at night, as the snowflakes started falling again.

Tovey was happy to see Carey when he came into the inn by the back door. He was tired and damnably hungry and found that Mr Allerdyce wanted a word with him as soon as he felt well enough. He sent Tovey out to fetch the ordinary up on a tray and sat cross-legged on his bed in his shirt, wolfing down salt pork stew and wonderful fried sippets. After a while Mr Allerdyce came in, apologised for the lateness of the hour, commiserated with him for the fever, remarked on how ruddy with it he looked, and hoped he was well-recovered.

"I'll be right as rain by tomorrow," said Carey. "Once the fever's gone I always am."

"Ay," said the Mayor, "it's just I'm worried about Mrs Carleton and her son…"

"Oh? Why?"

"Naebody's seen them, either of them, since she went off to the island on Sunday, the day you told her that ye thought Joachim Hochstetter may have killed her husband."

Suddenly Carey's appetite disappeared and he put the bowl down.

"Nobody's seen them for nearly a week?"

Allerdyce shook his head.

"What does Frau Radagunda say?"

"She says she hasn't seen them either and assumes that Mrs Carleton simply ran away."

"Ridiculous! Why would she leave the smithy? It's a going concern and all she has to do is marry one of the journeymen to make it official."

"Ah wis wondering, did you take her to Carlisle?"

"No, of course not, I was sick of an ague. The last time I saw her was with you, in fact. Have you searched the lake?"

"The what?"

"Have you checked the lake for a dead body or two?" Carey

asked, "That's what I'd do."

"Ye mean suicide?"

"No, Mr Allerdyce, I mean murder. What if Mrs Carleton went and accused Hepburn of killing her husband and he decided to shut her up the quickest way?"

"Good God! But…"

The trouble with country bumpkins was that they were slow.

"I've told you that Hochstetter or Hepburn likes killing."

Allerdyce clenched his jaw. "We'll search after sun up tomorrow," he said, "but I'm sure she's just…gone somewhere for a few days."

After the Mayor had taken his leave, looking troubled, Carey polished off the stew absentmindedly, moved the tray to a chest, rolled into his bed and pulled the blankets over his shoulder. Five minutes later he was trumpeting through the night.

Tovey returned, found the tray, sighed at the noises coming from Carey and, after taking the tray back down to the kitchen, sat over his wonderful book again which he had finally managed to wrest back from Mr Anricks. Mr Anricks was an amazing man, despite not looking very impressive. He had read everything, even Maimonides, and was a merchant with the strange hobby of tooth-drawing. He was staying at the Oak Inn as well, in one of the expensive bedrooms, like Sir Robert and was surrounded by piles of books which he was reading at a ferocious rate. Every day he had a lesson in Deutsch from Mr Ullock, who had a father who was a Deutscher. Sometimes he would walk through the town and had allowed Tovey to come too and had even begun to teach Tovey Portuguese. John Tovey already had quite a bad case of hero-worship of Sir Robert, and now he had a second hero because he had dared to ask Mr Anricks about the scars on his palms and after a moment, Mr Anricks had told him about his time in the galleys—no, it was a galleas—during the Armada. And Mr Anricks always called him Mr Tovey.

Still Mr Anricks was apt to keep books, and Tovey was very

glad he had finally got the *De Re Metallica* back. He spent a long time admiring the woodcuts showing all the magical machinery that kept the mine working, until the candle guttered and went out. When he lay down to sleep he was still wondering why, for instance, were there three enormous bellows in a row, pointing into the mine, being moved by men treading on planks? Why did the air go bad if you didn't force new air into the mine?

SATURDAY, 3RD FEBRUARY 1593, KESWICK

In the morning, Carey was up and dressed in his respectable olive brocade, tall hat, and furlined cloak, before the sun had done more than dirty the sky with blood. First he asked the inn's landlord where the town stews were and whether it was the men's day or the women's day, and after finding that today was the men's day, decided not to use the stews for the miners in the north of town, but the smaller, more respectable ones in the south. He found Anricks in the inn parlour, reading a book of Chancellor Melville's sermons in Scots and chuckling occasionally which surprised Carey. Melville, the Chancellor of St Andrews University and a stern Calvinist, was notoriously the most boring preacher in Scotland, a hotly contested honour.

"Oh, I enjoy the way the Chancellor tortures logic and yet never hears its cries of pain," said Anricks primly. "Alas, the most interesting of Mrs Burn's books are in Deutsch and I can't make head or tail of them yet. I have nearly recovered from my journey and so I shall be leaving soon. But not until I've read all Mrs Burn's books and found her a good dry place to keep them until she has a household of her own again. And perhaps I may stay longer still to learn Deutsch without having to go to Allemayne."

Carey took Tovey to attend him who, unlike Dodd, had visited the stews at Oxford while he was a poor student there and missed them when he came back to his little village where the duckpond was the best washing place. Although Tovey had gone very pink at the ears when he confessed to visiting the Oxford stews.

The Keswick stews seemed respectable and there was a changing room with shelves for clothes and an old man with one leg looking after the place. Unlike the Oxford stews, these were not on the Turkish model but the more usual English system. In the bath-room there were five large wooden bucks, with stools to sit on in the water, which had a plug in the bottom to let the dirty water out, and were refreshed with buckets of boiling water as and when they were needed. The price was a very reasonable 2d. Carey had an extra bucket of boiling water poured into his buck which was just what he needed to unkink his muscles and bones. He stretched out and got Tovey to scrub his back and in his turn scrubbed Tovey's pitifully skinny spotty back. There were very few other people there so early in the morning, which was why he had come at that hour. He had almost dozed off when somebody new arrived and got into the wooden buck next to him and had boiling water poured into it.

"*Grüss Gott*," said Mark Steinberger, soaping his legs carefully.

"Er…good morning,"

"You are better of your ague, Herr Ritter?"

"Yes, much better, Herr Schmelzmeister!" said Carey brightly, wondering if he could get some mulled ale brought to him. In London it would be complimentary, but…"Thank you for your concern. Tell me, can I get a drink here?"

Steinberger nodded, beckoned one of the stews servants, and mulled ale—clearly from the brewery on the island—arrived a little later. The girl who would have accompanied the ale in London to ask hintingly if he needed anything else at all and possibly recite her prices for him, was unaccountably missing. He found bathing much more relaxing without anxious tarts trying to seduce him. On the other hand, Steinberger was looking at him now with just as anxious an expression on his face as any whore.

"Do you…ah…know Frau Burn?" asked Steinberger heavily.

"Not in the biblical sense," said Carey quickly. "I met her

briefly while she was enceinte. She is a friend of my cousin, Lady Elizabeth Widdrington. A little while ago, I was also able to hang the murderers of her husband, which gave me great satisfaction."

Steinberger relaxed a little. "She iss moved into our house, she iss my sister-in-law and my vife, Annamaria, has insisted."

Carey had not in fact noticed the lack of caterwauling at the inn and had in fact forgotten all about the baby. "Oh good," he said enthusiastically, "that is so much more suitable than the Oak, don't you think?"

"I sink it is," said Steinberger heavily, "though off course the vet nurse is arguing with Annamaria about the best vay to swaddle the baby and my sister-in-law iss sitting and reading books which my wife does nott approve of and…vell, it's impossible for her to go anyvere else, but efen so, I vish…" He looked around with a harassed expression.

"Ah," said Carey sympathetically, rinsing his shoulders with a bucket of lukewarm water, "best leave them to it, don't you think?"

"*Ja*," said Steinberger after a pause, getting out of the buck and towelling himself down with one of the linen cloths. Carey got out as well and jogged Tovey out of his doze.

"I wonder," said Carey, wrapping his own towel round his middle and smiling at Steinberger, "have you seen Mrs Carleton? Mr Allerdyce told me last night that she went missing while I was…sick."

"I know she iss missing," said Steinberger. "I'm sure she is well."

"Where do you think she might have gone?"

Steinberger shrugged, a very different gesture from the French. "I'm sure she vill come back."

"I'm surprised at you," said Carey, choosing his words carefully. "She's one of your own, not just another Keswicker. Why don't you care about her?"

Steinberger's jaw set and he turned and left the bathing room in silence. Carey stared after him and then went into the changing room himself, followed by Tovey who had his towel round his shoulders, showing scrawny legs under it like a beetle.

They went back into town to get breakfast at the Oak and for Carey to change into his arming doublet which didn't matter so much if it got wet. There Carey found Red Sandy and gave him the third share of the proceeds from the cake of silver. "It's because you were here, backing up Tovey, instead of following the packtrain," Carey explained and Red Sandy looked stunned and pleased about it. That was worth doing, and what did he need a 6s 6d share of the stolen cake of silver for? Carey had much larger game than that in his sights.

Then they went to the lakeside to find Allerdyce shouting at some sulky-looking workmen who were poking around the boatlanding with boat hooks in an ineffectual way.

Carey sighed and went up to Allerdyce. "Tell me, Mr Mayor," he said, "if Hepburn killed Mrs Carleton and Josef, do you think he wants the corpses found?"

Allerdyce's face went from puzzled to embarrassed and he flushed.

"Mebbe he buried her?"

"In this weather? No. Why not start this side of the boat landing and work your way round, or perhaps have two boats. Better yet, do you have a sleuthdog?"

Allerdyce didn't have a sleuthdog as such, but he did have a couple of hunting dogs he used for wildfowling in the rushes, not that he got many these days, since the kobolds had scared the fish away.

Once the dogs had been fetched and let off the leash they instantly splashed into the icy rushes where they set up some moorhen and the heron. They dove into some more rushes and came out chewing something noisome. They bounced around setting up wildfowl and one attacked an old oar that was floating in the rushes and chewed it until it broke.

Allerdyce wanted to give up then, but Carey was watching intently as the dogs barked and snuffled their way around the reeds, splashing busily in and out and retrieving the sticks Allerdyce started throwing for them. There was one area of dense thicket which they avoided and so he went back to the boat-landing and took a boat, got one of Allerdyce's men to row him into the middle of the patch of reeds that the dogs didn't like. He picked up a boathook, stood and stirred around in the water and eventually the hook snagged on something soft. With infinite care, he brought it up to the surface. At least it was not a boy's hand, although smaller than a man's hand.

"Mr Allerdyce," he called sadly and once the Mayor got to him, he lifted the hand which was still attached and not rotted at all despite the nearly week of time it had probably been there. Mr Allerdyce stared at it as if he had no idea what it was and then he suddenly bent over the side of the boat and puked up his breakfast.

The workmen were called and many boathooks released Mrs Carleton from the pile of rocks holding her down. There was a woman, Carey thought was Frau Radagunda, watching impassively from the island. Mrs Carleton had been strangled and there was a slit in her stomach as well, perhaps to let the gases out. Not that that was a problem with the hard frost. Her face above her ruined throat was white, her cap still on and tendrils of blonde hair round her face like a delicate kind of waterweed.

Mr Allerdyce himself helped the workmen haul the sodden body up into the boat and there were tears in his eyes. As they rowed to the boatlanding, Carey said, "We'll have to go back and search for her son too."

"Oh, he wouldn't..."

"Why not, Mr Allerdyce? He certainly wouldn't want to leave a witness."

Mr Allerdyce was nearly as pale as Mrs Carleton when they handed her body up to the makeshift litter of oars to take her into town, to the church. Then Allerdyce turned the boat around and they searched for two more hours and found no trace of her son. By that time the waterdogs had gone to sleep and Carey had been joined by Bangtail and Red Sandy, looking happy.

"D'ye think the boy is still alive?" asked Mr Allerdyce finally.

"I'm afraid not, Mr Allerdyce."

The Mayor looked at the floor of the boat, his lips tight. "Why doesn't…Joachim Hochstetter just leave Keswick?"

Carey felt sorry for the Mayor—this was a far worse problem than the murder of Stoltz. "Why should he?" he answered. "This is his home. You wouldn't have found the body without my help."

"Well, damn it, where is he?"

Carey gestured at the island where the bald boatman was sitting watching them, his pipe lit. "There," he said, "at his mother's house probably."

"We'll have the inquest tomorrow," said Allerdyce, scowling, "or no, we can't, it's Sunday tomorrow. I'll swear you out a warrant now to search for the killer of Mrs Carleton and Mr Carleton too. Bloody Deutschers."

"Can you give me any men?"

"I can. Will five do?"

"I want to get on that island before it gets dark, any chance of that?"

"Ay."

And astonishingly, it was so. The piece of officially watermarked paper was in Carey's hand within the hour and he had his mixed bag of Borderers and Keswickers on three boats that belonged to the town. They went across as the sun was westering, which was a pity but couldn't be helped so far north.

Frau Radagunda was there on the boatlanding, cold fury on her face. "*Was soll dieses Eindringen bedeuten?*" she demanded. A scared-looking girl, her youngest daughter Elizabeth, translated for her—"What is the meaning of this invasion?" Carey had given the men his instructions and they trotted off round the island until one man was stationed every fifty yards or so. There were very few men on the island, and the women gathered near the tenth house and watched; the older ones with horror, the younger ones with interest. Carey had also taken the precaution of bringing every single boat from the Keswick side boatlanding to the island and setting a guard, so that nobody else could get on or off the island.

"We are looking for your son, Joachim Hochstetter," said Carey to her, "on suspicion of the murder of Mr Carleton, Mrs Carleton, and possibly her son."

"Ridiculous!" snorted Frau Radagunda and a great deal more in Deutsch.

On his signal, Carey had his men walk inwards from the island's margin, poking in bushes. He personally inspected the brewhouse with its gleaming copper vessels and the bakehouse, which was quiet so late in the day. He went into each house and carefully up through the rooms, tapping the walls, checking the floorboards and ceilings, measuring the ovens in the bakehouse and the malting floor at the top of the brewhouse.

Frau Radegunda was now standing with her hands on her hips in front of a brightly painted and carved house front, the last and biggest. "*Hier kommt ihr nicht herein. Das hier ist mein Haus und meine Insel. Verschwindet!*" The girl translating was staring at the ground and her voice trembled, "You cannot come in, this is my house and my island. Get out!" she muttered.

"Frau Hochstetter," Carey said carefully, "you know that by this warrant I have the authority to search this house and pull it apart if I so choose,"

She ripped it from his fingers, tore it up and stamped on it.

Carey sighed and became very cold. "He is here, isn't he?" he said conversationally to her. "But you're trying to delay me." Her face flinched before the translation was finished which confirmed Carey's belief that she knew much more English than she admitted to. "Pick her up and bring her with us," he said to Bangtail and Red Sandy who did it with considerable effort while Frau Radagunda shouted Dutch at him.

They broke the door lock, and went into the house which was shining and neat, through the hall, quick look in the blameless parlour and the shining kitchen filled with copper pans out the back, up the stairs and through the bedrooms, found a narrow spiral stair in a cupboard and followed it to three attic rooms for servants, the largest of which had a made bed with a half tester, a white velvet cloak hanging on a peg, a chest and a remarkable collection of books among which was a copy of *De Re Metallica*. He checked the chest which was full of polite conservative clothes that a merchant or engineer might wear, and a couple of workmen's hemp shirts and a leather mining tunic. Then he clattered down the spiral stairs again.

He smiled at Frau Radagunda who had stopped shouting and struggling and was standing stiffly in her hall.

"*Vielen Danke, mein Frau,*" he said to her, the only Dutch he knew and probably wrong. He swept a shallow bow to Frau Radagunda, who spat at him, walked out of the house and hurried to the boat landing.

"Sir Robert," came an old man's voice behind him, "may I speak with you?"

He turned, looked at a skinny old man in a respectable woollen suit and scholar's gown. "Will it help me find Joachim Hochstetter?"

"It might."

"And you are…?"

"Israel Waltz. I am the pastor here and also the barber surgeon."

"And?"

"Perhaps I can help you find Joachim?"

"Excellent. Where is he?"

"You know that most of the women here are Anabaptists?"

"No, I didn't."

"The menfolk go to church in Crossthwaite. The women stay here or come to the island if they live in Keswick and they pray together in the tenth house."

"Why are you telling me this?"

"The men too are infected, but the women also pray to Saint Sophia and the Theotokos, the God-bearer and the Holy Wisdom of God made manifest in the World."

"They are Papists?"

"No, Herr Ritter, I suppose you could call them Gnostics, if you know the word."

"I don't, I'm afraid. Now Pastor Waltz, this is all very interesting but…"

"Joachim is very close to his mother who is the daughter of a noted Anabaptist pastor. As happens with heretics, he started studying dangerous texts. The last time I spoke to him he laughed at me for being faithful to…to God. He said that the God of the Bible, Jehovah, is a monster. He says that if a man said and did the things that the Bible says that God said and did, we would call Him a madman or a demon and spurn Him. His mother and the other women are crazy to whine after God, or Jesus Christ, for that matter. The Devil is the only real power and men should do his will, even though he is evil and seeks the destruction of everything good."

"I never heard anything more perverse. Now, Pastor…"

Waltz nodded. "But persuasive. There are many passages in the Old Testament that make me feel Joachim may be right…"

"So where is Joachim Hochstetter?"

Waltz was staring fixedly at the ground. "He says the Catholic church is clearly the Devil's creature…"

"There I can agree with him…"

"So he says it doesn't matter if he pretends to be a Catholic and it doesn't matter what he does."

"Herr Pastor, will you get to the point?"

Waltz grabbed his arm. "What do you think? Do you think it's right that God is really the Devil?"

Carey sighed and shook him off, his eyes scanning the island for anything unusual, any sign of Joachim. The last thing he wanted was an abstruse theological discussion with the poor confused minister. But he could see nothing, all was quiet, Frau Radagunda standing with her arms folded and a ferocious scowl on her face, the boatman fishing peacefully in the reeds, still smoking his pipe, the Keswick men he had borrowed looking bored and wanting to go home.

He blinked and put his hand on his sword and wordlessly asked the Lord Jesus for help in rescuing a bewildered soul.

"Pastor, look at Satan in the Gospel where he tempts Our Lord," he said slowly. "He's a trickster, a coney catcher, a liar. He tries to get the Redeemer to bow down and worship him—and Jesus says, "You shall worship the Lord your God." If Satan was actually God, why would he have said such a thing? And the Son of God would be likely to know if he was God anyway. Instead Jesus just says, you shall worship the Lord your God—clearly different."

Waltz was looking strained. "Then why is God so cruel?"

"I can only say that perhaps He seems cruel from our perspective but not from a heavenly perspective. So, where is Joachim?"

He could see Bangtail coming towards him from the Frau, probably to ask him when they could go back to the inn, and then saw Bangtail's expression change to alarm and horror. He started sprinting towards him, shouting, the words indistinct and then Carey heard "Ware the gun!" just as Bangtail cannoned into him and Carey heard the boom of an arquebus behind and to the right of him. Bangtail knocked him over and landed in the mud on top of him. Carey rolled out from under, got up and chased the boatman who was trying to reload the arquebus he had hidden under a sack.

Just as Carey came near the reeds, picking up and throwing stones at the boatman as he went, the man dropped his weapon and dived full length into the icy lake, ducking down and swimming into the reeds. Carey found himself floundering in the rushes, striking round him with his sword. He lost sight of the boatman and when his men arrived he had them search, knowing that they wouldn't find anyone.

Then he heard a howl from where he had been standing to discuss theology with the pastor, a terrible animal-like cry. He ran back cursing, drenched to the waist and the arming doublet completely ruined with its second dousing, so it was just as well he hadn't worn the olive brocade, and found Red Sandy kneeling beside Bangtail, tears pouring down his face.

He looked at Bangtail's chest and there was a hole, surrounded by splintered ribs with the blood bubbling out. A jack couldn't keep off an arquebus ball at that range, good though it was against a sword or axe, even an arrow at the end of its flight. That was the exit hole.

The bubbles in the blood said Bangtail would die, was dying, while Red Sandy clasped the English Graham to him and howled like a dog. There was no point trying anything, Hepburn or Hochstetter's aim had been good. So Carey stood there, his sword in his hand, turned his back on Red Sandy and Bangtail to give them some privacy, sick at heart and angry with himself for falling for Pastor Waltz's patter, absolutely enraged at himself for not spotting Jonathan Hepburn in his disguise as the boatman.

After what seemed like a short time, Allerdyce came hurrying up, his face strained. "Is he...?"

"Ay," said Carey, "my man is dying. A good man, shot by Jonathan Hepburn or Joachim Hochstetter, disguised as the boatman. Did you know it was him?"

Allerdyce shook his head. "Nay, d'ye think I'm that good at lying?"

"I don't know, Mr Allerdyce. Is it really Hochstetter?"

"It is. It's Joachim, all right. Two of my men recognised him, bald though he is now."

Maybe he was telling the truth. Everyone on the island must have known, though. All of them. And every one of the

Hochstetters, including Annamaria Hochstetter's husband, Mark Steinberger.

Carey heard footsteps, turned and found that Waltz had wisely made himself scarce. Emanuel Hochstetter was getting out of the same boat that had brought Allerdyce and was approaching slowly, with young Mr David behind him. Carey advanced on him.

"The boatman was Joachim Hochstetter, your brother, Mr David's brother," he said to Mr Emanuel. "I won't ask why you didn't betray him to me. I know why. He was one of your own, your kith and kin, and he had such plausible stories about how I had falsely accused him of the assassination attempt on the King of Scots and that all he would do here was lie low. He has just tried to kill me and by the...act of God killed my man instead."

Mr Emanuel swallowed. His anxious face looked fifty years old or more.

"You've had time to get a letter from Leith Steelyard, that there was such an attempt and that Joachim disappeared from Court just before it happened," Carey went on relentlessly. "His assistants went through Leith but not Joachim himself. You know that Mrs Carleton was killed..."

"No, it was suicide..."

"You should stop listening to Joachim. Look at the body, Mr Hochstetter, and then perhaps you can enlighten me on how Mrs Carleton strangled herself and afterwards travelled to Derwent Water, lay down there in six feet of water, and then piled rocks on her own body."

Mr Emanuel said nothing, looking down.

"We're convening an inquest for her on Monday and reopening the inquest for Mr Carleton, and if we can find young Josef's body, we'll convene one for him too, make a nice set of it, and the murderer of all of them will be named as Joachim Hochstetter," said Allerdyce coldly. He was glaring at Mr Emanuel. "And Sir Robert's man too. Why d'ye think we dinna like ye Deutschers, eh? Apart from the way yer kobolds ruin the woods and land?"

Carey coughed and hoped there wouldn't be any riots. He turned back to Red Sandy who had laid Bangtail's body down, his own chest all covered with blood, and was shutting Bangtail's eyes with shaking hands. Leamus was approaching with a litter of oars, his statute cap held against his chest and his face solemn. He and Red Sandy heaved Bangtail's corpse onto it and returned to the boatlanding. Red Sandy was silent now and grey-faced, stumbling after the litter into the sunset.

"Ay," said Allerdyce, watching them go, "it's hard to lose a friend."

Carey caught himself and hurried after the litter. "Red Sandy," he said to the man who seemed not to hear him. He was muttering fiercely to himself.

"Where's the bastard gone? Eh? Where? He's thought it through, he allus does, he likes killing. Dinna fancy getting killed for sure. He knew where he was swimming for."

Now that was true and interesting to contemplate. Carey nodded and then touched Red Sandy's shoulder. "I will never forget what Bangtail did," he said, "because he saved my life. He was..."

"...nobbut a reiver, a Graham..."

"Yes, he was. And also he was a brave and generous man who took that arquebus ball for me."

Red Sandy sighed from his guts, shook his head as if to clear it, stumbled on after the litter, helped to move the corpse gently into the boat and then knelt on one knee beside it to go across the water. Once he looked back and shouted, "Ay, he's gone somewhere warm."

Of course he had but where?

Carey lifted his head and breathed, "The smelthouses."

They were surrounded by a stout wicker fence with two gates in it to let the road through. The gates were locked, the charcoal fires burning and reeking inside like the mouth of Hell and Carey hammered with his fist on the gate and Mr Allerdyce stood with his thumbs in his belt. "Open in the name of the Queen!" bellowed Carey and took an axe to the gate, hit it once with a satisfying crunch.

Mark Steinberger put his head round the gate and two of Allerdyce's men blocked it open with polearms. Allerdyce waved the warrant in his face and shouted something complicated in Norman French, then Carey and Allerdyce both shoved through and the men of the town's Trained Band spread out through the smelting houses. Carey waited in the central yard all piled with sacks of charcoal. A shout went up, Carey hurried over and found a broad patch of damp that had been part-mopped by a boy, and the boatman's clothes held out on a pincer, still smoking from the fire but not quite burnt yet.

Carey sat down next to the cold cupellation furnace and stretched his legs. "Bring me Mark Steinberger," he said. The man came in with one of the Keswickers, his face closed, shut tight. Carey considered him for a moment and then looked away, waiting patiently. Steinberger cleared his throat, but wisely kept silence.

"I don't believe that you approve of Joachim Hochstetter, Herr Steinberger," said Carey. "I think you are foolishly indulging your mother-in-law's dangerous doting on her son. But the matter has gone beyond family feeling. Joachim threatens all of you, you know? He's a killer and already at the horn in Scotland for attempting to kill the King of Scots."

Steinberger said nothing.

"You have made your home here, bringing your wonderful mining skills and incidentally excellent beer and bread, you have brought prosperity as well as kobolds to this land. But now the Keswickers will remember that you are foreigners and speak a foreign tongue, and Sir Robert Cecil, the son of my Lord Burghley, a chief shareholder in the Company of Mines Royal, is starting to ask questions."

Still Steinberger said nothing.

"I wasn't ill of an ague, you know, Herr Steinberger," Carey added conversationally. Steinberger's face didn't move.

Carey shook his head and leaned back in his still damp clothes. His heart was now beating slow and hard with anger and sorrow at Bangtail's death. "No," he said, "I went north and east following Wattie Graham's special midnight packtrain, the one that left from here about five days ago. I'm not sure why it left when I was in town. Perhaps there was some kind of emergency at the destination in Scotland."

Steinberger seemed to have been turned to stone where he stood. There was a rustle at the other end of the room. Carey ignored it, it sounded like charcoal settling.

"I wondered where they were going, so I followed them with a couple of my men," he explained, "all the way to Carlisle and past it, into the Debateable Land and on into Scotland where they brought the silver straight to Ritchie Graham's tower of Brackenhill."

Steinberger said nothing.

"That's the silver you cupellate from the lead, once you get the lead and silver out of the copper, and then you cupellate again to get the gold out to give the Queen, as you have ever since you came here, perhaps. You admitted the copper and gold, noted it in the accounts, but you forgot the silver and sent it north through Wattie's good offices to Ritchie Graham of Brackenhill who needs the metal for coining."

"He says he has a warrant."

"He does not have a warrant."

"He showed me it, from Henry VIII."

"That warrant expired when Good King Henry died." Steinberger contemplated the floor again. "And none of that silver ever sees a customs officer. It comes back, some of it, as sixpences and shillings and pennies to pay the miners; some of it I'm sure goes into your coffers. Maybe some of it even goes to Augsburg. For Goldscope mine, like Gottesgaab in Allemayne, is a rich gift from God."

"Not as rich as …"

"You and the other Deutschers are still here, Herr Steinberger. It's rich enough. Perhaps the juices have hardened into equally rich veins in some of the other places where you're mining. Don't the damnable lying accounts say you are busy digging at eighteen different places? But not a penny of God's gift of silver have you paid the Queen."

Silence.

"I probably can't catch Joachim Hochstetter until you give him to me," said Carey. "He knows the area, he knows the people, perhaps he's swived more of them than poor Mrs Carleton."

"Mrs Carleton?"

"The smith's wife who went missing a few days ago. Haven't you heard?"

"Ve have two smelting campaigns running, I haf been very…"

"Mrs Carleton was throttled to death and then dumped in the lake with rocks on her. Maybe three or four days ago."

For some reason that seemed to hit Steinberger hard. He stared at the floor, clearly thinking. "Vould…the man who did it, he might be vet?"

"Wet? I should think so. It's not as easy as you may think to put a corpse into water and then rocks on top. Why?"

Steinberger only shook his head. Carey waited, then went on.

"I have a letter already drafted in Carlisle which will be sent to London only if I do not return," he said, thinking about the letter to his father he had left with Bessie. He wasn't lying very much. "In it I recount what I have found out about the silver from Gottesgaab or Goldscope and how disgracefully you have cheated the Queen of her rights for years. It is addressed to Mr

Secretary Cecil and I suspect he will find it very interesting."

Steinberger's expression still hadn't changed, but a runnel of sweat ran down the side of his granite face.

"You are blackmailing us to give up Joachim for the silver."

"Yes," said Carey, "he's a killer, an outlaw in Scotland and in England, and will cause you nothing but trouble. Give him to me and perhaps I will not send the letter."

"Perhaps we could also arrange a small but regular payment to you as well, Herr Ritter," said Steinberger quietly.

Carey contemplated the man for a moment. "As you do for my Lord Scrope and perhaps Sir Richard Lowther, the other Deputy Warden." Carey thought that that would be very acceptable and quite appropriate but he was not going to deliberately make Steinberger's life any easier.

Steinberger moved speedily sideways to the door. "I must speak to my brothers-in-law and Frau Hochstetter."

"By all means, but I suggest you do not waste your time with the Frau."

Steinberger grimaced and was gone.

They called a hue and cry throughout the town for Joachim Hochstetter. The town crier cried a description of him at the market cross, the parish church, and Crossthwaite church, a torch beside him and a boy beating a drum before him. The whole of the little town was turned over in the darkness and the gold of torches. Carey had taken the precaution of setting a guard on the boats at the island and with Allerdyce he went house to house, checking outhouses and sheds, and found nothing, no trace of the man. Maybe he had run out of town into the white hills where he would die…No, he had a plan.

So Carey went back to the smelthouses with Tovey and his

book, identifying each furnace, each smelter and what they did, each channel and tank of water. He didn't insist on the men opening the ovens that were too hot to touch, but he looked everywhere else. You had to admit, the Deutschers knew how to build and work machinery, there was something very satisfying in the way the furnaces were arranged and how the ore came in at one end and came out the other as metal cakes. The whole place smelled raw, of the charcoal and the metals themselves. In the house with the cupellation ovens, two of the ovens were working and closed, the other two in the next room were cold and empty. Sitting there on the edge of a cold furnace, patiently listening, you could imagine the whole world turned into a smelting house, no trees or grass, just chimneys and great noisy machines, smoke everywhere.

Carey realised he had dozed off into a nightmare, and sat up. The fires were banked and the room was empty as the hue and cry moved away.

Except it wasn't empty. Carey had heard a sound like a dog at the mouth of one of the furnaces. It was hot from the fires burning next door and sweat was starting to go down his back. He sat and pretended to go to sleep again. He was in fact still tired from covering seventy miles on foot in a few days and returning on horseback. But he wanted to see what manner of dog slept in a furnace—and was it perhaps Joachim?

He heard breathing coming towards him, it sounded high-pitched for a man, but he gripped his dagger and prepared to jump the man, opened his eyelids.

A filthy boy stood there, staring at him with huge hollow eyes. "Josef, the smith's son," he said quietly.

The boy nodded and then remembered his manners and bowed.

"I am very glad to see you're not dead, Josef," Carey said gravely. "Who killed your mother?"

"Mr Joachim," said Josef, his fists clenched and his eyes shut. "He grabbed her and held her neck…her throat after she shouted at him for killing Father and I…didn't…I couldn't…"

Tears were carving channels in the soot on his face.

"I was afraid to try and stop him. I couldn't, I was too afraid. I hid in the reeds. I let my mother be killed…" He put his head in his hands and wailed. "*Ich bin ein schlechter Sohn!*"

Carey put his hand on the lad's shoulder, filthy though it was. "You couldn't have stopped him," he said thoughtfully. "You're too small still. All you could have done was to get killed as well. But tell me where he is and I'll kill him for you. I'm not too small, I'm as big as he is, in fact bigger, and I'm certain I'm a better swordsman because I'm the Deputy Warden of Carlisle and he's only an engineer."

Josef's eyes snapped open. "You will? But he's Frau Radagunda's favourite."

"How unfortunate. I am not only happy to kill him but I have His Majesty of Scotland's direct order that he be destroyed for trying to assassinate the King at New Year. Where is he?"

"I don't know for sure. I came here for I was afraid to go home, it's empty, the journeymen aren't there, nobody is there, Joachim might come and find me. Joachim is friends with everybody, nobody will believe he killed my mother."

The boy's voice trembled and he gulped several times and Carey saw that he was shivering. He took his cloak off and put it round Josef's shoulders, sat the boy down next to him on the ledge of the cold furnace. "Why not go to your relatives, do you have no aunts and uncles?"

"Mark Steinberger is my uncle but he works for the Hochstetters, he will never believe me, never…Nobody will…"

"I believe you Josef, and I think Herr Steinberger would too," Carey said, "but you have to tell me where you've been hiding. I was worried you were dead too."

"Oh." The boy looked surprised. "I've been sleeping here among the cakes of silver in the store house since…since my *Mutter*…I thought I was safe here, so long as I kept still when the men were working and sometimes I found food…But then…but then…"

He started crying into the fur of Carey's cloak, which made Carey sigh. "Did you see Joachim again?"

A nod. "He came running in here, an hour ago, he came running in, gasping, all wet and shivering. Dieter and him had an argument in Deutsch, Dieter was telling him to leave, he didn't want him here and he laughed at Dieter and said, "Silver?" He took off his wet clothes and Dieter fetched him a shirt and breeches and jerkin and a mining tunic with the padded hood and clogs. And he made Dieter give him a gun, a small one for wildfowling, and the powder and shot."

That was smart. There were so many miners and they all looked so similar in their mining tunics. "So? Where did he go?"

"Dieter asked him and he said, "Gottesgaab, I have business there."

"Do you think he was telling the truth?"

Josef looked down, shrugged. "I don't know."

"He is going to hide in Gottesgaab mine at least?"

Josef was shivering again. "If you follow him, you'll die because he knows the mine and you don't. But he's frightened of you. When he was alone, I heard him cursing you."

"And you're sure it's Joachim?"

"Yes. He shaved off his curly hair. But it's him."

Carey smiled his hunting smile. "Do you know the mine well enough to guide me?"

Josef swallowed. "I have been down with my father when we were working on the great waterwheel and other times as well. It's very big, but I will try."

Carey called Tovey from where he was looking at the machines and measuring them and they hurried into town from the smelthouses, picking up Red Sandy at the gate. At the Oak, they found Leamus, and Carey went up to his room and brought down his matched pair of wheel lock dags in their carrying cases. They took ponies at a ridiculous hire price from the landlord because they were in a hurry and it was late at night, cantered out of town westwards towards Newlands and Goldscope mine, with Josef in Carey's cloak bumping up and down in the saddle and holding the pommel tight. Allerdyce was nowhere to be found and the men of the Keswick trained band had gone home at sunset, so that was all the men he could muster. Carey wished he had brought more in the first place, as usual.

The mine bell had long sounded and the valley was quiet apart from the chuckle of water going through the waterwheels which had been uncoupled from the stampers. The ore-roasting continued day and night and the smoke blew across the hills. There was one lantern lit on what looked like a bunkhouse and another at the mine entrance. It wasn't locked, which made Carey frown.

Josef shook his head and walked through to the main entrance, a place where there were many tools all laid out neatly on shelves, mattocks and hammers and pickaxes. On a higher shelf was an array of lanterns and candles on little trays with a ribbon that went round the neck. There was one lantern missing. Josef took one of the candles with a short ribbon and lit it from the entrance lantern, so Carey also took one and lit it and put the ribbon over his head. Damn it, he didn't have his helmet, only his tall hat. He took it off and put it on the shelf and Josef gave him a workman's statute cap, stuffed with wool which he put on reluctantly.

The boy was already standing at the top of the stout ladder which plunged down into utter darkness.

"I don't know that I should take you with me," he said to the boy, though from the look of it, they would be the other way around, with the boy taking him.

"You should," said Josef.

"If we find him in here, he'll be all the more dangerous, because cornered."

"I know the mine too. I do. From when I was a little boy I came here with *Vater*."

"Yes, but…" Carey was looking down the hole. He did not want to go down the ladder into that darkness which looked so thick and physical, with all his heart he did not want to.

Did it really matter so much? Maybe he could let Joachim go? After all, he hadn't actually killed the King of Scots…

Ay, in two ingenious attempts, by sheer luck and the grace of God. He had murdered three people, at least, Carey thought, and I told the King I would deal with him. Am I to be foresworn?

There was also the undoubted fact that Joachim held the upper hand, alone though he was. Not only was he on familiar ground but he could simply wait in ambush at some underground chokepoint and jump out with an axe. And he would.

"Are there other entrances to the mine?"

"Ay," said Josef, "they are not sure how many. There's one round the other side of the hill where they bring in the ponies and places the water escapes…"

"Where are the ponies now?"

"In their stables with Hans to watch them. They work the machines."

"Leamus, will you go around the hill and wake the man who's looking after the ponies? Red Sandy, will you keep a watch here with Mr Tovey?"

He reached out to put his hand on the ladder and found his hand wouldn't obey him. He did not want to go down the ladder into darkness, even with a lit candle on his chest. He didn't want to do it, and how long would a mere candle stay lit, down there in the dark? Also he would get candlewax on his doublet.

Maybe Joachim was waiting there, just out of sight, waiting for legs to come down so he could cut them off…

"This is Furdernuss shaft," said Josef, "It's not very deep, only eighty feet, and under it is the great waterwheel…"

"What—bigger than that one?"

"That one is small. The great waterwheel is twenty-two-foot round to bring up the water from deep below."

"And it's down there?"

"Yes."

Too much information, Carey didn't want to know any more. Maybe Joachim wasn't even there. Maybe he had only taken the mining tunic as a ruse, only pretended to come to the mine, maybe even persuaded young Josef to lie and draw Carey in and then…

I am afraid, he thought suddenly, looking at himself as if he were a stranger. I don't want to follow Joachim into the mine, not only because he might ambush me but because I'm…because I'm scared of the dark in the mine…

He was immediately angry with himself for the fear and grabbed the ladder in defiance of it, but at the same time, something inside him baulked absolutely. What was wrong with him? His spirit was willing to climb down the ladder, find Joachim and kill him. But his body was not. His body said no.

His mouth was as dry as a smith's leather glove.

An earlier time came back to him, last year when he was in France and leading men through the cramped mine tunnels dug into the side of a fortress. He had gathered the engineers' maps and learned them as well as he could, and had his men practising crawling on their hands and knees. They had gone in and crawled through the stifling darkness with little candles on their chests and broken through to the counter-tunnels and found them empty and…

The older Captain of Engineers had immediately ordered a retreat, over Carey's orders and to his annoyance. Carey had been the last man scrambling out just as the petards in the counter-tunnels had exploded and that whole side of the hill had slumped into ruination, nearly taking Carey with it. He had been so appalled that he had apologised to the Captain of Engineers who only grunted that Carey was a young fool, but seemed capable of learning.

He needed more men. He couldn't go haring into the mine after Joachim; he needed men who were expert in it and could go cautiously and methodically, just as the Captain of Engineers had done and incidentally saved Carey's unworthy hide from being buried alive.

But would the miners be on Joachim's side, wouldn't they want to protect him?

They might, true. But at any rate, he could not go climbing down into a mine where eighty foot of ladder was just the start and not with only courageous young Josef with him, because that might be brave and dashing but would play into Joachim's hands and he and the boy would die.

"Where do the miners sleep?"

"The men who have the first shift tomorrow and the bachelors sleep in the bunkhouse, so they don't have so far to walk."

"Who is the captain?"

"Ulrich Schlegel. He has his own little cottage."

"I remember. He doesn't speak English, does he?"

"He understands it. I can translate. Will we not go into the mine?"

"No, Josef. I'm too ignorant and Joachim is too clever. Can we lock it up?"

"Yes, there is a key to the door but we never lock it…"

They found the large iron key and locked the door, which would slow Joachim down and then Carey followed Josef to the little carved wooden house nearby with the small tidy garden around it, locked up tight for the night.

It was late, at least nine o'clock. Without a doubt the mine captain was in bed. Carey knocked firmly on the door, knocked again. Josef shouted anxiously in Deutsch.

At last there was a grunt and the sound of the bar being moved and the middle-aged greybeard in a nightcap and dressing gown peered out of the top half of the door with a mattock in his hand.

"Herr Steiger Schlegel," said Carey formally, "I'm very sorry for troubling you at this time of night but it's urgent…"

Schlegel's eyes fell on Josef and he exclaimed, put down the mattock, opened the lower half of the door and hugged Josef, who muttered something in Deutsch and the greybeard waved them volubly into the little house where they sat by the covered fire. Mrs Schlegel was sitting up in a cupboard bed near the fire. She jumped out of bed, talking nineteen to the dozen in Deutsch, started sharpening the fire and pulled a stockpot on a bracket over the flames. All this time Josef was talking in their peculiar language. Sometimes Carey thought he could understand bits of it but then he realised that he still couldn't make out what was being said. He heard the name Herr Joachim though.

By the time Josef had finished, Frau Schlegel had given him a wooden bowl of soup, offered some to Carey, been told off by her husband, then offered him some beer from a barrel in the corner instead, in a large pewter mug that she mulled skilfully with the poker.

It sounded like Herr Captain Schlegel was swearing, for Frau Schlegel said, "Now then, less of that, Mr Schlegel." Her comfortable Northern tones surprised Carey.

"You're English?"

"Ay. I speak to him in English and Dutch, he speaks to me in Dutch and we get along very well. Did Herr Ingenieur Joachim really do all that and kill poor Mrs Carleton?"

"And more, Mrs Schlegel," said Carey, very relieved. "He killed Mr Carleton too because the smith knew too much about how Hochstetter had planned to kill the King of Scots for the King of Spain."

"Fancy?" said Mrs Schlegel. "Both of them?"

"Joachim tried to shoot me with an arquebus today, missed, and killed one of my men instead."

"Och."

"I believe he may have taken shelter in Goldscope mine and I want to find him before he gets out and goes to Workington. There will be good tracks in the snow if he comes out again, but I want to find and stop him now."

"And ye need a guide," she said, her eyes narrowing, "a miner to see ye through the mine."

"Yes."

"But Mr Schlegel isn't a fighting man. He might get killed."

Schlegel himself interrupted at this point and they had a big argument, Mr and Mrs Schlegel going at it hammer and tongs while Josef gulped the soup and Carey sipped the hot beer. At last Carey stood up and went softly out of the house, Josef trotted after him like a stray dog.

Carey was just going to tell the boy to go back to Mrs Schlegel when Ulrich Schlegel came out wearing his leather coat with the pointed tail and the pointy hood and a lantern in each hand. He was looking extremely mulish. Mrs Schlegel was getting dressed, pulling on her kirtle and she shouted something from the middle of it.

"What was that?" he asked Josef.

"She said she knows the kobolds won't like Joachim, he doesn't respect them."

Schlegel jerked his head at Carey and Carey followed him, feeling very relieved. They unlocked the double doors into the mine, found everything as it had been, Schlegel put one lantern on a shelf and took a candle. He went to the ladder which was bolted in place, diving deep into the earth. Without hesitation, Schlegel shook it, spat down the hole, and stepped on it, his hands and feet going down smoothly and quickly.

Josef went down too and Carey followed. "No two feet on one rung," came the soprano yell from Josef and Carey remembered the same from the Master's Mate of the ship *Elizabeth Bonaventure*, Cumberland's pride and joy. He changed the way he climbed down, eighty rungs, came to a tunnel that was chipped out of the rock for someone shorter than he was. He followed Schlegel along a tunnel with running water in a drain carved beside it, past a kind of waterfall where water plunged down a shaft to a cistern, and then uphill for a long way until they came to an opening where a stream was running into the mine. Schlegel lifted his lantern and looked for footprints in the snow, but there were only rabbit and fox prints, no boots. A young voice called in Deutsch from the rocks above, Schlegel answered. Then he grunted and turned around, gestured for Carey to go back the way they had come.

Now it all became mazelike and confusing. They went back down to the waterfall, stepped past it on a narrow track and listened to the water going down under its grill. They went on past the bottom of the Furdernuss shaft and on where the tunnels were just big enough for a man of average height to walk. Carey was sweating and his neck was already aching and he had hit his head a couple of times. Schlegel shoved past him at a wider point where another tunnel joined at right angles, and walked quickly along it. The next thing was the sound of his feet briskly going down another ladder in a deep shaft.

It was horrible. His lantern made practically no impression on the darkness and Carey's heart was pounding. Too soon he came to the ladder, offset from the main passageway, again plunging down into even thicker darkness. He could hear Schlegel far below, and Josef's lighter steps, and followed, swearing under his breath and promising Jesus Christ to completely stop all future fornication if He would only let Carey out of the darkness.

"Might Joachim be in one of the higher tunnels?" he asked breathlessly at the bottom, more to say something.

"They are dead ends," explained Josef. "They end at the veins."

They walked along in the black velvet darkness, Schlegel swinging his lamp, Carey's boots and his in the trickle of water.

The roof came down suddenly and Carey caught his head again, which was partly padded by his statute cap. The pointed hoods were a clever solution, Carey thought dizzily, you would feel the roof getting lower. Schlegel muttered something that sounded rude. The tunnel was so narrow, just wide enough for Schlegel and tall enough, which meant Carey had to keep his neck bent and walk sideways. He couldn't even turn his shoulders. Every so often Schlegel would stop and hush them and Carey asked him what he was listening for.

"Shh," he said sharply, "Joachim und kobolds, off course."

There were sounds, all strange and distorted. Dripping water but occasional bangs and creaks, the echos of their feet, water tumbling below them. Carey opened his mouth and tried to quiet his breathing. Schlegel was talking to Josef.

"Herr Mine Captain is worried about the great waterwheel. He's worried about the mine flooding, it sounds wrong."

They passed a shaft full of falling water, went on a little and Schlegel started down yet another ladder plunging into darkness. "Oh, Jesus," Carey said to himself, fighting down the fear in his stomach as he climbed down the ladder himself. How deep would they go? Was Schlegel working for Joachim, perhaps? Maybe he was deliberately leading Carey and Josef into the deepest part of the mine to betray them...

They walked back on themselves along a slightly wider though still low-cut tunnel where the noise of water got louder and louder, as if the Thames was falling into a hole above them and the floor became awash with water. Schlegel looked down and suddenly speeded up, saying something that sounded like "*Scheisse!*"

They came at last to an enormous waterwheel, taller than Carey, creaking round and round. Schlegel said, "*Scheisse*" again and Carey realised that while the huge waterwheel was turning under the pressure of the water splashing down from above, the bucket chain that plunged even deeper into the mine was not working and no water was being tipped into a channel that led downhill and out of sight. Even so, the channel was filling with the waste water from the wheel.

He blinked at it in the light of the lantern, Schlegel snarled some orders, and Josef grabbed him. "We have to clear the blockage," he said, "otherwise the mine will flood. Herr Capitan will find out why the bucket chain has stopped. Quick!"

"Christ," said Carey, "but…"

"If it floods, we will die," said Josef and led the way into the channel filling with water. Schlegel pressed some kind of tool into Carey's hand, and Carey followed, bent double, the freezing water over his ankles, the lantern guttering, his sword scraping against the side of the channel. He bumped into Josef who was at a blockage made of rocks, pulling them out. Only one person could work at a time and it was so cramped, Carey had to kneel to get at the rocks with his mattock.

"Take the rocks out," said Josef, "or when the water comes, the blockage will go back."

Carey pulled his furlined cloak from Josef's shoulders, started piling rocks into it, then backed up the tunnel on his knees, into the open space around the great waterwheel, found what looked like a metal box on wheels, oh a truckle, heaved and tipped the rocks into it, glimpsed Schlegel climbing around the wheel, ignoring the sheer drop with the bucket chain beneath him, went back, filled the cloak with rocks again. His head was throbbing; he couldn't seem to catch his breath. Suddenly Josef pitched forward into the water which was at waist level, and so Carey towed him backwards along with the rocks, got to the waterwheel, then went back and attacked the pile of rocks again, though his freezing wet hands and his knees were sore and he couldn't see and the lantern was going out leaving him in the velvet darkness, up to his chest in water and unable to say why he was there. Except he knew there had to be an end to the blockage somewhere and so he dug and scrabbled and panted and finally…two rocks broke apart and were swept down the channel, others followed. Carey held the walls against the current and breathed the air that was coming in from where the water poured out of the rock somewhere far away.

Shaking, he climbed against the flow and heard a creaking and a clattering which was the bucket chain moving, pulling up water from the deeper depths of the mine, pouring it into the drainage channel he had unblocked.

He stood there dripping and gasping, while Schlegel patted young Josef's cheek until his eyes fluttered open.

"*Ich versteh' es nicht*," Schlegel was saying over and over.

Josef sat up, coughed. "He's saying he doesn't understand why Joachim would flood the mine if he's in it. Why?"

"Samson? Pulling down the mine on top of himself…" Carey suggested, still breathing heavily. "No, that's not Joachim. Why didn't he break the wheel if he wanted to flood the mine, instead of just uncoupling it?"

Schlegel asked Carey something and Josef translated, "How did you know he only uncoupled the bucket chain?"

"You got it working so quickly. The lower levels would flood but anything above that might stay dryish. What's he playing at?"

Schlegel took his lantern and started walking back to the ladder that led upwards and downwards to where the veins of copper ore were. He walked past and the passage went on with a kink in it, Schlegel said something about it and Josef laughed.

"What?" asked Carey, very tired of not being able to understand.

"Herr Mine Captain was one of the young men who dug out this adit from daylight to wheelpit and he says they were very happy when the tunnel driving in from the hillside and the tunnel driving out from the wheelpit met, even if the tunnel has a kink in it."

"Oh," said Carey who was looking in dismay at his hands which were blistered and bleeding.

Suddenly he saw a tiny light to his side where there was nothing. But there was another tunnel at right angles. The light disappeared again, came back. He could hear Schlegel and Josef ahead, but he turned and squeezed into the new tunnel, tried to peer into the darkness to see the light there.

And then he stopped because although he still couldn't see anything there was the sound of boots echoing from every direction, boots and shouts in Deutsch. Kobolds, he wondered? He was standing in the blackness wondering what they looked like, wondering how big they were…His heart was still hammering, he was stock still in a tunnel in the living rock where he had to keep his head bent which was making his neck so tired, and now he was frightened of being lost, of kobolds, of Joachim, of the dark…Christ's Wounds, it was so dark.

He took a couple of deep breaths, tried to get a grip on his fear. What he wanted to do was curl up into a ball and hide. But he had to find Schlegel and Josef again. That meant turning round and going back where he came from. So he carefully did that and after a short time, he was back at the kink in the tunnel and went on. There was a scraping noise and something that sounded like a soft laugh, so he went back and found there was no tunnel entrance next to the kink. There was what felt like rocky wall there. He stared at it, blinked his eyes shut, opened them, tried banging on the rocks and they sounded solid.

But by that time there was another young man coming along the tunnel from the ladder up, carrying another lantern and with a candle on his breast. The young lad who had come along the tunnel was speaking to Schlegel in a concerned voice.

"Where's Joachim?" Carey asked.

"Ay, we're after him but we've got to get the bellows working," said the lad in comforting Cumbrian tones.

"Why?"

"Bring air in, listen, can you hear them?" There was another sound magnified by the tunnels, a whoomf whoomf sound. "That's the walking bellows, they're getting Ox to put him in his harness."

Carey felt unusually stupid. "Ox?" he asked.

"Ay, he's the bellows pony, very strong."

"Have you got the exits covered?"

"Ay, Frau Schlegel did that first, it's why there's only two of us in the mine and two at the bellows, your men, in fact, the skinny clerk and Red Sandy, because you don't need to know anything to step on the bellows. Everyone else is as at the daylights in twos."

"Good," said Carey, feeling a little better.

Schlegel meanwhile had cleared another blockage and the young man was piling the rocks into a truck at high speed. Schlegel gestured to Carey to follow and they started walking downwards and the water running along a channel to one side was getting faster. His boots slipped on the wet rock.

"Might Joachim be here?"

"*Nein*," said Schlegel and laughed.

Carey sighed and turned back along the passage. He was exhausted from being hunched over and his head was hurting.

"We are looking for him, though?"

"Ay sir," said Josef, "Herr Steiger said. We think he's still in the mine. When we have all the exits, then we work inwards."

"You've done this before?"

"Yes, sir, whenever somebody is lost or injured."

"Ah."

"This is the last exit." The lad motioned Carey to go ahead and at last they came to a fissure in the rock where there was a channel and the water came out and was gathered into a pool. The dam was in place and a large uncoupled wheel stood silent in the moonlight, snow like sugar everywhere. Carey raised Schlegel's lantern high, looking for tracks, found some fresh ones in the new snow. Then he saw another greybeard standing there, Herr Moser, the other mine captain, with a crossbow in his hands. That lightened Carey's mood a little.

"Where's young Josef?"

"I sent him back to the Furdernuss shaft. He is tired."

An exchange of Deutsch and the greybeard lifted his hand in salute. They turned away from the silver moonlight and the snow and headed into the dark again, and Carey needed to summon up every ounce of courage to do it.

What's wrong with me, he wondered, it's only darkness. Why am I so afraid?

Schlegel was talking and he waved the lad back to translate. "Now we move inwards with lanterns. Now we catch him."

The shouts from miner to miner echoed through the rock, distorting and sometimes sounding near, sometimes distant. They moved methodically, checking each side tunnel and only going on when they found them clear.

And then they were at the central ladder of Furdernuss shaft again, the ladder plunging upwards into the darkness, and there were three miners and Schlegel looking at each other and arguing in Deutsch and Josef still there, looking anxious.

"All right," said Carey, "how did we miss him?"

"Impossible," said Schlegel.

"If he was here, he's still here," explained the lad who had replaced Josef as translator-in-chief.

"Yes. But where?"

Carey tried to think and pay no attention to the shadows licking hungrily round the edges of the lamplight. "Are there tunnels Joachim might know of that you don't?"

"*Nein.*"

"Do you know all the tunnels?"

"Off course," said Schlegel indignantly, and said much more in Deutsch.

"He's saying he has helped dig every part of this mine, he has been here since he was a *Junge* and came here with the first men from Augsburg…" explained Josef and the young lad in tandem.

"I know," said Carey wearily. "But couldn't Joachim have found another tunnel? Is that impossible?"

More angry Deutsch words but suddenly Josef said, "Kobold

workings! Perhaps there are kobold workings here. I thought I smelled fresh air."

Schlegel stopped and looked at the boy, then waved him ahead. "What are kobold workings?" asked Carey.

Josef said, "Places where somebody else dug for silver, a long time ago. Sometimes we find their tools, in other mines and open workings, made of stone or antlers or sometimes bronze-tipped. Sometimes we find falls of rock and the kobolds' bones."

"Some say they are the Fae," Josef added, "or maybe they are Romans or Greeks?"

"Much more likely."

"In most places where you find silver or gold, somebody was there before you."

"I thought I saw lantern light at the kink in the...what is it? Adit? Off to my right. As if there was a tunnel there..."

They went back down the ladders, Josef was sniffing as he went, came to where the tunnel kinked, the rock looked solid. "No," he said, "maybe I made a mistake."

Carey looked down and saw something odd. There was yellow dust sprinkled on the ground, like sand, and it stopped short under what looked like rock. But it wasn't sand, it glittered in the lantern light. Surely it wasn't gold dust? Was it? He lifted a little on his fingernail, smelled it, held it near the lantern. It looked like gold dust, shining in the dim light.

According to Agricola, where you find silver, sometimes you find gold, and you might find pure gold if the vein is rich enough. Was it possible that Joachim had come upon a vein of gold and hidden it with some kind of barrier? That would explain why he came back, for sure. Gold did that to people.

Carey waited a moment, then tested the rock beside him which didn't move. He tried pushing it, sliding it, pulled it... and felt something give. The section of tunnel moved towards him and he slipped sideways through the gap with his lantern, left it open behind him.

He felt his way through tunnels until he came to an open area.

There was silver light high up and he realised he was almost through to the other side of the hill, and that was a hole letting the moonlight in.

On the nearest wall was what looked like a river of brightness flowing through the rock which picked up the moon's colour but was yellow, not white. It was in a deep channel that had been chipped out of the rock. Carey looked at it and did not believe what he was seeing. Maybe it was pyrites, fool's gold.

There were steps cut in the rock, ancient and slippery. Carey looked down, tried to see. "Where is Joachim?" he asked himself, like a child playing a game, to give himself courage.

He started down the steps carefully and found another hole in the opposite wall where moonlight came in. He looked through the hole. There was a platform and a sheer drop of fifty feet, some snow had come in through the hole recently.

He looked back and saw the steps cut in the rock, leading downwards and a new scuff on one of the steps and so he returned and went down holding his lantern tightly, sometimes needing to sit and feel his way down the steps until he came to another small stream of water, heading purposefully for an unseen exit.

All he needs is one exit, he thought to himself, just one. And the water's got to come out somewhere.

And suddenly he thought, Why did he come back into the mine now? Because it's a good place to trap me? Maybe a good place to hide too, we made the town too hot for him. But still he could have come back later, when the hue and cry had died down a little...No, this is a trap, specially for me. That gold dust on the ground was bait.

Carey paused then, looking up at the hole where moonlight was coming in. It was a gift, a gift from God, Gottesgaab. Somehow seeing it gave him courage.

He followed the stream, bending, sliding past narrow places, the flame sometimes going low in the lantern. Did that mean bad air? He pushed on through a crack where the rock changed and became crumbly. Suddenly he came out in a larger space that smelled of metal and earth and strongly of fox, a place that already had firelight in it, on a ledge. His own lantern flame got stronger and he looked up and around in a great space like a cathedral. He saw lines and stipples in orange, black, and white on the walls and blinked and suddenly saw the animals on the walls, thousands of them. There were deer and creatures like bulls and what looked like a ridiculous made-up elephant with fur on him, all galloping for one place where there was a bald man in a miner's tunic working, moving rocks quickly out of the way with a spade.

Above him, looking down on him from a flat piece of wall, was something that made the hair stand up on Carey's neck. It was a huge beast-man, part-painted in red and black, part carved, with animal legs and human hands and penis, and above his strangely calm face, tall stag antlers that swept up from his head. Joachim was exposing his pawlike feet and from the piles of rock all around him, it appeared he had been doing it for a long time; perhaps he had spent years at it.

Carey's mouth dropped. For a moment he wondered if he was dreaming this because the image of the Devil seemed to move as the lanternlight flickered. Was it the Devil? The expression on its face seemed mournful, rather than evil.

"There he is at last, all of him," came Joachim's voice, deep and soft, "The Devil. When I first found him as a lad, there was only his face and horns visible behind piles of rock and I looked at him and knew him. The Devil. Whoever you think you serve, really you serve him."

Carey drew his sword.

"I dug him out whenever I could, at night, on Sundays, so I could see more of him, to thank him for the gold he gave me. He's magnificent." Joachim laughed. "Now…well, whenever you kill or fornicate or take what isn't yours with some excuse about how you should have it, you worship him, the Devil. Whenever you lie and claim you follow the crucified fool, and burn Jews or Protestants or Catholics or heretic Anabaptists, he's there laughing at you. Do you think you fool anybody with your piety and wailing after Jesus? No. It's the Devil there in the Mass and he's in your dreary Church of England too, it's always him in blood and semen and shit and piss, he owns the world and we all worship him whether we realise it or not."

Carey was trying to advance across the rocks and pillars of the floor, picking his way. Joachim was backing carefully, seeming to aim for one of the shadowed curves in the wall, where the animals rioted above.

"But recently I've begun to think that he's just another thing we've made up, like God and Jesus. I think that he is just another shadow cast by men," said Joachim smiling, "which is why I'm still here. I have an experimentum to conduct, Sir Robert, and you're going to help me."

Joachim raised a pistol and Carey flung himself sideways, deafened by the explosion. But Joachim hadn't been aiming for him, but for the nearby brazier which spilled coals onto a network of slowmatches curling across the rocks. They started to hiss and travel and Joachim put the dag down, picked up a ready-loaded caliver.

He aimed it at Carey, but Carey was already charging him, jumping like a goat from one rock to the other and after the explosion was still moving, no holes in him, and he laughed because this was fine, this was not God-damned darkness but light and the animals on the walls seemed to move by themselves in the multiple flames of the slow matches. He felt like one of them, like the great grey wolf in the lead, shaped in a buttress of rock and he snarled and showed his teeth and attacked, a whirling thing halfway between animal and man himself. Joachim gave up trying to reload his caliver, flung it up to parry Carey's first onslaught with the sword, dropped it, met him with a mattock.

They rattled up and down over the rocks, slippery with escaping water, while the slowmatches hissed. Carey fell, rolled, was up on one knee, gasping.

"I've laid charges to destroy you. Don't you want to put the matches out?" panted Joachim, behind a pillar of rock.

"No point," said Carey, "too many of 'em." He charged again laughing madly, sword against mattock. Joachim was tiring but he was not, he pressed to the attack again and pushed Joachim up against the rocks where the Devil stood, felt his boot go into a space and lurched backwards.

Joachim looked down once, smiled at Carey and jumped down, feet first, through the hole, seemed to land heavily and his feet pelted off. Carey didn't pause, didn't think, just followed him, jumped down the hole to land six feet down on something soft and stinking…

Fluttering flying things were all about him, ah, the soft stuff was clearly bat shit, and he waved his arms, cleared a space, saw moonlight and ran out of the cave as the rock shuddered and the bellowing explosion above him took out the whole outer wall of the cave. He ran the fastest he ever had in his life as rocks rained down around him, leaping and bouncing, as that whole side of the mountain slumped and turned to scree and ruin, and he ran and ran and into blackness as a rock under his feet went sliding out from under him…

He came to again and he was outside, half buried in rubble. All around him the bats swooped and flapped in distress at the loss of their home. The waxing moonlight shone down on him, the air was sharp and cold and sweet and he was profoundly grateful to be in the open, out of the tunnels, away from the mine and the water…And still alive. He stayed where he was, gasping for breath and saying thank you, even while he wondered if he was broken and the pain just hadn't set in yet.

"Herr Ritter!" came the faint cry from above, and he could see Schlegel and young Josef standing on a ledge.

He lifted up his hand with an effort, shouted something back, started struggling out from the rocks. The eastern edge of the sky was lightening with dawn.

SUNDAY, 4TH FEBRUARY 1593, KESWICK

They climbed down to him. Astonishingly, although he was bruised and battered and would hurt tomorrow, nothing seemed to be broken. The strength that had come to him in the cave with the animals painted on it seemed to have left him completely, and he was weak and wobbly. Had there actually been a cave painted with animals and a huge rough painting of the Devil? Or had it been some kind of dream? He felt the whole of the night had been a nightmare in that terrible place of tunnels and rock and water, so why balk at the further dream of the Devil on the rockface?

He accepted a flask of aquavitae and strong arms helped him to his feet. He poked around and found his sword, also miraculously unbroken, sheathed it, stumbled and slipped in soaked boots the short distance down to the silver beck tumbling over the rocks. The miners helped him the whole way, along the side of the hill to the roasting ovens and stamping houses, a little up the valley from the mine and the well-built wooden houses where the miners slept.

He was so grateful he didn't have to climb up the ladders in the dark, or walk bent over along the endless tunnels, he felt almost like laughing, then thought better not, in case the miners thought him crazy.

Herr Mine Captain Schlegel shook his hand, all the miners gathered round him in wonder. Josef smiled and chatted in Deutsch which sounded muffled to him, until finally Carey said, "Gentlemen, I have to confess that I didn't kill Joachim. He ran away before the gunpowder exploded."

They tutted and Schlegel shrugged and said something in Deutsch that sounded rude.

Josef said something else Carey couldn't hear. "What?"

"At least you are alive, Herr Ritter!" Josef shouted.

"Well, yes, but are you not disappointed that he's slipped away again?"

"No, well, yes," yelled Josef, "but it's that we are talking about the idea of using gunpowder in a mine. Nobody has thought of using it to break rock before and everyone is excited at it."

Well, if he was crazy, he wasn't as crazy as that. "What?"

"Gunpowder can blast out rock. This is a great discovery!"

"Er…Joachim is loose? We still have to find him?"

"Yes, yes, but this will transform mining, you will see. We just have to learn how to do it." And the conversation began again in Deutsch, going hammer and tongs.

Carey left them to it.

He walked to the entrance of the mine, stumbling occasionally and limping as his bruises took their toll, found Tovey and Red Sandy drinking beer but no longer stepping on the bellows to blow air into the mine. Frau Schlegel was there and gave him some, which was very kind of her and probably stopped him from falling over. His ears were hurting and he couldn't hear very well, had no idea what she was saying, and he was feeling utterly exhausted at the idea of running Joachim to earth again and finding a way to kill him. In fact he thought that he would have about as much chance at killing Joachim now as a puppy would have against a hound and didn't think he would even have the energy to get on a pony and go back to the inn and sleep.

In fact it was Tovey who saved him because he started to climb on his pony but was also tired from stepping on the bellows for hours and Carey gave him a leg up. Red Sandy mounted and Leamus emerged from a cubbyhole where he'd been asleep but had woken to the sound of gunpowder. A pony was missing, the one called Ox who had been tethered outside, not harnessed to his wheel yet. Carey retrieved his tall beaver hat. And so they went back to Keswick, across the Derwent Bridge, heading for

Crossthwaite and the row of houses near the Greta Bridge just as the sun came up fully.

SUNDAY, 4TH FEBRUARY 1593, KESWICK

Joachim was shocked at what had happened to the cave where the Devil danced. He hadn't been sure what would happen when he lit the charges to see if the Devil could protect himself from the gunpowder. It hadn't occurred to him that the gunpowder would actually destroy the whole cave—which he had to admit was amusingly stupid of him since he had become quite expert with fireworks at Court. But rock was hard, rock was eternal, earth was soft, masonry was brittle, the living rock endured. If he had thought about it at all, while he brought in the gunpowder barrels and slowmatch, he had assumed that rocks would always need to be painstakingly chipped out by miners with hammers and chisels. That was why he had gone along with the encouragement of the persistent voice in his head which had called for the dramatic explosive trap against the courtier. If the voice was the Devil, why hadn't it known his cave would be destroyed?

At least he had the rolls of gold dust chipped from the seam tied round his waist. They would help him go to New Spain where they urgently needed mining engineers, a final gift from…what?

The voice was gone for the moment. Surely the bloody man was dead? Joachim had jumped down the hole as he had practised before, into the cave with the bats, and sprinted as fast as he could out of the cave, down beside the beck. The blast was supposed to kill Carey, not ruin the place. But then he heard the muffled sequence of booms and then a roar. He risked a look over his shoulder to see the side of the hill suddenly crumble and fall into chaos. He stopped and stared, but then smiled. Nobody could live through that if they were inside, surely? He sped up, past the roasting and stamping houses, past the mine entrance where he grabbed the first pony he found, climbed on and kicked it to a gallop along Newlands valley. There were people there but they were staring at the side of the hill where there were rocks still falling. Nobody noticed him, and he found himself still smiling as he rode away. Was the Devil still helping him? Maybe, maybe so. Or maybe he was just lucky as he always had been.

He had a place he was going to, the last place, the only place, despite it having been violated…except no, that was a bad idea because an island could be difficult to leave without a boat and he did not want to swim through the icy lake again. Once had been enough. Also the heavy gold around his waist would sink him. No, there was a better place he could go. He stopped and worked on his dag, finding the powder flask on his belt, the bullets in a little bag, the wads in his pocket. It took him a while because he was an engineer, not a man-at-arms, not a soldier, but eventually he was satisfied that the gun was loaded properly.

The pony was pawing the grass and cropping it, so he mounted again, changing course slightly, aiming for the houses near Crossthwaite church where many of the second generation Deutschers like himself lived. Women were moving around in the street, a line of cows being led into town by a plump fair-haired girl, knitting as she went, one-handed with a needlecase on her belt, and singing in a high true soprano.

He walked past her and banged on the door of his sister's house. He knew there would be only women there because his brother-in-law would already have left before sun up to go to the smelthouses—or perhaps to see what had happened at Goldscope. A woman whose name he couldn't remember opened it, and he shoved her indoors, shutting the door behind him and slapping her hard across the cheek when she screamed. She fell over, crawled away. There was a sturdy-looking woman sitting on a low chair with a baby to her breast, Annamaria was coming in from the kitchen, somebody was following her but stopped and ran away before he could see her.

"Joachim!" Annamaria shouted. "Mother of God, what are you doing?"

They were always wailing after the lying little trollop who had borne Jesus Christ.

"Good morning, Annamaria," he said politely. "Still as fat as a pig, I see. I want clean clothes and a good horse..."

"No," said Annamaria, "I am not *Mutti*. We don't have anything for you. Go away."

"I'll settle for Mark's clothes," said Joachim with a grin. "Or anybody's, really, I'm now ready to leave town and I'm sure my brothers will be oh so happy to hear that."

"No," said Annamaria again. "My husband told me about you, how you were soaking wet when he tried to talk to you in *Mutti*'s house, how that was the day you killed Rosa Carleton, my friend, and put her in the lake. And you killed her husband as well. Get out of my house and don't come back."

Joachim pulled the dag out of the front of his mining tunic and pointed it at Annamaria. It had a snaphaunce lock and no need for a slowmatch that would eventually burn down.

She went satisfyingly pale and started to gobble, and then she had to sit down. There was a minute's complete silence, in the back of which was a woman's voice shouting in the street. The wet nurse still had the baby to her breast, although it was starting to fret and fuss. Joachim looked down at it and frowned.

"Whose is the child? Not one of yours, is it, Annamaria?"

"If you want to know whose baby it is," said the wet-nurse in English, loudly and clearly as if to an idiot, "it's Mrs Burn's babby, the poor fatherless wee mite."

The baby stopped nursing, looked around and started to roar. Joachim pointed his gun at the wet-nurse. "Make it stop that noise!" he ordered in English, and the wet-nurse looked scornful.

He advanced on Annamaria, starting to feel fear, starting to feel the world sliding out from under his feet. People did what you ordered when you pointed a gun at them. His head was suddenly aching from the earsplitting noises the baby was producing.

"Make it stop!"

"I can't feed him while you're waving a gun around," sniffed the nurse contemptuously. She was a Liddle from Liddelsdale and had seen guns before.

Someone opened the door behind him and came through from the street, strangely with a pile of clothes in her arms, and stood to one side of the door which had closed again. He looked and saw Little Rady or Poppy, who had gone with him when he left, who had kept house for him and then run off with a minister of the church; his favourite sister, who had so foolishly written the letter in code that had somehow ruined all his carefully laid plans.

"Here are some clothes for you, Joachim," she said calmly. "And I'll help you get a horse."

He looked at her, saw betrayal in her face, in her voice. She had betrayed him once, hadn't she, when she went off with the minister? And again with that idiotic letter.

He moved sideways, bent and grabbed and had a handhold on the baby's swaddling clothes. There was a smell of cinnamon from it and for a moment it stopped screaming and stared at him curiously, swinging from its bands like the worms hanging in the trees that turned to butterflies.

"Is this yours?" he asked and pointed his gun at it. It was such a pity he only had one shot. There must be a way to make guns fire more than one bullet, it wasn't as if there was a shortage of bullets...Damn it, what was wrong with him? Why couldn't he focus?

Poppy watched him, she had gone very still. "Please," she said softly, "I would rather you killed me than my baby."

Joachim shrugged. "That's because you're weak and foolish," he said, and turned the gun on her. "But all right, just as you wish."

Strangely she relaxed and smiled at him. "Oh, Joachim," she said, "I feel so sorry for you."

He started to laugh, "Why? You're the one who's going to

die." Then he wondered why his back was feeling cold. The baby started making that awful noise again.

English suddenly intruded. He was so tired he actually had to make an effort to switch mental horses to the different language.

"Joachim," shouted Carey hoarsely from the street, "put your gun on the table and then your hands on your head…" The courtier was aiming one of his wheellock dags at him from a distance of about three yards while his man with the plait down his back was crouched by the door he had eased open, moving away.

Joachim spun to shoot the courtier and in that moment, Poppy grabbed something from between the clothes and launched herself forward onto Joachim, stabbing hard up at an angle in his side with the kitchen knife in her hand. Both guns barked and Joachim looked down on his sister with the knife sticking out of his side and his shoulder destroyed by Carey's bullet. He had been right not to trust her, but his bullet had gone into the wall when she stabbed him and when he tried to raise the gun to hit the caterwauling baby with it, the weapon simply dribbled out of his numb fingers.

Quite gently, Poppy caught the screaming baby-parcel as he dropped it and put it on her shoulder, stepped back so Joachim could keel over, breaking a bench as he went because of the heavy gold dust bags round his waist.

Mary Liddle tutted, took the baby from his mother, and marched into the kitchen, muttering about foreigners. Poppy sat down next to her brother and patted his hand while he writhed on the floor. "*Gott behüte dich*," she said to him softly and he took breath to argue and then stared up at the shelf beside her as if there was a person there. "*Du?!*" he said in disgust and his eyes rolled up.

Carey came in cautiously with his second dag pointed at Joachim. There was no need for it, and Carey released the lock with a whirr and put it carefully down. He looked absolutely exhausted, poor man, was covered in mud and gravel, and seemed ready to keel over himself.

"Poor poor Joachim," said Poppy. "Poor *Mutti*. So clever and so stupid."

"Are you all right, Mrs Burn?" Carey asked wearily, since she had run to his horse in the street to tell him Joachim was in Annamaria's house with a gun, and he expected her to faint or cry or something.

Poppy looked up at him and smiled, not realising that she had blood sprayed on her face and her hands wet with it. "I'm remarkably well," she said consideringly and then noticed her bloody hands and made a grimace of disgust. Freda, whom Joachim had slapped and knocked down, was bringing a bowl of water for Poppy to wash in. "*Danke*," she said and then shook her head at Carey. "But, Sir Robert, I think you need to get some rest."

Radagunda Hochstetter came into her kitchen, feeling frightened and confused. There had been an explosion at the mine early in the morning. She had heard it while she was copying the adjusted figures into the account books to show the shareholders. Then later there had been a further loud bang from Crossthwaite.

She had gone outside, peered northwards, trying to see what was happening in Keswick, sure it was something to do with that very unpleasant young Englishman, Herr Ritter Carey. Or Joachim, who had been like a desperate man in the last few days, though he wouldn't tell her what was wrong and shouted at her if she tried to probe a little. He had fallen out of his boat late at night a few days ago and tracked muddy wet footprints all across the clean kitchen floor, always mopped last thing at night. She didn't think he had been drunk, he had denied it in the morning, and it wasn't like him. The disgusting Englishman

Carey had invaded her island, searching for Joachim, making ridiculous accusations and so the whole house had to be cleaned and scrubbed from top to bottom as well as the door-lock replaced. And Maria had gone yesterday, claiming she had a cold, back to her mother in Keswick.

So she came in from the back courtyard and found the kitchen full of her children, Annamaria and Mark Steinberger, Emanuel, not Veronica who was living in Newcastle with her husband, the Mayor, nor Susanna who was also married, not Joachim for some reason, Daniel, David and not Elizabeth, who was still a maid… All her strong grown children of whom she was so proud—and Little Rady, or Poppy, as she preferred to be called..

Radagunda swelled with anger. What was that evil unnatural child doing in her sacred kitchen? It would all have to be scrubbed again.

She pointed at Poppy and hissed, "Get out! I don't know you, you are not my daughter!"

"Why?"

"What?"

"Why am I not your daughter? What have I done?"

"You…you went off with your brother, no doubt you disported yourself with all the men you met, you found one of them that was stupid enough to think of marrying you, you married him like a peasant, pleasing yourself, and then you killed him…."

"No, actually," said Poppy, cutting across her, "it was Joachim who did that. Joachim told Lord Spynie that it was James who had tried to kill him and Lord Spynie sent two assassins to murder James in his own manse."

"Nonsense."

"Also, have I killed men? Have I tried to kill the King of Scotland as Joachim did? No. Did I kill poor John Carleton? No, Joachim did that with a red-hot swordblank. Did I kill Rosa Carleton, his widow, making his son an orphan? No, Joachim did that."

"I met him here," said Mark Steinberger, "in this kitchen late at night on the day that Mrs Carleton was killed and dumped in the lake, with rocks to keep her down. Joachim was wet through."

"No, he fell out of his boat…"

"He tried to kill the Ritter Carey with an arquebus but missed and killed his man instead…"

"He was defending this island from invasion…"

"Herr Ritter had a warrant from Mayor Allerdyce. Which he had because of the killing of the Carletons."

"Ridiculous. Joachim would never…"

Emanuel sighed and all eyes went to him. "You are utterly blind about Joachim, Mother. I have always wondered why you love Joachim more than me, than all your children. Is it because he's like you…he was like you, in caring for no one but himself? Well…?"

Emanuel rubbed his eyes. "I have worked so hard all these years to do your bidding, to…deserve your love." He smiled sadly. "I should have asked you if you deserve my love. Well?"

Radagunda couldn't think what to say. She was bewildered. Why didn't she like him as much as Joachim? It was true he was the most dutiful of sons, but…

"But thank God," said Poppy coldly. "God helped us resolve the problem of Joachim, because Joachim died this morning, at Annamaria's house, where he was threatening to shoot my baby."

Annamaria, whom Radagunda trusted, nodded at this. "He was, *Mutti*. He was like a madman, demanding clothes and a horse and…"

"And aiming his pistol at wee little James Postumus Burn." Poppy's voice had iron in it. "He was holding him up by his bands and threatening to shoot my baby who had never done him any harm."

"Yes," said Annamaria, "and you told him to shoot you, not the baby."

It wasn't precisely that Radagunda didn't know what to say. It was just that the breath was stopped in her throat at the thought that Joachim would do such a thing. She couldn't understand it.

"So I hid a knife in a pile of clothes and offered them to him and when he saw Herr Ritter in the street aiming his dag at him, he turned and I stabbed him. Herr Ritter shot him at the same time and he died."

Now Radagunda felt that her heart had been hit with an axe. She couldn't breathe, couldn't think. Her little Joachim, stabbed and shot at the same time? He was dead? It was too much.

"Your precious little Joachim was a cold killer," said Mark Steinberger, "who never cared for anybody but himself and had no respect for you either. I say good riddance."

And all the people there except Radagunda herself, nodded. She couldn't believe it, couldn't believe that they would say that about their own brother, her own son, her own…

"He always used to laugh at the way *Mutti* called him 'her own little Joachim,' didn't he?" said Annamaria casually. "Do you remember, Poppy? He said it really annoyed him, but he let *Mutti* do it because she always let him get away with things."

Poppy nodded. "Do you remember, *Mutti*, I wrote you a letter when I first went away with him and I was keeping house for him in the Netherlands, and I said I was worried because he would say he didn't like someone and the next thing you knew, they were dead?"

Radagunda said nothing. That was the first of Poppy's letters that she had burned. Had Joachim really said that about her, that he didn't like it when she called him lovingly "her own little Joachim"? Was it even possible he…he didn't love her?

If Poppy had told her such a thing she would never have believed it. She didn't believe that nonsense about people dying in the Netherlands. But Annamaria had no imagination and…

"Do you want to view the corpse, Mother?" asked Emanuel, wearily. "Annamaria has got it into her parlour and she and her gossips will lay it out this evening. Do you want to be there?"

Slowly Radagunda shook her head.

"The funeral will be in a few days, but it will be a quiet affair with no paid mourners, just family."

"Oh, no, we must have…"

"Oh, yes, Mother," said Emanuel with a firmness she had never heard from him before. "Yes. We will have no procession, no wailing or black cloaks, it will be simple, for Hochstetter family members only and we will bury Joachim respectably in Crossthwaite churchyard and there will be an end to his wickedness."

Once again she couldn't speak, the words cramming her throat so none could get out. It was too much, she couldn't stand it. She stood up and all her children stood with her, showing respect (as Joachim didn't very much, that was true). "I…" she started, shook her head. "I…" she tried again and then she gave up trying to speak and walked out to the courtyard. Behind her she heard the scrape of chairs as her children sat down again to thrash out the order of service for…for her little Joachim. Strangely, they were also speaking of gold, Joachim's gold, and what to do with it.

She felt utterly alone, utterly bereft. Why was God punishing her like this? The child she had nearly lost unbaptised to the measles, the child of her heart ever after because he had nearly died, was he really the killer they said he was?

She thought back to the time when they had visited the Queen's palace at Whitehall, when Joachim had been eleven years old. There had been a consequence to that trip, when Joachim had disappeared for a few minutes, one she had never ever told him about. A week afterwards, she and Daniel, her husband, had been summonsed to appear before the Board of Green Cloth in Whitehall, a mysterious committee of men that administered the Queen's Court. Neither of them had known what it was about and she had been a little annoyed at the high-handedness of summoning her as well as her husband. Women didn't appear in court; they had men to do that for them.

She had stood behind her husband and listened without understanding to the quick English from the snowy-ruffed, bearded men. Daniel had then turned to her and asked if Joachim had gone missing while they were at the palace of Whitehall.

Instinctively she had lied. No, she had said as definitely as she could. He had been with her the whole time.

CThis is serious," Daniel had said. "A stableboy was killed, stabbed in the stomach by another boy wearing green brocade and furs like Joachim. The Board of Green Cloth must investigate any violent death within two miles of the Queen's person or her palaces, so they are asking us about it because you were there and the clothes sound like Joachim's."

Her mind went immediately to the guide. Had he told them what had happened? She wanted to ask about him but also didn't want to tell them about him if they didn't already know. "Why are you accusing my son of such a terrible crime?" she asked, playing for time, allowing tears to come to her eyes. "He's a good boy."

Daniel turned back to the committee and spoke in English for a while, listened and then turned back to her.

"Nobody admits to being with you. Did you have a guide?"

She didn't let her breath puff out of her body or relax, because the cold eyes of the Englishmen were on her. "No," she lied, "and Joachim was with me all the time," she said. "You know I would never let him go exploring." She found her handkerchief in her sleeve and wiped her eyes.

Daniel turned back to the men and spoke for a time, with just the right mixture of respect, deference, and firmness. There were a couple of further questions from the Englishmen, probably about Radagunda's truthfulness. She knew Daniel would be able to answer well, she was always truthful and she was a good wife to him, she knew that.

When Daniel had finished speaking, the men talked quietly to each other and then the one in the middle leaned forward and spoke at some length with a small smile. Daniel bowed low again so she curtseyed as well and they were led out of the panelled room and out into the passage.

Daniel had waited until they were back in the boat, on the way back to the Steelyard, before he asked her quietly if she had told the truth. For just one moment she thought of telling him what had really happened, but it would only be a burden to him and worry him and...No. She lied again and smiled at him and laughed at the idea that she could have let Joachim explore in a strange place like Whitehall Palace, until he smiled and kissed her fingers and left the subject.

As soon as she got back to the lodgings, she went upstairs to the boys' room and checked Joachim's dirty shirts, tangled on the floor, of course, not in the laundry bag. Yes, one had a little dabbling of brown on the right cuff, as she had spotted on the night they came back from Whitehall. She took it and folded it and put it in a basket, went out to the meatmarket at Smithfield where she sent her woman to look for liversausage and then stuffed the shirt behind a counter when no one was watching. She ordered a quarter of a sheep to salt down for the winter and came home again, her heart still hammering, waiting for God's vengeance.

She had known that Joachim had killed something because he had been unusually calm and loving after the Whitehall trip, but she had thought it was only a dog or a bird again. That it had been a boy...Well, the boy had presumably been baptised, although like all non-Anabaptists he had gone straight to Hell anyway. And really, when you thought about it, did it matter if a heretic died earlier or later?

And so she had managed to forget about it, for surely Joachim had a good reason to do it, if he had indeed stabbed the stableboy. It made her feel even closer to him, because she had been able to protect him again, just as she had by her prayers against the measles. So she had endangered her immortal soul by lying about it to her husband; what did God expect? She was his mother.

She looked down. There he was, beside her, curly hair flying, cap lost, arms up to embrace her and she picked him up and felt him nuzzle her neck and say, "*Mutti, Mutti, Mutti.*" She stood there and hugged her little Joachim to her and slowly he changed in her arms into a block of stone and then faded away.

She knew she would never ever see him again, not even at the end of Time when Jesus came in Judgement, because he would go to Hell for killing a fellow Anabaptist, Rosa Carleton, while Radagunda would go to Heaven. That was fact. Never, never again would she feel him nuzzle her neck and say "*Mutti, Mutti, Mutti.*" Her heart slowly changed from steel to lead.

TUESDAY, 6TH FEBRUARY 1593, KESWICK

The inquests were held the next day and Bangtail's funeral was set for the day after. Carey paid for Bangtail's shroud and the gravediggers and the sermon which was read by the curate at Crossthwaite church. Pastor Waltz was there, who had tried to distract Carey so he could be shot. His face looked guilty and Carey hoped he felt something. At least he had turned up, but Carey saw no need to speak to the man.

Red Sandy stood like stone through the service, his face more like his brother's than it ever had been before, his jaw clamped. Carey invited him to say a few words by the grave and he stood like a post for so long, Carey wondered if he would ever speak. Then he said, "Bangtail Graham wisnae my friend last spring for I thought him a fool then. But we made friends later in the summer and he was the best friend I iver had. I loved him. God rest him."

He dropped crumbs of earth onto the corpse and turned away. Carey's throat ached for the man.

They went to the commonroom of the Oak Inn for the funeral ale and found all the drovers there. Carey watched while Red Sandy downed quart after quart until he passed out.

The following day, with his whole body black and blue with bruises and hurting like hell, Carey had a tense but fruitful meeting with the remaining Hochstetter brothers and Mark Steinberger, from which Frau Radagunda was absent. She was busy with the accounts, they said. Among other very satisfactory decisions regarding a pension for him in silver, they gave him a valuable green velvet cloak lined with marten that was much better than the fur-lined cloak he had lost in Goldscope mine. They also dealt with the question of Josef Carleton, the smith's son, who had been orphaned by Joachim. With the help of the Mayor, the Hochstetter family would find and appoint a smith from the area who could make the tools they needed, who would work from Carleton's smithies as a paid man. Josef could either stay with him, or, if he chose, with his uncle Mark Steinberger, to complete his apprenticeship and journeying, until he was old enough and experienced enough to take over the business himself.

Carey had ordered his men to start packing up. Since Bangtail's two horses had nothing to carry, on Mr Anrick's suggestion, they bought four kegs of the Deutsch dark double-double beer to sell to Bessie, and twenty pounds of the meaty spiced sausage as well, funded ultimately by Mr Secretary Cecil.

Mr Anricks had not yet finished reading all of Mrs Burn's books but thought he would in a month or so. Carey sat with him in the parlour over two silver cups of aquavitae.

"How did it go with Young Hutchin?" he asked.

"Ah, yes," said Anricks, "the young devil is made for intelligence work, although he can't read and write. He is well-settled in the large Widdrington stables, on the grounds that you want him away from Carlisle and the malign influence of his uncles. I imagine he'll be running all the boys there in three months. I advised him to put his time at church to good use and follow the readings in the Book of Common Prayer, and left him a hornbook so he can learn his letters."

Carey nodded. He was confident that if Elizabeth could stay at the King's Court and away from her husband, she would be very well until her husband finally died of his gout. But would her husband let her stay, that was the question? It made his sleep a little easier at night that he now had a man—well, a youth—placed in the Widdrington stables who could ride for Carlisle if need be.

FRIDAY, 9TH FEBRUARY 1593, CARLISLE

They set off into the hills north and east for Carlisle again, planning to stop at an inn on the way, the sky heavy with snow clouds but Carey thought it was too cold to snow yet. Still he moved them on, Red Sandy silent and tightlipped, Tovey bouncing awkwardly, and Leamus off his horse which he said was a little lame, his big bare feet slapping on the rocks and grasses and the hummocks of snow. His boots and hosen were packed onto one of the spare ponies.

Eventually, next day, Carlisle loomed into sight and when they came back into the keep, Carey found Janet there, waiting for him.

"He willna wait," she said to Carey. "He wants to fight Wee Colin and he's nowhere near ready. Wee Colin will wait, he won't. Will ye come and talk some sense intae him?"

"Where is he? Stobbs?"

"Nay, he rade hame like he said he would, on Whitesock, and it half-killt him. That was last week. This week he's been trying to wield a sword and it's half-killing him again."

Carey was appalled. "He must still be wood," he said. "Is he hoping Wee Colin will go easy on him and then he'll kill him that way?"

"Ay," grunted Janet, "that'll be it."

"I'll come," said Carey. "Tomorrow, with his brother."

SATURDAY, 10TH FEBRUARY 1593, GILSLAND

Red Sandy was an uncomfortable companion on the sixteen miles to Gilsland, saying barely two words the whole way. Carey was a little surprised at it, but it seemed that the Dodds were silent when they were upset.

At Gilsland Carey found a weak and scrawny Dodd in shirt, woollen breeches, and a jerkin, all of which flapped on him, exercising with a veney stick while Janet stood and watched with her arms folded and her hands in fists. Red Sandy watched for five minutes, then shook his head and scowled. Carey picked up one of the veney sticks and attacked Dodd when the young cousin of Janet's gave up, got a fighting grin from him and then they exchanged some blows until Carey got bored, pressed Dodd, disarmed him, and when he came back with his dagger, tripped him so he landed on his back and lay there gasping for five minutes.

"Ye're dead, Sergeant," said Carey conversationally. "In fact, you're dead twice over and ye know it. I've never fought Wee Colin but I know he's better than a milkmaid—and so are you when you've not got a half-healed wound in your back."

Dodd pushed himself up to a sitting position, still heaving breath into his lungs.

"Ye bastard..."

"Do you want another bout?" asked Carey. "I don't like beating up a sick man but I'll do it if I can drive some sense into that thick stubborn head of yourn."

And he put himself *en garde* because you never knew with Dodd.

"Ye're telling me I canna fight Wee Colin?"

"Not soon. Or not with swords," said Carey smoothly.

Dodd stopped heaving for breath for a moment. "What are ye saying?"

"Ye can't fight Wee Colin this year with a sword. Maybe in 1594 but not this year. But if you're so desperate to get the fight over with that you don't care if you live or die, you could fight him with a pistol."

"Whit?" said both Dodd and his wife together. Carey ignored Janet who was looking daggers at him.

"I've heard of a duel being done this way in Allemayne. You use matched pistols. Fortunately, I have a pair. Each is loaded. You select your weapon, pace off ten paces, turn and shoot. If you hit the other man, he's probably dead. If he hits you, you're probably dead. Or both of you might die, so it's just like a regular duel."

Janet started to speak. "Oh no," she said. "No, we dinna want..."

Dodd creaked to his feet with his hand to his back. "D'ye mean it?"

"Certainly I do. We'll ask Wee Colin if he's willing for it and if he is, we could have the duel in a month."

"Why not sooner?" demanded Dodd.

"Because, Sergeant, you need to practise every day with the pistols so your grip is at least as strong as a milkmaid's, so you can stand straight and aim and fire without dropping the bloody thing, which you might, and I don't want my nice dag damaged."

Carey got the first real smile he had seen from Dodd since Dick of Dryhope's tower.

"Ye'd do that?"

"I think it would be better if you concentrated on getting well and fought Wee Colin in a year's time..."

"Ay, and I think..." said Janet.

"Ah canna wait that long. Thinking of Wee Colin would... would wear me down, so it would."

Janet rolled her eyes. "He's no' such a bad man, Wee Colin," she said, "and if he wisnae yer blood enemy, ye'd likely be friends."

Surprisingly, Dodd looked down and his thin face was suddenly sad. "Ay," he whispered, "but since he is ma blood enemy, Ah havetae fight him as soon as I can."

She rolled her eyes again.

"Right," said Carey. "I'll send a messenger to Wee Colin to ask for a meeting to discuss the duel and see what we can arrange. I want you practising with calivers, so you get used to a bigger kick. I bet you haven't got anything except serpentine gunpowder here, have you? I'll bring you some milled, once you can actually hold the weapon straight for five minutes."

SATURDAY, 3RD MARCH 1593

Three weeks later at the start of March, no sign of spring, in the coldest wettest part of the year which had forced a postponement the day before due to driving rain, Carey and Red Sandy and Wee Colin and two of his brothers and Dodd, of course, met on the Border on the Tarras moss. There was nothing visible for miles save brown soggy hills and brown soggy valleys. The wind was blowing hard, but Carey had chosen the fighting ground with care so there was protection in a dip in the land. Neither Wee Colin nor Dodd was wearing his jack because what was the point of armour against a lead ball?

Carey had brought the folding table he used for musters and a camp stool, sat down and loaded both his pistols with the little waxy grey balls: charge and wad and ball and wad, taking infinite pains with the ramrod and using the finest milled powder. They would use one charge and Wee Colin's second, his brother, was happy with this.

When both were loaded to his satisfaction, Carey offered the guns to Dodd, since Wee Colin was the challenger. He took the nearest and it looked a little less clumsy in his hand now he had spent every day for three weeks learning to shoot. Wee Colin took the other and Carey stepped back, his cloak flapping in the wind and a grim expression on his face.

The two men backed each other and paced ten paces. They turned and faced each other. Carey was watching Dodd closely: he saw Dodd take aim, pointing his finger the way Carey had taught him, and then saw him move the heavy barrel infinitesimally and fire. Wee Colin fired at the same moment and the two disappeared into white smoke.

Red Sandy ran to his brother who was still standing, looking down at himself in surprise. Wee Colin was also looking surprised.

"Gentlemen," said Carey, moving between them, "do you want to take another shot, since ye both missed?"

Dodd shook his head once. After a pause so did Wee Colin.

"Ay, it was a wonder neither o' the wheel-locks jammed nor misfired," said Wee Colin. "I prefer a snaphaunce lock meself, less to go wrong. But no."

"So do I," admitted Carey, "but these were so expensive, I can't abandon them."

"I think ye could convert them into snaphaunces," said Wee Colin. "I know a man in Dumfries ye could ask."

"That's uncommon kind of you, Mr Elliot, thank you. Sergeant Dodd, are you happy that honour is satisfied?"

Dodd looked up at Carey with a very odd expression on his face, and moved his boot a little. "Ay," he said. "Ah am."

"Mr Elliot?"

"Ay."

Carey collected his dags and put them in their cases on his pony. Red Sandy had lost his tense miserable expression and Dodd seemed to be trying to swallow a smile of relief.

"A toast, gentlemen," said Carey, producing little silver cups for everybody and pouring out from a flask in his doublet pocket as the wind strengthened and the rain started to fall again. "I give you The Dodds and The Elliots, may the peace hold and friendship grow."

Wee Colin raised his cup. Dodd did the same, everyone drank the whishke bee.

The Elliots went north and the Dodds and Carey went south.

"If only we could deal with all feuds on the Border like that," said Carey brightly, as they came in sight of Gilsland. "Just the headmen, fighting it out in a duel, clean and quick, not fifty riders each side thundering into battle. My life would be so much easier."

Dodd fell back a little and tilted his head at his brother. "What's sae funny?" demanded Red Sandy, seeing his lips twitch.

Dodd showed him a little ball of paper that was singed and torn. Red Sandy took it and it was the size of pistol shot and coloured with blacklead and wax.

"That bounced off o' my doublet," said Dodd, with a grin. "The courtier loaded Wee Colin Elliot's dag with a wad of paper. That's what's funny."

"Yes, but…" Red Sandy began and then swallowed his words. "Ay," he said, "that's funny."

"That pays for Dick of Dryhope's tower," said Dodd. "Even though I missed Wee Colin, that pays for it."

"Ay," said Red Sandy, pokerfaced.

They came to the gates where Janet was standing with strain and tension written all over her face that melted away to nothing as she saw her husband riding towards her and ran to him and kissed him.

SUNDAY, 4TH MARCH 1593, CARLISLE

Carey reached Carlisle late the next day after doing a deal with Dodd for a good load of stones from the Giant's Wall on his land to mend the Eden bridge again.

He went up the stairs of the Queen Mary tower, whistling and feeling very pleased with himself and stopped when he found John Tovey standing there, looking anxious.

"What's wrong?"

"There's a girl here, sir. She says her name is Jane and she has a message for you."

"A girl?"

"She says she's come all the way from Widdrington, sir, and from the looks of her she has…"

"How the devil did she get here? Who brought her?"

"She says nobody, sir, because Young Hutchin's locked up and so she came herself because she loves Lady Widdrington."

"But it's nearly a hundred miles…"

"Yes, sir. She said she walked and ran like you did when you went from London to Berwick and it worked and she's here now. She's in your study, sir…"

"Well, that's not suitable. I can't have a maid in my chamber…"

"Bessie's there as well, sir, so it's respectable."

"Oh. Well. Very good, Mr Tovey."

"She says it's about Lady Widdrington, sir. She won't say what's wrong with her."

Carey strode into his chamber and found Bessie sitting on the chair and a sturdy looking girl with brown hair and rather a square face and a muddy kirtle and hob-nailed boots, sitting on a stool, clearly near to dropping with tiredness. Both of them stood up and curtseyed as he came in. Bessie was flushed and had a dab of flour on her chin.

"Ah have never heard such a tale from a maid," said Bessie, "but ye'd best hear her message yourself."

"Are you Sir Robert Carey?" asked the girl, looking up at him.

"Yes, I am," he said. "I remember you. Weren't you in the dairy when I came to Widdrington a few years ago?"

She flushed to her hair roots. "Ay, sir, I was, I am. Young Hutchin wanted to come but Sir Henry locked him up, so I said I'd carry it."

She stood up, felt inside her stays for a pocket and brought out something shining. Jane gave it ceremoniously into Carey's hand. He looked at it as if he didn't know what it was, but he did know. It was half of Elizabeth's handfasting ring. There were two slim rings, one with a male hand on it, one with a female hand. You put them together and they clasped each other. He was holding the female hand.

He went to ice immediately. Just as he had sent the Queen's emerald ring to Elizabeth when he had desperately needed her assistance at the Scottish King's Court the previous summer, so she had sent her part of her handfasting ring to him. It was a mute cry for help.

He stared at Jane who was scowling. "What happened?" he asked quietly.

GLOSSARY

"at the horn"—outlawed

"out on the trod"—out in pursuit of reivers

ague—malaria; quartan ague—four-day cycling malaria

Allemaynes, Deutsch, Dutch—Germans

Anabaptist—a type of German Protestant who believed in adult baptism among other revolutionary things; the Catholic Church did its level best to wipe them out.

aquavitae—brandy

arming doublet—the old doublet you wore under your armour or jack

arquebus—large and heavy hand gun, with a long barrel which you usually needed a tripod to hold up

Ars Mathematika—the art of mathematics

assaying—testing an ore to find out what was in it

bag pudding—steamed savoury pudding, often made with suet

baldric—the shoulder strap for a long sword

belladonna—a poison

blacklead/plumbago/waad—graphite

blackrent—protection money

blankmanger—medieval dish made of almonds, cream, and chicken

Border reiver—a member of the riding surnames, persistent cattle thief, horse rustler, murderer

bread trenchers—slices of whole-meal bread used as edible plates, saved on washing up breeks—breeches; fighting breeches were made of leather

brimstone—sulphur

buck—very large wooden tub, big enough for two or three people to sit in

buffcoat—thick leather sleeveless coat, one down from a jack, in terms of protection

caliver—smaller hand gun

Calvinist—variety of Protestant who follows the teachings of John Calvin

canions—straight breeches to the knees

carlin—old woman

churching—forty days after she had given birth, a woman would be "churched," or allowed back into church, after her period of ritual uncleanliness; during the period before her churching she could not do housework or cook anything

codpiece—a flap of cloth tied at the top of the hose, to hide the privates; often stuffed to look larger (of course)

cramoisie—very popular colour in Elizabethan times, dark purple-red

dag—smallest kind of firearm, a large gun firing one shot at a time, with a heavy ball on the bottom of the grip to balance the barrel and hit people with when you missed

double double beer—very very strong beer

duds—London slang for clothes

earthcoals—what we call coal; what they called coal, we call charcoal

Entschuldige, Maria. Stell es einfach auf die Truhe—I'm sorry, Maria. Just put it on the chest.

falling band—plain linen collar

farthing—a quarter of a penny

fewmets—deer droppings

Four Last Things—Death, Judgement, Hell, and Heaven

French pox—syphilis

fried sippets—thick slices of bread fried in bacon fat, delicious galleas—cross between a galleon and a galley, there were four of them in the Armada

gallowglass—Irish mercenary, allegedly from Gallway

Geht es dir gut? Wo bist du denn gewesen? Was hast...—How are you, where have you been, what...?

gossips—a woman's best female friends, her god-siblings

Gott behüte dich—God protect you

Grüss Gott und einen guten Nachmittag, Schwager—Good afternoon, brother-in-law

half-testered bed—only half a roof over the bed, as opposed to four-poster bed

hammerbeam roof—magnificent roof for a hall as at the Inns of Court or Oxbridge colleges

Hansa Steelyard—private dockyard for the exclusive use of ships from Hansa (North German) cities

harbinger's warrant—a harbinger was a type of herald who found food or drink while the Court was on Progress and paid for it with warrants which promised that the warrant would be paid in the unspecified future at a very advantageous rate for the Crown

Heilige Mutter Gottes—Holy Mother of God

Herr Ingenieur—(German formal address) Mr Engineer

Herr Kaufmann—(German formal address) Mr Merchant

Herr Schmelzmeister—(German formal address) Mr Smeltmaster

Herr Steiger—(German formal address) Mr Mine Captain

Hier kommt ihr nicht herein. Das hier ist mein Haus und meine Insel. Verschwindet!—You cannot come in. This is my house and my island. Get out!

highman/lowman dice—dice weighted to normally throw high/low

hobby—small sturdy horse or pony, native to the Borders

Hobson's livery stables—a successful chain of livery stables, where you couldn't choose which horse you hired, hence "Hobson's choice"

Ich bin ein schlechter Sohn!—I'm a bad son!

Ich versteh' es nicht—I don't understand it

infield—fields nearest the tower or farmhouse

insight—the contents of a house that were moveable, pots, pans, blankets, etc.

jack—two meanings: 1) a leather mug, 2) a padded leather coat with no sleeves and metal plates   between the leather layers to ward off blows

Jeddart axe—type of axe popular in Jedburgh

kern—Irish mercenary

kine—old plural of cow

kissing comfits—hard sweets

kobold—German mine-demon

liege—a feudal lord, often meaning the King for complicated reasons to do with William the Conqueror

livery—a great lord's uniform for his servants

lungfever—pneumonia

manchet bread—best white bread, made of sieved flour

marchpane—hard almond paste

marker stones—notorious for going wandering, they marked boundaries

maslin bread—second best bread, with the wheatgerm and some bran left in; very nutritious

masque—ceremonious playlet usually about Greek gods, sung and danced by the Court

Mews—where falcons were kept

milled powder—stronger and finer gunpowder than serpentine

minister—Protestant priest in Scotland

mithered—annoyed, cross

morion—curved helmet of the period

neck-verse—before the Reformation, the clergy could claim Benefit of Clergy if they were facing hanging, by reciting a verse of scripture and getting away with a lesser punishment

neeps—root vegetables

New Spain—the Americas

oil of vitriol—sulphuric acid

orangeados—a Seville orange skin stuffed with sugar

outfield—rough pasture, further away from the tower or farm-house

Papists, recusants—people who refused to go to a Protestant church because they were Catholics and got fined for it

pattens—wooden clogs to lift your shoes out of the mud

pele tower—small fortress very common on the Border

pelican—alchemical device

petticoat forepart—the pretty triangular part of a petticoat that was deliberately displayed

poinard—long thin dagger with a very sharp point

postern gate—small gate in a bigger one to let in one person at a time

pottage—thick soup made with beans, vegetables and bacon (if available); standard peasant food

procurator fiscal—Scottish lawyer

rammer—the thing you rammed a cannonball into a cannon with

retting tubs—where flax was soaked in water and lye to separate the fibres to spin linen

roodscreen—the wooden screen between the altar and the congregation in an old-fashioned Catholic church

roughshod—a horse shod with spiked shoes for frosty weather

Sea Beggar—independent Dutch Protestant ship

Secretary script—the other kind of Elizabethan handwriting, differing from Italic by normally being unreadable to modern eyes

serpentine powder—basic ordinary mixed gunpowder, quite weak. If you wanted to shoot a four-pound ball, you needed four pounds of serpentine powder.

small ale—the weakest kind of drink, about 2 percent by volume, no hops; what children, women and invalids drank

snips—ancestors of scissors

sweet oil of vitriol—ether, made by pouring sulphuric acid into strong wine

swordblanks—what you make swords out of

thrawn—stubborn

Tollbooth—Edinburgh prison

toothdrawer—early dentist

Trained Bands—the men of a city or town would train together to fight, often as pikemen or arquebusiers

truckle—small bed on wheels

vitriol—sulphuric acid

Warden Raid—the Warden would raid a particular area and burn down towers to teach the reivers better manners. There is no evidence this ever improved anybody's manners.

Was höre ich da? Joachim ist der Mörder meines Mannes?—What is this I hear? Joachim is the murderer of my husband?

Was soll dieses Eindringen bedeuten?—What is the meaning of this invasion?

wean—child

whishke bee/uisge beatha—whisky

wood—woodwild, mad

AUTHOR'S NOTE

There is a wonderful history book to be written about the Hochstetter family, Haug and Co of Augsburg, and the Company of Mines Royal, telling the story of early water- and horse-powered industrialisation and the first tentative steps towards capitalism. Unfortunately, I am not the person to write it because I can't speak German and most of the rich original source material is in German, as are the accounts.

Briefly, Daniel Hochstetter, the son of Joachim who got gold out of Crawford Moor in Scotland for Henry VIII, came to England in 1563 with six others with permission to survey the mineral resources of England. He came back in June 1564 with twelve workmen and took them to Keswick, where they had found copper ore which also contained silver.

He came back in October 1566 to deal with one of his men, Leonard Stoltz having been murdered by the Catholic earl of Northumberland, just possibly for being an Anabaptist. English copper was made in September 1567 and the Company of Mines Royal was officially incorporated on 28 May 1568. A law case over the rights to the ore between Northumberland and the Crown was settled in the Crown's favour, to nobody's surprise apart from Northumberland's, who rebelled shortly after.

And from November 1571 to May 1572 Daniel Hochstetter brought his wife and family all the way from Augsburg to England. They stopped over the winter in London, where they went sightseeing, and went north in the spring. They settled on

Vicar's Island in Derwentwater, where they built a brewery, a bakery, a mill, and planted orchards and made a pig farm. They built stamping houses for crushing ore at Goldscope mine in Newham, smelthouses for smelting and assaying in Brigham and started mining for coal at a small village nine miles away called Bolton Low Houses. Many of the original miners went back to Germany in the 1570s when the mines were allegedly "failing of ore" but the Hochstetters stayed, although Daniel himself died in 1581. Mining continued in Keswick right into the seventeeth century, to the Civil War.

I have based my account of sixteenth-century Keswick on *Elizabethan Copper* by M B Donald (1955), *Elizabethan Keswick* by W G Collingwood (1912), and *Goldscope and the Mines of Derwent Fells* by Ian Tyler (2005). The last is a rare, lively but, alas, footnote-free book, and I used Ian Tyler's original sketchmap of Goldscope mine for Carey's adventures underground. Agricola's book on mining, *De Re Metallica*, in President Herbert Clark Hoover's translation became my bible for the metallurgy and the astonishing wooden machines. There is in fact a major clue to the mystery towards the end of Book 3 of *De Re Metallica* and Wattie Graham of Netherby did in fact own Borrowdale woods, for some mysterious reason.

Joachim and Poppy replace two of Radagunda Hochstetter's children who died in childhood and I have, of course, used my authorial licence pretty freely throughout the book. I think it's possible, though, that something similar to my account was going on in Keswick in the later years, especially as the Graham headman, Ritchie Graham of Brackenhill, did in fact have a thriving counterfeiting business in his pele tower at Brackenhill. By the way, Brackenhill tower has been rebuilt and is apparently available for rent.

I have to confess to having invented the various superstitions around the smith and his smithy, unless I simply read about them a long time ago somewhere obscure and forgot, as I did with the incident I stole from C S Forrester—Karen L Black, you got me bang to rights!

And if I was running the charming and helpful Keswick Museum, I would have a whole standing exhibition devoted to the forgotten history of the German miners in Keswick in the sixteenth century. I'm sure it would fascinate modern Germans. It certainly fascinated me!

Acknowledgments

As always I owe enormous gratitude to all the people who have helped me with my book. If I've forgotten anybody, I hope you'll forgive me.

Ian Blakemore of Rosley Books actually got me a little tour of Vicar's Island itself, and showed me round Keswick.

Andrew Gordon very generously allowed me to borrow his house while he was on holiday, so I could career around the Lake District and Carlisle, and among other treats, took me to Whitehaven to look at the place (before I realised Workington was the right port).

Keswick Museum and Threlkeld Quarry Museum were generous with their help.

Markus Baur has been my alpha reader who supplied correct German formal address and some snippets of German, as well as advice on German customs, proof-reading and excellent suggestions.

Stephen Michael Stirling has read an early draft and given his usual valuable and measured advice.

My beta readers are heroes. It's not easy to read a rough early draft of a book and give your thoughts within two weeks.

Here they are, in no particular order: Lynn McMillan, Lorna Toolis, Michael Skeet, Fiona Middlemist, Lori Walker; Kier Salmon, Chris Luke, Frank Luxem, Lorraine Neill, Sallie Blumenauer, Hadas Kozlowsky, Gereg Jones Muller, Diana Britt, Hilarie Berzins, Robin Mclennan, Clay Foard, Karen L Black, Kendall Britt.

Thanks are also due to Sophie Robinson at Head of Zeus (my UK publishers), and Barbara Peters at Poisoned Pen Press (US publishers). Nowadays it's rare for publishers to take as much care over editing as they do.